EVERLASTING

TMONIQUE
STEPHENS

DEDICATION

For my daughter Cyre`. Thank you for your love and unwavering faith. We've taken this journey together and I couldn't have done any of it without you. You are my sunshine.

ACKNOWLEDGEMENTS

A special thank you to author Kathyrn Bain and Karen Herbin. I am very lucky to have you as friends and critique partners. Thank you to the friendliest, funniest, and most nurturing romance chapter in the world, Ancient City Romance Author, ACRA.

An extra special thank you to Charitee Gerow for keeping me sane at work and making me leave my writing cave for a few hours of fun.

Let me not forget my best friends, author Michelle De Leon and Diane Rora. Thanks for your continued love and support. You guys always tell me what I can do, not what I can't.

OTHER BOOKS BY TMONIQUE STEPHENS

ETERNITY: Descendants of Ra Book 1
EVERLASTING: Descendants of Ra Book 2
EVERMORE: Descendants of Ra Book 3

CHAPTER ONE

His firm lips kissed the delicate spot above her collarbone. Did he know that would drive her crazy? She grabbed his broad shoulders. Her nipples tightened. Desire coiled low in her groin. His long, midnight hair brushed the back of her hand. She threaded her fingers through the silky strands and arched, bringing her nipples into contact with his hard pecs. Need shot through her.

His lips stroked up the column of her neck. She turned her head, giving him complete access to the sensitive skin. He chuckled, a deep, sensual sound that reverberated through her and made her want to hear him laugh.

A velvety touch circled the shell of her ear. She giggled and twisted her head to get away, bringing their lips within centimeters of contact. Would he finally kiss her? Through the fall of his hair, she glimpsed his eyes. Deep ocean blue. She struggled for air as she drowned in their watery depths.

His hands tightened on her bare hips. Her legs parted and slid up his muscular thighs. She was more than ready for him.

He said her name. Whispered it. "Alexis. Wake up."

Detective Alexis Lever shot straight up in her bed. Her breath hitched and her heart ran a marathon in her chest.

Wow.

She'd dreamed of him before, but never so vividly. He was always shrouded. Shadows masked his face and a great distance separated them. Tonight, she felt his touch, glimpsed his face.

"It was just a dream." She heaved a disappointed sigh and adjusted her twisted sweatpants.

A breeze fluttered the curtains and stirred the surprisingly thick October air. A putrid odor flooded the small bedroom. Gagging, Alexis pressed a fist to her lips as her heart kicked into another gallop. Her gaze darted around the moonlight-dappled bedroom of her grandmother's house.

No one lurked.

The hair on the back of her neck rose. She reached for her gun, slid the covers off, and slipped from the bed. Her thoughts turned to Daniel Nicolis, the Village Strangler. The last time she had seen him he was climbing out of the freezer at the M.E.'s office like it was an Olympic sport. The department was in deep denial. They claimed he must not have been dead. Yeah, it'd happened before, but how many walking dead had taken a header out of a high rise building? And the person that gave him the final shove was stashed here, sleeping in the opposite bedroom.

It could be him, back to even the score.

She opened her bedroom door and eased out. The dim hall smelled of carpet freshener from a recent vacuuming.

Alexis raced across the hallway. Please don't tell her she had led Stella Walker, the only survivor of The Village Strangler, into a death trap. If anything happened to Stella, Alexis Lever, NYPD detective, could kiss her career bye-bye.

She yanked open the door to her childhood bedroom and flipped on the light.

Empty. The bed neatly made.

Stella Walker was gone. Not only was Alexis not supposed to take a witness into her home, she damn sure wasn't supposed to lose her. So much for her good intentions. She slammed her fist onto the dresser, rattling the antique perfume bottles. If Stella had stayed in protective custody and hadn't decided to go it on her own, Alexis would still be asleep.

The rumble of an engine drew her to the window. Headlights off, a sleek sports car crept down the street. It circled the cul-de-sac and parked across from her house. The car door swung open and Roman Nicolis exited the dark interior. The weak streetlight didn't soften his hard face. Nor did the leather coat hide his muscular frame. How had he found them at her grandmother's house?

The floorboards squeaked in the living room and the rusty hinges of the front door squealed. Stella raced from the house and into his arms. It was amazing how some women fell for a criminal. And make no mistake, Roman Nicolis was a criminal.

He held Stella close. Not even air separated them. Then he kissed her.

Must be nice to have someone care that much. Someone who would follow you to the end of the earth and back. Wouldn't be her, though. That helpless female thing some women did wasn't her style. Major General Martin Lever and her three older brothers had made sure she wouldn't need rescuing.

Alexis ran down the stairs. Stella wasn't under arrest. Alexis didn't have the legal right to stop her from leaving, but she couldn't let her leave with Roman. The man was a mercenary, his brother Daniel a serial killer. Maybe a dose of common sense would make the woman reconsider departing with a man she barely knew.

As she stepped off the last stair, that smell slammed into her. *Rotting. Decomposing...death.* The moonlight slicing through the window above the double sinks cast shadows that loomed and concealed the room. Her hand stroked the wall and brushed the switch. Fluorescent lights flickered on. Leftover cartons from the Chinese takeout place littered the countertop.

She moved forward. The Glock led the way to the back door. Midway in, a low growl froze her. A sliver of fear stabbed her heart and flipped her stomach. Her muscles quivered ready for flight.

The back door to the kitchen exploded. Lifted off her feet, she landed against the back of the sofa in the adjacent living room. Wood and glass narrowly missed her.

Alexis rolled to her knees. "What the hell?" Where was her gun? Patting the ground around her, she skimmed the muzzle poking from beneath the sofa.

The light had shattered. The kitchen door was a black hole to the backyard. Foul air wafted in and smothered her. Alexis doubled over and hurled chunks of Chicken Lo Mein. When she stood, she wasn't alone. A monster had stepped through the opening.

She saw it in pieces where the moonlight touched. A flash of a crocodile face. A glint of razor sharp white teeth. And a glimpse of claws as long as her fingers. Before she could raise her gun, a beefy hand grabbed her throat and snatched her close to those rows of teeth. Its fetid breath buffeted her, ruffled her hair. She couldn't breathe. Terror sapped her strength.

This had to be the flip side of her dream. Things like this didn't exist outside of sleep. She brought her gun up, but the monster knocked the weapon from her hand, sending it clattering to the linoleum floor.

A tongue snaked from its mouth. It lapped her face. Thick saliva coated her cheek. "You're not her," the beast hissed.

Did that mean she wasn't dinner?

Its head whipped towards the front of the house. The claw holding her loosened, allowing her to take a wheezy breath. One eye with a vertical pupil rotated and studied her.

"Next time." It threw her.

Alexis flew over the sofa and crashed onto the oak coffee table. Through a fog of pain, she glimpsed the beast crashing through the front door. She rolled and landed between the table and the sofa.

Stella. Had she escaped? Please God, let her be safe. Clutching her side, she lurched to her feet, freed her backup gun from her ankle holster, and made her was to the destroyed doorway.

She paused against the shattered frame. Twos and threes of everything wavered, but then her vision cleared. The monster was there, closing in on Roman and Stella in their fleeing car. Strength waning, Alexis fired. She took a step and stumbled over a piece of the broken door frame. Weightless, the pain skittered away, leaving her euphoric. Her vision cleared and the stone stairs leading to the front of the house rushed toward her.

Or was it the other way around? Not that it mattered. She didn't have enough strength to brace for impact.

CHAPTER TWO

"Your brother is in danger. Only you can save him."

Reign Nicolis refused to take the bait Nephythys, the Egyptian Goddess of the Dead had laid. His shoulders were embedded in the wall of her palace on the sacred Isle of Chemmis, his feet dangled off the floor, over a pool of his cooling blood. His chin didn't move from its place on his chest. "My brother is dead."

"He is alive, for the moment," Nephythys said.

She stood before him. Her voice filled with faux concern for the brother he hadn't seen in two millennia. He wouldn't meet her gaze or give her anything she wanted. But he couldn't stop himself from answering.

"You lie." His voice vibrated with anger. Her words and everything between the crown of blue hair on her head to the tips of her toes were a deception. That's how she had tricked him to Chemmis, the home of the Egyptian Gods. With subterfuge and innuendo. He wouldn't fall for it again.

"You know I cannot lie."

That much was true. Nephythys dealt judgment to all followers of the Egyptian Gods. Her words determined their final resting place in the underworld. Either ascension to the stars or perpetuity roasting in *Duat*.

"Come, I will show you." She waved her hand.

Reign dropped to his feet and slumped against the same wall that had imprisoned him. His bones creaked and his muscles ached. Whether days or years, he could not guess how long she'd left him hanging until he obeyed. He'd tired of her games long ago. Using Roman was a new tactic in her latest attempt to bend him to her wishes.

Two thin, translucent strips of linen stretched across her small breasts and lean hips. Her display didn't inspire the lust she sought to invoke. Cold contempt was all he could muster. Nephythys turned and led the way through the dim passages of her white palace to a sunbaked room. So long in darkness, the light stabbed his eyes.

"Look into the Scrying bowl. The first waters of the Nile will show you the truth." She pointed at a bowl waiting on a table in the middle of the room.

Made from beaten gold, with hieroglyphics carved into the surface, Reign couldn't ignore his interest. He wanted to see, needed too, but— "How will I know it is not a memory you have stolen from my mind and manipulated?" He took in her alabaster skin and pale blue hair. Once, her petite body enthralled him. He'd gladly become her slave. Now...

She glided closer. Her whisper-thin linen coverings showed more skin than they hid. The delicate fabric molded to her curves, drawing attention to her pert nipples and the vee where her thighs joined. This display was beneath her station. He almost wished he could feel something other than disgust and betrayal when he looked at her.

"You will know, Reign. Have trust." Her lips curved.

He laughed. A brittle sound, which surprised even him. Trust was not something he would ever do again with Nephythys. Her pouty lips trembled with artful dismay. He waited for a tear to fall just to see how long it would take for her to give up the futile effort. A full minute passed before she lowered her dry eyes. The Goddess of the Dead did not cry.

Reign turned to the bowl and looked into the muddy waters drawn from when the Nile was but a spring. An image appeared in the swirling liquid. His face on another man's body.

"Roman." Relief and sorrow tore through him. For the first time in two millennia, he saw his twin, who should have been long dead. How had he survived all this time? The image faded, but not before he caught a glimpse of a nightmarish creature that stalked his brother.

"No!" He grabbed the bowl. A force shoved him to the opposite side of the room. "Bring him back." He demanded.

"There is no way to reform the link. You have destroyed it. But I can give you more than a watery image of your brother." She rushed through her words as if she read from a prepared script.

"Give me? You let me believe Roman was dead." He struggled against the power confining him.

"You never asked if he was alive. You never cared to know what happened to him. All you had to do was ask."

"For a price."

Her words struck bone. He didn't ask, not because he didn't care about Roman's fate, but because the answer was too painful to face. Their last moments together were filled with acrimony after they'd both failed in their duty.

"There is always a price. To help your brother, I can send you back."

Reign stared at the bowl. He'd be a fool to trust her. "He has survived this long without me—"

"Anubis's champion stalks him."

"Why? What could he have done to draw the attention of your son?"

"Anubis believes I sent you to stop his involvement in the human realm. He thinks Roman is you. Your brother fights your battle. And he is losing."

That was not possible. Other than him, none surpassed Roman on the battlefield. "My brother is a warrior—"

"He is not the man he once was. Time has softened him. You saw him. He ran *from* the battle, not toward it."

Though it pained him, he couldn't deny her words. "You do this out of the kindness of your heart?" He chuckled at the absurdity. As Judge and Jury of the pantheon, she had no understanding of kindness.

"I have a price." Nephythys released him and then sidled closer. "All I need is a promise that you will return to me—"

"—to be a slave to your whims?" He couldn't let her get that close to him again. "No."

"Then your brother will die." She leveled a steady gaze at him.

He'd always protected Roman. Always. Right now, Roman was fighting for his life. Reign clenched his hands to keep from hitting something.

"I want a willing, attentive lover."

"You want a pet," he said through gritted teeth.

"I want you. With love in your heart and passion in your body."

"And what will I get?" When she didn't respond, he had his answer. He turned away; ready to return to his gilded cage.

"I will free you from the Vanquished. No longer will your demons haunt you."

To be free of his tormentors. What would he give to have that relentless torture cease? Their voices silenced forever? Anything. And she knew this. "You had this ability all along and withheld it. To punish me, bend me to your will."

No emotions showed on her face, but her coiled hair quivered in response to her agitation.

Whispers gathered in his head. The Vanquished, his constant companions, had awakened. Quickly, their wails rose from incoherent babble to mournful screeches which tore at his sanity.

"Negotiations are over. Do we have an agreement?" Nephythys folded her arms under her breasts, plumping them.

The choice should be simple: freedom from The Vanquished and a chance to save his twin. And all he had to give up was his soul. Not like he had used it in last two thousand years. Still, he had to know. "Let me touch you." He stretched a hand toward her.

Immediately, a soft glow shielded her body, protecting her from any physical contact.

"You know you cannot. All are forbidden to touch me."

Nothing had changed. To relegate himself once more to her version of love left a chasm in his gut. But, he had no options. He couldn't let Roman die because of him.

A null raced into the room and stumbled into a low bow. "Great Goddess, The god, SET, approaches." Breathless, the servant trembled.

Reign almost smiled. SET had granted him a reprieve from a lifetime of servitude. Reign leaned into her. He brushed her protective barrier. She retreated. He followed, backing her into a wall, crowding her. She couldn't haggle with SET about to make an entrance. "One day. That is all I will give you."

"No, this is not a negotiation." The tips of her hair flamed.

"I have changed my mind. One hour is all you will have."

Her attention snapped from him to the open archway, and returned. "No. You will give me what I demand."

"Then we will wait for your husband's arrival." He leaned his naked body against a wall.

Anger flashed in her eyes, but she looked to the archway again.

His lungs tightened, searching for the air that suddenly vanished from the room. Reign wobbled. His muscles jellied and he slammed into the table for support.

"All right! I agree." A copy of Nephythys separated from her body and cupped Reign's face.

He didn't have the strength to push her away when her lips covered his. In a rush, some of her power transferred to him.

"Until you return to me, I give you part of my *vis*'Ra, my energy. It will grant you immortality, the ability to fade and flash, and care for your needs." An icy wind circled the chamber. "They will not last long," she stammered, glancing at the doorway. "Goodbye, my love."

Her *vis*'Ra coursed through Reign's veins, a poisonous brew that propelled him from one realm to the next. He materialized on a black road with a yellow line dissecting it. Small dwellings lined either side of the road. Was this freedom? He glanced down at the strange clothing covering his body. The rustle of leaves drew his attention to a sickly tree. He studied the leaves flapping and strained to feel the wind on his face, but no breeze caressed him. Was he real? A metal monstrosity crept down the road and rumbled to a stop a few feet away. He braced for attack. The door swung opened and Roman appeared. Stunned, Reign couldn't move as his brother strode by without pause.

"Roman?" he called and received no answer. How could he not see him, know he was here? Had time and distance truly destroyed their bond?

The door to the house behind him opened and a woman ran into Roman's arms. Fury pulsed through Reign. He expected to find his brother engaged in battle, not entwined in an intimate embrace. He bargained his life for this? Once more, his brother placed what lay between a woman's thighs over family. Too many times drink and women came between his twin and his duty. As mercenaries, their honor lay in their ability to wield the sword in their hand, not the lance fools hung their pride on.

Roman swung the woman up and carried her to the waiting conveyance. Unlike the other women his brother had wasted time on, this one he held close and tenderly kissed. Had he found the one who had caused him to lose his soul?

No woman was worth that. Nephythys proved that.

"Roman, I am here."

Still, his brother ignored him. Reign grabbed Roman's shoulder. His hand passed through. He wasn't real. What had Nephythys done to him? Behind him something crashed. He spun and saw a beast, the hybrid nightmare he had glimpsed in the Scrying bowl. The beast Anubis created and the Goddess ordered him to defeat.

The gods and their petty games. Reign could kill it now, save his brother and return to his cage secreted in Nephythys's palace. He gagged at the thought of being subjected to her idea of love, but that was the bargain he'd made. Whether now or later, the price had to be paid. He would do this for his brother and the woman. At least one of them would have peace and their line would continue.

Roman entered the metal carriage. It roared much like the beast, then settled into a throaty rumbled. The rear wheels smoked the black road. The beast leaped from the wooden structure and landed inches from Reign. It paused and studied him.

It *saw* him when his brother hadn't.

Reign's hand itched and a weight rested in his palm. A sword. Jagged. Dark as night, sharper than sin, and larger than the one he used to wield in battle, was clasped in his hand. He lifted it.

Heavy, good for cleaving.

Roman and the woman sped away, cloudy fumes trailing behind. The beast followed. Its claws dug into the black road, leaving chunks behind.

Reign charged after both. Fast and agile, the beast pulled away. Nephythys's *vis 'Ra* surged in Reign's veins. His atoms shifted, separated. Panicked, he couldn't stop his body from dissolving. Suspended in the air as a heavy mist, Reign quelled his terror. If the gods could do this, then he could too. With a thought, he chased after his prey, closing the distance within a matter of seconds. A little closer and he would have him.

A force yanked Reign to a stop, reeled him back, and slammed him to the ground. Pain ripped through his head. The Vanquished, his personal army of demons, shrieked inside his skull. He'd thought Nephythys would have alleviated the curse so he could return quickly to her servitude. He wasn't surprised fortune didn't favor him. It never had.

For countries, for kings, and for emperors, he killed. To honor the Nicolis name, he killed. And to protect the one person he loved—his brother—he killed. Too many to count fell beneath his blade, but each victory came with a price.

Roman must return. Without his brother's easy temperament to balance the darkness in Reign's soul, the Vanquished ruled, and he would become a madman, no better than the beast he chased. Soon he would lose rational thought and descend into madness. He hadn't traveled all this way to become the thing he would destroy. *No.* His fingers cracked the hard surface of the black ground, searching for earth to hold onto and center him. Sometimes touching the ground from which all things sought sustenance helped suppress the riot in his brain. But there was no dirt beneath the surface of this strange ground. An ashy, gray substance covered his fingers instead of fertile earth.

A distant whimper reached Reign and gave him the strength to turn his head a fraction. A woman stumbled from the house. She wobbled on unsteady legs. A wild, curly mass of hair obscured her view. She rested on one of the wooden columns. One wrong step and she'd trip on the scattered debris and tumble down the stairs. He had to get to her before she fell.

Fighting the invisible demons weighing him down, Reign forced himself to his knees. Then he crawled. With each step, the cries of the Vanquished lessened, replaced by calming silence. If he were pious, he would offer a prayer that she stay put until he reached her.

She pushed away from the column. Her knees buckled. Seconds before her skull would've smashed onto the ground, Reign materialized. He dove beneath her and absorbed the brunt of the fall.

Damn the gods.

The feel of her solid form blasted through his petrified center. He hadn't realized how much he missed this. Human contact. The simple act of touching and being touched. Warmth and the softness of a woman. So long denied, now he feasted.

He buried his face in her mass of curly hair and inhaled jasmine and honey. A moan ripe with longing ripped from his throat and he fitted her lush curves more intimately to him. She shivered and her breath curled in the air. Gently, he rolled and let her slide from his arms to her back. The pale glow of artificial light bathed her face and he forgot to breathe. Something so lovely couldn't be real. Wasn't real. Touching her shouldn't be allowed.

Desire to taste her luscious lips—this one time—dug its claws into him, and drew him near. He brushed her wild tresses from her face and stroked a finger down her cheek, leaving a bloody streak. A quick search and he discovered a gash on the side of her head. He hadn't saved her. And while he pawed her like an untried youth, she lay dying.

The sound of shuffling feet whipped him around, ready to defend her.

"I called for an ambulance." An elderly female pushed open the short wooden gate. A halo of silver hair gave her an angelic appearance.

"Can you help her?" Reign asked when she kneeled opposite him. The elder stared, her gaze bore into him, and he couldn't turn away from the intensity of her watery eyes. Beneath her glare, something inside him wanted to retreat, slink away, and hide like a chastised child. Then her withered face stretched into a smile.

"Alexis will be fine," she said.

"Alexis." He repeated the name and returned to study the woman he'd saved.

"She's stronger than even she realizes," the elder said.

Her voice soothed him in a way he couldn't explain until the quiet drone of a distant wail caught his attention. Another slightly different wail joined it. They approached. Together, they set his inner demons on edge. Red, blue, and yellow lights dissected the night and two metal monstrosities screeched to a halt a few feet away. He stood, ready to defend.

"It's all right. They're here to help." She looked up at him. "They'll take care of her."

He wanted to care for her, but that wasn't his mission. "I will leave." It pained him to say those words. Leaving was the last thing he desired, yet he had to. He lingered a moment longer before stepping into the shadow of the house and fading away.

***

Stretched out on a gurney in the emergency department of the county hospital wasn't how she planned to spend the evening. So much for following where your conscience led. She should've left Stella Walker alone and maybe her grandmother's house and her head would still be intact.

"Keep still, Detective," her doctor ordered while probing her scalp.

"Sorry," she mumbled. She had a concussion and an inch long laceration on the left side of her skull. So far, that's all they'd found wrong, but the MRI results hadn't returned yet.

"What bed is Detective Lever in?"

Alexis cringed. The one person in the world she didn't want to see was a few feet away on the opposite side of the privacy curtain. Her partner, Lead Detective McCabe. She didn't know his first name. Didn't think he had one since no one dared call him anything but his surname. He didn't like her gender, didn't like her style, and hated her youth. She was twenty-four, not two.

Maybe McCabe would take the drawn curtain as a sign she wanted privacy and leave. The curtain snapped open. Even though she expected it, she flinched.

"Please, keep still. I'm almost done."

She didn't believe the patience in the doctor's voice. In the parted opening stood her partner, Lead Detective McCabe, all two hundred and eighty five pounds of him, and that was a low estimate. His impersonal gaze swept over her before meeting her eyes.

"You okay?" he asked though his gaze didn't meet hers. Instead, he studied the equipment with what looked like trepidation, though she could be wrong.

"I'm fine. Once the doctor finishes I'm free to go."

"You need to spend the night under observation, Detective," the doctor interjected still piecing her back together.

"Thanks. I prefer my own bed," she said, then glanced at her boss. "How'd you know I was here?"

"The desk sergeant got a call from New City PD and your neighbor, Mrs. Margie Kelly." He stepped fully into the room. "She gave the sergeant more info than New City did."

She wasn't surprised her eighty-year-old neighbor had phoned 911. Honorary member of the neighborhood watch, nothing got by her rheumy, insomniac eyes. But a Nicolis calling for the cavalry? Hard to believe.

"Your neighbor's out there, by the way. She was so concerned she hopped in her Buick and drove the speed limit to get here despite her cataracts. Her words, not mine." He spoke to her, but stared at the doctor.

"She's a fixture in the neighborhood, but her heart's in the right place."

Awkward silence enveloped the small space. McCabe stuffed his hands in the pockets of his khaki pants and started jiggling his loose change. It had to be the hospital and not the crusty blood matting her hair that had him on edge. The man was the lead detective in The Village Strangler case. He waded in body parts and guts.

"All right." The doctor peeled off his gloves and dumped them in a nearby red bin along with a stack of bloody gauze and disposable instruments. "I'll be back with your MRI results."

"So what the hell happened?" McCabe snapped the moment the curtains swung back in place.

Yeah right, like she was going to tell him about the animal that demolished her grandmother's house.

"My guns—" She had dropped both during the fight.

"I have one. The New City PD found it in the living room, unfired. They have the other for testing. Answer the question." McCabe pinned her with a hard stare.

Don't shift. Make eye contact. Be sincere, but not ingratiating. "I don't know what happened."

His eyes narrowed and his thin lips compressed into a slash. "You're in deep shit, detective. Can't blame you for zipping it shut. If it were me, I'd do the same. But just to let you know, Internal Affairs will be all over this. You see, that busybody neighbor of yours told us all about your houseguest, the petite brunette you brought home." He imitated Mrs. Kelly's voice. "Though Nicolis failed to mention he was squiring away our only witness and you failed to mention you were taking her home. If anything happens to Stella Walker, your career is over."

"Because I helped a witness?"

"Because you keep fucking up. Should I list all the ways?"

Alexis gritted her teeth and lowered her eyes. *Great.* Her one act of kindness would leave her unemployed.

"Are you listening to me, Lever?" McCabe leaned closer, crowding her with his bulk.

It was his favorite interrogation technique. She forced herself not to lean away. "Yeah, every word."

"Another thing, you've been reassigned to Vice."

She swallowed her bitter response but couldn't mask her grimace.

The curtain opened and the doctor slipped back to her bedside. "Your MRI is normal."

"So I'm done?" She started pulling leads off.

"I really think you should stay the night, detective, but I can't force you. Let me get the nurse to discharge you." He left again.

"My gun?" She stretched out her palm to McCabe.

He placed it on the bed. "I'm gonna give you some advice, Lever. Straighten your shit up. You don't get unemployment when you're fired." The curtain swung closed behind him.

His words had a definite ring of truth. The sane part of her wanted to listen. To dig a hole and pull the dirt in behind her. Be the good girl, the team player, follow the rules and maybe they would like her, give her a dram of respect.

And that thing. It had tossed Alexis aside. It didn't want her. It hunted Stella. Did she and Roman get away? Coupled with Daniel Nicolis, The Village Strangler still on the loose, the woman was in deep trouble. She should've told McCabe about it.

Yeah, and end up heavily medicated in a strait jacket. She doubted her strait-laced supervisor believed in anything paranormal. She didn't either. Ghosts, vampires, werewolves, fairies, gnomes that reserved airline seats for savvy travelers, none of that shit was real.

Except for the monster that grabbed her by the throat and looked her in the eye. The monster that chose not to kill her, passed her over for better prey.

And all of it was no longer her problem. Right? She gave a mental nod. She needed a shower and a sleeping pill. Maybe after a few hours of unconsciousness, her world would right itself. On an ordinary night, she would've listened to the angel on her right shoulder and taken the cautious road leading back to her grandmother's house. Thank God Nana wasn't alive to see her home wrecked.

Another thing on her list to take care of.

Alexis wrestled the safety rail down and swung her legs over the edge. Next came the leads and the IV. She couldn't return to the desecration of the one place she always felt safe without doing something.

By the time the nurse arrived with the discharge papers, she was dressed and the gun was in the pocket of her sweatpants. She hadn't made it far when the shrill voice of Mrs. Kelly reached her over the din of the emergency department.

"My dear, where are you off to when you should be resting?" She hustled over to Alexis with a surprising amount of energy for a woman her age.

I'm off to make a bad situation worse. "You didn't have to come, Mrs. Kelly."

"Of course I did! Your grandmother would've haunted me if I didn't."

Alexis smiled. She'd forgotten how close they were. "I'm fine. Can you give me a ride back to the house?" She could return to her apartment, but—

"Certainly. I parked in the garage."

Alexis followed, trailing slightly behind. Not because she was tired, though her feet did drag, but because she kept looking over her shoulder. They weren't alone. There were voices filtering from other levels of the garage, footsteps echoing, car doors creaking open and slamming shut.

That's not what put the chill at her back and made her hair stand on edge. *How did I survive that fall?* A vague memory of arms cradling her surfaced. It seemed so real.

Lingering traces of the dream she was enjoying before she woke filtered through her brain. A man waited across the room. Shirtless, his perfect pecs and brick stacked abs flexed as he closed the distance between them, stalking her. Predator versus prey. The bed dipped under his weight as he stretched across it, erect and ready. Her breath came in anxious little bursts as she strained to glimpse his face through his fall of midnight hair. She couldn't. All she could see were deep ocean blue eyes.

"A dream, nothing more," she murmured.

"Huh? Did you say something, dear?" Mrs. Kelly glanced at her.

Alexis shook her head.

"I'm parked over here." Mrs. Kelly pointed to a white Buick at the top of the ramp.

"Coming." She hurried after her. Mrs. Kelly had the car door opened, ready for her to slide in. Alexis paused. "Did you...see anything?"

Mrs. Kelly's eyebrows furrowed. "Like what dear?"

Like freaking Godzilla! "Oh, anything."

"No, nothing, dear."

"Did you see a man?"

Lips pursed, Mrs. Kelly tilted her head and thought for a moment. Her silver hair glinted in the underground lights. "Yes, I saw a man and your lovely houseguest drive away in his car. They seemed so much in love." She sighed.

That wasn't the man Alexis was referring too. "No one else?"

"No. Why?" Mrs. Kelly leaned closer. The yellow lighting of the garage reflected off her milky eyes.

Just like she thought, a dream. "Uhm, no reason." She slid into the car. She didn't have a lot of time if she was going to do what she planned.

***

Reign couldn't walk away. He had to be certain she would recover. When they loaded her into the larger of the conveyances he climbed in, convinced she needed his protection.

New to this world, everything confused and overwhelmed him, especially the place they took her. The bright lights, the noise, the people clogging the passageways, it was battle without a foe. He thanked the gods he could pass through the crowd unencumbered. A buffer of cold surrounded him and chased many away. Stationed by her bedside, he watched them care for her until he was certain she would survive. Even then, he lingered, his empty arms strangely aching.

He turned away and passed Mrs. Kelly holding vigil on the other side of the closed curtain. Through the maze of corridors, he made his way outside. Once there, he tapped into Nephythys' power and materialized. He breathed in a lungful of fresh air and stiffened his resolve. The time to leave had long passed. Behind him lay a woman he didn't know, would never know. Ahead waited Nephythys, the most vainglorious creature that ever existed, and the bargains he had made. The first thousands of years ago…and the last a few hours past.

Reign ignored the well of regret threatening to flood him, stretched his senses, and searched for his brother. He must find Roman. Together they would find a way to destroy the beast and defeat Nephythys. Since birth, their bond had never failed to guide them to each other's side. Within moments, he located him and allowed his atoms to follow where his senses led.

He slammed back to the same spot beside the medical facility, except Alexis stood over him. Her chin tilted and a breeze brushed the hair off her shoulders. He reached for her, but she and Mrs. Kelly walked through him.

Confused, he climbed to his feet and watched their retreating backs. Why did he return to this spot? The beast must be near and its pull was keeping him here. Had it come back for him or Alexis? He searched the area and then followed the women. Staying to the side, he watched their conveyance until it turned a corner.

He'd moved a few steps when the Vanquished dropped him to his knees. Their tortured screams ricocheted inside his skull and tore his sanity apart. Against his will, his atoms shifted and he flashed into the rear seat behind Alexis.

"Did you turn the air on? 'Cause it's freezing in here." Alexis hugged herself.

"It has turned chilly." Mrs. Kelly fiddled with some knobs. "The heat's on. It'll warm up soon."

Damnation. It wasn't the beast that kept pulling him back. It was Alexis.

CHAPTER THREE

SET wanted nothing more than to feel life in the body of his wife. A smoky tendril stretched out from his gaseous form and skimmed the empty shell she'd left him. But what a beautiful shell. Her dusty pink nipples topped globes of taut flesh. A flat abdomen led to trim hips and a smooth mons. If only her legs would willingly open, cradle him, welcome him into her dark recess and their sensual embrace. Angry, he vibrated and a jagged strike of red lightning flared in the center of his mass. Per their agreement, for three millennia he abstained from enjoying carnal delights with his wife. At council meetings, her sparkling presence reminded him of what he didn't have—had never had. Nephythys, the woman his minuscule soul was attached to. In all their time together never had she graced him with a smile, a willing touch, a moan of pleasure. Those precious acknowledgments she reserved for anyone but him.

He'd hoped all this time apart had softened her, made her long for his attention, *any* attention. Perhaps now she would allow him a foothold into her heart. After so long, her bitterness must have healed.

His optimism withered when he entered her bedroom and beheld this still nakedness sprawled on the bed.

This is all she would give him. A corpse. Parts of him lashed out and shattered the pretty things she collected.

He pulsed with the desire to crush her, leave nothing but a bloody, broken body. One of the many dark pleasures he enjoyed.

He couldn't, not to her.

The bedroom disintegrated as tendrils sprang from his gaseous body and whipped about the room. Nothing escaped swift destruction except the soulless form on the bed.

SET drew his expanded self together and calmed, reined in his darkness. Once composed, a tendril wrapped around her waist and dragged her limp body to the edge. He transformed from his preferred state to a more solid form, his dark swirling essences momentarily trapped beneath a barrier of thin, translucent skin. He could be anything, male, female, or animal, but he made himself into a form he knew she would desire, a tall, muscular male. He looked down and studied his member jutting proudly forward. Cylindrical, the appendage had none of the features that completed the male anatomy. No sacs, no hair, no veiny sinews, and no bulbous head with a slit opening.

Not his favorite form, he tolerated it for Nephythys. His gaseous state was much more functional. The boundaries of flesh disturbed him. Limited him. Made him vulnerable to all the vagaries humans suffered. Never would he bind himself into human form. She would have to accept this substitute.

SET spread her legs apart and studied her opening. Dry, no moisture wept for him. In his gaseous form, her arousal didn't matter. He could penetrate every part of her body, simultaneously filling her repeatedly until all his frustrations were excised.

He touched the jutting part of him to her opening and felt her shriveled membranes brace. This will hurt, he thought with a cruel grin. His essences pulsed beneath the translucent skin, taking pleasure at the thought of her pain. But physical pain healed while a wounded heart festered.

Somewhere on the island, her spirit waited for his departure and the ritual cleansing to be completed. Once the nulls removed all evidence of his presence, only then would she rejoin her body. Nothing of his visit would remain.

Angry, he thrust inside and buried as deep as the appendage allowed. Something pricked his eyes and a bead of moisture rolled down the slope of his face. He touched the strangeness, smoothed it between his fingers.

Tears. He jerked away from his wife and reverted to his gaseous state.

This is why he never took the disgusting form. Quivering in annoyance—or maybe fright—he fled the destroyed room and ended up in the alcove.

Thank Ra she wasn't here to witness the display. It would give her pleasure to see him so weak. Her laughter would ring in the council chamber. The God of Evil would not suffer humiliation. Agitated, he swirled about the room, brushing every surface, filling every microscopic crevice. He brushed something.

The remnants of a man.

CHAPTER FOUR

Instead of going home and resting as she promised Mrs. Kelly, Alexis changed out of her sweat clothes into jeans and a sweater, hopped in her car, and headed downtown. The last place she should be was exactly where she was going.

Luckily, her precinct was large. Not everyone knew everyone. She showed her badge to the desk sergeant, who gave her a cursory glance. A swipe of her ID card unlocked the door to the employee entrance. She said a quick prayer they hadn't moved her junk yet, because she couldn't remember where Vice was located.

The back stairs to the second floor ended a few feet from her desk. Alexis opened the heavy fire door a fraction and peered into Homicide. Someone had dimmed the overhead lights and most of the desk lamps were off.

As she suspected, Homicide was empty. The manhunt for Daniel Nicolis continued. The public and press bought the lie that he had fabricated his death to escape justice. Only a dozen, including her, knew the truth.

She stepped in the room. A snore halted her. Four desks back near the right side of the room, Detective Yates's face was planted on the blotter. In the brief quiet between snorts, she heard voices drifting from the conference room. They were having a meeting.

Damn. She didn't waste time guessing how long she had before the room filled with detectives again. Quickly, she logged into her computer and searched for animal attacks. Pages of dog attacks loaded. It wasn't a damn dog that stormed through her home. It was…a lizard man, thing.

Someone laughed. Another joined in. The snoring stopped replaced by a protracted yawn. The rollers on a chair squeaked. Alexis ducked low in her seat.

Snap, crackle, pop. Yates must've stretched every muscle in his body and cracked every bone. A chill swept over her and pebbled her skin. She spun around, sure that someone lurked behind her. No one was there. So why did she feel like she wasn't alone?

A file slapped against the ground, bringing her back to the five W's: who, what, when, where and why. She peeked around her computer and watched Yates pick up the file and stumble toward the bathroom.

Time frame: One week ago. She typed in the name she remembered, Irma Barker. Last Tuesday, the retired transit worker reported a wild beast lived in the factory across the street from her. She gave a vivid description of a giant lizard man. The only reason Detective Henry took the report and didn't chase her out of the precinct and back to Rockland County was McCabe. Suddenly, the bastard had a heart. She scrawled the info on a Post-It and peeled the yellow square from the stack. Somewhere out there, this thing stalked Stella Walker. Maybe this lead would help find her.

Thirty seconds later, she was back in her car and on her way to Rockland County. Fresh New York City air never smelled or felt so good. Plus, the rushing air kept her alert. The pre-dawn traffic was light. She sped along the West Side Highway just above the speed limit. Within the next hour, this stretch of road would be a parking lot, as would all the highways in NYC. Rush hour started at five in the morning and ended at ten at night. Focused on her destination, she didn't enjoy the moment. Her thoughts were on what she would find. Not one for wild flights of imagination, she refused to assume she'd find anything. Rather, she hoped she wouldn't find anything.

"You have arrived at your destination." Her GPS intoned and she parked. Mrs. Barker lived modestly in a small frame house fourth on the block, sandwiched between two foreclosed properties. Her home and possibly the sixth house were still inhabited. As the report stated, the factory lay across the street. The structure and the surrounding parking lot encompassed more than five acres of real estate in New City, a small township a few miles from the Bronx border.

Judging by the abandoned industrial park, the recession had hit the town hard. The sign indicating what it manufactured had been removed, but it looked like a textile factory. Three stories with a faded, red brick shell, the large windows on the first level were boarded.

Alexis exited her car and adjusted her gun on her hip. She retrieved a flashlight from the trunk and paused. The glow from the few streetlights cast enough shadows to leave dozens of hiding places. This was probably a waste of time. And a looming disaster. Lately, every move she made helped further her slide into the sinkhole she called her life. Still, she jogged across the street to the shuttered factory.

Carefully, she slipped through an opening in the rusted gate and caught her jacket on a sharp edge. She swallowed a curse and stuck her finger through the hole, making it worse. *Damn, I just bought the thing a week ago.* Patting it down didn't make the hole disappear, though she pretended it did.

Instead of cars, abandoned pallets, barrels, and a trove of gears and machine parts littered the parking lot, as if they'd forgot to load them on the last wagon train out of Dodge. A police car crept by and she ducked behind a pallet of barrels. Her cell rang. *Damn it!* She forgot to silence the thing. She dropped the light and fished it out of her jeans.

Her mother's phone number appeared on the screen. At six a.m. only death would have Gloria Lever calling anyone. "Gloria?"

"Alexis?" She breathed heavily into the phone.

Was that trepidation in her mother's voice? Other than her only daughter failing epically at every task she had set in front of her, her mother feared nothing.

"What's wrong, Gloria?" Calling her *'Mother'* had ended after the last disastrous pageant when Gloria had all but disowned her. Alexis suspected losing the moniker didn't bother her mother at all. She had never been the type of parent you'd call 'Mommy' with childish glee or 'Mom' or 'Ma' as a teenager. A formal woman, Gloria Lever was always—*said somberly, reverently*—Mother. The boys still addressed as such. To Alexis, she was just Gloria.

Alexis waited. "Oh God, is it Dad?" She supplied her own answer when she heard nothing on the other end.

"No, your father is fine. He's sleeping upstairs."

It must be one of her brothers. Army, Navy, Air Force, each represented a branch of the military. "Is it one of the boys?" she whispered, needing the info now instead of later.

"No, the boys are fine also."

Then why the hell are you calling me at the crack of dawn? "Gloria, I'm a bit busy right now." She peeked from behind the barrels. The street was deserted again.

"Are you all right?"

Her mother had never asked that before. She'd never been the warm, hug you before bedtime, baked goods after school— kinda mother. Cold, distant, and controlled were her forte and she wasn't selective. "Yes, ma'am."

"Margie called…but I had a dream."

Great! Just want she needed. "I'm fine, Gloria. I really have to go." She repeated hoping the words would sink in.

"I said I had a dream." Gloria repeated.

And? Alexis wanted to say, join the club, but didn't. Her mother's dreams were…different. Sometimes things happened around Gloria Lever. Nothing bad, at least not to the family, but sometimes a last minute change of plans saved a family member from injury or brought a fortuitous meeting which always worked in their favor. The men in the family benefited from her mother's premonitions. While Alexis-

"Whatever you're doing, stop. Leave." Her voice took on a desperate edge that was so unlike her polished mother. Until today, she'd never called her with a warning, or suggestion to change her plans. She always knew Gloria had abilities, yet never asked.

Alexis glanced behind her at the building. A faint streak of sunlight illuminated the brick frame. It was now or never. And she had come so far. A cold breeze caressed her, gave comfort when it shouldn't.

"Dreams are foolish. An illusion only a useless mind creates. We live in the real world, with consequence. I have no

dreams and neither should you." Gloria often said when Alexis voiced an opinion other than what Gloria had implanted.

But she did dream. Her dreams, fantasies, and longings bled into nightmares which terrified her until around the age of twelve she stopped dreaming. That is, until recently when a tall, dark, shadowed man filled her head, and her nights.

"I have to go." After years of not caring about her whereabouts, now she cares? Alexis shook her head and swiped the phone closed and powered it down. She didn't have time to examine her mother's motivations.

Alexis circled the perimeter, testing each door. She jerked on the last one. Like the others, it had been sealed tight. But the dumpster off to the side would be the perfect ladder to reach the window with the broken board.

Okay. One quick peek. She touched her weapon, making sure it was on her hip and tossed her flashlight onto the top of the metal bin. She winced at the loud clang it made. One hand on the lid, one foot on a discarded cart, she started to haul herself up.

A loud bang whipped her around. She pulled her gun, strained her arm reaching for the flashlight, and ran around the corner toward the sound. One of the doors was open. She slowed and scanned the deserted lot. The door squealed and she pivoted, ready to fire. A hard, cold wind slapped her and slammed the door against the opposite wall. The noise echoed across the lot. She cringed and used her body to block the door from slamming closed.

No damage to the frame or knob. Could she have missed it? After last night, anything was possible.

She crept inside. Gutted of anything valuable, the spacious factory held nothing but a concrete floor and a discarded mattress in one corner. Squatters, though nothing else claimed inhabitants. She looked up through a hole in the ceiling to the second floor.

With her gun and flashlight leading the way, she walked deeper inside the factory and swept the area searching for the monster.

She was about to call herself stupid when she jerked to a halt.

That smell. All of her muscles trembled. Her breath fluttered, trapped in her lungs. Her stomach clenched in defense. Though she wanted to, Alexis didn't gag or cover her mouth and nose. She fought the fear and inhaled, drawing within her the rank air and unlocking the forgotten memories of last night. The little details came rushing back, flooding her senses. She blocked them all but couldn't dismiss the smell. The same odor clung to the beast that had charged through the house and flung her out of the way.

The hair on the back of her neck and beneath the soft fabric of her shirt rose. Her hand, steady a moment ago, trembled.

The beast was here. She had found it.

***

Fate had hung a dangerous predicament around Reign's neck, bound to two women: one a needy, selfish goddess, the other…how to describe Alexis? Unlike Nephythys, she was tall for a woman. Pale, but with a smattering of dainty freckles on her face. Her lips were thin because she constantly grimaced. Relaxed, they distracted him with their pouty seduction. All of her distracted him.

Damnation. He came here to save Roman and with any luck, himself. He had to find a way to cut the tether binding him to Alexis and kill the beast as Nephythys demanded. The Egyptians and their petty games. A growl burned the back of his throat.

Alexis whipped around and pointed her weapon in his direction. Had he spoken aloud? Her coppery eyes skimmed over him. He hardened. All of him. Then she turned and continued her searching.

She should be resting, he thought, watching her circle the outside of the building, searching for an entry point. The entire night he'd spent by her side waiting for her to yield to those ordering her. Alexis ignored them and followed her own path. He admired her tenacity.

Alexis. Her name lay heavy on his tongue, wanting to be spoken.

Reign shoved the thought away. Roman needed him. As for the goddess, Roman would help him thwart her because he could not go back to Chemmis, a slave to her whims. He would not. Nothing and no one could make him choose that hell again.

He stopped. Alexis had vanished. Had he been lost in his thoughts that long? No. She couldn't have gotten far. The tether wouldn't allow it.

Reign rounded the nearest corner and spotted her. *What was she doing now?* She dragged a crate next to a large metal box and paused, studying the shattered window above. He had to stop her before she hurt herself. But stopping her meant revealing himself and he wasn't ready. There were still too many unknowns in this new world. He needed more time.

Reign flashed to the nearest door. He could use his sword and carve an opening in the metal, but that would leave many unanswered questions. He could tap into the power the goddess gave him, but he wanted nothing from her he didn't absolutely need. A quick glance confirmed Alexis still studied a way to climb the container. He grabbed the handle, turned hard and jerked. With a grinding snap, it swung open. He stepped inside the shadowy interior. A wave of energy halted him and kept him from advancing any further. He couldn't pass through, but he glimpsed what the barrier protected.

He turned to slam the door closed, but she was already there. Face scrunched, she studied the opening. So unlike the women of his time, Alexis's fearless nature intrigued him. Nothing swayed her determination. This would. The barrier would keep her from entering.

She peered inside the building and then passed through him and the barrier unrestricted. Warmth suffused him, starting in his heart, and spread to each nerve cell. She'd touched him more intimately than she'd touched anyone before.

Her soul brushed his, yet she calmly continued to navigate the intricate pathways and skirted the danger lying inches from her. She didn't see the open pits lining the floor with the beasts nestled inside. He couldn't understand her blindness. She paused and disgust washed over her features. In his invisible state, he could only imagine what she smelled. Weapon shaking in her hand, she swung around and stumbled over her own feet.

Heart hammering, he beat against the barrier. It didn't budge. Next, he pushed. The threads of energy woven together into a pattern of weaves, gave a little, but didn't break. He pressed harder, leaning into it, only to be repelled eight feet away. Slammed to the ground, he groaned and climbed to his feet and rushed back.

Somehow, Alexis kept to the pathway. Too many times, she came close to disaster, flirting with the edge of the danger while searching each dark corner. Regardless of the consequences, he had to get in there. He charged at the weaving, only to be repelled with equal force.

He flashed back to the doorway, roaring in frustration.

Alexis spun and ran toward him. A chunk of plaster tripped her. She fell, right into the open pit and the beasts lying within.

Power rolled through him. Nephythys's *vis*'Ra ripped his insides apart and leaped from his palms in crimson threads. He grabbed onto the barrier, fingers sinking deep. The weaves crackled, melting like heated wax.

He flashed across the room a fraction of a second too late. Alexis fell but no further than the floor. She twisted and landed on her side. Her weapon aimed at his heart. A different, multicolored weave of energy protected the pit.

"Don't you move!" she shouted.

Damnation. He had forgotten to fade.

"Hands over your head."

He did as instructed.

"Where'd you come from?" She eased to her feet.

"No where you have ever heard of." Her weapon never wavered. So small, yet she trusted it to protect her.

"Take one step forward." She motioned with the gun and angled the light to bathe his face. "Oh fuck!" Alexis gasped, slack jawed, eyes wide.

A lady in his time would never dare to think such a word and never allow it to pass her lips. Though he did like the way she bit her bottom lip right before the curse exploded. She stepped back, over the pit. He had to stop himself from reaching for her.

"You're not real," she whispered and closed her eyes. "I've finally lost my mind."

The plaintive notes in her voice touched his conscience. Wondering about your sanity was not unknown to him. The

Vanquished were quite real, though they only interacted with him.

"Police! Come out with your hands up."

Alexis turned toward the sound. He should disappear, fade by the time she turned back around, and shatter her already fragile state. No, he couldn't do it, not to her. He strode to the door. She watched, weapon trained on him.

"I am real. You are not crazed." He opened the door and stepped out.

Two officers in uniforms similar to those worn by the men who Alexis worked with, stood behind the open doors of a patrol car, their weapons aimed. He raised his hands as ordered. The Vanquished screamed inside his head and his palm itched, ready for his blade to appear.

"On the ground. On your belly," one ordered.

Reign heard Alexis's footsteps behind him. He fought the instinct to push her back into the building and attack the men. The Vanquished urged him on, goading him toward violence.

"NYPD," she said, exiting the building. She cut a wide berth around him. He angled his head and watched her weapon still trained on the center of his chest. The badge dangling around her neck glinted in the headlights.

"Alexis? What are you doing here?" one of the men asked.

"Paul?" Her head jerked around and her mouth slipped open in surprise. "I-I'm checking out a lead in the case."

"Without stopping by the station and letting our chief know you're here?" One of the officers approached. He studied the badge hanging around her neck. "We got no word you were in our jurisdiction."

"Sorry about that." She glanced at Reign and seemed unnerved to meet his gaze. "On the ground! Hands behind your back!" She yelled at him.

Reign stretched out on the pavement.

"Anyone else in there?" The officer approached the building cautiously.

Alexis shook her head, but the man went inside to secure the building anyway.

"What's his story?" Paul secured Reign's hands behind his back and patted his clothing, searching.

On the cold ground, staring at her shoes, Reign wondered what she would say.

"I found him inside, trespassing."

"What case are you working?"

"One of the neighbors filed a report at our station. There was a possible connection to the Strangler case. I came to check it out, but didn't find anything."

Paul nodded and he seemed to study her with appreciation. "I didn't know you were assigned to the case."

Alexis shrugged. "It's not something I open a conversation with."

Hauled upright, Reign ignored the screaming tendons in his shoulders. Paul opened the backseat door. Together they tried shoving him inside. Reign didn't budge, not until she looked at him once more.

"Get in the car or I'll mace you," Paul threatened.

Didn't sound like something he would enjoy. Nonetheless, he waited. The other officer had returned from the building. Both men squared off around him, weapons aimed. Once, an army had tried to move him and failed—these men would fair no better.

Finally, she looked at him. A quick glimpse from her coppery eyes and he allowed himself to be squeezed into the backseat. He would humor them, for a while, before fading, or until the tether drew tight and yanked him back to her side.

"We'll take this guy in and book him for you," Paul said.

"And take the credit for the collar?" Her voice dripped acid. "Thanks. I'll follow you." She started for her car across the street.

"It's just trespassing. What's the big deal?" He blocked her way.

The man stood too near, with a familiarity that made Reign boil. Blood pounded in his ears, drowning out the rest of her words. He had felt rage before, but none like this. He ached to wrap his hands around the man's throat and twist. He snapped the restraints, ready to materialize between them.

"You. Are. The big deal. Don't help me, Paul. It makes me nervous." She walked around him and jogged across the street.

Paul watched her.

Reign watched Paul.

***

Trailing behind the police car, Alexis couldn't keep her gaze off the back of his head and broad shoulders. Every single thing about him embodied the fantasy lover she'd created, then forgotten and remembered again just days ago. She had dreamed of his naked body covering hers, wrapping her legs around him, and begging him to take her.

Somehow, he shifted his big body around and stared at her from the caged back seat, as if he knew where her thoughts strayed. A shiver raced down her spine. Heat pooled low in her groin and released in a whiplash of pleasure. She clenched the wheel with suddenly sweaty palms and tried to hold onto the tendril, all the while his gaze remained locked on hers. "Thank God," she sighed when they pulled into the police station parking lot.

It seemed the entire police station had stopped to stare at the new arrival. She couldn't fault the women for gawking or the men for unconsciously touching their weapons. Immense and overwhelming, he stood at least six foot eight with shoulders as wide as a linebacker with the pads. Black cotton stretched tight over massive shoulders and molded to perfect pecs and brick abs. Even stretched behind his back, his biceps bulged. When contracted, they'd probably peak like mini Mount Everest. His eyes, electric blue, peered through his shaggy midnight hair, watching her approach.

Palpable menace seeped from his pores, polluted the air, and set everyone's nerves on edge. The man was a killer. He wouldn't wax poetic like a comic book villain. No, he'd kill you and move on to the next combatant before your body hit the ground.

Her heart suddenly ached. The embodiment of the man she dreamed about most of her life now stood before her and he was probably a criminal. And for some weird reason, she cared. Her life had plopped into the crapper yet she cared about a criminal she had met fifteen minutes ago.

Then he pivoted that body so she got a full frontal and whipped his hair back with a snap of his neck. Alexis sucked in a sharp breath. That face. There was nothing pretty about him or even handsome. He demolished her senses like a freight train smashing into a two seater. He was almost too much to look at, yet she couldn't turn away. She didn't dare.

Exhaling slowly, Alexis didn't back down from his stare. His eyes seem to deepen into dark drowning pools when she approached. His hard, lean face softened and an increment of his fury abated, lessening the overall testosterone level in the room.

"No ID and he won't tell us his name," Paul's partner told the desk sergeant.

Her prisoner's—that's how she thought of him—lips curled slightly in a mockery of a smile.

"Reign," he said.

Oh, shit. She had to lean against a wall. His rough voice kicked off a pulse deep in her groin making her imagine something else rough and deep.

"Run his prints and take him to holding. I'm sure he's in the system," the sergeant said. He offered no resistance when they led him away.

Paul took her arm and pulled her off to the side. "I could cover for you."

Alexis gave the hand on her arm a scathing glance and looked at Paul. He dropped his hand. "Why so helpful?" He leaned closer. His nearness made her skin crawl.

"I'm just trying to help."

"Yeah." *Right.* She nodded, not sure if he was trying to help her or himself. She tried not to follow Reign's progress through the department. Once he was out of sight, her brain cleared. She glanced at Paul. He seemed earnest enough. Taking him up on his offer would lower the level of crap she was wading in. "All right, Paul. Thanks."

A smile stretched across his face. "You seem pretty attached to the guy." He squeezed her arm and leaned close to her ear. "Haven't fallen for a criminal, have you?"

Alexis yanked her arm away. Damn, his words hit a little too close to home. She stepped outside the police station and tilted her face into the sun. A wave of exhaustion swamped her. She needed a shower and sleep ASAP.

Her thoughts strayed to Reign again, but she fought the urge and focused on getting home. Her shift started in a few hours and she had to see the damage to her grandmother's house. She rolled down the windows and hoped fresh air would keep her awake.

When she parked in the driveway, she saw men on the porch with Mrs. Kelly. A panel truck from the local hardware store was parked in front the house. Her neighbor met Alexis before she exited her car.

"Where have you been?" She scolded. "You needed rest, not a joy ride." She pulled Alexis down and examined her wound. "You're not bleeding. Are you in pain?"

"No, just tired." More like dead on her feet. Alexis yawned. "You didn't have to do this, Mrs. Kelly."

She waved her hand, dismissing Alexis's statement. "Did you get my message, dear?"

"No. Sorry."

"Oh, well I called your father and told him what happened. I knew you wouldn't be up to handling everything so he gave me permission to have the carpenters come out and get an estimate and fit a temporary door. I hope you don't mind." She patted Alexis's shoulder.

That had to be sympathy Alexis saw in Mrs. Kelly's watery eyes and gentle smile. She didn't mind her calling the carpenters. Her father, on the other hand, she wished the woman had left him out the loop. *Damn.*

Better to call him before he called her. She skirted passed the workers and fished her phone from her pocket. Her cell rang before she dialed. "Lever."

"It's Paul. The guy we brought in escaped."

CHAPTER FIVE

SET sank deep into the bowels of the Underworld where he was first formed. Where the first evil was committed so long ago that only he remembered. Once there, he wallowed in the corrupted essentia, drinking in its purity and forming a plan.

There were long forgotten parts of *Duat* only the oldest inhabitants remembered. Deep subterranean cells retaining *Malum,* old evil no longer permitted to walk the earth. Evil he caged as protector of the human race and as a pretense to gain Osiris' council, would serve him again.

A ripple of delight swept along his changing form. So many layers with nooks and crannies, caves and wells, to cast friend, foe, and the discarded dregs off and forget they existed. Through many layers of sediment and rock he passed, slowing as he approached each ward. Some created by him, others by Osiris. A few were a combination of the four council members: Nephythys, Osiris, Isis, and himself. He passed through the final ward and set foot on the ancient corridor. Created from the very first sands of Egypt, the inky glass pathway led to equally dark glass chambers housing the enemies of the Pantheon.

At the end of the pathway, Osiris's crypt rested. Not like the crypts of the pharaohs, no furnishings, trinkets, bodies of slaves, or feasts were housed to take him to the afterlife. Encased in stone, frozen to his council seat, the god had chosen his fate and accepted his sentence. There he waited for the one person that could free him.

But never would.

His mind wandered to his son, Anubis. How could a joining between Nephythys and him produce a weak-willed, spineless being? She had birthed Horus, a true prince of the Pantheon, for her lover Osiris and let his wife, Isis, claim maternity. It was the only way SET would let the child live and mature into his godhood. And it was the only way Nephythys would agree to be his wife.

What a poor bargain he had made when he commanded Hathor, the Goddess of Love, to join them together.

Too late for regret. Now was the time for vengeance.

As he walked the pathway, SET peered into each chamber, searching for the one he wanted. In the middle, situated between a Chthonic demon and a Sumerian, Khuket—Goddess of Darkness and Chaos—resided. Curled into a tight ball in the shadowy corner of the room, SET listened to her labored breathing. She suffered. Eternal hunger gnawed her insides and reduced her to this mewling being. He would never know that hunger. The abundance of evil precluded that possibility.

SET swept his hand along the hieroglyphics lining the doorway to her chamber. The glyphs hummed to life. Their patterns changed, realigned, allowing the barrier to thin and him to pass. Her breathing hitched and her head craned on her neck. Her dark pixie hair was at odds with her ashen skin. Red rimmed, pitted eyes glared at him before she rolled onto her back, heaved a breath, and rolled once more onto her side.

A pert nipple peaked through the tattered remains of a gown showing vast stretches of flesh. A tight abdomen, the curve of her hip lay bare. The gown dipped into the valley between her slim legs, outlining her sex. All would've stoked a fire in any man. Regrettably, SET wasn't a man and his embers burned for one who cared naught. If he could, he'd kill Hathor, the Goddess of Love, for binding him to his beloved wife, even though she did so at his command.

The conquered Goddess of Ogdoad studied him with hostile eyes. No less than all he deserved for his part in her pantheon's defeat. The desire for revenge swam in her jade eyes. A fruitless endeavor. Death held no advantage over him or him over the final judgment. Besides, there were worse things than death—defeat. A condition she should be well acquainted with.

"Forgive me, Great God SET, for not welcoming you as you deserve. What brings you to my palace?" she rasped.

He stopped a smile from forming. "You do, Goddess." His *vis'*Ra ebbed from his pores and gathered in a murky ball, hovering in the center of the cell. Khuket lurched to her feet. Sparks flared briefly in her eyes as she tracked the energy.

"I thank you for the recognition, but I am no longer a goddess." She trembled.

SET waited for her to crumble, crawl, beg. She didn't. "Though caged, I will not deny your true station, Khuket, Goddess of Ogdoad, the kingdom that came before my own."

She sank gracefully to her knees, then genuflected and stayed bowed in that submissive position. He wasn't fooled. Energy depleted, she had not the strength to gain her footing once more. He palmed the ball of energy and hurled it across the cell. *Vis'*Ra coated her, soaked into her. Khuket collapsed onto the earthen floor. Body arching, mouth agape in a silent scream, she thrashed. Her fingers gouged the ground until she banged her head once, twice leaving flecks of tar-like blood quenching the dirt. A shudder raced from the tips of her hair to her toes. Then, she stopped. She dry heaved once, twice, gritted her teeth, and bore down. He knew his energy didn't quite suit her, but she needed it. She wouldn't regurgitate his precious gift.

Khuket, the last remaining deity of The Eidos, a race of elementals who thrived in the first eons, gave a last shudder and stood. A flame flickered in the depths of her eyes. No longer wan and pasty, a thousand candles seemed to illuminate her from within. Edges of the tattered gown seamlessly knit together. The threads of her power stroked him, subtly shifting his emotions. Her steady gaze cooled to a smoldering ember when she met his gaze and her slight smile washed over him. He threw back his head and laughed.

"You are exactly what I need. I will grant you your freedom now and forever if you complete one task for me." Her startled expression pleased him.

"You would free *me?* Once your enemy?"

He nodded.

"What is the task?" Suspicion edged each word.

"I need you to kill a human."

"Why can you not kill this human yourself?"

He suffered her questioning stare for a moment. He wouldn't her tell that he couldn't leave Chemmis. By caging Osiris, he had caged himself. "You will find this human for me. Destroy him. Then bring him to me, alive."

A feral, eager grin split her face. "Who is this man that has earned your wrath?"

SET pushed all the knowledge he had of his nemesis into Khuket's mind. Her lovely face lost all trace of emotion. "Are you up to the task or do you doubt your abilities?"

"Your will shall prevail, but this will take time, my lord." Her level gaze didn't skirt away from his.

She challenged him with the truth. "What is time to a god? Do you accept?"

"Yes, my God SET. I agree to your terms for my complete freedom. There are many ways to destroy a man. Do you have a preference?"

He did. "Make him love you. Then use that love against him." As Nephythys used his love for her. Khuket's jade eyes assessed him, searching for a way in. As if she had a chance of discovering anything he didn't want her to know.

"Is that all?"

Demure and acquiescent, she portrayed the model servant. He liked that. He told her the terms and she accepted without haggling. Not that she had a choice. SET moved his hand along the hieroglyphics, causing them to glow. The sealed glass doorway turned back into its natural state, collapsing to the ground as golden sand.

Khuket crossed the threshold and sighed deeply. He noted a different look in her eye. Amusement? Curiosity? Both danced within their depths.

"What will stop me from leaving this place and doing as I please?"

SET changed, turned into a Typhon, a jackal-like mystical predator Ra defeated when he'd first conquered earth. The Greeks learned of the legend, created their own beast, and named it such, though nothing so magnificent as he. Sleek, coal colored fur covered his body. Multiple rows of canine teeth populated his mouth. Small openings for ears and four pitted eyes comprised his head. Eight claw-like feet and a forked tail, all ten feet of him surrounded her.

He batted her back into the cell. Khuket skidded to the middle of the room and didn't move. In this form, he had to battle to keep his more primitive impulses under control. He wanted to pounce and play with her before devouring her in delicious bits. Instead, he stalked her and pinned her to the floor. He crouched low and brought his snout close to her face. He liked the fright in her eyes and the way she trembled.

"I am SET, the God of all Evil. Wherever evil goes, hides, lives, I am drawn to it and it to me. You, defeated goddess, will never be able to hide from me. Your dark chaotic essence is the very thing which will lead me to you. Run. I need a good hunt." He growled, drooling onto her face.

Her fear seeped into him, satisfying the rage her challenge stirred. He retreated and returned to the SET who had greeted her earlier. "Follow me." He turned and again crossed the threshold of the cell. He glanced once more on Osiris's crypt, swearing the god's eyes followed him. Khuket paused and studied the occupant of the cell next to her.

"Fail in your oath and this prison will house you again," he said.

"My oath binds me to your will, Great God SET. You will have your vengeance and I will have mine."

Her form faded into the foundation of the prison. SET didn't give chase. He let her believe she had achieved some small triumph because it wouldn't last. And in the end, victory was much sweeter when you destroyed your opponent's dreams. Instead, he listened to the sweet chimes of her laughter ringing in his soul.

CHAPTER SIX

Alexis didn't expect a warm welcome from Vice, but the silent treatment was more than worn out. The men of Vice had the sensitivity of a sea sponge and the women weren't much better. Praise traveled slowly while news of a screw-up rode the bullet train. Jokes, everyone had jokes. Why couldn't they talk behind her back like normal folk? Nope, cops got in your face, up close and very personal, so they could see when it hurt.

And she'd had plenty of hurt. A rookie and the youngest detective on the squad, she was a pariah. When the legal department threw out the last detective's exam rather than face a lawsuit from the Justice Department for discrimination, they agreed to open the test to every applicant, regardless of time on the job.

She hadn't studied, but took the exam for future reference. Scoring in the top percentage drew attention she never sought or wanted. The department had to offer her a position, while encouraging her not to accept. Her pride wouldn't let her turn it down. And she was glad. She loved the job. Well, maybe not all aspects of the job.

From the back of the squad room, she listened to her new lieutenant drone on about tourist complaints, target zones, and the joint task force with other Vice squads around the city. No surprise they put her on the hoe stroll her first day. As a patrol officer, she'd had a few assignments with Vice when they were short on female detectives. She remembered the drill.

Alexis squeezed into a pair of low-rise skinny jeans and stiletto heels. The racer back tee with shelf bra she had dug out from the bottom of her workout bag barely held in her rack—but she guessed that was the point—slutted her up. Pimped out by the department all in the name of lowering the crime rate. The principle behind the idea was great, until you dragged in the tight clothes and clear heels, and strolled up and down a seedy avenue hoping someone liked you enough to throw their family and career down the gutter. She loved catching the Johns with their lame excuses. She hated seeing the teary-faced wives bailing out their cheating spouses.

God, she never thought she'd be in this position again. Whether it was on the stroll or on stage, she despised being on display, judged for your body parts.

Raised in a family of military men, she wanted to wrestle, play baseball in the summer and basketball in the winter, not take ballet and piano lessons. She wanted to learn how to shoot and take karate lessons. Her life wasn't about what she wanted. Forced to watch from the sidelines, to be the cheerleader instead of the jock, she did what she was expected to do, follow in Gloria's Miss Florida 19-whatever footsteps. Why? Because Alexis Lever was the next Miss America.

Groomed from birth to be the epitome of grace, beauty, style, and class, she failed at each one. She was clumsy, awkward, and color blind so her clothes never matched. All she ever wanted was the respect of her father and brothers.

The disappointments in her failures were spread equally around. Her last stab at a title, any title, was at twenty when she competed in the Miss Westchester County pageant. She purposely gained weight, sang badly, and ate chocolate until her face looked like a pepperoni pizza. When it was over, she joined the police academy. Gloria didn't speak to her for a year. Her brothers laughed. Her father was appalled at her joining the police academy one month after the pageant loss. He wanted her in the military, the family business. She didn't need to walk the same paths her brothers had chosen and fail in comparison. Doing this job proved she was as good as any of them, brothers, coworkers, anyone.

Her father's praise proved it. Finally, he acknowledged her accomplishment; she'd made it without using his name. Still, Gloria barely spoke to her.

Alexis shellacked on a thick layer of make-up and was surprised at the outcome. She hadn't done a half-bad job. Maybe her time on the pageant circuit wasn't a total waste.

No longer the fresh innocent girl teetering on the brink of womanhood that Gloria strove to portray, she looked like a woman with a story to tell. Too bad no one wanted to listen.

She snatched up her make-up and threw the kit into the back of her locker. It ricocheted before she slammed door closed. A few catcalls were expected, not the stone cold silence following out the station and into the unmarked surveillance van.

"Hey, I need to place the electronics," Delaney said.

She gritted her teeth and refused to meet his eyes when his chubby fingers slipped between her breast and his hand traveled up her shirt. How hard is it to place a strip of tape and a microphone? Three tries and he was still fumbling. He'd only been on the job fifteen years. She was sure he'd seen a set of tits in that time.

An arctic wind circled the interior of the van tossing papers into the air, sending goose bumps streaking down her spine. She glanced at the windows, but they were both closed.

"Done. Sorry about that." Delaney murmured. He stepped away and wiped the sweat off his upper lip.

Damn. Delaney was a quiet and unassuming guy. Probably the nicest guy in the building. He didn't deserve her unkind thoughts.

"Thanks," she said and exited the van. Her heels clicked on the pavement like gunshots in her rush to escape. "Lever!" The lieutenant's voice hissed in her ear. "Get your ass back here! You're too far to cover."

"Yeah, Okay. Roger," she mumbled into the mouthpiece.

Three hours later she had four arrests to Dalton's nine. It's not a competition; she lied to herself as she glanced at her partner. She had to admit Officer Dalton looked stunning in her Lycra cat suit with cutout abdomen. A petite woman at 5'4" 34-24-32. Ass high and tight, boobs pointing towards the sky. Her glossy blond hair glowed under the streetlights, which complimented her porcelain skin and pale hazel eyes. Standing next to her, Alexis felt every inch of her tall, inadequate frame.

Her double d's, freckled skin and hair that should have been wavy but instead was unruly and frizzy.

Swollen feet and an aching back had her leaning against a parking meter. The four-inch heels were not the Easy Spirit walking shoes she wore every day to work. She'd give anything for a massage.

11th avenue was usually a hodgepodge of denizens. Now, foot traffic had died down except for her, Dalton, and a few other brave streetwalkers on the stroll. Dalton glanced her way from the lamppost she had guarded for the last twenty minutes. They'd ignored each other all night.

"Lever." Dalton nodded and walked over to her.

Alexis returned the rookie's nod.

"I hate details like this." Dalton covered her mic and whispered. "This is a waste of time." Dalton started. "I'd rather be looking for the Strangler."

As part of the few who knew the truth, hunting down Daniel Nicolis, Roman Nicolis's adopted brother, was what Alexis would be doing right now if she were still in Homicide. One moment he was splattered on the pavement fifteen stories below Stella Walker's apartment. The next his body, vanished from the morgue. Well, headquarters told the world he had vanished, but she'd seen the video. Getting up and walking out of the morgue's cooler is very different from '*vanishing.*' Then there was the Egyptian guy that helped Daniel and then disappeared in a whirling vortex.

Alexis covered her mic. "Where do you think he is?" she asked, letting Dalton draw her into the conversation.

"Cozumel with margaritas in each hand." Dalton laughed at her own joke. "He knows we're onto him. He's been smart enough to evade us so far. I don't think he's interested in killing."

"What is he interested in then?"

Dalton shrugged. "Power, control, dominance, the usual things men want."

She hadn't said anything Alexis didn't know already. Alexis walked away, but Dalton followed her.

"I'm right; it's the same anywhere you go." Dalton matched her steps.

"I think you're wrong," Alexis said. She couldn't stop herself from correcting the rookie as they strolled down the street. "This isn't the usual man. His motivations are different. Like all serial killers, he doesn't *just* like killing, he needs it." She remembered the eviscerated remains of his last two victims and fought to keep down the *Big Mac* she'd had for dinner. "Everything indicates he's spiraling down toward a crisis or a mental break. But now he's gone to ground. Daniel's an extremely motivated, trained killer. Also, he doesn't have a type which puts everyone at risk."

"Was he a victim of child abuse?" Dalton asked.

"Not confirmed, but it doesn't matter. Abuse doesn't turn you into a killer. It's a decision you make. But I'd like to know what turned him. I'd also like to know how long he's been killing. He didn't start this spree this summer. He's been killing for a while."

"Then he's hidden the bodies well," Officer Dalton stated.

"He could've been killing bums, indigents, prostitutes. We don't know where his job at Nicolis Security has taken him." Once again, everything revolved around the Nicolis family. Damn, she wanted back in the chase. "But I'm sure the feds and the department have things well in hand." They had stopped in front of a bodega. "I'm dying out here. Let's get some water." She tapped her microphone. "We're getting some water."

"Roger, we're calling it a night," the Lieutenant replied over her earpiece.

That gave them a few minutes before the van picked them up. The bell dinged when they entered the small corner store. Salsa played over the radio and the attendant watched them behind bulletproof Plexiglas. They were hookers, his usual clientele, so he watched for a second then turned back to his twenty-inch flat screen. She passed a mirror in the corner of the ceiling and stopped. Loose and wild, her hair resembled a mane. The clothes and a ton of makeup made her into another woman, a woman with a heavy past and dark future. What would Paul think of the re-made version of Alexis Lever?

He'd love it. She could see the smirk on his always-charming face. Ugh! She pushed the unwanted thoughts away and stopped herself from grabbing a roll of *Bounty* and wiping her face clean. She couldn't wait to get back to the precinct and wash the goop off.

Reign had seen her without all this crap. By his smoldering gaze, he didn't find her lacking. She thought of her missing criminal and her insides sighed and turned liquid. Impossibly tall, impossibly big, impossibly gorgeous. His face, all hard angles, and planes. His electric blue eyes. She never liked men with long hair but on him, it was a requirement. Everything about him made her want to come over and over and over again. What would he think of her dressed like this?

The bell over the door broke her concentration. Three men entered the store and spread out. One stood by the door, another went to the cash register where the attendant waited, and the third wandered back to eyeball them. His gaze flickered between her and Dalton, sizing them up.

Her gut clenched tight and her heart thudded heavily. Alexis glanced at Dalton, but she was focused on the diet drinks in the freezer. Alexis looked at the attendant. His gaze darted between the man in front of him and the one by the door.

Alexis's fingers curled. In her time on the force, she'd drawn her weapon once. She'd never had to fire. Would that streak end tonight?

***

Reign's blood simmered in his veins. All night he watched Alexis and fought to control his desire and rage. Her decadent attire tantalized him and worse, distracted him. She was a warrior, not a courtesan. Courtesans of his time dressed with more clothes than the average female of this present day. Men ogled her. They touched her and darkness so foul filled him until he trembled with the desire to destroy them. They talked to her about inappropriate things. They laughed with her over tasteless humor, and they laughed at her when she wasn't within hearing. She wasn't his to protect, he reminded himself every minute. He came here to save one person, Roman.

Repeating the statement kept him from shredding someone. He also ignored the part of him, which wanted to find the creature and eliminate it, *for her*. That meant returning to Nephythys. Not an option to consider. Once he found Roman, together they'd decide what to do. But first, he had to find a way to leave her. He must sever the link they shared without hurting Alexis.

For now, he'd traded one enslavement for another. He ground his teeth together and slowed his breathing. His anger fed the Vanquished and their agitated voices swirled in his head, churning his emotions into a toxic stew. It didn't help that her lushness lured him closer.

She ignited a hunger of pleasure and need he had buried and thought forgotten. Alexis was danger wrapped in a silken package, carnal temptation to a man that had lived in a sensual vacuum. He couldn't have her and just wanting her threatened her safety. He had to get away from her before lust led to blood and retribution.

A sudden sense of danger whipped him around. Mired in his thoughts, he had lost track of her. Only a few yards away, he found her rooted to the spot and staring right through him. Sweat beaded her brow and she panted through parted lips. Her eyes were wide and afraid, but her hand steadily crept to her weapon.

Why is she reaching for it?
***

Alexis didn't have time to react. Without hesitation, one of the men pulled a gun out of his jacket pocket and rushed over to Dalton. A warning would've helped, but Alexis couldn't find her voice. Head still in the freezer studying shelves of ice cream, Dalton didn't notice him. And a half-stocked display of Corn Flakes blocked Alexis from running to Dalton's aid.

In Alexis's peripheral vision, she glimpsed two guys at the front of the store, one guarding the door. The other had his gun aimed at the attendant, who'd opened the cash register and was stuffing a paper bag with bills.

She heard a smack and a crunch. Dalton screamed.

Alexis pulled her weapon, thumbed the safety, and cocked it in one smooth motion. She pivoted. The gunman loomed over Dalton. The butt of his gun rose over his head, ready to strike her again. She lowered her chin to the microphone between her breasts and prayed they were still connected to the surveillance van. "Officer down."

"Police! Drop your weapon." Alexis shouted to the guy about to brain Dalton. She prayed his five seconds of hesitation was enough to allow Dalton to retrieve her weapon and level the playing field. Otherwise, the man on her right had a clean shot of her.

She may die. But she wouldn't die alone. Alexis aimed for her target's center mass. She slowed her breathing.

And blinked a final time.

A wall dressed in black stepped in front of her. The blare of gunshots drowned out everything but her blood pounding through her arteries. She looked up and up, and saw long, shoulder-length silky black hair that was more than familiar. Spasms choked her lungs. She backed up and brushed the display.

It couldn't be! Just couldn't!

She was awake. This wasn't a dream.

Her hand reached up and threaded through his hair. A slight turn of his head and his blue eyes captured her. Vaguely, she heard the door open and the men run out.

Disbelief made her blink. Hard. "How are you here?" she whispered. A siren wailed and tires screeched outside the store.

"Where you go, I follow." His lips curled in a wry smile.

"Huh?" She shook her head, because she must've misunderstood. No criminal stalks his arresting officer and then saves her. He turned and faced her. "Are you hurt?" He had to be injured.

She skimmed his body, searching for blood and lurched to a halt when she saw the sword gripped in his hand. Alexis jerked back. She raised her weapon and pointed it at his chest. Was it contempt that spread across his features before he spun away and charged toward the front door?

"Don't!" she screamed and he halted.

He whipped around. His muscles bulged. His face twisted in fury. "They would have killed you. For that they die."

"You're under arrest." The words were thick in her throat.

"You would punish me for protecting you?" he snarled, baring his teeth.

She remembered the mic clicked between her breasts and slapped her hand over it. "You're an escaped criminal and my prisoner." Though her insides trembled, the gun didn't waver from his chest.

His eyes turned flinty. A vein in his neck pulsed ominously in time with the glowing crimson blade gripped in his palm. "Truer words have never been said," he sneered. "But neither you nor anyone else in this realm will ever chain me." Reign faded before her eyes.

The door burst open. The bell above it was discordant as officers poured in.

Blood drained from her brain. Her muscles surrendered to gravity and Alexis fainted into a display of Corn Flakes.

***

Alexis woke to muffled sounds and strobing red and blue lights. An EMT crouched on one side of her. On the other side, a detective from Vice's lips moved, but she couldn't process his words. Someone had placed her in a vacuum, a protective cocoon where she could see, but not hear a thing. Or maybe she had turned deaf, and dumb and blind was planning an ambush around the next corner.

A part of her registered that she should be afraid. Too busy studying the crowd scurrying around her; she didn't have time for fear. The EMT beside her waved his hands in front of her face. She tracked the movement. He snapped his fingers, breaking the protection bubble surrounding her. A cacophony of noise assailed her. Confused, she pushed away from the EMT.

"Lever." Someone shouted. Hands pinned her to the ground. "It's okay."

Her senses realigned and the confusion faded. A quick mental check confirmed she had all her body parts and there were no bullet holes ventilating her chest. Cold penetrated through the back of her denim jacket.

I'm on the floor. Her gaze darted around the room. She didn't have a chance to question 'Where am I?' Memories flooded her system.

"Where's Dalton?" Mouth dry, tongue heavy, her words came thick and slow.

"She's fine. The EMT's are taking care of her. What happened here, Lever?" He gripped her shoulders hard. His face filled her vision. Detective Michael Cavaugn, one of McCabe's cronies.

Alexis wrenched free and pushed herself up into a seated position. The room tilted and her stomach heaved. She gritted her teeth. Blowing chunks at another crime scene was not an option. The first time was humiliating enough.

"Lever, can you tell me what happened here?" Cavaugn pressed her.

Sure, I can tell you everything that happened. "Did you catch the guys that did this?"

He shook his head. "No. We're canvassing the area."

Lever climbed to her feet. Cornflake boxes littered the floor along with shell casings.

Shit! It really did happen. What could she tell them that would be close to the truth? "Dalton and I came in to get something to drink. Three armed men, one black, two white, walked in. Two had .38's one had a sawed off shotgun. Dalton had her head in the freezer and didn't see them enter. One grabbed her and knocked her on the side of the head. I pulled my weapon and trained it on him. Two had their weapons on me and…" *Reign appeared.*

Bigger than life. Taking a chest full of bullets meant for her.

Then walked away.

No. Vanished.

"That's all I remember," Alexis mumbled while the scene continued to unfold in her mind.

"Did you fire a shot?"

"Huh?" Lost in thought, she hadn't heard him.

"Did you discharge your weapon?"

Almost, but Reign appeared. "No, I didn't."

"So they fired at close range and neither of you were hit. I'd say that's an unexplainable miracle."

She was about to agree when she spotted a camera mounted in the corner of the ceiling facing her. Her blood went cold. This miracle wouldn't be unexplainable for long.

"Their surveillance equipment doesn't work. Been out of order for months the clerk said." The detective pointed to the camera.

Good. The last thing she needed was digital proof she cooperated with a fugitive. *The mic!* Her fingers dipped into her cleavage and pulled the microphone from between her breasts.

"What did the clerk say?" she asked.

"He hit the floor after the first shot. Says he didn't see anything. We collected the microphones from both of you. The techs already checked and they didn't pick up anything after you called for help."

This was more than a miracle. Alexis opted for the precinct over a ride to the hospital. She had a report to file and she knew others were waiting to grill her.

Several uniformed officers stopped her and asked about her welfare as she walked into the building. But as she made her way through Homicide to her desk in Vice, the snickers started. Whether real or imagined, their mumbled words reached her.

Incompetent, foolish, out of her depth, rookie. The last word summed it all up. No matter how long she stayed on the force, they'd treat her as a rookie.

Why? "Because some liberal got the detective test thrown out on the grounds of discrimination!" McCabe's voice screamed in her head. No one respected her. She was too young to be a detective. Too inexperienced. Lousy shot. Slow as hell. She couldn't keep up. Didn't know enough. And worst of all, she was nice. That's what they thought of her. Incompetent and nice. The words should be synonyms.

Exhaustion dragged her down until her knuckles scraped the linoleum. Punch drunk from too many events happening too close together, Alexis plopped herself in her rolling chair. The box containing her belongings from her desk in Homicide blocked her computer screen. She pushed it to the side and logged onto the secure website.

Five minutes later, she sat back, pressed print, and listened to the quiet whine of the printer as it spit out a single sheet of paper.

"Lever." The captain's bellow jerked her around.

She would've liked a chance to reread it, edit it a bit, but she folded the sheet once and rose. Still dressed in hoe stroll best,

Alexis crossed the room, swept past her captain, and placed the sheet on his desk. She didn't bother to sit.

He walked around his desk and snatched the paper up. "Good. I'll approve it immediately," he said after reading it. "Time off is exactly what you need. This is the smartest thing you've done in a while."

She wouldn't thank him for the insult. Purse, keys, badge, no gun because they confiscated it, no matter. She had another one at both her apartment and granny's. She collected her things and made her way to the exit, her car, and home.

CHAPTER SEVEN

Free! Khuket's essence floated on the heat radiating from the lava pits and the smoky updrafts from the smoldering pyres. All of her dormant senses surged and expanded outward in a glorious explosion of energy. Chaos. Its shadowy presence surrounded and throbbed inside her, bringing her back to life. So long denied, she basked in the dissonance, absorbing the frenetic energy chaos created. There were infinite threads in *Duat*, none she could use to fulfill the contract she had made with SET. She continued on, moving through each layer of the Underworld, until she entered the greeting room of a palace.

The presence of her benefactor touched every aspect of the home. But this wasn't where he dwelled. Evil—like chaos—preferred gloom and this cathedral so near the surface of the world wasn't dark enough for him to rest. She actually favored her desolate cell. This could be the reason she survived while other members of her Pantheon had withered and died.

The Egyptians had descended from the night skies in overwhelming numbers, dividing the planet amongst them as if none called this land home. They stole The Eidos' powers, crippled and enslaved them. Those who succumbed lived. Those who fought died. She was all that was left of the Elementals.

Anger rippled through her, but she'd learned to let none show on her features. Imprisonment taught her the value of hiding one's true emotions. Though she projected chaos, violence didn't dwell within her. After so many years of solitude and meditation, she conquered the emotion what once was her foundation.

She moved through the palace, exploring the pristine rooms, touching the cool marble. Traces of SET lingered, but this edifice was too clean and smooth. The God of Evil would decry perfection in all things, living or inanimate. This monument was built for someone else.

A woman perhaps. *Hmmm?*

SET fascinated her with his bluster, no joy. He didn't delight in his true nature as she did. The joy she received in the subtle machination of the chaos she wrought, satisfied her as nothing else could. She sank onto a cushioned marble bench. Velvety softness surrounded her. Too long, she'd been denied any ease. Her hand trembled as she smoothed the aged, once tattered fabric instead of ripping the cloth from her body. With her restored powers, she could array herself as she pleased. Khuket refrained. No comfort or raiment would she seek until she fulfilled her oath. The cloth served to remind her of her precarious freedom. And though she had her powers, she was still enslaved.

If given a choice, she would stay here in *Duat*. Maybe, afterwards she'd return and conquer the powerful SET. After all, there was an unoccupied cell.

Khuket halted. Awareness shrieked across her senses, leaving her quivering. She raced to find the source and paused in front of a barrier of energy. Intricately woven ethereal weaving pulsed, blocking her way.

Cursed, Egyptian magic. It surrounded her. Caged her. Her cold core swelled in anger. Her nails lengthened, SET's *vis*'Ra collected in her palms. She grabbed the barrier. At first, the weaves resisted, but SET's donated power mixed with her fury allowing her to force her way through and into a room. Chaos pulsed from the trapped souls lining the walls in canopic jars. Some were dense and multicolored; others were thin, erratic tendrils fluttering inside the funerary ceremonial containers.

She was no prophet. The future remained a mystery to her, but she was certain these jars held the key to her goal. And her revenge.

"Who are you?"

Khuket spun, ready to flee. Freedom tasted too sweet to have it snatched away so soon. A woman's wide eyes met her stare. She gasped and quickly lowered her eyes. "Never did I think I would meet one of my own deities again." She sunk to the floor and bowed low.

Khuket scrutinized the woman. She was an Eidos, but from a lower caste. Stripped of all her energy, she now existed as a slave. Fury whipped through Khuket, causing jars to dance on the marble shelves. Fear leeched from the woman cowering on the cold marble.

"Stand and come to me." The goddess demanded. The woman crossed the barrier and waited inches away. "What is your name?" Khuket asked.

"I'm a null. I have no name other than what my master Anubis chooses to call me and he calls me null." Hands folded meekly in front, her chin rested on her chest.

Khuket reached for her, but the woman backed away smoothly.

"Don't touch me. It's forbidden. Once touched, we can be owned, and we're no longer trusted by our masters. The punishment is severe. You must leave, Goddess. Anubis will be here to see who breached his barrier." Her hands never parted and her chin never rose.

Khuket grabbed the Eidos's bare shoulder. Memories flowed from the slave into her mind as she ruthlessly mined for knowledge to start her revenge. "I am your new master. I shall call you Neith, because you and I come from the same place." She transformed into her essence—a turbulent mist—and forced her new servant to do the same.

A god materialized in the room. He jerked to a halt. Shock twisted his sharp features. Neith trembled next to her.

Khuket glided in front of her subject. She wasn't strong enough to fight, but an impressive display could cover a necessary retreat.

SET loped into the room in his Typhon form. The unknown god dropped to his knees in front of SET and bowed low.

SET's gaze swept over her and then seemed to dismiss her. "Did you know of my wife's betrayal?" SET rasped.

"No, father." Anubis shook his head. His chalky face flushed.

SET's barbed tail smashed into the marble next to his son. The boy yelped. SET clucked and hooked his enormous head. "I can smell the lie in your words."

Khuket smiled. Family dramas were always exciting. "SET, come see what endeavors your seed has been up too." She reformed and moved aside.

"My son seeks to build an army. He thinks to overthrow me and rule in my place. I allowed him his foolish dreams for a few centuries. Now it is time for my child to learn his place in the world." A glee glowed from SET's canine eyes. His tail wrapped around Anubis's neck and dragged him. SET stopped before he left the room.

Do not forget our deal, goddess. His voice filled her head. Then he was gone.

"Quickly, take everything." Khuket said to Neith. She didn't have time to speculate why The God of Evil left the souls unguarded. She needed to take what she could and leave.

Together, they enveloped all the jars in their clothing and arms. Some smashed against the floor, the souls wafting like ash caught on a breeze. Khuket paused, their malevolence attracting the darkness inside of her. She watched them flash away and followed a second before their trail disappeared.

Like stepping into another room, Khuket left one dimension, and entered the next. A dark, cold place illuminated by a sliver of moonlight. She had traded one cell, for another.

"It's a factory, Goddess." Neith followed behind. "Abandoned a long time ago."

The word had no meaning for her. "You know of this world?"

"Yes, Goddess. Anubis didn't want all of us ignorant. The nulls are his only companions in Chemmis."

Her slave had value. She studied the woman with new appreciation. "Is he as incompetent as his father believes?"

"I don't know things of that nature, Goddess." Neith stared vacantly into the darkness.

She lied, but Khuket understood the slave's loyalty to her master, even if Anubis was no longer that person. Something scraped and dripped behind them, then lumbered their way. The null looked at her for guidance and protection. A long time had passed since Khuket had protected another being. She wasn't the only one left who remembered the war and her failure. But this was a new world, a different earth, and she had a new chance at victory.

She swept into the sweet darkness, unafraid. The dark held no mystery and kept no secrets from her. Pits lined the floor of the room protected by the same barriers that had guarded the jars in the Underworld. At the edge of a pit, three beasts waited.

Her breath caught, delighted at their magnificence. Swirling around their hulking forms, she had no words to describe them. Thin, black chaos threads ebbed and flowed around their huge bodies. Khuket drew closer and peered into their dim souls. The essences from the shattered jars dwelled inside them. This is where they had led her.

Together, the beasts sank to their knees. She glanced into the pit. More of their brethren lay dormant at the bottom. She had an army. And secreted in the folds of her gown were the rest of the jars, and the way to activate them.

Glee bubbled within her belly, raced up her throat, and burst from her mouth as pure laughter. A sound so foreign to her ears, for a moment she failed to realize the joy emanating from her. Sinking to her knees, Khuket thanked the cosmos for their divine providence.

"They are called quimaera, but Anubis only named the first. He called him Alamut." Neith stood next to her. "He placed their bodies in Alamut's care to hide them from SET."

"Why didn't Anubis bond with them?" Khuket asked.

"He's a coward. He wants his father defeated, but doesn't want to be the one who wields the sword."

Khuket's lips twitched. It seemed Neith had made a choice. Better to have a willing slave. She stepped close and placed her hands on the quimaera's bowed heads. Nothing but anger filled them. The rest of their souls were empty vessels awaiting instruction.

Again, she tapped into SET's *vis*'Ra, enveloped them, and shifted their chaotic patterns to match her own. She restored them to the state they once inhabited. Men. And gave them their first set of instructions.

Her limbs trembled. She had used much of SET's donation. Still, nothing would sway her from this path. She stiffened her resolve and gave the order.

"Find for me Nephythys's lover."

CHAPTER EIGHT

Reign caged his emotions to keep from burying his fists in the nearest wall. Fury pulsed from him in cold waves, which left Alexis shivering in the elevator next to him. She wanted to cage him. Visions of Nephythys and two thousand years of her *special* torture clouded his mind. Once more, he tried to leave only to return to Alexis's side more enraged than before.

She rejected his protection, aimed her weapon at his heart, and demanded he comply with her wishes. Two women, realms apart, yet the goddess and Alexis had more in common than he first guessed. Or maybe it was something he brought out in women that made them want to enslave him. He couldn't be around Alexis without wanting to wrap his hands around her neck.

Alexis walked into her apartment and entered her bedroom. He was grateful she was out of his sight. The Vanquished gnawed at him.

You hide from a woman, they mocked, and he couldn't deny the truth in their collective words. The few days here in this realm had offered plenty of opportunities to show himself and enlist her help to find his brother. Instead, he stayed away, wasting time.

His jaw clenched and he ground his teeth. No longer.

Reign passed through her bedroom door, but she wasn't there. The steady beat of water striking tile guided him to another door. He jerked to a halt, unable to look away.

She was naked. Gloriously. Her creamy skin glowed.

Heavy breasts with pink pert nipples balanced on top of a delicate rib cage that narrowed to her waist then flared into curvaceous hips and a tight rear. Between impossibly long legs, a strip of reddish curls shielded her core. Transfixed, blood drained from his head and rushed south. He knew she would be beautiful, but never guessed she hid this perfection under her clothing.

Alexis shivered, wrapped her arms around herself, and glanced up at the slotted metal grate in her ceiling. She sighed and disappeared behind a glass stall. Tethered by lust, he followed.

Then lurched to a stop.

Reign forced his eyes closed. And though everything in him wanted to step further into the room, he pivoted and returned to the bedroom.

He listened to a door open and close. The water pattern changed from splattering against tile to the wet slap of droplets on skin. He imagined caressing her slick limbs, swiping her soaked hair to the side and tasting the curve of her neck.

What would he give to be in that room with her? Nothing. A pent up groan eased from him. She wasn't his to have. For a moment, he wished he were like Roman. No reserve. No conscience to oppose his desires. Taking what he wanted regardless of the consequences.

The water ceased, drawing him from his ruminations. The click of a door opening almost had his neck craning for a peek of her. Slapping feet warned of her approach. Once again, he turned away, listening as she crossed from the bathroom to the carpeted bedroom.

He had to leave or what little honor he had would vanish in a torrent of need. Just before he left, he caught a glimpse of her. A towel shielded her body while her hair cascaded in orange flames down her back. His limbs leaden. The ache caged in his pants barred rational thought. Reign nearly collapsed against the wall on the other side of her bedroom. Battle was easier than fighting this unwanted desire.

A knock on the front door snapped his attention away from his cock.

"Just a minute," she called and dashed into the living room dressed in a clingy robe. Wary, he followed. He didn't like how she squinted through the spy hole in the door, and then paused before reluctantly opening it.

"Hey." Paul, the bastard who handcuffed and shoved him into the police car, leaned against the door frame. His gaze landed on her breasts covered in the silky fabric.

A predatory growl rumbled through him and his palms itched for the man's blood.

"What are you doing here?" she asked. Her eyebrows furrowed and her mouth was agape.

"Can't say I was in the neighborhood." He gave a dry chuckle. "But after the other night, I thought I'd check on you."

Revulsion washed over her face, though that didn't stop her from stepping to the side and granting him entry.

"Did I interrupt you?" He grinned, and Reign fought the urge to plant his fist between the cop's eyes. "Damn. You keep it cold in here."

"Uhm, yeah. The air conditioner isn't working properly. Want something to drink?" She led the way to another room with Paul trailing after her, and Reign trailing Paul.

"Yeah, any beer?" He scanned the room.

She opened a small metal door and tossed him a bottle.

"You still have my favorite," he smiled a wide toothy grin Reign wanted to rearrange.

"Excuse me? I introduced you to microbrew." Head cocked to the side with one eyebrow lifted, she folded her arms tightly under her breasts, which enhanced their voluptuousness.

"You introduced me to lots of things," Paul said in husky voice. Her entire face turn rosy and her chin dipped to her chest. "I've missed you." He stepped closer to Alexis.

And death.

"Not enough to call though?" Alexis shrugged. Her lips thinned in a grimace.

"I wanted to, started to a few times." Paul rubbed the back of his neck. His eyes pleaded for understanding.

"What got in your way?" She smirked and leaned against the counter. Her hand played with the belt of her robe.

Reign's gut clenched. If she opened it—

"My stupidity." He took a swig of beer.

"And my gold shield?" Her eyes had narrowed.

Paul sputtered. He backhanded the beer trickling down his chin before it landed on his shirt.

"So how do you like New City?" She continued.

"It's a good department. Not as busy as NYPD, but okay." He gave her a slow once-over and lingered a second too long on her breasts.

Reign's blood boiled.

"Listen. I apologize for everything. Like I said, I was stupid." His hand landed over his heart.

"Yeah, very." Her full lips pursed.

He took another step toward her, his grin matched hers. "Did you miss me? Maybe a little?"

She stared at Paul, seeming to drink in his features.

Reign's heart shouldn't be racing painfully in his chest. His blade shouldn't be clutched in his palm. And the Vanquished shouldn't be ordering him to cleave the man into chunks.

"Yeah, I did..." She sighed.

Rage rolled through Reign. She moved within inches of the man. Her lips pouty. Her eyes molten.

Reign turned away. He'd survived centuries of torture without breaking. This slice of hell he couldn't handle.

"I got over it," she whispered.

But Reign heard every word. He spun. The tightness in his chest unfurled.

Alexis walked around Paul and passed through Reign. Her soul brushed his, entwined for a brief moment, but long enough for her emotions to stain him. Betrayal, not love suffused her senses.

"Thanks for checking on me." Her voice held no emotion as she opened the door.

Paul sauntered to the door and paused at the threshold. "Are you sure you want me to leave? We had some good times together."

She smiled, yet no warmth reached her eyes. "Yeah, but not enough to take you back. Enjoy the beer." The door closed behind him.

Bells chimed incessantly from the bedroom. Alexis ran into the room and snatched a device from the table.

"Hello. Yes, I'm Alexis Lever...tomorrow at four at headquarters. Yes. I'll be there." She tossed the object onto the table and plopped on the bed. Shoulders slumped, her chin buried in her chest.

That alone was enough to make Reign ache to pull her into his arms and shelter her from the storms battering her life. He'd rather fight a war than see her cry. He crouched in front of her, ready to reach out and lift her face to his. Though she cried over another man, he wanted to comfort her. Her chin shot up and light bathed her features. Her eyes were watery, yet no tears rolled down her cheeks.

Alexis shot to her feet and disappeared inside the room containing her wardrobe. Seconds later, she tossed some clothes on her bed and returned nude. Reign froze. Honor demanded he leave. Lust rooted his feet, peeled his eyelids back, and made him watch her fascinating dance.

A flimsy bit of lace glided up her thighs and settled between her legs. A thin strip disappeared between the twin cheeks of her delicious rear. A similar piece of lacy cloth harnessed her breasts. Next, she shimmied into a tight pair of leathers and a half top that left her limbs bare and the juicy globes of her breasts nearly spilling out.

Several hard blinks and he finally tore himself away and returned to the adjacent room. With grim realization, he recognized a new prison caged him. On each side a dilemma: Nephythys, Roman, the Vanquished...and Alexis.

Lost in his predicament, the jangle of keys snapped his head up. Alexis had exited the apartment.

Where in the hell was she off to? From drooling fool to guard dog in an instant, he followed, trying in vain to ignore the swish of her tight ass.

CHAPTER NINE

This was the world long denied her.

Hovering above New York City, Khuket savored all of its wonder. Her Pantheon had ruled a barren, molten lump with only the rudiments of life beginning to germinate. Never had she imagined this was what she would discover when SET released her. The sights. The man-made objects intrigued, but the natural wonders fascinated her, especially the oceans. The calm surety of the tides juxtaposed the rage of a hurricane. The volcanic world she'd left behind had cooled and turned into this. Her eyes couldn't absorb it all.

She inhaled a deep, intoxicating breath. No longer did sulfur burn her lungs and ashes clog her throat. This world didn't smell of molten rock. The flora held a rich bouquet of clashing fragrances, which delighted her. Metallic beasts of burden roamed the land and the air, screeching, belching, honking, the noise buffeted her. She became a leaf, tossed about in the chaotic storm this world created. Still, it was better than the silence she had endured.

And the creatures, humans, they were an easy breed to manipulate. Everything they did, thought, touched, created chaos. Ropey strands in a kaleidoscope of colors. A tug, a subtle pluck or added tension on the strand and they danced. Like a kitten with a multicolored ball of yarn, so many choices, so many outcomes, awaited her gentle influence.

As the first dwellers, her people welcomed the Egyptians as equals. Their guests soon became their masters. Ra descended from the heavens with his consort Nu and stole their dark world from them. Now she was bound to SET until she completed her oath. But once she accomplished that duty, she'd be free to reclaim this world and gather her descendants. She would rule this world. Foolish Anubis had provided an army and the means to control that force through the souls residing in the canopic jars. Below her, the first three of her new army waited, their true forms masked beneath a human guise, and her servant, Neith.

Hunger gripped her, gnawed on her soul. Wafting on a gentle current of air, Khuket dove to a rooftop. Her insides twisted, she dropped to her knees. Pain sucked a gasp from her and left her dizzy. She'd nearly depleted the energy she'd siphoned off SET. She hadn't survived imprisonment and traversed two realms to end up as drifting particles in the stratosphere. She gathered her strength and climbed to her feet. At the edge of the roof, she scanned the immediate area. Plenty of chaos surrounded her. None suitable to digest.

Like a fisherman casting a net, she stretched her senses as far as her waning strength allowed. Less than a mile of rainbow colored chaos weaves illuminated the night. A shame only she could see it. Each strand had a meaning. The different hues of blue denoted loss. The many hues of red signified pain. Physical pain trended towards the lighter pinks at the end of the spectrum while emotional, the opposite end. Love was a bright red shade while obsession and lust were thick crimson cords.

The weaves blurred and nearly evaporated. Exhaustion nipped at her, causing her form to flicker. Frantic, she searched for that one particular strand that would nourish her. Her gaze swept each quadrant of the city and found nothing. But where one was needed, many would have to do. She needed a gathering, humans congregating in mass numbers. A great battle would be ideal, thousands of humans killing each other. The chaotic energy they generated could be adapted to sustain her.

There. Along the farthest edge of her weave, she found a small cluster. They would have to do.

Ravenous, Khuket pushed off from the roof. The breeze was to the east, in her favor. Good, less energy expended to reach her destination. Beneath her, three quimaera and Neith followed. She'd ordered them to find Nephythys's lover, but this world distracted her. A welcome diversion, though she didn't have the luxury to dawdle. Her freedom waited. After she fixed SET's marital problems, she'd have all the time to explore and conquer.

She sensed the bodies crammed inside the rectangular building long before spotting the lines of humans snaking outside. Khuket passed through the wall and entered a room. By the densely packed weaves, she expected weapons to be drawn and spilled blood coating the floor. Instead, they moved, pushing, rubbing, sweating, against each other while noise blared from every direction. Next to her, a male and female stroked each other intimately. Their lips locked, but they weren't ripping each other apart. They melded together, trading fluids, both enjoying the invasion. Bright, silky red strands of chaos flowed.

All around her energy leeched from straining bodies and blended with the other strands. The room filled with sweet and supple power. Rainbow colors shattered and gathered with each throbbing beat, claiming her body in a languid grip. First, her head bobbed from side to side. Then her shoulders dipped, alternating the movements with her head. Finally, her hips swayed, caught in the rhythm surrounding her.

Khuket threw her head back and supped. She drew the delicious strands through every pore until the backwash spilled out of her. Stuffed, her thoughts muddled. Never had she felt like this, sensual and, alive. Her pulse thickened and rose to match the throbbing beat of the noise surrounding her. She swayed, stumbled, regained her footing, and swayed again. Her head swam, lost in the noise and strobe lights.

A man approached. He rubbed his body against her. She pressed back and didn't protest when his hand grasped her hip and guided her between his legs. He rocked his pelvis into her. A ball of need burst to life in her core. Her limbs turned loose. Not even when hunger seized her in its talons and reduced her to an animal had her wits failed. Now, she couldn't string more than three words together.

"Hey, you okay?"

He touched her bare arms, sending a jolt through her body. The fog cleared from her mind. She looked down and realized she wasn't faded, and then glanced up at the human. Thin, with a mop of black hair mixed with bleached streaks. Skinny of frame with sallow skin, metal pierced his ears, eyebrows, and lips. Chaos swirled around him in a lazy, unfocused pattern.

"You're cute." He leaned closer.

Cute? She had mastered enough of the language to know what cute meant. But her stomach heaved and she doubled over.

"Oh, looks like you're gonna be sick." The man backed up and disappeared into the crowd.

Her form flickered. In a rush, the energy she'd absorbed bled out of her pores, eyes, nose, and mouth. Poison. None noticed in the dim room the dying Goddess in their midst. The injustice of leaving this world, so soon after gaining her freedom, fired her senses and generated a burst of energy. Her essence spread from her dark center and circled the room, weakening with every rotation.

Her body dissolved and rained as a mist upon the oblivious humans. She'd returned to her Elemental form. SET had lost his slave. Her revenge against the Egyptians was thwarted.

A mass of chaotic waves jolted her. Particles suffused her with delicious darkness and dragged her back from the edge of oblivion. She coalesced, hauled her weak body off the floor. Jarred back to life by the succulent taste of a man, she trailed the only source that could keep her alive.

CHAPTER TEN

Alexis adjusted the gun hidden under her jacket, in the small of her back. She bent and retrieved her helmet from the chair next to the front door. Caramel, butter soft leather stretched across her ass, making her aware of each movement. The thong caused *just* enough friction to remind her why she loved being a woman. She hadn't felt this sensual in years.

Good 'cause she needed the distraction. The call from Internal Affairs had face-planted her into a wall, and she had yet to pick the drywall out of her teeth. The department hadn't wasted any time boiling the oil to dip her in.

She'd screwed up again. And so hot on the heels of her other screw-ups. They'd searched for the three gunmen. They'd called in the K-9 unit and a helicopter, but were more concerned about frying her ass.

No one had seen Reign. Dalton and the attendant were down on the floor. The store had no surveillance equipment and the microphone had recorded nothing discerning, only muffled voices. Other than her eyes, there was no proof he was ever there. Just like that day at the morgue when Daniel went missing. On a monitor in the security office, McCabe and the other detectives had watched video of Daniel rising unaided from the refrigerated drawer. But Alexis had seen a different image. A man, dressed in clothing found in an Egyptian history book, opened the drawer, and assisted Daniel. Then a vortex sucked him away, leaving Daniel stumbling and naked.

And didn't that make her crazier? The threads of her life were pulling apart, but she wouldn't sit around waiting for the men in white coats to straitjacket her and cart her way.

She marched into the apartment's parking garage, passed her Altima, and swiped the protective cover off her baby. Black with gleaming chrome, sleek, built for speed and all hers. *Hayabusa.* The bike made her want to bow and pay homage.

Too many weeks had passed since the last time she felt the fine-tuned hum between her thighs. Among other things missing between her legs. She was gonna get on this bullet and ride until vanishing men and the department were in her side mirrors.

Alexis swung her leg over. Leather to leather, crotch met seat. She turned the key and cranked the throttle. The bike roared to life and the vibration thrummed through her, cranking her own engine.

Good girl rules be damned. Reign appearing...then disappearing. Her brain lurched. People didn't vanish. Fainting into boxes of cornflakes, the reaming from her lieutenant, then Paul showing up, and lastly the phone call completed the disaster list. Tonight, she needed more than Duracell.

She needed release, a few seconds of oblivion, to take her away. Tonight, she needed a drink and a man, then another drink. Exactly in that order.

She had just slid her helmet over her head when twenty feet away, a shadow peeked around the concrete column.

Her heart fisted. *Reign?* "Who's there?"

A kid, maybe twelve years old, stepped into the light and leaned against the column. Senses on high alert, she pulled the helmet off and glanced around the parking garage. It wasn't unheard of to use a kid to distract while another snuck up behind. Alexis balanced her helmet on the tank and cut the engine. "Hey, are you okay?"

Hands shoved into his jean pockets, the dull brown hoodie shielded his face. But she knew him.

"Hi, Dougie. A little late to be out?"

A careless shrug gave his answer. As little brother to the leader of the local street gang, the words 'bed' and 'time' were not to be in the same sentence. He pushed the hoodie off his head. Dark-skinned and baby-faced, lanky, Dougie Woodard shuffled forward. "Hey, Detective. Can I talk to you for a sec?"

Talk? She managed to hide her surprise behind a cough. "Yeah, what's up?"

He twitched and his gaze darted around the garage. Fear had replaced his usual bravado. What the hell was going on?

"Why so jumpy?" Hell, his twitching was starting to infect her. He must be desperate to break the cardinal rule and come to her, an officer, for help.

"Ruthless is missing. Dante, too." He stepped closer. "Dey went missing 'bout two weeks ago. Searched ev'rywhere. All I found were their bloody shirts. Thought it was the other gangs, but dey gots people missing, too. Been happenin' for a while."

Dorian 'Ruthless' Woodard. One-time high school basketball star, now street corner entrepreneur and HNIC-Head Negro In Charge-rumored to have killed two rivals as his initiation to the gang and dragged the middle brother, seventeen-year old Dante, with him. Afterward, he tattooed 'ruthless' down his arm and seemed determined to live up to the moniker.

"Did you report it?" Missing gang leaders could lead to a turf war.

"Tried to. Police don't care." He sneered. Tires squealed in another part of the garage. Dougie flinched and ducked.

Alexis climbed off her bike and went to him. "Is someone chasing you?"

The boy's spine stiffened and his shoulders squared. "No. No one's chasin' me." Swagger back in place, except his chubby cheeks and soft brown eyes didn't quite hold the malice he would've liked. Alexis wasn't sure about Dougie's parents, but with both his brothers missing, the boy was vulnerable. And he was a good kid. She had checked out the entire family when Ruthless drew the attention of law enforcement. Dougie was a 'B' student and when he wasn't slacking and running his mouth, his teachers thought he had potential. She agreed with them.

"Where were they last seen?"

"They were headed to Central Park."

"Why down there? Out of the neighborhood. Aren't there enough street corners here?" A scowl tightened his face and she regretted her scorn. He came to her for help, not ridicule. Alexis crouched next to him. "Let me take you home."

"And let ev'ryone see me wit you? A cop." He darted out of her grasp. "Nah." He strolled away, arrogance cloaking him like a bulletproof vest.

She wasn't surprised he rejected her help, but was glad she tried.

Cruising onto the street, Alexis replayed her encounter with Dougie. Police ignoring missing gang members, maybe, but you couldn't search for someone you didn't know was missing. Well, now she knew. And what the hell was she going to do about it? Waltzing in and opening an investigation when everything she did was under the microscope wasn't the way to get back into the good graces of her chief. Then again, with her track record nothing she did would ever get her back into that lofty status.

Darius Woodard. The last time she'd seen him was the night she'd hauled him in for questioning. The guy who'd shattered his knee was killed in a drive by. Darius had laughed, not with joy, but a hollow chuckle, which denied nothing. She'd never forget the guilt in his eyes and his dry laugh. If I.A. didn't skin her and take her badge, maybe she'd get a chance to investigate.

As soon as she hit the highway, Alexis opened the throttle. The bike roared and she roared too, screaming beneath her helmet. The October wind whipped her, tore at her body and jacket. She didn't care. She needed this bit of freedom, this madcap dash down a mostly deserted highway before the noose tightened around her neck.

Everything she'd sweated for—all of it—could be a memory in a few hours. What would she do then? She didn't have a backup plan because being a cop was her backup plan.

Mired in thoughts, she didn't see the pothole until the last second. She swerved, jerking the handlebars sharply to the right, then overcorrecting to the left.

Her heart plunged to her lap and every muscle cringed. *No,* she cried, more worried about 'her baby' than her body kissing the asphalt. She tried to regain control, but one hundred forty pounds of muscle couldn't match the combination of ninety miles per hour and a three hundred fifty pound bike. There wasn't time to be afraid, or review her life and the multitude of mistakes. There wasn't even time to pray as the bike tipped and her butt lifted off the seat.

Something yanked her back. Her ass landed hard on the leather seat, jarring every bone in her body. The bike wrenched to the right and still tried to skid out from under her. She grabbed the handlebars and countered the tilt by shifting her weight. Her baby shimmied, straightened, and continued to race down the highway.

Damn, Evel Knievel could kiss her ass! Nothing like escaping death to make you feel alive. Her heart returned to the space between her lungs and did a happy dance only to lurch to a halt.

The wind no longer beat at her, but glided by as if she sat in a glass cockpit. And behind her, something solid pressed against her back.

Her lungs stopped working. She couldn't take her eyes off the road. The bike weaved unaided between three cars in its path. Fear warred with higher reasoning, which warred with her sixth sense. She wanted to look behind her, but if she saw 'him' she might faint again. Though she doubted passing out would be fatal. Her personal guardian angel wouldn't allow it.

Alexis took the next exit. She pulled into the first parking lot she came across, *RedZone* nightclub, and hopped off her bike.

Nothing was there. Rather, no *one* was there. Not finding a body sitting on her bike was just as bad as finding one. Circling the machine did nothing but stretch her legs instead of giving her a clue as to why she wasn't dead. She should be road kill, or at least broken and bloody, waiting for rescue to fail miserably at keeping her alive long enough to be an organ donor.

She backed up until a parked car stopped her retreat. Slumped against someone else's vehicle, Alexis braced her hands against her knees and concentrated on breathing. *In and out, in and out.* Anything more and her brain would short circuit.

Laughter broke through her survival instinct. She sucked in a fortifying breath and straightened as a gaggle of girls strutted by in micros and stilettos. They glanced her way, laughed a little harder, and paraded on.

Yeah. The last time she'd been to a club, she was seventeen and it was the night before a pageant. Only one dance and Gloria had barged in and dragged her back to the hotel.

Funny how a smell, a sound, the glimpse of something from the corner of her eye, could dump her back into her childhood. She didn't go to clubs. Her body didn't dance. The whole sweating to music thing annoyed the hell out of her. She went to bars for billiards or sports. No dancing allowed.

Alexis wiped a hand across her sweaty forehead. *God, I need a drink and here's as good a place as any. And maybe some anonymous man would get lucky tonight.* Her last sexual escapade was eight months ago and not worth remembering. All of them were like that, except Paul. Initially, they had clicked on so many levels. Her first partner, he'd taught her how to handle herself on the streets and in the squad room. Then he'd handled her in bed. It worked for fourteen months, until she'd gotten her gold shield, and he didn't.

She checked her gun and wallet and tucked her helmet under her arm. Her lungs emptied on a hard sigh as she walked to the front of the line and showed her badge. The bouncer moved out of her way. The perks of being NYPD.

House music. Damn, she hated house music, but the gyrating crowd squeezed onto the dance floor didn't have a problem with the DJ. Not the typical nightspot, the club boasted a large dance floor, an equally large stage, and stripper poles off to the right. She veered away from the hooting men waving cash.

At the bar, she gave her helmet a seat and stood. The only woman not showing yards of skin, the bartender spotted her immediately. Tequila, no ice, no umbrella. She couldn't stomach drinks that mimicked smoothies. She sipped instead of throwing it to the back of her throat and gulping. *Gloria would be proud.* Her brothers wouldn't. Those three jarheads had corrupted their little sister with lessons in liquor, poker, and how to make a guy regret touching you.

The mirror behind the bar reflected the writhing bodies. Technically, she was in their age group, the twenty-somethings, yet whatever remaining exuberance secretly stored in her atoms was buried deep and unreachable. Coming here made her feel ancient. Her membership card in the exclusive club had been revoked when she'd joined the academy and the notice had landed in her inbox years ago. She finished her drink with a smooth gulp and upended the glass on the bar.

Alexis picked up her helmet. This bad idea needed to end before anything else happened. Skirting the edge of the crowd, a column and secondary bar station blocked her way. She glanced around the room for another escape route. She had to reverse directions and squeeze by the dance tables and a man blocking her path, if she was going to make it to the exit. Her gaze snapped back to the man. It wasn't his obnoxious or drunken conduct that drew her, but the blank, glazed stare as he watched a dancer spin around the pole, legs spread eagle, upside down.

He stood off to the side. No emotions on his slack-jawed face, though from the bulge in his pants, he was interested. His hands were relaxed and empty of weapons. Yet instinct warned her to keep her gaze on him.

Alexis threaded her way through the crowd. Her senses screamed at her to do something. Maybe it was the smoldering, dark aura whirling around him. She blinked and damn, that aura still surrounded him.

What the hell was in that tequila?

A bead of sweat collected at her temple and rolled, unchecked, down the side of her face. Concentrating on her breathing, Alexis fought the panic clawing its way up her throat.

No one else seemed to notice him. Still…he hadn't moved. In fact, he seemed rooted. He stared, unblinking for a full minute before his bottom eyelid rose to meet the top.

Her breath caught. Humans didn't blink like that.

A pack of people parked themselves between her and the man, blocking her surveillance. A crowd and a gun equaled stampede. She needed to get him out of here, away from innocent lives. She pulled out her badge and pried her way through the people.

"Sir, please step away from the table and come with me." She yelled. A few feet away, *That Smell* slapped her. The unmistakable rancid odor. Adrenaline pumped into her system. Her heart bolted like Secretariat out the gate at the Kentucky Derby.

His head turned slowly. Eyes latched on to her. She sucked in a breath. Vertical irises. Inner translucent lids that blinked from left to right.

Alexis's hand crept to the small of her back.

***

Reign followed Alexis when she stormed inside the building. Confronted by the narrow entrance, he faltered and struggled to place one-step in front of the other. The dark narrow hallway closed in. The curving walls shrank around him, squeezing, reminding him of his time spent in the bowels of *Duat*. Decades blended into centuries until Nephythys *rescued* him into slavery. People pressed themselves against the walls to avoid him, repulsed by the cold wave he generated. Good, they needed to stay out of his way.

His breath seized, trapped in his chest until he burst forth into an open area. A cacophony of throbbing sounds deafened him while colorful, pulsing lights blinded him. When his blurred vision cleared, his jaw hit his chest.

Men and women—barely clothed women—jerked, grated, grinded, touched, kissed, palmed each other in a frenetic, decadent orgy. He'd heard of things like this. Knew this happened in the camps of the followers as men, women, and children offered the only true commodity they had—their bodies. He and Roman refused to allow women to be used and mistreated in any camp they stayed. In all these centuries, nothing had changed. Men still warred with weapons that killed hundreds of thousands instead of one at a time and women still used their bodies as a lure for protection and survival.

Temper stretched thin, he searched the crowd for Alexis and spotted her crown of red hair just as a mist circled the room from a machine overhead. He opened his mouth and her name almost slipped from his lips. He wanted to call, have her turn, and smile at him. Instead, he closed his mouth. Neither friend nor lover, she wasn't his to call out her name.

A man crossed his path, a burn covered by intricate ink stretched over his muscular arm and shoulder. A beefy brawler with short hair walked close behind. A Nubian trailed behind the brawler. By their stance and the way they surveyed the crowd, they were warriors. The voices of the Vanquished rose in his head. They wanted blood.

Reign fought it. So close to the abyss, his soul couldn't accumulate any more. He came here to kill one being. Just that one and no more. He focused on the vow he had made so long ago. On his knees, he had bowed before a prophet and swore to lay down his weapon and retire his sword. Before a fortnight had passed that vow laid ground into the dust, mixed with the bones of the prophet and a legion of soldiers. He had failed on every level.

Had that failure lead to his downfall? Centuries of questions and he still hadn't secured a single answer.

Screams pierced the heavy music. People streamed by, rushing for the exits. He spun, searching for Alexis and glimpsed her in the strobe lights. Heat seared his palm and his fingers wound around his sword in a tight hold. The metal hummed as he lifted the weapon. The crowd jumped back and Reign surged through the throng.

Then he saw her.

And the beast.

The same creature that had crashed through her home and nested in the pit.

Alexis shouted, but her words drowned beneath the music and the thunder of the mob. The creature lunged. She ducked. Then swung around and smashed her helmet into its face. Stunned, the beast stumbled backward and quickly regained his footing.

Reign's mind snapped. He forgot to flash and tore through the surging crowd, flinging bodies out of his way, his eyes trained on her and the animal.

Alexis dodged and scrambled away. The beast snagged her jacket and hauled her back. Claws rushed toward her frightened face.

At the last second, she raised her helmet. Claws slashed the surface, causing sparks to fly mere inches from her cheek.

Reign flashed in front of her. Claws sliced into his raised forearm. The Vanquished roared, feeding off his pain. They begged to join the fight. He buried his sword deep in the beast's gut. The edge of the blade glowed crimson and the flesh surrounding it sizzled and smoked. He glared into the beast's sinister eyes. His blade blazed hotter and evaporated the animal from within. Immediately, another weight was added to his soul, dropping him to one knee, dragging him closer to darkness.

Reign shouldered the burden, as he shouldered all the others. Nothing mattered but the goal at hand—protecting Alexis. He whipped around. She crouched behind him, ready to fight.

He reached for her. His palm open. His heart willing her to trust him. She didn't hesitate to slap her hand into his. He pulled her to her feet and scanned for injuries. "Are you injured?"

"Look out!" Alexis cried.

He shoved her against the nearest wall and spun. Another animal leaped, slashing inches into his shoulder. A kick to the scaly middle sent the animal flying backwards. Mid-air, it flipped and landed on all fours. Claws gouge the concrete floor as they found purchase. The beast raced toward him again.

The Nubian he'd passed earlier burst into the fray. The beast knocked him into the crowd with a swipe from a barbed tail.

The blighted energy of the Vanquished ignited, burning him with their hatred. Without his twin to balance him, Reign couldn't control the fury sweeping through him. It wielded him and turned him into *de Mortem, the Scourge*. He became Death, the name they had once whispered when he walked onto the battlefield because that was his gift to all enemies.

The reptile scurried forward on all fours, the mist partially obscuring it. Reign succumbed to the vehemence coursing through him. Piceous power plowed through his veins. He latched onto the addictive energy of the Vanquished. It seared through every barrier and restraint, until Reign was no more. Only Death remained.

And he wanted blood.

The blade became a part of him, and extension of his arm and his will. Two swipes across the abdomen eviscerated the beast. Though its entrails spilled, it charged.

Reign barreled into it. He grabbed the beast by the neck. But the animal's tail swept Reign's feet from under him. He landed on his back. His head *thunked* hard against the floor. He faded and passed through the center of the animal. Behind the beast, a swing of his blade sliced off a leg. A bellow mixed with the thumping music. The beast collapsed onto the floor and tried to crawl away.

Reign grabbed the barbed limb and flung the animal into the wall. With a plank from a broken table, he stabbed it through the heart, pinning it there.

A warning prickled his senses. He pivoted. A fist smashed into his temple. An uppercut to his chin rocked his brain. Slammed to his back; his head bounced on the floor. Stars exploded behind his eyes. They danced with the colored lights swirling around the room. He had to rise. Flat on his back in the middle of a battle ensured death. He lifted his head and spotted, through the mist, the animal stalking him.

A chair flew over him and crashed into the scaly body. To his right, Alexis had grabbed a metal stool prepared for battle as people darted around them.

Outstretched on all its limbs, claws glinted in the colorful lights. The animal leaped for her. Reign flew between the two, his sword up, singing in his hand.

Alexis stumbled back, slipped, and went down hard. Her head clipped the base of a fallen table. Reign speared the beast's neck and dragged the blade from stem to stern; splitting the creature in two, leaving the halves to sizzle and evaporate. Another weight added to his soul.

His chest heaved, bloodlust sizzling through his veins. Three beasts had attacked—two were now dead. It wasn't enough, the Vanquished wanted more. A few feet away, the last one thrashed, trying to extricate itself from the wall. He glanced at Alexis. Groaning, she clutched her head.

He marched over to the beast. The barbed tail swished, narrowly missed impaling his thigh, but connected nicely with his blade. It flopped to the ground. He grabbed the spiked tail and planted it in the center of the animal's head. Again and again and—

"Enough! Kill him and be done!"

Distantly, Reign heard the command, but nothing could stop him now.

Bleed him dry, the Vanquished ordered and he gladly obeyed. Blood spurted and splattered. The beast's death cries shivered over his skin. The dull thud of flesh giving way filled his ears with the sweet song of slaying, answering the dark call of his demons.

A force wrapped around Reign and separated him from his prey. The Nubian stood in his path. "I won't let you do this." His hand hovered above Reign's heart.

"Who. Are. You?" Reign sneered, wanting the name of the man he was about to kill.

"Tyrone."

"Move. Or die." The words were whispered, but by the widening of the Nubian's eyes and grim line of his mouth, Reign knew he heard him above the throbbing noise.The Nubian shifted subtlety, braced for attack.

To the right, the beast had removed the stake from its chest and began climbing out of the wall. Reign cocked his head to the side. "Me or him?"

The force which immobilized him, released. The Nubian turned toward the beast, to finish what Reign started.

Reign planted his fist in the man's jaw, lifting him a foot off his feet. He hauled him back for two more bone-crunching blows before tossing him aside. Then he stalked his true prey.

"Stop." The Nubian groaned behind him. "Don't do this."

Reign couldn't stop. Fury burned his veins. The Vanquished ruled not him. Their howl disintegrated his last sliver of sanity. The sword in his hand screeched. He struck.

A blow to the back of his head dropped him to his knees. His sword vanished. He staggered to his knees. A kick to his ribs sent him flying into a wall.

Plaster rained from the ceiling. Had the crowd joined in on the beating? He pulled free and landed in a heap.

The Nubian placed a hand on his chest. "Control yourself."

Reign didn't hear. His attention focused on the hand touching him, keeping him glued to the ground. How was it possible for a man inches shorter, fifty pounds lighter, to wielded this much power? He couldn't move and only breathed in small panting breaths. He thrashed against the invisible bonds holding him, but they tightened, making him struggle more.

The man leaned close and whispered in his ear. "Don't make me hurt you."

For a second, Reign thought that might be possible.

CHAPTER ELEVEN

"Isn't that Detective Lever?" EJ Nicolis said to his brothers Avery, Quin, Brayden, and their best friend Tyrone Gregory. EJ downed a shot of vodka as he pointed at a woman striding through the crowd. From their table in the back, their gazes followed her until she disappeared in the crowd

Tyrone followed Avery's finger, his gaze trailed the tall red head.

"Hell, yes—" Quin upended his empty glass onto the table. He whistled low and stroked his goatee. "What's she doing here?" He stroked a match against the table and brought the flame to a cigar pressed between his lips.

Avery grabbed his shot glass. A grimace twisted his face as his burned skin stretched tightly over his bunched bicep and shoulder. He pitched the drink down his throat. "Maybe she's here for the same reasons we are. Little bump, little grind."

"With all that leather hugging her ass, I'll give her more than a *little* grind." EJ tossed back a shot of scotch. He chased it with a gulp of beer.

"It's slim pickin's here tonight." Avery scanned the crowd.

"Since when are you picky, hijo? What happened to your 'quantity' motto?" Quin chuckled.

Avery's eyes narrowed. His mouth twisted as if words struggled to slip out. Then he shrugged, pushed away from the table, and headed toward the bar.

"What's up with him?" Brayden asked EJ

"Nothing." EJ jumped up and followed his sibling.

"What's up with them?" Quin glanced between Brayden and Tyrone.

"Who knows? Secrets run thick between those two," Tyrone murmured. Hell, they all had secrets. He had more than all of them combined. Besides, it wasn't Tyrone's place to mention the object of Avery's obsession worked here.

Quin stood. Tyrone noticed his knives peeking from his waistband. Undetectable high-grade polymer plastic, Quin never left home without something sharp.

"Something's brewing. I better go and keep an eye on them." Quin stalked after Avery and EJ Brayden jumped up and followed Quin.

Tyrone faltered. A strange energy had entered the building and had taken a razor to his senses. His submerged *vis'*Ra awakened. A growl started in the back of his throat. He shook it off, reined himself in, and focused on the erratic patterns which circled the interior of the club. He tried to focus, but with so many bodies, and the manufactured mist, he couldn't pinpoint the origin. Some of the energy swept over him, giving him a chance to study the weaves.

They weren't completely unfamiliar. Traces of the pattern were definitely—*Egyptian!*

Tyrone spun. His mouth dried to desert sand. *An Egyptian was here! In this realm.* After all this time, they had finally found him.

The club erupted. Fist connected with flesh, chairs and bottles flew through the air, and the crowd stampeded. He spotted Brayden decimating an opponent's teeth. As always, Avery and EJ fought back to back, leaving all comers planted. Quin stood in the middle of the room doing his best Jet Li impersonation, smiling as he flipped and landed a kick to a guy's sternum. At least he hadn't whipped out his knives and sliced anyone open. This disaster was manageable.

Tyrone spotted a huge man standing in the middle of the crowd. Waves of *vis'*Ra energy radiated from him in a pattern Tyrone had never seen before. Sinister, edged with crimson flames, the man's *vis'*Ra beat against his senses. The beer rolled in his stomach.

Then he saw what shouldn't be. The quimaera. Three of them. Soldiers of the Egyptian Pantheon. Here in New York City.

What The Fuck!

He glimpsed the man again. A sword clutched in his hand, lifted into the air, ready to kill the quimaera stalking him. His aura vibrated and he seemed impossibly larger.

He smelled them. A fetid meaty odor. He had to get the people and his brothers out before the police arrived. And he had to kill the quimaera.

Tyrone shoved through the shifting throngs in time to see the man's sword glow crimson as the blade impaled the beast. Smoke curled in the air. Flesh sizzled and evaporated.

A chill raced down Tyrone's spine. Egyptian legend told of an ancient blade that sang as it drank the blood of its master's enemies. That was one of the stories his mother told him as a child that he never believed, until now.

From the day of his birth, he'd listened to the dire warnings against using his *vis*'Ra. Moderation and caution. And above all else, never draw attention to yourself. Tyrone looked around the club. Although fights were still in full swing, maybe this disaster could be mitigated.

Screams echoed from a rear exit. A mob had gathered, causing a bottleneck in the narrow doorway. Only one side of the double steel doors was open. He used a bit of his *vis*'Ra to open the blocked door and free the trapped people.

He turned back to the club and automatically searched for his brothers. Three were engaged, having fun as they gave better than they received. He glimpsed Avery near the bar blocking a chair from crashing into the woman he couldn't keep his gaze from all night. Avery pushed the woman toward the exit then stalked the unfortunate fool who had thrown the chair.

Tyrone swept the room, searching until he spotted the Egyptian through the mist. The quimaera was a bloody mess, ready to be put down, but the man continued his pummeling, clearly intent on reducing the beast to something a Shop Vac could suck up. He was no better than the animal he tortured. And less sane.

Tyrone had no choice but to delve into his dormant energy. He bound the man, temporarily halting the onslaught and turning the focus onto him. Soulless eyes glared out from a man's face—an eerily familiar face. They studied him. Tyrone's muscles clenched. He braced and poured more energy into the restraint immobilizing the man.

The beast pulled itself from the wall. Unable to stop both of them, Tyrone released the man and turned his attention to the quimaera. Fists snapped his head back. He crashed onto the concrete, his jaw hanging at an odd angle.

He grimaced, anticipating the pain and snapped his jaw back into place. Painful, but just until his limited *vis'*Ra flooded his system and healed him. He climbed to his feet in time to see the last quimaera incinerated in a bright blue flame.

The bastard with the sword turned and searched the club for someone new to kill.

"No," Tyrone shouted.

The man stalked away.

Tyrone flashed in front of him. "Control yourself," he said.

Dull lumps of coal peeked through shaggy hair, eyes that wished to hide in the man's haggard face. The sword, still clutched in his hand, quivered with constrained energy. A low-pitched whine rose from the blade not as an off-key violin string, but chanting in the language of Tyrone's mother.

'Hal Manah Eirbo Na'al Cu. I am the bringer. Face me and be judged.'

Tyrone gritted his teeth. His jaw answered with a throb. He wouldn't allow the shedding of anyone's blood. He released a third of his *vis'*Ra and pinned the man to the floor of the club.

Ra! The man was strong. As his opponent struggled for freedom, Tyrone's power faltered. His muscles trembled from the effort to restrain him.

Who the fuck is this guy?

He had to make a choice: Either use more of his *vis'*Ra to stop the man or release him to kill. Neither option was good; each had its own disastrous consequences.

Tyrone looked deep within and found the pathway to the locked door holding his true self, the powers his mother had warned him to never use. Yet, she had still trained him in their purpose because one day he would need them for both their protection.

A sealed door at the end of a bright hallway guided him forward. He walked the path. Touched the knob.

"Tyrone! What is it that you do?" His mother's thoughts joined his.

Before he could answer, her essence blocked the door and pushed him back.

"Mother, you don't understand."

"Then explain it to me."

"I don't have time." Sweat covered his straining body. He only had seconds left.

"Time matters. Make time." She demanded.

"I must do this." He strained.

"Why? I will not move until you tell me why you are ready to free your vis'Ra and let the Pantheon know you live."

The man had gained his footing. He faced him.

"If I don't, many will die! Starting with me."

His mother looked through his eyes and saw his opponent.

"Leave Tyrone, he is not human!"

"I will not! Now move and let me be what you created me to be!"

For a second, his always-decisive parent faltered. *"Take my vis'Ra."* Her energy began flowing into him.

He pulled away.

"No, mother!" He tried to sever their bond, but he was no match for her.

"Better they find me than you. They can only punish me. You, they will kill."

Her *vis*'Ra flooded him. In vibrant hues of red, it blazed out of his extended hand and enveloped the man in binds. He raged, flexing against the restraints.

"Tyrone?" Brayden loomed near with Avery, EJ and Quin gathered close.

"What the hell are you doing?" Quin clasped his knives in his hands.

"Bro, what the fuck are you?" EJ's eyes popped wide. Avery stood beside his sibling, one gun trained on the man, the other on Tyrone.

Before Tyrone could answer, sirens sounded and warbled to a halt outside the club.

"Now is not the time boys, we have to go," Brayden stressed.

"Release me." The man interrupted their discussion.

"Don't." The group behind Tyrone chorused.

He didn't want to, but as his opponent struggled against the bonds, his mother's donated powers started to fail. She weakened. The ruby threads frayed. She was formidable, yet in her current form, she was too old for this great display. He couldn't continue much longer or this loan would cost her.

"Are you calm?" Tyrone prayed silently to Ra the man was, because he didn't have power left to stop him.

No answer.

Energy dropping fast, Tyrone released his opponent slowly, lowering his vis'Ra in increments until the man rose to his full height. God, he was taller than all of them.

The man eyed them all. An unspoken challenge? By the hard set of his jaw and flinty eyes, he wouldn't back down. Not now. Not ever.

From his peripheral vision, Tyrone saw his brothers line up next to him. Not true siblings, though they couldn't be any closer. Shoulder to shoulder, together they faced this new threat. Silently, he thanked Ra because he had nothing left. His mother's vis'Ra had winked out, leaving him with just his own paltry energy. Though they probably didn't stand a chance against him, they would all fight to the death. Together.

The man approached, his boots landing like grenades on the concrete floor. The bright lights snapped on. Though Tyrone couldn't see all of his face through the long hair, there was no denying who the man was. Same build, same intense blue eyes, same damn face. His brothers cursed. They saw the resemblance too.

He stopped a nose hair from Tyrone. "You stink of them. Which god do you call master," he gritted out, for his ears alone. Tyrone stifled his gasp. Only Brayden knew his most guarded secret.

"Do they know what you are?" the man hissed.

"Do you know what you are?" Tyrone challenged.

"I am what I have always been, *boy*. Do that to me again and I will kill you." Then his eyes turned to the rest of the men.

He glared at each of them before he spun and walked over to the detective.

He paused and pivoted to his right. Tyrone followed his gaze to a corner of the room. He didn't see anything, but tonight, that meant nothing. His faith in his abilities had diminished since entering the club. Tyrone gathered the minuscule amount of power he had left.

The door to the club burst open. "Police! Nobody move!" Weapons drawn, the police entered.

The man swung Detective Lever's limp body into his arms and vanished.

Tyrone sagged. Hands braced on his knees, he sucked in a deep breath. This was worse than bad. This was the Titanic, the San Francisco earthquake and the Japanese tsunami rolled into one fucking colossal disaster.

"Tyrone, we gotta go." Brayden cut through Tyrone's ruminations.

"Yeah," he nodded. "I know."

"Don't forget the security tapes," Brayden whispered.

Tyrone had enough energy left to do both. He fried the electronics and flashed them all a block away.

Avery doubled over and threw up in the gutter.

EJ stumbled over to a light pole and held on for support.

"Dios Mio!" Quin slumped against a parked car, breathing deeply as he prayed. Unaffected, Brayden stood next to Tyrone.

Quin pointed a finger at Brayden. "You've done this before, haven't you?" He accused between wheezing breaths. "None of this is new to you."

Brayden shrugged. "He's my best friend."

"Who was that guy?" EJ asked, climbing to his feet.

"Couldn't you tell? He's Roman's lost twin, back from the dead, ready to kick ass." Avery swept the back of his hand across his mouth.

"Kicked our asses," EJ mumbled.

"But you kicked his." Quin pushed off the car and sized him up as if he'd never seen Tyrone before. "How'd you do that?"

More police cars squealed to a stop outside the club, along with a news van. "This is not good." Tyrone looked at Brayden. "We need to go."

"True. We need to get home and tell Roman. And I am not playing 'Beam me up' again." Quin pulled himself together and stalked to their car.

"The man's getting married tomorrow. This little tidbit can wait until he says 'I do'," Avery muttered. A round of agreement circled the group.

Mother? Through their bond, Tyrone reached for her, but received no answer. Though she appeared seventy-ish and in good health, she was a lot older. And not long for this earth. Dread bloomed in his chest.

"I can't go back to RockGate. I'll catch up with you guys later." He vanished before they could question him more.

CHAPTER TWELVE

Safely above the riot, Khuket watched the human SET sent her to kill, destroy her quimaera bodyguards. He moved with a fluidity that belied his tall, well-muscled body. The image SET implanted in her head did not do him justice. He was more than human. He was a warrior god, sent to conquer and destroy. Raw energy bled from him in waves as he decimated the beasts.

And the sword. The blade lived.

Somehow, the warrior had channeled his fury into the jagged steel, making it a weapon unlike any other. The sword wielded the man instead of the man wielding the sword. Yet they were one. His eyes glowed in harmony with the pulsing crimson aura sheathing the blade.

The chaos generated from the panicked crowd poured into her, quenching her parched soul. Greedily, she gorged on the most basic of human emotions: fear, until she could hold no more of the delicious banquet within.

Stuffed, she almost missed trailing him when he lifted the woman into his arms and flashed. For a second, she looked for Neith. She spotted the former null speaking to a girl with spiky blond hair, but Nu couldn't linger. She followed the warrior across the city and waited a few moments before passing through the outer wall of a dwelling the humans favored. Faded, Khuket hovered in a corner of the ceiling peering at the tender scene below.

He placed the woman on the bed. Straightening her limbs and smoothing the hair from brow, he lingered over her. The hunger on his tormented face conveyed all she needed to know. The woman was his weakness. Through her, he could be slain.

SET wanted him to suffer. To lose all that he loved. If she could turn his lust onto a deadlier path, SET would have his vengeance and she would have her freedom. Never would Khuket, Goddess of Chaos, be bound again.

Her weaves unfurled from her body and reached for the warrior.

He spun. His blade appeared, glowing in his fisted hand. His eyes followed suit. He placed himself between her and the unconscious woman.

Immediately, Khuket withdrew. Wrapping her weaves tight about her form, she shrank. A small, invisible target wasn't easy to find and harder to kill.

Minutes ticked by as the warrior guarded the woman, his gaze sweeping the room. He stepped halfway into the hallway, then returned and checked the room again. For a moment, his gaze and the blade lingered where she huddled.

Did he see her? She shuddered in excitement. Could he kill her like he killed the quimaera? Terror replaced excitement. To come so close only to fall short of her goal? The fallen Gods of Ogdoad would weep if they could.

Just when she thought he had discovered her, the sword disappeared and the warrior turned away. Back to the bed, he stood over the woman. Her clothes vanished, leaving a flimsy material covering her breasts and groin.

By the sharp intake of his breath, either he relished what he saw, or he was in pain.

He grabbed a cover from the end of the bed and spread it over her. After he left, Khuket waited before moving from the corner. She passed over the inconsequential female, drifted from the bedroom into the short hallway, and floated into the living room. She found her prey standing by the windows, gazing at the sleeping city.

She kept her distance as she watched and wondered about the man that she was destined to kill. But maybe she didn't have to kill him. If she could turn him, make him take up her cause, be her champion, and lead her fledgling army, the

Pantheon would tremble. All that was taken from her would return.

Not all. Her family would never return or the other Gods. Gods whose names she couldn't remember.

Khuket pushed the memories away. She'd spent enough eons brooding on the past. Her future was now, and either way it began with this man.

The warrior sat in the nearest chair, stretched his long legs, and let his head fall back. When his chest rose and fell in a steady rhythm she crept closer, ready to dart away at the first instance he became aware of her presence.

With his guard down, Khuket's weaves encompassed him. Her mind touched his and brushed up against a smooth, gray barrier. Even in sleep, he guarded himself. She searched for a way around the mental shield. Probing carefully for a weak spot, she stroked the surface until an area softened and she slipped in.

She found herself standing in the back of a vast room. But she wasn't alone. Thousands of men, dressed in various military attire stood at attention in precise rows. They all faced one direction, a corner at the opposite end of the room.

Khuket threaded her way through the silent sentinels. Seconds or days, the journey seemed endless, the men countless. She pressed on and focused on the pinpoint of darkness emanating from that corner.

Back against the wall, butt planted on the floor, Khuket found a child. The hollow-eyed, shrunken boy resembled nothing of the man she saw earlier in the night.

Shadows shrouded him, but she could clearly see the dull rusted blade resting in his open palm.

No. Not rust. Blood coated the metal.

Focused on the gutted soldier lying at his feet. The boy didn't acknowledge her. Even when she cupped his face between her hands and tilted his head up. Was this her warrior?

The shadows parted, skittered away like dislodged maggots feeding on the corpse revealing gray tinged flesh stretched over a skull. No muscle. No lips. No lids or eyes. Just empty sockets. His mouth dropped open, mocking a scream. No tongue moved to voice his pain.

Khuket plunged into his mind. "Reign." She discovered and whispered his name as she searched through his past.

"Ahhh," she sighed, reveling in the violence wrought at his hands. Battle upon battle, he killed and maimed. His unparalleled skill brought victory to those who paid his price and death to all others. But instead of joy at thrusting his blade into yielding flesh, he abhorred his skill. So much so, the men gathered were manifestations of his guilt.

Khuket's weaves ripped into him. Disgusted by his weakness, she poured chaos into him. At the same time, she shifted through his memories, searching for anything she could use against him. Images of Nephythys surfaced.

Only a few days past her incarceration and already humans repulsed her. So many conflicting needs and wants clogged their minds. None greater than love that skewed, fleeting emotion.

To her utter disappointment, she discovered that this warrior was no different. He willingly gave up his freedom to be a slave for a transient moment of bliss with the goddess, Nephythys.

The fool.

Hate was the only true emotion that held any value. Constant and everlasting.

The boy struggled. He pulled away from her invasion, but Khuket held tight, even when feet shuffled behind her. She pushed the memories of Nephythys aside. Neither the goddess nor the unconscious woman he guarded mattered. If she unleashed enough chaos within him, she would control him like she controlled the quimaera.

Barriers popped up as she delved into his mind. She blasted through each one. So close to gaining everything she needed, nothing could stop her now.

The men behind her shrieked. She glanced over her shoulder in time to see them lunge. Thousands of hands grabbed her. Tossed into the air, her weaves snapped.

These men weren't apparitions. They were remnants of the slain men somehow attached to the warrior. Khuket slammed into a wall and slid to the floor.

Weapons drawn, the warrior's private army threatened her. She looked at him. Still in the guise of a child, in the same corner, he was slumped over with shadows creeping closer.

She moved. A sword pressed to her throat. Very real. Very pointy. She had to leave. If Reign awakened, he would feel her presence in his mind. After what he did to the quimaera, she wasn't ready to face him or his blade.

She glanced at the child again. Shadows blanketed him. Only a lump remained until the shadows rolled away revealing an empty corner. The men tore into each other.

Khuket slipped away. But before she vanished, she searched the corner again for Reign. Only an inky stain on the gray floor remained.

A deflected sword missed her by inches. Khuket retreated and once she was free of Reign's mind, she hovered to study her handiwork. A grimace had replaced his peaceful expression. His hands fisted, clutching air.

Khuket smiled. Chaos had taken root.

***

The goddess Nu, co-creator of the Egyptian Pantheon, floated through the corridors of the mansion unseen. The house was UN-warded, unprotected. The child could not live here until the situation was rectified. She stopped on each level blessing, cleansing, warding.

She turned her attention to the grounds, which were beautifully decorated in white and gold for the coming nuptials and glided to the tree line. Making sure to cover every inch, she brought up all the dead things. Bugs, rodents, animals. Dead for a day or for one hundred years, she removed their lingering spirit and reburied them. She needed to do the entire woods, all of the property, but she couldn't. She was too weak for a true warding. Instead of imposing her will, she cast spells like a novice priestess.

Nu lifted her head to the heavens and chanted. The earth beneath her feet, the wind caressing her face, the water from the lake on the property and the animals dwelling nearby, nature answered her call. They gave her their spirits and joined with the essences of the dead. Blended and bound together, she wove the strongest protection spell possible. The colorful weaves weren't as strong as she'd like, still, only those of the Nicolis line, her line, could cross the boundary. When they did, she would know.

For now, this was the best her weakened form could do. Reborn as an infant, her unlimited *vis'*Ra were bound to that child's form and the energy its small body generated.

Pitiful.

In the past week, she had drained the body almost to the point of no return. Now, the child lay unprotected and vulnerable.

Unacceptable.

The child's death meant Nu's death. Until she ascended, she was as weak as any mortal. Except when her spirit broke free of its human confines and some of her *vis'Ra* was at her disposal. This was Ra's punishment for abandoning the Pantheon. One she gladly accepted. Without Ra's guiding hand, the Pantheon became treacherous.

The children she'd birthed had turned on her and had tried to bind her to the Isle. Born from the spirits of the universe, she'd escaped their confinement by releasing her energy back to its home. Now on her third reincarnation, she couldn't believe Ra had crippled her by attaching her essence to a child. Nu sighed. Cursing her erstwhile consort would serve no purpose other than blighting the land around her.

Immediate grounds complete, she returned to the house and the place housing pieces of Daniel. She descended to the vault where the head lay covered in a steel case. She didn't have the energy to open the door and see the evil SET and Anubis had wrought. Damn her son and grandson.

What was she to do? Undo the five children she brought into the world near the beginning of time? And what is good without evil?

Although she abhorred everything about SET, he was necessary to the balance Ra set in stone before he created all. She loved her children. But SET wanted more than to be free. For now, he concentrated his effort on the Pantheon and his errant wife. If ever he turned his attention to this realm, she had to be strong enough to defend this world or all would be lost.

She was tired. Her *vis'*Ra had started to ebb. It was time to return to her host. Nu sighed as her spirit floated through the house and over the grounds once more. Soon, all of her plans would come to fruition.

***

Alexis's eyes slid open. She blinked back sleep and stretched before sitting up. Sunlight streamed through the curtains and caressed her face. She squinted into the light and didn't care to check the time. It was daytime. That's all her brain needed to know right now. In the bathroom, she emptied her bladder and splashed cold water on her face. Then braved the mirror.

"I look like shit." She leaned against the rim of the sink. Her body ached like road-kill still twitching on the asphalt. She threaded her fingers through her hair, but didn't tame her bed head. Her teeth were furry, her tongue as flexible as a brick.

How long had she been home? She wondered, brushing her teeth. She'd forgotten something. Something important had slipped from her memory. Alexis scooped up a handful of water, rinsed and spit. Then ran her tongue over her smooth teeth and sighed.

Alexis slowly sifted through the jumbled mess in her mind. The information didn't want to surface. A headache burst behind her eyes and spread, deflecting her focus. She doubled over and pressed her fingers against her throbbing temples. Images of Reign flickered. His face, body. His huge blade.

Nothing else. She slammed into a big fat mental roadblock. Zilch made sense. She needed liquor, no ice, no glass. Good thing she kept a bottle of Jack in the kitchen for this kind of emergency. She slipped a black satin robe over her bra and thong, and shuffled to her living room.

Reign, sprawled on her worn sofa like an erotic ornament, snored softly. Her gun and handcuffs in his lap. The headache evaporated and details of the night flooded her brain. The bike, the club, the animals attacking her, and Reign. He had been there.

Her knees jellied, but she didn't go down. She crept across the room until she stood in front of her sofa. Her breath caught. Not because he was gorgeous or living, breathing, real. Her breathing ceased because whether awake or asleep, the man was deadly. To her career, to her body and especially to her senses. Being around him threw her off-kilter.

Not good. Whatever he was…wait. She gave herself a mental slap and let the thought settle into her psyche. Yeah, okay. *Whatever he was,* he had to go. Once in custody, the CIA, NSA, Area 51—they could all get together and figure out what the hell he was. Away from her.

She eased her gun and cuffs from his lap. Stepping back would've been wise. Instead, she leaned forward to study his face. Pale, tight skin stretched across sharp cheekbones and a broad forehead. His short beard effectively covered his jawline and softened his features a bit. No wrinkles, no crow's feet, no freckles marred the perfection of his face.

Her fingers tingled. She longed to touch him, but stopped herself from brushing the tangled hair resting on his forehead. So unlike her wiry, coarse, Brillo head, his was spun silk.

His eyes snapped open and their gazes collided. She brought her gun up and stepped back. The Glock never left the center of his chest. Still, she felt like prey instead of predator.

"Get on the ground," she ordered.

Him, on the ground and immobilized was the only way she would get out of this alive.

He didn't move. His gaze never left her face. Those intense eyes did something to her, threw her off balance even though she had the upper hand.

A grimace tightened his face and his jaw shifted as he grounded his teeth. For a second, his blue eyes glowed. Didn't they? She blinked hard to get her bearing.

His gaze took a slow drift south. Heat suffused her body, baking her from inside out. She wanted to glance down to see if her hastily thrown on robe had opened, revealing way too much.

"On. The. Ground."

He stood and she moved further away, out of his reach. He filled the room until everything shrank in comparison. A muscle flexed in his jaw. His eyes darkened or was it just the lighting in the room? First glowing, now darkening.

What's wrong with me?

A sliver of fear shafted her. She squelched it and backtracked her way around the coffee table to the clear space near her bedroom. Reign followed, then dropped to his knees and lay flat on his stomach. It wasn't a hardship staring at him stretched out on her living room floor.

"Hands behind your back." Alexis prepared her handcuffs while she watched him rotate both hands behind him. Carefully, she approached, completely aware of the tiger by the tail cliché. She dropped her knee—hard—into the small of his back. He grunted, as if her five feet, eleven inches, one hundred and forty pounds meant a damn thing.

Alexis had a single cuff around one of his thick wrist when he rotated his hand and grabbed her forearm. He tugged and twisted onto his side. Pulled forward, her knee slipped from his back and her legs straddled him. An arm banded around her waist and flipped her onto her back. His big body pinned her to the carpet. Air whooshed out of her lungs. Her gun was still clutched in her hand. Only now, it rested above her head, secured by one of his.

Every inch of him touched her. Chest against chest, abs against abs and groin—

"Get off!" Her intended yell came out as a desperate hiss.

He eased up and shifted, causing his chest to brush her nipples through her robe. To her horror, they pebbled, hard little bullets tenting the satin. If he noticed, he didn't react. Through the curtain of hair, she could see his eyes. They were clear now, and deep blue. She also glimpsed the sharp planes of his face. A lapsed Catholic, she didn't hesitate to say a quick Hail Mary while waiting for his next move.

"Hello, Alexis."

Her name was rough on his lips. "How did you know where I live?"

"I know many things about you."

"Really? I know nothing about you. How did you get in here?" She waited for him to answer, but he made no reply.

"Do you remember nothing of last night?"

His rumbled words vibrated within her. "It's a little mixed up in my head." A headache flared between her eyebrows. "You were there, at the club." Her limbs trembled annoyingly.

"I remember you." A picture of him moving with the fluid grace of a big cat floated in her head, and nothing else. Her stomach flopped and her skull threatened to split open. "How did you know where I live and how did you get in here?" She repeated.

He took the gun from her hand and effortlessly scooped her from the floor. Held against his body was no better than being beneath him. At least her stomach settled and her head decided to stay attached to her neck. She glanced up and met his gaze again beneath the fall of his tousled hair.

"Are you unwell?" he asked.

His accent was exotic, fucking erotic. The man was a drug she refused to take. "I'd be better if you let me go," she snapped.

Slowly, she slid down his body. The satin bunched under his hands and cool air fanned her ass. He released her and backed away. "Do not fear me, Alexis. I would never harm you."

"So says the man holding my gun." She met his steady gaze without flinching.

Reign glanced at the weapon clutched in his hand. He marched forward, holding her gun in his palm like a waiter carrying dessert. She backpedaled into the opposite wall. He crowded her until she couldn't see anything but him. Then he grabbed her hand and pushed her weapon into her palm.

"You think this protects you from me? Use it. Many have tried to kill me. Perhaps you will succeed. I have lived long enough to earn my patch of earth," he whispered close to her ear.

A shiver raced through her. Blood pounded in her veins. Bitterness edged his words, but his hair hid his face. She needed to see him, to read his expression. So many emotions could be contrived, but real bitterness was hard to manufacture. If this wasn't a pretense to intimidate her then she wanted to know what happened to him.

"I don't want to kill you. I want to arrest you, send you back to jail."

He jerked and flicked his hair back, exposing a furious face.

"Send me back?" The room hummed with his anger. "Never—" he vowed inches away from her lips. "—will I return to that place."

Alexis stared into his angry face. Her free hand crept up and she touched his cheek.

Reign flinched. She almost drew away, but he closed his eyes and turned his face into her palm. A sigh ruffled her hair, stroked her temple. He jerked away, stalked a few feet to the opposite side of the room, and paced.

Why did I just do that? Shaken, her body and senses couldn't sort themselves out, so she clung to the only thing she could. Alexis extended her gun and reached for her cordless phone on the end table. "You're under arrest."

He stopped-and disappeared.

Choking on nothing but air, Alexis crumbled. She slid to the floor. With her knees to her chest, she buried her face. Finally, she'd done it, lost her fucking mind. Everything that just happened was a figment of her imagination. Her career in the NYPD was over. Hell, her whole life was over.

Hands grabbed her arms and pulled her to her feet. "You're not real," she whimpered. "I need to be committed 'cause last night didn't happen and you're not here."

"I do not know if I am real or not. I came here to save my brother and kill Anubis's champion, yet there are beasts roaming the streets." His chest heaved. "Then, there is you."

She pulled away, struggling against his hold, until she looked into his eyes. "You're not real."

Pain spread across his face. "Though I acknowledge I am different, I believe I am as real as you. Your mind is sound."

She still had her doubts; however, she kept her opinion to herself and pulled her arms from his grasp. Distance. The more space between them the better. She needed to not be near him. She crossed to the other side of the room.

"If you're real, answer my question. How did you disappear like that?" She heard the hysteria in her voice and fought to quell it.

"I don't know. My will makes fading happen."

"Fading? Is that what you call it?" Reign nodded. His answer didn't make her feel better. "Is that how you got out of jail? You faded and walked right outta there?"

"Yes."

His cold eyes studied her, picked her apart. More pieces of last night flooded her brain. She remembered him lifting her, carrying her out of there. Didn't he? "You brought me here. How did you know where I lived?"

"I am always with you. I cannot leave your side."

She shook her head. "Huh? I-I don't understand."

"Since the night I arrived here from Chemmis days ago, I have not been able to leave you."

"That's impossible. I would know if you were here," she blurted. He disappeared again and a familiar coldness chilled her skin. The cool air bathed her, snaked beneath her robe, and caressed her intimately. He appeared again, inches away.

"I cannot leave you. I have tried, yet I cannot."

Her thoughts scattered like a deck of cards tossed into the air. Wordless, all she could do was stare.

"Please, do not fear me."

"Tell me what you are." Instead of a command, her voice was a thready, breathless whisper.

"I am Reign. Born in the city of Tempyra in Thracia more than two thousand years ago. I am immortal." His stony expression betrayed nothing.

Woodenly, she nodded, but it was too much. "Can you please leave, disappear, go, do whatever it is you do? I need a m-moment." She blinked and he was gone.

With her gun by her side, Alexis searched every room of her apartment. She was alone, but she wasn't. He was still here. Somewhere. She sensed his presence in the cold air surrounding her.

He said he'd been here for days, in her apartment, attached to her. Days. That meant he'd been in her grandmother's house also. If he couldn't leave her that meant work, the factory, Eleventh Avenue, and the bodega. Had he been in her bedroom? Seen her change?

She glanced down at her body and that's when it hit her. She hadn't stripped out of her clothes last night, leaving only her bra and thong.

He had.

And there wasn't a damn thing she could do about it.

CHAPTER THIRTEEN

Alexis was wrecked. Not drunk. Just a wreck. Yet, somehow she dragged herself up, barricaded herself in the bathroom to shower and throw on some clothes. She slapped on some make-up to hide the duffel bags under her eyes.

Yesterday started with a prayer, strolled into a good idea, then turned bad quick before decomposing into a stinking mess. She called her union rep and asked to push back the meeting. He called five minutes later with a no-go. Internal Affairs wouldn't reschedule.

Great. She hopped in her car with her personal air conditioner riding shotgun. Maybe if she ignored the invisible man next to her he would go away. Not likely.

She cruised by the club to see if her bike was still in the parking lot and lo and behold, it was gone. Either towed or stolen. The latter would be easier to explain. She'd have to check impound after IA.

She made it to police headquarters with ten minutes to spare. Then through security, the elevator, the receptionist, and inhaled a ragged breath when her butt eased into a chair in the Internal Affairs conference room. The rectangular mahogany table gleamed under the fluorescent lighting. Her throat dried when she saw a water pitcher and glasses an arm's length away near the center. On her right sat her union representative, on her left, her attorney. Across the table were Harold Roberts, the Chief of Detectives, and Edgar Wallace, her captain. They were already here, early. Beneath the table, her fingers twisted her pants leg and her foot jiggled.

A breeze caressed the back of her neck, calming her. *He's here. In the same room.*

God she hoped she wasn't the only one who could see him. If they saw him, then they wouldn't think she was crazy. Maybe they'd help her get rid of him.

"Are you listening, Lever?" The Chief pounded the desk.

Yanked from her thoughts, Alexis flinched and nodded, "Yes sir, I am."

"You ignored the rules of this department and common sense. You took a witness into your private residence and then lost her," the Chief continued.

I didn't lose her. Stella Walker left on her own accord while I barely survived. Not that anything she did was right in the department's myopic eyes. She could handle sexism. Growing up in a military family with three older brothers, sexism was the toast at breakfast. Since when had being a good test taker become a handicap? Oh, yeah, since joining the NYPD.

Intelligence can only get you so far, Lever, McCabe had intoned the first day she showed up with her gold shield clipped to her waist. Like he would know.

"Can you tell us what the hell happened at the bodega on Eleventh Avenue two days ago?" The Chief's flat tone gave nothing away.

When in doubt, tell the truth, her father always said. She couldn't tell them the man who had escaped custody in New City was now stalking her. Oh, and he's invisible. And standing behind her. Not if she wanted to stay out of the psych ward at Bellevue Hospital.

She opened her mouth, but her attorney spoke.

"My client will not be commenting on the incident until she's seen a physician."

The Chief nodded. His eyes narrowed a fraction, assessing her. "I was going to give you a reprimand and let you return to work. Then you pull this shit upstate and faint on duty. Some think you're a loose cannon, Lever. I think you're a danger to yourself, and worse, a danger to my department."

Danger? She wasn't a danger when she'd found the evidence linking Roman Nicolis to the attack in Central Park. Stella Walker didn't think she was a danger when she called her for help. Last night when she'd faced those beasts, *she'd* been the one in danger.

Reign had saved her. She didn't remember everything, but she remembered him stepping in and taking a blow aimed for her head. She had checked the news before she left the house. There was a report about the brawl at the club, though nothing about the beasts. Reign killed the three that were there. More lurked, she was sure of it. Could they hunt down the rest, together?

"I could've fired you after the stunt with Stella Walker, but damn Roman Nicolis! He pulled in a lot of favors to keep you employed. After yesterday though, you're on indefinite suspension pending an investigation into your conduct."

"Huh?" She leaned forward. Somewhere in the course of her mind wandering, she'd missed a key point of info. "W-what did you say?" The union rep tried to shush her. She ignored him.

A cold wind circulated the room, casting the loose papers comprising her employment folder into the air. Her hair whipped about. Alexis ignored the men chasing papers. She swiveled and focused on the arctic storm at her back. An outline of a man showed through the swirling wind.

Please God, not here, not now. She ignored the fact only moments ago she wanted him to be seen.

"Where the hell'd that come from?" The Chief tried to fix his comb-over. When no one answered, he cleared his throat. "Let's get this meeting over with, Lever."

Refocused, Alexis turned her chair around. "What does Roman Nicolis have to do with these proceedings?"

"He bailed your ass out of hock, that's what." He closed the file on the table.

"Nicolis did what?" She lurched to her feet and banged her knee into the table. Her lawyer grabbed her arm and tried pulling her back into her chair. She yanked away.

"I got a call from Judge Grayfield and Senator Orley over your bullshit!" The Chief bellowed. "No one tells me what to do."

But apparently, they had. "Sonofabitch," she gritted.

"Daniel Nicolis' body is missing and Roman Nicolis is concerned about your welfare," Captain Wallace stated. "He pulled a lot of strings. I don't know what you *did* for him to leave such a positive impression." He sneered. His cold gaze assessed her.

"That's uncalled for, Wallace," her attorney defended her.

Wallace's mouth snapped open for a reply, but the Chief cut him off. "I can see what you're thinking, Lever, and let me say this. Roman Nicolis is the only thing keeping me from firing you. You drive up to his house and piss him off if you want." He leaned forward with a sick grin plastered across his face because that's exactly what he wanted her to do.

She couldn't lose her job.

"This'll go into your permanent record. I can't imagine how disappointed your parents will be. Hopefully, it won't ruin their anniversary," the Chief added.

She plopped back into the chair. Of course, he would remember their anniversary. It was only days away. Frenemies and rivals with her father since boot camp, the Chief would probably be there. Fuck! She'd forgotten. Her mind shuffled through her repertoire of excuses, searching for a way out of the looming disaster.

"We're done here. You're suspended with pay until further notice." The Chief gathered his papers and left. Wallace trailed behind him.

They might be done. She wasn't.

Alexis grabbed her purse and marched to her car. She tossed everything into the backseat, slid behind the steering wheel, and slammed the door. Reign sat, crunched in the passenger seat.

"You will take me to my brother." He whipped his hair back, away from his face. Those eyes of his drilled into her, demanding she comply.

Oh. My. God. The height, the build, the facial structure, and those blue eyes. How could she have been so blind?

"Yeah, I'll take you to him." *And leave you on his doorstep.*

CHAPTER FOURTEEN

Alexis planned on pounding on Roman Nicolis's front door and demanding entry. Unfortunately, his front door was open. Well-dressed women and handsomely attired men wandered between the house, the garden, and the maze. The grounds were resplendent, decorated in white and gold and nature's brilliant fall colors. A server handed her a flute of champagne when she crossed the threshold into the large marble vestibule. Good. She needed it. The first sip left her taste buds thirsty. She emptied the glass and grabbed another.

The grand staircase waited to her right, guarded by a man in livery uniform. Four corridors branched out from the rest of the room, but everyone seemed to gravitate to the hall on her extreme left.

Whatever they celebrated, she couldn't care, but she did pillage the plate of mushroom caps before making her way further. Reign walked next to her, solid and so real. At the next fork in the road, she ditched him. They both sought the same man. Let's see who reached him first.

"He manipulates my life and then parties the night away," she grumbled, while threading through the guests. She passed a solarium and a library before ending up in the ballroom at the back of a crowd.

She knew he was rich, but *damn.* "Who has a ballroom in their house?" At the edge of the room, she easily spotted the tallest man. Roman stood head and shoulders above most of the onlookers. Whatever event he had going on, she'd piss on it. Alexis elbowed people out of her way. What she had to say wouldn't wait for privacy.

She nudged the last body out of her way as *At Last* by Etta James began to play. Roman pulled Stella close. His arms wrapped around her slender waist and they began to sway.

Alexis's jaw swung loose and she gulped a mouthful of air. This wasn't a party. It was a god damn wedding reception! Stella looked exquisite in a silk organza mermaid wedding gown similar to the one Alexis had drooled over in a bridal book when she and Paul were dating.

She watched them dance, both completely ignorant of how they destroyed her life. Her conscience twinged. Could she tell a man off on his wedding day?

Yeah, she could.

One step onto the dance floor and her cell vibrated. She fished it out of her pocket and glanced at the screen. *Shit! Her father.*

Had the Chief informed him about the suspension? He'd wasted no time. A bead of sweat collected at her temple. She could ignore him. But one didn't ignore Major General Lever. Hell, there was no way she could hear him with the crowd and music. Alexis made her way from the ballroom and through a side door. The newlyweds would have to wait a moment longer for her wrath.

The sweet smell of fresh cut grass and the late afternoon sun calmed her nerves before she answered her phone on the final ring.

"Hello, Sir." She grabbed a lock of hair and worried it between her fingers.

"Alexis." Full of reprimand, her father's voice stiffened her spine.

Oh Lord, whenever he started a conversation stating her name like that meant trouble. She snapped to attention, ready to salute. "Sir?"

"The bill for the repairs landed on my desk an hour ago." Immediately, she knew the call concerned her grandmother's damaged house. The domino effect of one lousy choice kept accumulating.

Damn! Her logical father wouldn't believe a story about a wild beast and an invisible man. Quickly, she fabricated a story about vandals and a fallen tree. So much for telling the truth.

Alexis braced herself for the coming barrage. Retired Major General Lever didn't yell. He didn't need too. Precise wordage and a deadly tone whipped the men under his command, and his family, into compliance.

"This bill is outrageous—"

"I'll take care of it, Sir." She cut him off, and then sucked in a sharp breath. No one cut the General off. You waited your turn to speak, if it ever came.

"Good answer."

Had his voice softened? No, must be her imagination.

"Your mother and I have come to a decision. We're not placing your grandmother's house on the market. In this economy, it won't sell. However, if you make the repairs and pay the property taxes, we'll consider willing it to you after we die."

A smile spread across her face. Her grandmother's house and her family's respect were the two things she wanted most. Now, she had one. "In writing, Sir?" She didn't want to have to fight her brothers in court years from now over property they never wanted.

Her father taught her well. Nothing was real unless you had proof on white paper with black ink. Or as the NYPD preferred, a color video with perfect lighting on a full frontal with the victim pointing a finger at the culprit saying, "You did it."

"In writing," he agreed and Alexis caught a hint of pleasure in his voice. A group of guests passed her, drowning out her father's voice, and bringing her back to her current dilemma, Roman Nicolis.

"I have to go, Sir."

"Your mother wants to speak to you."

What was it lately about Gloria wanting to speak to her at the most inopportune times? She tried to keep frustration out of her voice. "I'm at a crime scene. Tell her I'll call her later."

"Understood," her father said before the line went dead. If there was one thing her father understood, it was work. His work—the military, the mission—came before family, friends, even God.

She threaded back through the crowd and stopped at the last place she'd spotted Roman. Of course, he wasn't there. She spun. Nope. No Roman or Stella. *They could be anywhere in this f-ing mausoleum.* She started wandering, hoping to run into him, when her phone vibrated on her hip. *Dad again!* She darted back outside. "Sir, now is not—"

"It's not your father, dear."

Her wily mother called on her father's phone because she knew Alexis wouldn't dare ignore him. "Yes, Gloria?"

"You didn't listen to me," she hissed.

Oh hell, what now? Since her last debacle, she purposely hadn't listened to her mother. "What are you referring to?"

"Did you see him?" She continued as if Alexis hadn't spoken.

Her heart lurched. '*Him*' could refer to anybody. "Who?"

Silence. Except for heavy breathing, Gloria didn't reply.

"Never mind, Alexis. I-I'm being silly. Sorry for pulling you away from work."

Through a side window, she spotted Roman striding through the house. She didn't have time for this. She came here with one objective, to confront Nicolis. Not be a guest at his wedding and deal with her parents. Alexis followed his movements, but by the time she entered the house she'd lost him.

"Mother fu-fudge!" *Shit, cursing was unladylike.* "Gloria, I gotta go. I'll call you later." She was about to press the end button when she heard her mother's voice.

"Please be careful." She hung up before Alexis could reply. Never one for sentiment, the concern in Gloria's voice threw her. She studied her phone. Her finger hovered over the contact app and debated calling her mother back when she glimpsed an object rushing toward her. The crowd surged. No time to duck, she caught it.

When the women around her attacked, she huddled her mysterious package close to her body and protected it. Only when they stopped tugging and pulling on her, did she finally see what landed in her arms.

Flowers? She turned the bouquet around. No, roses. A huge bouquet of battered red roses. Alexis looked up. Stella glided from the middle of the staircase toward the landing where Alexis waited, clutching the kryptonite arrangement.

"Congratulations. You're next." Stella smiled and pulled her into a hug.

CHAPTER FIFTEEN

Reign wandered through the maze of opulent rooms, searching for his brother. He could feel him, somewhere in this home, amongst the mass of people milling about. His twin was here.

A tingle of evil raced along his spine. People walked around him as he froze in the center of the room, searching for the malevolence teasing his senses. Yet, there wasn't a focal point.

Then it hit him. The same presence that had greeted him the night he came to this realm and met Alexis. Anubis's champion was close. Reign swung around, searching for the monster and found a mass of chatting people. He followed the invisible trail, leading him through the house until the sensation faded, sliding away like a slick of oil on a watery surface.

A round of laughter interrupted his thoughts. A crowd had gathered in the back of the house. Head and shoulders taller, he easily peered over everyone and saw Roman.

In the midst of a group of men, all dressed in similar attire, his twin raised a glass high. "We've come through much, weathered many storms. We are more than family."

These were the same men who'd challenged him nights ago: The scarred one, the brawler, the Spaniard and the dark haired one. The group now included a blond he had never met. Fury pounded through his veins in time with his beating heart.

"You all know me better than anyone else. Almost as well as my beautiful wife." He saluted a woman standing to the side. Reign followed his stare to Stella Walker. His bride.

"We are brothers. I'd lay down my life for each you," Roman continued.

"Starting to get sappy," the Brawler grumbled to the crowd's amusement. "Wrap it up before you embarrass us."

"Let my husband have his moment," Stella yelled from the sidelines.

Roman chuckled at the ribbing. "To the men I trust and hold closest to my heart. I raise my glass to you all, those present and far. You have my eternal gratitude and loyalty."

The shivering crowd parted in front of Reign.

"Oh my, where—did—you—come—from?" a woman asked.

The words rushed past Reign. Betrayal wedged in his heart. Roman laughed while his new brothers slapped him on the back. He embraced each brother as he'd once embraced Reign after a hard battle. A cold wave rolled through his gut. Those spectators closest to him fled for warmer environs, but Roman…his head snapped around.

Their eyes locked.

For the first time in two millennia, Reign met his twin's stunned gaze.

And turned away. He swallowed the cold lump of desolation lodged in his throat and strode through the house. Faded again, people darted out of his way, blowing warm air into their cupped hands and wrapping their arms around their bodies. His palm itched. The sword wanted to appear and cleave flesh from bone. He yearned to bathe his anguish in blood. The temptation ate at him. Teased him to comply. To surrender to the horrid gift his father had bestowed. A trained killer. Mercenary. Monster. No better than his quarry.

Though cold, he never truly felt the chill, until today. Looking at his brother's happy family, the men he'd surrounded himself with, sucked the remaining heat from Reign's heart. The Vanquished raged inside his head. The urge to kill something nearly smothered him, but a shock of titian curls and a glimpse of Alexis's fine profile diverted his attention from murder.

Reign swerved to intercept her. He wanted to pull her into his arms, bask in her warmth, use her to chase his demons away.

A tendril of evil brushed his senses and yanked his focus. Translucent, worm-like tentacles, coiled around his ankle before slithering away. *Alamut.* The beast's name filled his head. At times, the Vanquished whispered. His tether to Alexis stretched too far, causing him to double back and lose the tendril. Eventually, his senses led him to a door. He passed through the wooden barrier to stand at the top of a staircase. The wood creaked beneath his weight as he descended into the dark lower levels of his brother's home.

Stale air circulated between the rows of weathered wine racks. The scents of musty earth, wet concrete, and things long forgotten combined to fill the space with palpable malice. He walked down the main isle between the many rows of stacked bottles. Alamut drew him. Like a hook deep in the throat of a fish, it tugged on his senses and reeled him in, guiding him toward the wine barrels on the back wall.

The sword appeared and he gripped the blade tight, reassured by its weight. He passed through the door and materialized. Lights clicked on. The room was filled with metal racks holding pictures, pottery, gems, jewelry, parchment, gold, silver, and many more things he didn't understand. He didn't waste time trying. He focused on one thing as he walked deeper into the vault and stopped in front of several cylindrical containers of various sizes.

The smallest of the six vessels drew his attention. Round, yet flat on the bottom and top. He flipped the latch on the side. With a pop and hiss, the vacuum seal broke. He lifted the lid and peered inside, then reached in and grabbed a fistful of black hair. Ice swept through Reign's veins. He ground his teeth to keep from them from clicking. The Vanquished responded to the chill touching his core with a mournful wail. Reign had to stop himself from opening his hand and stepping away.

A hard tug pulled the head free. Trepidation made him pause before turning the head to see its features. This wasn't Alamut. Only a man who'd suffered a hard beating. Bruises covered his jaw and right cheek. Dried blood trailed from his forehead into his eyes. He flipped open the rest of the nearby containers and found the assorted remains of the man's body.

While that thought stormed his brain, another joined. The corpse wasn't cold or clammy, and decomposing. This hacked body still had warmth, as if, life continued to flow through it.

He grabbed the head again. Its eyes flipped open.

Damnation. He dropped the head and slammed into the shelving behind him. Items clattered to the floor, the clank magnified in the confined space.

The head wobbled across the floor and stopped face up. Cold eyes of the deepest blue, much like Roman's and his, glared. "We meet again." Rasped through bloodless lips.

Reign's eyes narrowed. "We have never met." He picked up the head and held it at arm's length.

"Don't remember me?" The features contorted, becoming the grotesque monster he faced in Alexis's ancestral home.

"Aye, I see you now. Who had the pleasure of dismembering you?" A feral grin stretched his face.

"Your brother," the head hissed.

"I have no brother," he growled and pushed thoughts of his twin away.

"And Stella," Alamut added.

"A woman? Anubis chose poorly when he made you his champion." He chuckled.

"Yet, I am still here." One corner of Alamut's lips curled in an imitation of a smirk.

"Your master's magic keeps you alive," Reign said.

"As does yours."

"I have no master," Reign barked.

"You stink of Nephythys. You're her lap dog, ordered to kill, but you find you no longer have orders to obey," Alamut sneered.

"You are still alive, Alamut."

"Do you call this living? Trapped in a steel prison without an hour's reprieve?"

"Should I feel sympathy?" Reign's eyebrows stretched to his hairline.

"No, you and I have unfinished business. Reassemble me or do you intend on letting your brother win your battles," Alamut goaded.

"I fight my own battles." He shook the head and propped the stub on a shelf.

"Then fight me and complete the oath you gave Nephythys," Alamut taunted.

"What do you know of the oath I gave the goddess?"

"It's the same oath I gave Anubis, to serve, obey, and defeat you. We have both failed. My punishment's obvious." Alamut cast his gaze toward his limbs and torso in the other canisters. "What will your punishment be when Nephythys discovers your failure?"

"My death." The words left a void inside Reign.

"Not eager to die now that you finally live? Maybe you won't. Nephythys may reclaim you and your life with her will continue as it has for the last two thousand years."

God, to be trapped with her again. Bound, buried, manipulated, and lied to, all for the sake of her pride. He'd loved her once, long ago. In the beginning of their tortuous relationship when he thought, he died and she'd saved his soul.

"Reign?"

He spun.

The door to the vault stood open and Roman blocked the exit. His expression stunned as he stared at his brother. Slack-jawed, he rushed forward until his gaze shifted to the head perched on the shelf. He stopped and the joy on his face vanished, replaced by a calculated stare.

"Who are you?" Roman demanded.

After two thousand years, his brother no longer knew him? Had the resemblance ended when their separation began? Reign touched the bristly hairs on his cheek and had a moment of surprise. Nephythys preferred him clean-shaven. His whiskers must have grown when he left Chemmis.

"Roman—" Reign began but then Roman's new family appeared in the doorway. Four men filed in and fanned out behind Roman.

Again, his palm tinged. The sword called, wanting death.

Like the buzz of a million bees nesting between his ears, the Vanquished whispered, growing louder until they roared.

Alexis.

The tether had stretched too far. Reign closed the distance between him and Roman.

"Out of my way." He grabbed a fistful of his brother's wedding clothes and shoved. Roman shoved back. The screams inside Reign's head escalated. His knees threatened to buckle. Someone grabbed his arm. Anger whipped through him. He spun and grabbed the man who dared touch him and tossed him into a shelf. Ready to brawl, he pivoted, fists swinging toward the next enemy. Roman blocked his punch. Stunned, Reign didn't fight when his brother pushed him aside to protect someone other than him.

"You protect him...over me?" Reign's blood boiled and the dark sword manifested in his hand. Roman's gaze shifted to the blade. The Vanquished demanded war, yet Alexis pulled on his soul, taking him an atom at a time back to her side. In the last seconds, he caught Roman's startled expression as he faded before their eyes.

Reign rose from the lower level to the ground floor. He darted through celebrants and the structure of the house, continued higher until he found her in a bedroom.

A scream rent the air. He spared a look at the bride darting away from him to the opposite side of the room.

"Can't you knock! Stella, it's all right. I can explain," Alexis shouted.

His brother's wife stopped before escaping out the door. Her gaze darted between the two of them, and then settled on him. Her mouth parted as her eyes widened. She stepped closer, a question pursed her lips. Yet before she could ask, the door burst open and the room filled with Roman and his brothers.

Reign looked at the men fanned out around him, weapons at the ready. All prepared for battle, but none more than him. Deep inside, a moan echoed through his gut, transformed into a wail as his hungry ghosts appeared. They filled the room, surrounded the men and his twin. For a moment, he thought his personal demons were there to protect him. But their anger filled him and magnified the simmering rage he battled to control.

"Brother, are your men prepared to die?" Reign sneered.

"Brother? You are no brother of ours," the blond said, stepping closer.

"—Who are you—"

"—How did you get in here—"

"—Leaving in a box—"

Voices filled the room and competed with those in his head.

"None here question me," Reign spat. Crouched in a fighting stance, his black sword gave a mournful cry as it manifested in his hand.

"Everyone back away." Alexis stepped in front of him.

Reign faded, passed through her, and solidified once more. The men braced for attack. Knives and guns palmed in their hands, aimed at him. Neither they nor the fists beating his back would stop him. He took a step forward. Roman blocked him, still questioning, still not believing.

His black sword raised a fraction of an inch, ready to attack his twin.

Roman's eyes narrowed. He raised the sword clutched in his hand and took another step closer.

Wild fury surged through Reign, demanding vengeance for the unspoken challenge. But this was his brother. Locked together in their mother's womb from conception until the day of the curse. They'd beaten each other senseless plenty of times, but not like this. Never had they lifted their hands in true anger against each other.

Now, he could barely control the urge to hack into his twin, quarter him the way Alamut's body lay in pieces below. From the glint in his brother's gaze, Roman craved the same.

"Stop this!" Stella cried and rushed between them. The train of her gown snagged on her heel and she fell into Reign's body. Instantly, his sword vanished. He steadied her and set her back on her feet. Roman snatched her from Reign's arms and examined her. "Are you all right?"

"I'm fine." She looked over her shoulder, tentatively testing his name. "Thank you, Reign."

He bowed his head. "You are welcome." His gaze shifted to Roman. "Your bride is beautiful, brother, and has manners."

"All it takes to get your attention is to trip into your arms?" Alexis stood beside him, mouth grim and eyes full of annoyance.

Was she jealous? Reign pushed the thought away. Now wasn't the time. He returned his attention to the situation at hand.

Fear. From Roman's slackened mouth to his concerned eyes, fear leached out of him and buffeted Reign. Once again, they were connected. Did his own erratic emotions buffet Roman?

Too painful to see Roman's worried expression. Reign turned away and ran into a wall of hostile stares. None of the men had lowered their weapons. Mutual hate simmered, threatening to boil. This time Reign won the battle to control it.

"Bring your pets to heel, Brother. I answer to none." There were growls and muttered curses around the room.

"You will answer to me." Roman warned. The hard determination in his tone replaced any previous trepidation.

Answer to him? Born ten minutes after his brother, he never answered to Roman. Now, his twin thought to order him?

"Follow me." Roman commanded Reign. En masse, his men prepared to follow their leader, but Roman shook his head once.

"Roman, I don't think it's wise—"

"No, Thane—" he cut the blond off. "Everyone stays here."

Reign waited as Roman met each man's gaze and received an answering nod. Older, Roman had abdicated his senior role, preferring Reign to lead and shoulder the responsibility and conscience for both of them. Irresponsible and impulsive, Roman fought, drank, and whored his way across each battlefield until the sword in his hand and the lance in his pants competed in notoriety. Now somber and sober, he led this group of men.

Resentment made Reign grit his teeth. A modicum of responsibility and maybe they would never have suffered the wrath of the merchant who hired them. Failure to protect his family began this cursed journey, but damn it this wasn't the end, at least not for him.

"Reign."

Pulled from bitter memories, his gaze returned to his brother. Roman waited by the door. Reign took a few steps to join him then paused at the blond. Thane, his brother named him. Several inches shorter, Reign looked down at the man from his six foot eight inch height. Thane didn't flinch or look away. Yet, Thane was afraid. Reign hadn't survived decades of battle without learning to spot weakness in an adversary. Something caused this man's insides to tremble, but he didn't think he was the cause.

Temptation rode Reign hard to test out his temporary powers. He wondered how much of the goddess's energy had transferred when her illusion kissed him. He glanced at Alexis. Her eyes had narrowed into slits and her fists were balled.

"No," Reign said to Roman. He returned to Alexis's side and the Vanquished quieted.

With another nod, Roman's men filed out of the room, but his wife stayed.

"You've trained your pets well, Roman," Reign smirked.

"They are not my pets." Roman's voice vibrated with restrained anger. "They are my family, my brothers."

"I'm your brother." Somehow, he contained the rage roiling inside.

"How are you here?" Roman asked.

A bitter laugh escaped Reign. "This is your greeting?"

"Where the fuck have you been and how the fuck did you get here?" Roman stepped closer.

"Sweetheart." Roman's wife touched his arm, but he refused to break Reign's stare and tried to move her behind him. She slipped from his hold and moved to Alexis.

"Thank you for taking me in and I apologize for leaving in the middle of night." Stella hugged Alexis.

Reign watched a tepid smile cross Alexis's face and she patted Stella's back.

"I appreciate the apology and understand why you left," Alexis said when they parted. Then she looked at Roman. "You bastard! How dare you interfere with my life. Do you know what you've done?"

"Save you from being fired?" Roman answered.

"Instead of being fired, they stuck me in Vice. I'll be on the hoe stroll for the next five years if I'm lucky!"

"Detective Lever, I'm so sorry." Stella went to Roman's side. "We thought we were helping you. When I left your grandparents home that night, we had no idea you were hurt or the repercussion with your job. I never would have left if I knew."

Alexis blew out a harsh breath and braced her hands on her hips. Reign reached for her and then stopped when he took in her dark scowl. Stella stepped forward, but Roman halted her. When she protested, he shook his head and silenced the budding argument.

Reign looked at the graceful woman who had wedded his brother and wondered how Roman's fortunes had changed. The house, the men, the wife—this was not the brother he remembered.

"Our guests are probably wondering if we've started the honeymoon." Roman whispered to Stella.

She nodded and glanced between Roman and Reign before departing.

Reign watched as Roman looked at Alexis with an unspoken plea for privacy.

"Fine," Alexis grumbled before stalking out and slamming the door behind her.

"Still the manipulator, brother?" Reign moved to the other side of the room.

"I do what I must to keep those I love safe. How do you know Detective Lever?" Roman asked.

"Why do you care?" He tensed.

"I know her."

Jealousy stabbed deep, threatening his control. His brother had *known* many women. Was Alexis included in the count? "She is under your protection?"

"No—"

"Then she is my concern, not yours." He refused to address the sudden rush of relief flooding his system.

"Detective Lever is a guest in my house and therefore under my protection. My brother would understand."

"You protect her now? After you left her alone in her home with a beast? Odd way to show your concern for a woman."

Roman's eyes narrowed while his nostrils flared. Reign knew his brother's memories had returned to that night. The night he retrieved his woman and left Alexis to die.

"How do you know—"

"I was there, Roman. I saw your concern for your woman and the lack of for Alexis," he spat.

"Daniel wasn't after her. He hunted Stella. I made a choice. I chose to save my wife."

"And left an innocent to die? The brother I remember would never have done something so heinous."

"She's not an innocent. She's a cop. I thought she could take care of herself. In any war, there are hard choices. I would do the same again," Roman said.

Two thousand years later, Roman had finally grown enough to make the hard choice he often left to him and others to do. Reign closed the distance between them, stopping inches from his twin. "Who killed Alamut?" he growled.

Surprise crossed Roman's face. "How do you know his name?" Suspicion laced his tone.

"Answer the question, brother." Reign demanded and waited.

"I did." Roman's brows lowered.

"You fought that *man*?"

"Yes, Stella and I stopped, quartered and contained him," Roman sneered. "A sword is the only thing that stopped him, not kill him."

Nephythys's assessment of Roman's skill was wrong. His prowess hadn't diminished over the years. Or the goddess lied. Manipulating him once again to do her bidding. No matter. The *thing* still lived. As long as Alamut was alive, Reign would remain free. Something unfurled in his chest and he released a low sigh. "He wasn't yours to end."

Roman tilted his head. His eyes narrow. "What do you mean?"

"Alamut was mine to destroy." He pointed to his chest. "And remains so."

A knock sounded and Stella entered. "Sorry to disturb, but I need you, sweetheart." She apologized to both of them before her gaze settled on Roman.

Reign approached her slowly. She turned to him. Her gray eyes held questions, but never left his face. No fear showed on her face. Good, because he would never hurt her. He dropped to one knee and kissed her left hand.

"Sister, with my life I will protect you."

"Uhm, thanks. Please get up now." Her cheeks blushed a rosy pink.

Reign stood and looked at his brother. Roman smiled and took his bride's hand.

"Thank you, Reign," he said. "The obligation of a bride and groom haven't changed much in all these centuries. Stay, I'll return in a moment."

***

Roman left the bedroom more confused than when he entered. After everything, Reign's last act of dropping to his knee and welcoming Stella into the family? Unexpected.

"That's your brother, right? Even with the beard and the long hair, it's him?" Stella pressed when they left the room.

Roman ushered her into a secluded alcove. "I don't know. He feels like Reign, but after everything that happened with Daniel I refuse to take anything at face value."

"What do you mean he 'feels' like Reign?"

"We're twins. We have a connection. We've always been able to sense each other, know when the other is in trouble. For two thousand years, I couldn't feel him and now, suddenly, I do. But something's wrong, off. Like the pool is tainted."

How could he explain how his insides twisted when he saw Reign and Daniel's head talking to one another like long lost friends and the dark current flowing through him. When he looked at both, he could feel each of them, twined together, inseparable inside him. Bile churned in his gut.

Stella's soft hand stroked his cheek. "What do you want to do?"

That was the million-dollar question and he had no answer. Laughter filtered through the bedroom windows. Wedding guests still roamed the house. He swallowed a groan and looked at her. "This isn't how I wanted your day to end."

"Our day, and no, I wouldn't have planned this ending either. We also didn't plan on you reuniting with Reign, so the day isn't entirely ruined."

"Yeah? The night's still young," he muttered. Stella laughed and he hugged her. The scent of her filled him, grounded him, and gave him a reason for living.

"Shall I order the house cleared?" He couldn't care less about their guests.

"We only have the cake left. You deal with your brother. I can entertain our guests for a while." She stuck her hand out.

"Deal." Roman pulled her into a simmering kiss. By the time they pulled apart, Hector was waiting a discreet distance away.

CHAPTER SIXTEEN

Bianca wanted to stay away. Should've been easy. What scorned woman wanted to attend their ex's wedding?

A vengeful woman.

They couldn't have picked a more perfect day, she noted with a large dose of bitterness. The afternoon sun burned softly, filtered through an occasional cloud. A cool breeze ruffled her hair. The leaves on the trees and the hedges of the garden maze had started to turn yellow, crimson, and auburn, painted the ideal backdrop for a fall wedding. If only she'd brought along a blowtorch.

She'd arrived moments before the 'I do'. On the back lawn, next to a well-appointed tent, she clenched a glass of champagne as she watched Roman say his vows and tie himself to a woman other than her.

Afterward, Bianca grabbed another drink from the circulating servers and mingled. She didn't expect to stay long. As an uninvited guest, soon someone would spot her, then she and the exit would meet. But as a former resident of RockGate, she knew all the secrets to avoid detection.

Her back against the edge of the patio, Bianca listened to the brothers give their speeches and was sufficiently nauseated to turn away and return to the house. Soon after, Roman darted past her and raced into the second ballroom set up for the guests. Tempted, she started to follow and nearly collided with Thane. Only a quick spin and merge with a group of guests stopped her prompt ejection from the festivities. Like a freight train, Avery, EJ, Brayden, and Quin, swept through the crowd, following Roman. She trailed them at a safe distance until the last disappeared into the wine cellar.

Bianca loitered, leaning against a nearby column a few yards away, she kept peering at the door. Within minutes, Roman rushed from the basement, followed by his men.

Should she follow them and risk discovery? No. She had made it this far. Trying to eavesdrop at the scene of whatever crisis they were attending would only lead to an unceremonious and embarrassing removal.

With the crowd focused on the commotion, she slipped unnoticed through the open basement door. Quietly, she closed the door behind her and paused to let her eyes adjust to the dim lighting. Cool and damp, the subterranean space smelled earthy. A shiver ran through her. Anything associated with dirt or the outdoors was anathema to her, but that didn't stop her burgundy suede and python Pradas from click-clacking their way down the wooden staircase.

Never in all her times at the mansion had she ventured into the wine cellar. Now she understood why. Rows of dusty wine bottles filled the middle of the room, while barrels stacked the wall.

Bianca strolled the center aisle, noting the sparse lighting and shadowed areas. It didn't take her long to feel foolish. She came to the mansion searching revenge. Dumped by Roman less than three weeks ago, only a few months away from their wedding, she wanted nothing more than to see him and his new wife suffer in any way possible. She reached the rear of the cellar and realized nothing in here would help her achieve her goal.

Still, Roman had left his wedding and rushed to this room. She took another trip around, examining the shadowed areas.

Nothing. Frustrated, she turned to leave, and stopped. A memory surfaced. The vault was down here. She'd seen it a few times as a teen. Could that be why they ran down here? She studied the wine barrels lining the back wall. She remembered Hector pushing one of them to gain access. But which one? And what would happen if she pushed the wrong barrel?

She started pushing the barrels in the middle and worked her way. Risking embarrassment and eviction was worth achieving her goal. A moment later, she heard a click. An entire panel shifted, rolled back, and slid into a hidden recess on the right. A spotlight flicked on and landed on a steel door with a QWERTY keypad. She sucked in an excited breath and stretched her hand out. Centimeters from brushing the letters and numbers with her fingers, she paused.

Fingerprints, stupid! No one could know she was here. Leaving a print would dispute that. Her hand curled into a fist and dropped to her side. She stepped closer.

The password could be anything from the obvious to something completely random. Roman's name—her fingers twitched—or one of the men—her hand raised—maybe a combination of all. She could try. Type in a few names. She stopped herself again. This keypad probably kept a log of all entries. A few wrong passwords and the cavalry would come running.

Damn! She wanted in. Something in there would help her achieve her goal.

There is.

Bianca spun. Her gaze darted to every dark recess. "Who's there?"

No one is there, Bianca.

She swallowed hard. The voice hadn't come from somewhere in the cellar. It came from her. She'd finally gone over the cliff and landed in crazy.

You want your revenge? Unlock the vault and free me.

The voice had a familiar tone. But it couldn't be... "Daniel?" she whispered.

Free me.

She turned to the vault and backed away into a wine rack. The bottles danced, but didn't clatter to the ground.

"You're dead. Stella shoved you out of a window. I saw it on the news."

And you believe everything you see on TV?

Not today.

She touched the still tender spot on the back of her head. "How-how are you inside my head?

I learned a trick...or two. I can show you how to do it.

None of this was real. Couldn't be. "The last time I trusted you, I ended up with a concussion." She still couldn't remember all the details of that night.

The price paid for deception. Aren't you curious, Bianca? Or are you resigned to being the ex-girlfriend, ex-employee, ex-daughter. Free me and know real power.

Only one word registered with her. "What kind of power?" She moved closer to the vault.

The kind which make you a god.

She ignored his melodramatic speech and focused on the possibility he could be telling the truth. "Why would you share with me?"

Because you and I have the same goals. Make Roman pay.

Jealousy wasn't only a female trait. She could use him. Repay Roman for his betrayal. Hurt him. A delicious shiver raced up her spine at all the possibilities.

No. The offer sounded too good. "I don't believe you."

But you're interested. I can hear it in your voice. Feel it in your body. You want to free me but you're afraid. I promise I won't hurt you.

He was right. She wanted to release him. The compulsion was almost too much to resist. Finally, she stepped back. She must have crossed a motion sensor because the spotlight went dark and the panel slid back into place. Once more, the vault was hidden behind the wine barrels. A pent-up breath rushed from her before she returned to the exit.

I can give you everything you want, Bianca.

There was a catch. Had to be. An opportunity this good never fell into your lap without one. Besides, if he wanted something inside the vault, he could steal it himself, instead of freaking her out. She marched up the stairs.

Revenge. Glory. Money. All of it yours.

But not Roman. The basement door creaked like a bullhorn, but she didn't hesitate. She opened it and stepped boldly out.

No one spared her a glance. Bianca fixed a smile on her face, rounded a corner, and smacked into her father. Anger replaced the brief flash of surprise on his face.

"Daddy," she said and immediately realized her mistake. The last time she called him Daddy she was eight years old. He grabbed her arm and pulled her into an alcove.

"What the hell are you doing here, Bianca?" Dressed to the nines in his formal livery he looked the part of head butler of an English estate.

He must not have seen her leave the cellar. "I went to the cottage to visit you and I heard the commotion."

"Please, Bianca!"

"I swear I didn't know the wedding was today." She crossed her heart.

His eyes narrowed and his gaze swept from her head to her feet. "You come to visit dressed in Chanel and Prada? When did I become so worthy?"

She glanced down at the charcoal and burgundy dress and smoothed the silk over her hips. "Well, I couldn't show up in jeans, Hector."

"You shouldn't have shown up at all. Leave." He looked around. "Before someone throws you out."

"Of course," she whispered and lowered her eyes. "I apologize, Father. I just had to see for myself. Before, the break-up wasn't real...now it is." Though crying was the last thing on her mind, somehow she managed to generate enough moisture for two tears to travel artfully down her cheeks.

"Bianca, dear, you should go to the cottage and rest, make yourself comfortable, and I'll check on you when I get a chance." Awkwardly, he patted her shoulder.

Perfect. "All right, Father," she sighed and brushed her tears away. "You're correct. I shouldn't be here." The cottage was exactly where she needed to be. For a multitude of reasons.

***

So much for a homecoming.

Reign threw himself into a chair. It creaked under his weight, but held. He let his head fall back and closed his eyes. Nephythys, his blue-haired nemesis, once more her lies trapped him. Surprised? Yes. She needed him as much as he needed her.

He loved her once. Bile rose in his throat and he swallow it back down. Better not to think of that. He had stopped trusting her centuries ago. But then she showed him Roman in the Scrying bowl with Anubis's beast chasing him. She called Roman weak, told him his brother had lost his skill and had become like the other men in this current century, compliant and fearful. Reign believed her.

What a fool. In two millennia he had learned nothing. He should have died with his Prophet. Unlike Nephythys, who only wanted body and blood, at least *he* promised redemption and salvation. All he asked in return was faith and abstinence.

Reign choked back a laugh. Most men would have run from the word. But his Prophet didn't want him to abstain from temptations of the flesh. He asked him to put down his sword and follow him.

Sometimes, memories weren't good for the soul. Better to leave them buried. He came to find his brother. Not only was Roman well, he was happily married with a ready-made family. His brother had moved on while he lingered. Reign stood. It was time to find Alexis and go. The door opened and Roman entered.

"Nice trick back there in the vault," Roman said dryly. "How'd you do that?"

"Blessings to you and your beautiful bride," Reign said staring at the bookcase opposite him.

"Thank you."

"Do you love her?"

"Yes." Roman answered without hesitation. "I asked you a question." He crossed the room and stood in front of him. "How did you become invisible?"

"I don't know," Reign lied.

"Where have you been?" Roman demanded.

Anger rumbled through him. How many times had Roman disappeared for days of pleasure and returned smelling of liquor and women, with no explanation. "Question your men, not me."

"I have a right to ask." Arrogant, spoken like the leader he now was.

"You seek to control. Control the rabble you have gathered."

"They're not rabble. They're my family."

He almost said, 'What am I?' but held his tongue at the last second. "I am not part of your *family*?" He snorted.

"You're my twin," Roman said.

Reign studied his brother's face and noted the uncertainty in his eyes.

"You and I are more than family, we are one." Roman moved to lean against his desk.

Reign heard the hesitation in his voice. "So much so that it took four men to replace me."

"Yes. And it took more than that."

"Who are these boys?"

"All of the men here are family, most through Oria."

Oria. Their sister. Reign hung his head. Centuries ago, when Nephythys falsely showed him Roman's death, he forced himself to forget their sibling. Thinking about her life, how she survived their disgrace and disappearance, weighed heavily on his conscience.

"She lived a hard life. Our shame left her with nothing, but her beauty." Roman confessed.

Reign's head shot up. He gazed hard at his brother while his hand gripped the arms of the chair. "Sh—she was not a—a—" He couldn't bring himself to say the words.

"No." Roman sharply shook his head. "She married a farmer and had five children. All except one of my men are her descendants."

Reign remembered the Nubian he encountered and how Roman's men rallied around him. He must be the addition who was not their descendent. Their line continued. Some of Reign's anger ebbed and his shoulders slumped. Then he thought of the rag-tag group of men Roman had amassed, a useless bunch with little skill and no backbone. If this was the state of their lineage, then the gods help them.

Roman's grim face made Reign believe his sincerity. He dropped his guard, opened his senses, and felt the confused anguish hemorrhaging from his brother.

Too much. He severed the link they'd formed in their mother's womb.

Roman's head snapped back as if slapped. He grabbed his temples and looked at Reign. "I didn't know you could do that."

"There are a lot of things you don't know about me," Reign murmured.

"Then tell me. I'm here."

Reign opened his mouth, but the voices of the Vanquished filled his head.

What to tell him? Tell him how I, the greatest warrior, cried for centuries for my brother. Tell him how I begged for light, sound, a friend. How the flesh was ripped from my body, regrown, and ripped again. Tell him of my torture and how I came to love my tormentor.

He shook his head.

Tell him what a coward I am.

"Never!" The word ripped from his throat. Reign lunged to his feet. Rage and guilt boiled his gut. Roman retreated, a wounded look in his eyes.

"Brother—"

A knock sounded on the door. Roman's gaze never wavered from Reign, waiting for him to continue. "I'll start again. Where have you been?"

"Enslaved." Reign cursed. He balled his fist to keep his hands from trembling.

"Because we failed?"

No, I failed. "You were cursed for your failure, and I for mine." The memories came fast, too fast to block them. They dragged him back to a time when he still believed his actions could change things for the better. He could play the '*if only*' game. If only I had turned right instead of left. If only I had done this instead of that. For millennia, he tortured himself, repeatedly listing his failings, until death became his only recourse. But Nephythys's betrayal ran deep enough to keep him alive, regardless of his desire.

"The prophet you failed to protect? I wondered if I caused your curse."

Which one? The Vanquished or the enslavement at the goddess's hands? He swore and dragged his hands through his hair. When he looked back over the course of their lives, he wondered if they weren't cursed from birth. Nephythys promised to free him of his demons, but the price was too steep.

"No, the fault lay with me." Reign met his brother's inquisitive stare. "My failure enabled the goddess Nephythys to imprison me on Chemmis, the isle of the Egyptian Gods." He paused, waiting for Roman to say something. Roman stood in the middle of the room staring at him. Hell, he'd just told the man he was enslaved and his brother showed no damn reaction. This stoic bastard wasn't the brother he remembered.

Reign paced to the other side of the room. Arms folded across his chest, he leaned against a bookcase. "I am her champion and she has charged me with destroying the man you have quartered in your cellar. You have done my job."

"Is that a thank you?"

"No. You will keep him confined—"

"—until I find a way to completely destroy him."

Destroy Alamut and I return to Nephythys. Reign was about to order Roman to do no such thing, when he paused. His brother would want to know why. He couldn't tell him all his enslavement entailed.

"You don't know how to finish him." Reign chose his words carefully.

"And you do?" Roman's raised eyebrow mocked him.

Without warning, the Vanquished screamed and Reign dropped to his knees. His insides shredded and his atoms flew apart.

And landed in the passenger seat of Alexis's conveyance. From her down turned lips and drawn brows he didn't need to guess her emotions.

"Sorry for yanking you out of there, but it was time to go," she snapped.

"What has happened to upset you?" He demanded and shifted in the cramped seat.

She gripped the wheel tighter before shrugging. "Nothing."

Reign doubted *nothing* had her white-knuckling the wheel. He wanted to shake her and command she tell him. As they flew down the road, windows open, her hair whipping behind her, he didn't think taking that action would be wise.

"Tell me," he growled.

"No." She glowered and quickly re-focused on the road.

Frustration ate at him. The women of his time were never so stubborn. If they weren't in the car, he would make her comply. Thoughts of how hardened him. Her gaze shifted to his. Those coppery eyes challenged him in more ways than she probably imagined. Then her gaze strolled down his body.

Maybe she did know.

"As you wish." He faded, though it felt more like a retreat when he glimpsed the smirk that curled one corner of her lips.

CHAPTER SEVENTEEN

Reign's cold aura surrounded Alexis. He might be gone from sight, but his presence lingered in the dark interior. The vacant seat beside her lied. Dear God, she wanted to run and put this nightmare behind her. She couldn't do that with her personal stalker mystically attached to her rear.

She'd thought she remembered all the events of the night at the club. The averted wreck on her bike. The beasts' attack and Reign's appearance, until Brayden, Avery, and EJ cornered her in the mansion when she stepped out of the solarium. Their words repeated in her mind.

"You and Reign make a cozy couple." Brayden walked up to her.

Couple? Being magically attached to someone didn't make you a couple. It made you a *Lifetime Movie.*

"We're not a couple." The wind kicked up, whipping her hair about her face.

"Seemed like it at the club." EJ said from the other side of her.

The club? Yes, they were there fighting on the periphery. Why didn't she remember that before? "What were you guys doing there?" She pulled a pair of shades from her breast pocket to shield her eyes from the afternoon sun.

"Women and liquor." Avery snapped, joining the conversation. "And you?"

"Men and liquor." She snapped back. "Did you guys stop me to inquire about my social life?"

"Reign is a dangerous man, Detective Lever," Brayden said.

"Really." She knew that the first time she saw him, touched him, felt his hard body on top of her. He was danger in font sixty. She pulled her thoughts away from Reign and studied the men surrounding her. All were well over six feet tall, muscular, and aggressive as hell. An aura of deadly efficiency oozed from their pores. Would a gun protect her? Maybe? An image of Reign in the club wielding a sword popped into her head. In a fight against all three, she'd bet money on Reign.

"Aren't you all dangerous?"

"Enough talking," Avery said. "Reign decimated those beasts with his shiny sword. No one helped him."

"He was brutal. He beat one to a pulp before incinerating it." EJ grunted.

"The other he cleaved in two," Avery added.

She was there, so why didn't she remember? No matter how hard she tried to recall it, the memory eluded her.

"Detective, are you okay?" Brayden asked.

No. Since meeting this family, *okay* had taken a long vacation. "Fine," she said through clenched her teeth.

"You're not fine. Whatever connection you two have, sever it." Brayden continued.

Damn it. Tell me something I don't already know. Her nails digging into her palms kept her from screaming. Lately, every man she met thought they could tell her what to do. "Look, I don't take advice from the three brothers I already have, so you three stooges don't have a sinner's chance in heaven." She pushed her way through the men and stormed out of the mansion. Only to end up in a speeding car with her invisible stalker.

Alexis parked in front of her grandmother's house and looked at it. The contractors Mrs. Kelly hired had done a beautiful job on the repairs, though Alexis couldn't appreciate their efforts. The day had stretched too long. She exited the car, slamming the door behind her. Her keys jangled in her hand as she jogged up three stairs and shoved the key in the lock. She entered the house and smacked into Reign's broad chest. His hands steadied her.

"You will tell me now what happened at my brother's home."

His dark presence loomed over her in the small foyer. Goosebumps spread across her skin. Alexis yanked away and stumbled back. She flipped on the domed overhead light. His granite face and simmering gaze hadn't improved with illumination.

"What happened at the club?" she blurted. His eyes narrowed. She expected him to look away, the telltale sign of a person about to lie.

"I killed the beasts." His gaze never left hers.

"How?"

He grimaced. Then looked down. His open palm faced her. "With my sword."

A black blade appeared clasped in his hand. She blinked.

"How did you do that?" Rattled, she backed away.

His powerful shoulders lifted, then fell. "I don't know. I wanted it, so it appeared. When I no longer want it…" It vanished from his hand.

"Bring it back," she whispered. In a blink, the blade was back. She approached him cautiously. "Will it vanish if I hold it?"

"I don't know."

"May I?" She held out her hand expectantly.

He shook his head. "It is very heavy, Alexis. You will not be strong enough."

Her lips pursed in anger. "I'm stronger than I look. I don't plan to swing it around my head. I just want to hold it."

He turned the handle to her, then pulled back. "Only if you let me hold your weapon."

She leaped back and her hand went to her gun. He sighed in annoyance. "Woman, I have made no move to harm you."

"A police officer never gives up their gun. Never."

"A warrior's motto." He nodded and hair fell around his face. Reign approached. A frisson of fear shafted through her, sending her heart thumping. Alexis drew her gun.

"Still you point that at me?" he said.

Not once did his steps falter as she backed up, stumbling to keep an equal distance between them.

"I have been with you for many days and could have killed you a dozen times, but I did not." He crowded her until her back was against a wall and her gun was pressed into the center of his chest. His face was the only thing she saw. Her breath caught. Her insides fluttered.

"Do you wish me harm, Alexis? If you do, your weapon will achieve nothing. I do not know if my sword will achieve anything, but I dare say you would have better luck with my blade than with your gun." The word rolled off his tongue like a sensual sigh. She lowered her weapon and shoved it back into the holster.

Hilt first, he handed the sword to her and waited until she had a strong grip before releasing his hold. It pulled her down and thunked into the carpet. She tried to lift it, but couldn't. Reign smirked and sat on the sofa while she dragged the blade—cutting a slice in the faded carpet—to the chair. Well-polished and honed to a sharp edge, the sword glinted as she traced a finger over the intricate design. The cold metal tantalized as she imagined him wielding above his head while he charged onto a battlefield. The image was terrifying...and erotic.

Braided leather wrapped around the handle and scroll characters traveled down the blade. No, not characters, hieroglyphics. "Do you know what this says?" She stroked the metal. Puzzlement crossed his features, then a dawning awareness. She thought he was about to lie and say no. Instead, he nodded.

He stumbled over the pronunciations a few times before speaking. "'*I am the bringer. Face me and be judged*'. I have never read Egyptian before."

"How'd you end up cursed in Egypt?" Instead of answering, he looked away. *Okay. Next question.* "Why does the tether hold you here?"

His gaze swung back to her. "The Vanquished. When they come and I can no longer function."

"Who's the Vanquished?"

"Conquered warriors haunting my soul. They are my penance, my tormentors. The only peace I find is when I'm within one hundred feet of the one who balances my soul. You are that person."

She was about to say she didn't want to be *that person* when his gaze turned sultry, swept across her face, down the column of her throat and rested on her breasts. An internal switch flipped and she flushed. Her fingers stroked down the blade as images of him—of them—entwined and doing things she dreamed about flickered in her head. The positions, the thrusts, the licks, and touches. Orgasms after orgasms. She, crying out his name.

His gaze roasted her. Those oceany eyes kissed her lips, caressed her breasts, slid down her body and settled between her thighs where she ached. Her finger slipped on the metal and blood ran freely. The sharp sting seared all lustful thoughts away. Instantly, he kneeled in front of her and grabbed her wrist. She tried to jerk away, but he held her firmly, his thumb pressed hard on the wound.

"Apologies, your injury is my responsibility. I never should have let you—"

"It's okay. It's not that bad."

"It is. My nearness keeps causing you injury. That, I cannot allow." His eyes blazed full of anguish.

Strands of his long hair swept across his face, partially hiding his expression. Alexis brushed the wayward locks away. She skimmed her palm down his sculpted cheek and through his short beard. His eyes widened and...he stopped breathing. Amazed that she had actually caused a man to stop breathing at her mere touch, Alexis leaned in for a taste, that's all she promised. One kiss to settle the heat stirring in her blood.

Centimeters away from his lips, she paused, then drew away.

There's a reason you're celibate, Alexis. Too many relationships had soured quick and left her swearing off men for the past year. But if there was ever a reason to end her diet, Reign was it.

He waited. Not a muscle betrayed his emotions, yet a vein pulsed wildly at the base of his neck.

But he lied.

What if you approach this logically? You want him. Your panties are sticking to you, you want him so bad. So have him. Leave your heart out of it. Hell, men do it. You can do it too.

Screw him, let him work all your kinks out. Just don't fall in love with him so when the shit hits the fan—

I won't be the one cut by the blades.

She pressed her lips to his.

Holy hell! Nothing had ever tasted so delicious, felt as delightful as his firm lips slanted across her mouth. His whiskers gently brushed her skin, heightening her senses. His scent, woodsy with a hint of musk, filled her lungs. She leaned into him, parted her lips, and licked the seam of his closed mouth. He shuddered and his lips parted. His tongue darted inside her mouth and ignited her blood.

He wanted her. She didn't just feel it in his touch, but knew it as if she were peeking into his soul.

They yanked apart, she panting while Reign inhaled sharply and exhaled deliberately. His pecs heaved as his gaze devoured her. Nothing made sense, not the heat surfing through her body or the hunger gnawing at her soul. Kissing Reign erased the presence of every man who had ever touched her. Flustered, she glanced down and saw her finger still pressed between his.

He released her. She wiped away the smear of blood and found perfect new skin. "Okay, so how did you do that?" She held up the healed digit to his puzzled stare.

"I do not know." His gaze shifted away.

He's lying. Disappointment dissolved the lingering taste of him. *Wow, that didn't take long.* Alexis rose and strode to the bookcase to study her grandmother's ancient collection. "So, we have to find out where the animals came from and if there are more."

"I know where they are and yes, there are more."

Alexis pivoted. "There are more? How many more."

"Enough to be a problem."

"You knew where they were and didn't tell me?" She demanded, storming back to him. He rose to his feet, forcing her to step back to maintain eye contact.

"It is not a secret, at least not to me. And you have been there. You did not see."

"What didn't I see? Where've I been?" Her forehead dipped, drawing her eyebrows together in a scowl.

He held out his hand. "Come. I will show you."

Could she trust him? Did she have a choice? Everything the Nicolis men said about him circled her brain. They warned her to stay away. *As if that was so easy.* Reign claimed he was a warrior. Looking at him, she didn't dispute it. Bossy, arrogant, yet gentle with her.

She placed her hand in his and didn't resist when he pulled her closer. One moment they were in the living room. Then her atoms scattered. Next, she was back in the factory.

Alexis slumped against Reign. Parts of her still flew about. His arms banded around her and kept her from crumpling. Good, because she was about to shake apart. Her teeth chattered. Icy sweat covered her skin. She was freezing, inside and out.

"I have you," he whispered and pulled her flush against him. His steady heartbeat calmed her even while his breath teased her temple. Heat pooled low in her groin. Awareness of him— every sinful inch—flooded her. Her breasts pillowed against his chest. He shifted and lifted her. Abdomen to abdomen, pelvis to pelvis, all of him touched her. Warmed her. Placed her thoughts on a dangerous path.

She pulled away. "I'm okay. But don't ever do that again." His hands lingered on her waist.

"Then how will we return home?"

Home. He said the word like he belonged there. She'd opened her mouth to answer when *That Smell* slapped her. She buried her face in her sleeve and whipped around. Oh my god, she mouthed and threw herself back into Reign's arms. All around her were pits filled with the animals.

"Shhh." He hushed her. "They are dormant."

"How do you know?"

"They are not attacking."

She cut her eyes from him and peered around him at the pit. "They weren't here before."

"Yes, they were. You did not see them." He dropped to his haunches next to the pit.

Alexis crouched next to him. The oppressive odor made her stomach flop and threaten to hurl. She leaned over to get a head count and slipped. Reign's quick reflexes saved her from tumbling in.

"Have you seen enough?" He pulled her along with him.

"We can't leave them here," she protested.

"We cannot take them with us."

Now he wants to be a smart aleck! "I'm calling the authorities." Her explanation would come after the police saw this.

He snatched the phone from her. "Calling the authorities will ensure their deaths. Unless your men are trained in swordsmanship, their weapons will not work."

"How do you know?"

"Roman and I spoke of this."

"Still, we can't just walk away. A kid could wander in here and get hurt."

"Is there a record of anyone being hurt here?" Reign questioned.

They were in New City, not New York. She didn't know anything about this building. "Not that I know of. Is this why you came here? To this...world? To kill these things?"

"Uhm...yes."

Another lie. Her disappointment mounted.

"Then *you* go down there and kill them." She ordered. He had a sword, use it. She couldn't understand when he refused. He killed those animals, their remains vanishing in a wink. Brayden said as much to her before she escaped RockGate. "Or do I have to pay for your services? What is the going rate for a two thousand year old mercenary?"

His nostrils flared and a muscle flexed in his jaw, curling a corner of his lip. "You could not afford the price. Killing one may wake the others. I am skilled, but even I cannot battle all of these creatures at the same time."

Fine. Alexis scrubbed a hand across her forehead and dragged her fingers through her hair. She walked around and decided to do a head count. Twenty. She moved on to the next pit. Twenty. And the next. Fifteen pits with twenty animals nesting in each equals...wait. Her heart lodged in her throat, she returned to Reign and stooped over the first pit again. Three times, she counted and came up short each. Ten. Ten. Ten. There were ten animals in this pit while twenty slept in the others.

Three were killed at the club. Where were the rest? "We have a problem."

With Reign trailing her, she counted each pit again.

"I agree. We do have a problem."

The hard edge to his voice halted her. Fist clenched, muscles straining, he stared into the pit.

"Hey." She touched him. "Are you okay?"

Reign's head jerked to her. Alexis almost stepped back. His blue eyes glowed.

But then she blinked and the glow was gone. She shook her head. *I must be tired.*

"I am well."

At least one of them was. "How do we find the rest of them?"

"I do not know."

And neither do I. When did all this strangeness begin? She thought back to the fight at the club, but ditched that path. All of this happened way before that incident. Methodically, she retraced the last few weeks, examining each major event for any paranormal elements until she remembered the video tape at the morgue.

Daniel Nicolis's swan dive and resurrection, then the image of the Egyptian dude on the surveillance tape that only she saw. All of this weirdness started with him. Could the factory and the morgue be linked?

Only one way to find out. She glanced at Reign. He studied her with an intensity that left parts of her simmering.

Not now! She told her libido. *Correction. Not ever!*

Alexis cleared her throat. "I have an idea where to start."

One thick eyebrow stretched into his hairline. Though she hated riding the Reign express transit line, there were worse places to be than wrapped in the arms of a gorgeous man. "Can you take me to the morgue?"

His brows drew together. Of course, he didn't know what a morgue was. "Is there a way I can direct you?"

He nodded. "Possibly. If you open your mind when we flash instead of fighting the process. Perhaps you may enjoy it."

Not likely, but she didn't have a choice. He'd transported them to the factory and she wasn't about to walk miles home.

However, opening her mind to him? Bad enough he'd invaded her home. She wasn't about to let him roam her thoughts, learning every intimate detail about her.

"You keep your grubby mind to yourself and I'll do the same. Take me to my precinct. I have to pick up my bike. I'll ride to the morgue and you can tag along."

"As you wish." He sighed, but she didn't believe he was happy about it.

His arm circled her waist and pulled her against his body. Though she should be indignant of his manhandling, she didn't mind. She really should shove him away and make him regret his arrogance. Do something other than slide her arms around his neck and lay her head on his pec.

His chest expanded on a deep breath and his heart kicked into a gallop. "You are a stubborn woman."

Took him long enough to figure that out. "Yes I am. I'm ready to leave now."

Laughter rumbled through him. "As, you, wish."

CHAPTER EIGHTEEN

Daniel waited. Not that he had another choice. Confined in several different containers, the powers Anubis had gifted him were limited. Maybe the metal cylinders housing his parts kept him from fusing his body and destroying the two people who brought him so low. Reign freeing his head was the closest he'd come to freedom since Roman stuck him in the vault.

He should've obeyed Anubis and fulfilled his mission. If he'd killed Reign, as ordered, he'd be enjoying sunlight and leading the army of quimaera. Now, his fate rested on Bianca's vanity.

Though weak, Daniel was still connected to Bianca's mind. He followed her movements to her father's cottage. She thought of his proposal, weighed the pros and cons, sought an advantage. He knew her well enough to know what her answer would be.

And it only took twenty-four hours.

Through her eyes, he watched Bianca jog through the dark woods. She deactivated the security alarm at the kitchen entrance and slipped inside. She'd picked the best time, three a.m. The men were either asleep or out and the staff had yet to rise. A pen light illuminated her walk down the center aisle of the cellar to the third barrel on the right. With a click and a hiss, the panel slid back and moved right. Recessed lighting hit the metal door. One finger stretched out to punch in the numbers. Waiting.

07221970. He whispered into her brain.

The pneumatic motor hummed and the door opened. Without the huge slab of metal blocking him, Daniel pushed passed her mental defensives and took complete control of her body.

Bianca ignored the rolled documents, stacks of cash, paintings in pressurized frames, and weapons of all sorts and sizes. She headed straight to six metal containers.

She unlocked the first container. Air rushed in and though he didn't need to breathe, Daniel went through the motions of opening his mouth and inhaling. Bianca grabbed a fistful of his hair and yanked. Darkness gave way to fluorescent light. He squinted beneath the glare, blinking up at her.

Daniel used his power to calm her horror, and focus her on reassembling his body. She emptied each container and slumped against a nearby shelf. Daniel Nicolis, the human jigsaw puzzle. Humpty Dumpty had nothing on him.

Her glazed, unfocused eyes, roamed over his parts, but didn't seem to see him.

"Bianca! Snap out of it and get to work."

Her gaze shifted to his face. For a second, she broke his control. She gasped and sucked in a breath.

"Scream and I will kill you," he lied. He couldn't kill anything in this condition.

Her mouth clicked closed. She nodded a few times, dragged a trembling hand across her sweaty forehead, and then gingerly took hold of his right leg. She lined up his torso and played doctor with his body parts. Not quite the way he once wanted her to play with him. The longing he had for Bianca didn't last. It couldn't survive under her unwavering lust for power and for Roman.

He grunted through the torture of ligaments, tendons, and muscles re-growing, and reattaching. His power levels surged with each attachment. Daniel slowly climbed to his feet. He reached for Bianca who was still seated on the floor.

He stroked her silver blond hair away from her face. "Obey me and you will have nothing to fear." He cupped her chin. "Defy me, betray me, and I will set your head in the dusty remains of your body." His fingers dug into her tender flesh. Pain made her eyes pool and his reflection swim.

Energy hummed through him, setting off tingles throughout his body. Anubis's gift, the god's *vis'*Ra, coursed through his blood. Never did he want this to stop. He pulled her to her feet and kissed her perfect red lips. The best way to ensure loyalty was to make her an addict. Power, like cocaine, meth, and oxy had the same effect. But, only a taste.

She drank in the thimble of power and panted for more.

"Later, if I'm pleased, I will show you what true power is." He ushered her out of the vault. When it closed behind them, he pulled her close and flashed to the cottage, the home that Hector rarely used.

The perfect hiding place and only a few hundred yards from achieving his revenge.

***

Alexis parked her motorcycle a few blocks away from the Medical Examiner's office and prayed she didn't run into anyone. She cut the engine and dismounted. Quickly, she pinned her wild hair back into her professional bun. A few steps down the block and she wasn't alone. A part of her warned not to take comfort in Reign's presence by her side. A bigger part ignored the advice as she marched on.

She went around back to the ambulance bay entrance and saw an employee leaving. She glanced at Reign to tell him to vanish, but he was already gone.

"Hey, there. I'm Detective Lever," she called out before the door closed and locked behind the man. She jogged up to him with her shield displayed. A quick peek at her badge had him paying full attention. "I need some information about the night Daniel Nicolis's body disappeared."

Since no one except the department and the examiner's office knew the truth, she'd keep quiet about Daniel getting up and walking away.

"I wasn't here that night. Mario was. He's inside." He nodded his head toward the building. "But they just dropped off three bodies so he's gonna be busy for a while."

Perfect. "Well, I'll go inside and wait for him. Thanks." She scooted around the man and entered the building. The refrigerator room wasn't far. Though she knew the chances of finding anything in there was next to nil, still, she needed to see the room. Voices echoed nearby. Most likely from the examiner and Mario. She had to hurry.

Staring at the bank of metal refrigerated drawers, a sliver of fear stabbed her. It's the unknown laying on the other side. She could only imagine the anguish a loved one experienced waiting for the door to open and the drawer to slide out.

"What is this room?"

Alexis jumped. Reign stood next to her. Heart lodged in her throat, it took a second for her to muster an answer. "They keep the corpses in here."

"You do not bury your dead?"

She nearly laughed at his horrified expression. "Yeah, we do, but sometimes not right away. Not when they've died unnaturally or suspiciously." She walked over to the drawer Daniel had rented for a night and ran her fingers over the handle. She wondered if it was vacant, but she was too chicken to yank the handle and see.

"Why are we here?"

"I'm retracing Daniel's steps."

"Daniel?"

The interest in his voice turned her head toward him. "Yeah, weren't you listening when I spoke to the employee?"

Reign hesitated.

"Guess not."

"Why are we here for Daniel?"

"I think he may be the catalyst for all of this; the quimaera, possibly the factory. I need to…"

He stared at her as if waiting for her to continue.

"Daniel Nicolis was your brother Roman's adopted son. I really don't understand how a grown, single man adopted a bunch of boys and no red flags were raised, but hey, lifestyles of the rich and richer." She chuckled.

He didn't.

Should she tell him what she saw on the video? Maybe that would get a rise out of him.

A voice came from the hall. "Yeah, okay, I'll bring the next one in." The door swung open.

Reign vanished and a man entered the room.

"What the—" He skidded to a halt. "What are you doing in here?"

Alexis pulled out her badge. "Detective Alexis Lever, I was here the day after Daniel Nicolis's body went missing."

The twenty-something year old squinted at the gold shield. "I remember you." He gave her the once over and smoothed a hand over his green hospital scrub top.

A cold breeze circulated the room. Mario shivered. Alexis shot an annoyed glanced at the last spot Reign had occupied.

"I answered a bunch of questions already."

"I have a few more. You were here when the Nicolis body was brought in?"

Mario nodded.

"Anything unusual or strange?"

He shook his head. "Nope."

But he wouldn't make eye contact. She'd bet her paycheck he got away with answering only a few questions because of the VHS footage of Daniel rising from the dead. Why question a person when the police had video evidence, even if the tape lacked quality. Even with budget cuts, she still couldn't believe they hadn't upgraded to digital and stepped into the twenty-first century.

"Where were you when the body went missing, Mr. Gonzalez?"

"That body didn't go missing, no matter what you told the public." He sneered.

Hmm? "Mr. Gonzalez, did you see something?"

He shook his head hard, but looked away. Alexis moved closer to the man.

"I think you did."

"I didn't see nothing." His gazed shifted around the room as he chewed his inner cheek.

She leaned close and whispered. "I'm not trying to jeopardize your job. I just need to know what you saw, please."

A growl rumbled around the room.

Alexis coughed to mask the sound. "Are you sure you didn't see anything? This is really important, Mario."

"Well—" He pointed to the drawer where Daniel had resided. "I saw that door open and a man climb out, like something out of a bad horror movie."

Her heart raced. "Did you see one man? Or two?"

"Two of them?" he whispered. He pulled a rosary from his scrub pocket and began to pray in Spanish.

It was the last thing she expected from the young man.

"I only saw one zombie. Now you say there are more?" Eyes wide, he raked his hands through his lank hair. His jaw dropped open and his legs wobbled.

Alexis caught him before he dropped to his knees. "Sir, hey—" She shook him to get his attention. "This is not the apocalypse and zombies are not walking the earth." The last thing she needed was him fainting. She had to speed this up and get out of here.

"When did you see the tape? 'Cause I saw it that morning with the other detectives and we all thought no one else had seen it but us, so did you see it before we did, or after?" Alexis asked.

The man wasn't slow on the uptake. By his firm lips and narrowed eyes, Alexis figured he was weighing his options. Lie or tell the truth. She'd wait him out.

It didn't take long for him to whisper, "After."

"You made a copy?" She stifled a gasp when he nodded. "Still have it?"

He nodded again.

"Where is it?"

Mr. Gonzalez slipped his hand into his pocket and withdrew his phone.

She couldn't quell her excitement. "You made a digital copy?"

A smile stretched his lips. He pulled up the video and angled the screen toward her.

Once again, she watched Daniel's resurrection by a man dressed like an Egyptian prince. He entered the room, opened the drawer, did some mumbo jumbo, and Daniel Nicolis's eyes snapped open like he just woke from a good nap. Then the man vanished in the same swirly down-the-drain way she remembered.

She took the phone from him and sent a copy to her cell. "Why did you make a copy, Mr. Gonzalez?"

"I wanted proof I wasn't to blame for a body disappearing."

"Good call."

Someone yelled his name followed by a string of curses.

"I gotta get a body and get back. It was a bad night," he said.

"Yeah, I heard. Three dead."

Mario shook his head. "It's a lot more than three, detective."

Alexis glanced up from his phone. "What do you mean?"

"Three homeless were found dead in the Bronx. Two businessmen were found in Tarrytown. And four college kids were killed in Riverdale."

Mario grabbed a stretcher from the opposite side of the room and wedged it below a drawer. He yanked the handle. Metal grated before the door swung wide. Cold air curled and dissipated. Mario adjusted the stretcher, bringing it to the exact height of the lip of the refrigerator. He locked the wheels, reached inside and pulled. A black body bag slid onto the stretcher.

The bag was small. Too small. A chill swept through her. Alexis moved closer. "Is that a child?"

"No, this is what's left."

Alexis touched the bag. Random parts, moved beneath the surface. *Not a body.* Her empty stomach heaved. She swallowed a dry gulp and fought the nausea. "Were they all killed the same way?"

"The papers say they were. But these bums got the worst of it."

"The worse of what?" *What the hell had done this?*

"The papers say they were eaten."

All she could do was blink as her mind returned to the factory and the half-filled pit. But that made no sense. All those areas were not only separated by distance, but also demographics and affluence. The beasts couldn't be the link.

"Hey, you okay?" Mario touched her shoulder.

She handed him back his phone. "I would appreciate if you didn't tell anyone about our meeting and I won't tell anyone you made a copy."

Back on the street, Reign appeared. "Do you think the beasts were the cause of the killings?" he asked.

Yes. Maybe. "I don't know. Once the autopsies are filed, I have a friend that can get me the information." All of this felt wrong.

"What did that man show you?"

"Shush. I'm thinking." She had to get her thoughts in order. Something wasn't adding up. First, Daniel. Second, Reign, her stalker. Third, the quimaera. The three names circled her brain. Daniel and Reign had an Egyptian connection linking them together.

Alexis glanced at Reign and watched him subtly scan the area. The immortal warrior stranded in the wrong century. Men cleared out of the way as they walked down the street while woman ogled, drool almost leaking from their slack jaws as they stared.

She wished he'd stayed invisible.

When they reached her bike, she opened her phone and brought up the video. "Tell me what you see?" She placed her cell in his calloused palm. She didn't need to view it again. So she studied him.

The man would never be a poker player. Though not obvious to most, he had a Tell. A throbbing vein snaked from his neck and disappeared under his tense jaw.

"I see a man climbing out of the metal drawer."

Alexis waited for him to say more, but he didn't. Her heart drummed in her chest. "Really. That's all you see?" His gaze rose from the screen and met hers. She swallowed hard, trying to bury the denial surging up her throat. It didn't work. "You're lying." She snatched the phone from his hand and got on her bike.

It shouldn't cause her this much pain that he continued to lie. But it hurt.

"Alexis—"

"There are two men on that video. Daniel Nicolis and some Egyptian dude. Two!" She held up two fingers in front of his face. "Not one. And you damn well know it." She hissed because a crowd had gathered.

"Alexis, I am—"

She revved the engine, drowning out his voice. Reign grabbed the handlebars. Though she tried, the bike wouldn't move. Her gaze shot to his. She didn't say a word. Not a single thing. She bared her teeth and stared hard into his blue eyes. A sigh lifted his chest and his hands slide from the handlebars.

Alexis backed out of the space and raced down the street. No helmet, her hair escaped the pins holding it in place. For a brief moment, she was free and alone. The wind caught a tear before it rolled down her cheek and dashed it away.

One hundred feet and the wind no longer buffeted her. A presence brushed her mind, seeking a way in. She blocked it and concentrated on riding home and getting Reign Nicolis out of her life.

CHAPTER NINETEEN

Through the fog of sleep, Stella snuggled closer to the warm body of her husband. A smile tugged at her mouth. Husband, a foreign word, yet it repeated happily in her head. His warm lips caressed her neck and the curve of her shoulder. A calloused palm cupped her breast and brushed across her nipple. Her back arched, seeking more of the erotic torture.

"Good morning, wife." His thick voice promised sensual delights and stirred her sluggish body to life. He pulled her closer and she felt his rigid flesh against her bottom. Too tired yesterday to enjoy the pleasures of their first night of matrimony, they'd collapsed into bed and slept. But now, let the honeymoon begin.

The staccato knock at their bedroom door seemed to echo and amplify, impossible to ignore. Roman swore and threw back the comforter. Propped up, Stella stifled a giggle and watched his splendid naked ass stalk across the room.

He yanked open the door. "What?"

"Pardon the intrusion. I wouldn't have disturbed you if it wasn't absolutely necessary." Hector whispered from the half-opened door.

"Who needs me now?"

"You're not needed. Mrs. Breemer from social services is waiting in the great room to speak with your wife."

Stella clutched the sheet to her bosom and sat up. "For me? Are you sure, Hector?"

"Yes, she was quite specific," Hector replied.

"I will be down shortly to deal with her." Roman closed the bedroom door.

Stella was tempted to allow him to take care of whatever this woman wanted. As she watched him dress, she admitted this wasn't the way she wanted to start her marriage. She hadn't survived three attacks on her life less than two weeks ago to hide from her past.

She snapped the covers off and slide from the bed. "I'm going with you." She braced herself for an argument.

Instead, Roman smiled and waited for her to get dressed.

What could Social Services want? she wondered slipping into a pair of jeans and a sweater. The time she spent as a ward of the court ended six years ago when she ran away from her last foster home. The memory of her final night in the system replayed in her mind as she dragged a brush through her hair, until Roman took her in his arms and held her. His immense strength fortified her trembling body.

"You are not your past," he murmured. He repeated the words until she nodded and tilted her head up for a loving kiss. He held her hand as they walked through the mansion to meet their guest.

Seated by the fireplace, an older, slightly rounded matron sipped tea and munched on petit fours served on Waterford china.

"Hello, Mrs. Breemer. It's a pleasure to meet you." Roman gave a short bow. "This is my wife, Stella."

The china clanked painfully against the saucer as she returned it and jumped up to greet them. "Mr. and Mrs. Nicolis, the pleasure is mine. Let me apologize for interrupting your honeymoon. I wasn't sure if you were leaving on an extended vacation and this couldn't wait." Her pale cheeks flushed a bright red and her double chin wobbled.

"We understand." Stella shook the woman's hand, hoping to put her guest at ease. She sat next to Roman on the brocade settee. The woman's plain gray suit and sensible black shoes reminded her of the social worker who'd handled her case years ago. "How can I—we—help you?" She swallowed the lump in her throat.

Mrs. Breemer seemed to gather her strength. Her back straightened and her shoulders squared before she reached into her briefcase and removed a portfolio. She opened it and, from her angle, Stella could see a 5x10 glossy photo of a child. Mrs. Breemer stroked the picture with her thumb before she removed it from the paperclip and passed it to Stella.

"This little girl is your sister, Ember Walker. She's twelve years old." The woman cleared her throat. "Mrs. Nicolis, your sister's in a coma, and needs your help."

***

The last time Stella was in a hospital, she had pushed Daniel to his death. She shook her head and chased the memories away. Today would be hard enough to handle without dragging the man who tried to kill her into the mix.

Holding Roman's hand for strength, Stella walked onto the children's ward at Mercy Hospital. Cartoon characters decorated the colorful walls, giving the place a whimsical appeal.

A horn beeped. "Excuse me," a small voice shouted. Roman pulled her out of the way and a little boy on a black tricycle streaked with orange flames, swept passed. With each rotation of the pedals, engine noises rumbled.

"Slow down, Eric," a nurse called, but Eric kept pedaling. Mrs. Breemer waited at the end of the next hall. Smiling like a used car salesman, she pumped their hands and ushered them into the room.

The social worker had showed them Ember's chart earlier to prepare them for her medical condition, but still Stella's knees weakened to see the infant sister she'd lost contact with years ago. She was now a sick, comatose child. Ember's medical file was as thick as an encyclopedia, yet it held no answer. A foster child for five years, the state hadn't skimped on her care, yet still a diagnosis remained elusive.

She studied her sister's straight black hair, thick eyebrows, sooty eyelashes and pale, almost translucent skin. What color were her eyes? Gray like their father's or brown like Ember's mother's? Small framed and delicate, she looked like a porcelain doll about to shatter.

"She looks like you." Roman took her hand and squeezed gently.

"Is there anything she needs?" Stella struggled to keep her voice steady, but it cracked at the end.

"Code blue in room 1208. Code blue room 1208." Intoned from a hidden speaker in the ceiling. The nurses burst into a flurry of action outside Ember's room and a red and white crash cart whizzed by. Stella's heart kicked into overdrive. Was some poor family about lose what they held most dear?

"She needs a family. Since her hospitalizations have grown longer in duration, we've had to move her to a new foster home each time she recovers. It's as hard being with a new family as it is being comatose. She needs stability." Mrs. Breemer stroked Ember's hand.

"Have you had any success locating her mother?" Roman slipped an arm around Stella's waist and gave a reassuring squeeze of comfort and support.

"Last year her parental rights were terminated. Ember has no parents."

"How long has she been comatose?" Roman leaned closer to the monitors and studied the steady patterns.

"Two weeks. Odd. Until a month ago, these *spells* usually lasted less than a week. She's usually a normal, average fifth grader. Then, at any given moment, she slips into a coma lasting as short as thirty minutes to her current two weeks." Mrs. Breemer frowned and shrugged. "Her tests show she's stable and should be awake. All we're doing is waiting until she wakes up."

Stella sat next to her sister. "Hello, Ember." God, she couldn't say more, but she had to. "I'm your big sister, Stella. I knew you when you were a baby. The last time I saw you, you were six months old and cranky. I used to feed you at night when Dad was too tired and your Mom was…sleeping. I'd hold you until you fell back to sleep." The beeping machines filled the heavy silence.

Tears rolled down Stella's cheeks. Roman gathered her into his arms. Pressed close to his side, she looked at Mrs. Breemer through blurry eyes. "What do I have to do to make this happen?"

"What do *we* have to do to make it happen?" Roman corrected.

She gave him her hundred-watt smile and brought his head down for a kiss.

"Are you sure?" The social worker's voice held some hope, but her eyes were wary. "It's a lot of responsibility being a foster parent to any child, especially a sick one. There are a lot of rules and regulations."

"Are you trying to discourage us, Mrs. Breemer?" Stella's sharp tone seemed to startle everyone.

"It doesn't matter," Roman said. "We won't be fostering the child. We're adopting her."

Stella flung her arms around his neck. "I love you," she whispered in his ear. His phone made a muted ring between their pressed bodies. He kissed her and fished the cell from his pocket. He frowned at the screen.

"It's okay, I'll be fine." Stella turned back to Mrs. Breemer.
***

Roman stepped into the hallway and closed the door firmly behind him. He answered the phone. "Now is not a good time."

"Excuse me, Roman," Brayden said. "Sorry, but this couldn't wait any longer. We're waiting for you downstairs."

Roman tapped *End* and returned to his wife. "Stay here. I'll be right back."

Her brows furrowed, but she nodded. Her trust bathed his soul in warmth. They had been through too much for any doubt between them. He pulled her close for a chaste kiss.

Five minutes later, he exited the hospital and found the trio, Brayden, Avery, and EJ Their grim, urgent expressions set him on edge. Things were about to get worse, how much was the only factor.

"What's this about?" He studied their rigid features and waited for an answer.

"It's about what happened two nights ago," Avery said.

"And Tyrone," Brayden added.

"Two nights ago? And you tell me now?" he barked. A slow deep breath expanded his lungs and steadied the urge to strangle the three standing in front of him.

"You were getting married. We all agreed to wait." Brayden pushed off the car and stepped forward.

"Tell me." Roman ordered. His gut clenched, prepared for the worst.

CHAPTER TWENTY

Alexis parked in her grandmother's driveway. The protective shield around her vanished. Her shoulders slumped. Keeping Reign out of her mind exhausted her more than running around New York City all night.

Stiff and sore, she climbed off her bike and stretched the kinks from her protesting muscles. A shower, food, and sleep were what she needed. Her chances of getting all three were slim.

Mrs. Kelly waved from her porch. She'd read that the elderly didn't need much sleep, but why was the woman up so early when she didn't have to be?

Alexis returned the wave and climbed the porch stairs. The door opened as she reached for her keys. Reign's big frame blocked the entrance.

God, I'm too tired for this. If only she could shove him out of her way. She had about as much chance of doing that as she did moving a mountain. He stepped to the side, clearing a path into the dim recesses of the house. Sunlight filtered through the sheer ivory curtains hanging in the living room, beating the gloom back and lifting her spirits.

"Anubis." The word hung in the air.

Alexis turned. Reign stood in the middle of the room. Hands at his sides, his body, an immense unyielding wall.

"The god in the moving images you showed me, his name is Anubis. He is a lesser god, son of SET and Nephythys."

She noticed he snarled the last name.

"There is no love between mother and son or son and father. Daniel Nicolis is his pawn. I was sent here to stop him." He stepped closer to her. "I apologize for my deceit. It was meant to protect."

She studied the drawn brows above his deep blue eyes and the tight lines of his face. He seemed earnest. But then the best liars were. And if he lied about one thing, what else could he be lying about? "I'm not going to let you kill Daniel."

"I have no intention of killing him."

At least they got that settled. "I don't need your protection, Reign."

"Yes, you do. I am all that stands between you and those animals."

There was no arrogance in his statement. Just truth. She did need him. She also needed him to be honest. "And that's the only reason you're here? To stop the beasts?"

"I came to save my brother. But he does not need me."

"And afterward? When we find a way to stop those things, what then?"

"…I find a way to leave you." Tight voice, his rigid face held no emotion.

"Good. The sooner, the better," she mumbled through the lump in her throat.

His eyes darkened, but he said nothing.

"When you leave, do you go back to Chemmis?"

A cold wave hit her. His lips thinned into an angry line and his hands fisted. He nodded once. *Hmm? He held no love for the place.*

"I need to sleep." She walked around him and his fingers brushed the back of her hand. A jolt of sorrow caused her entire body to seize.

Then his fingers slipped into her palm. A dull ache welled in her center and spread to every cell, leaving a void in its wake.

The pain wasn't hers.

Alexis canted her head at Reign. To the world, he was a six foot eight inch warrior. Deadly to his enemies and her sense of self-preservation. Still, watching his bowed head, feeling the desolation seeping from his palm into her, she saw the truth.

Their gazes locked. Longing lay naked in the depths of his eyes.

"Reign—"

He claimed her lips with a scorching kiss. Raw and hungry, her head reeled. A hand cupped her head. Another gripped her hip and gave a gentle tug. She didn't fight him guiding her closer or the desire he ignited in her blood. His knee slipped between her thighs and he lifted her until she hooked a leg around his waist. Chest to breast, abs to abs, groin pressed against groin, she felt him lengthen. Her core blossomed. Alexis moaned and his tongue slid into her mouth. He tasted like Sunday dinner at grandma's, Christmas morning, and Midnight on New Year's Eve, while his body promised Disney World. His biceps flexed as his hand slid under her shirt and stroked up her back.

She moved her hand up his chest, feeling the cotton fabric, the tense muscles beneath, and the thud of his racing heartbeat. Then her fingertips brushed the bare skin of his neck.

A bundle of conflicting emotions slammed into her. Passion warred with frustration and a simmering rage. Terror and loneliness mixed with a profound hunger and a darkness no sun could penetrate. Betrayal had tainted his memories, leaving an anger that stretched centuries. All of this was woven together by bitter regret.

Questions cleared the lust from her mind. She tore her lips away, aching from pain belonging to Reign. Briefly, his hands tightened on her body. His head dropped into the crook of her neck before she could search his face for answers. Warm breath fanned her collar. She bit her lip to keep from protesting when his hands dropped to her hips and he set her on her feet.

Alexis darted up the stairs to the safety of her grandmother's bedroom. She stripped off her jacket and refused to think about the man camping in her living room. Yeah, right. As if she could order herself not to still taste him on her lips, remember his hands on her body and his tongue stroking her mouth.

How could she feel him, know his intimate thoughts? The good and the f'd up ones. There were a lot of f'd up ones. So many, he was a toxic stew, churning endlessly until he almost dragged her under.

Alexis gritted her teeth. She didn't have time to decipher The Reign Riddle when Egyptian Gods roamed New York, resurrecting bodies, and wild animals were running loose. If she read it in a novel, she would've pitched it into the nearest incinerator.

Her stomach grumbled, but she needed to wash before searching for food. Hot water pulsing out of the shower head swept away the remaining cobwebs and clarified her position. Those things needed to die.

Period.

There had to be a way and she needed Reign to kill them, regardless of her libido. It shouldn't be hard to get one man to do what she wanted. A spoonful of sugar went down a lot easier than a spoonful of salt, her Nana used to say. Nana should know. Her marriage lasted fifty-five years.

Alexis studied herself in the bathroom mirror. Once her pageant days had ended, she threw away her makeup kit and every form-fitting item of clothing she'd owned. Comfort and practicality ruled the day and every man she'd dealt with had better like it or else. Her single state summed up how well that worked. Memories of Paul tried to float to the surface. Now was not the day to stroll down that rocky road. She nailed the coffin full of memories of her ex closed and reburied the box.

Her stomach rumbled and cramped, drawing her away from introspection. Even though she'd snacked at the wedding, her last true meal was a bowl of cereal twenty-four hours ago. If she was starving, then her guest roaming downstairs must be too.

She opened her phone and saw she had a message. "Hello, dear. It's Mrs. Kelly. I see you're still staying in your grandmother's house. I have a list of contractors who are trustworthy to work on the house and update it a bit. I left the names in your mailbox. I hope you don't mind. Just trying to be helpful. I also made a chocolate cake and left it for you in the kitchen. Figured chocolate would help to make some of what you've been through better. Call me if you need anything. Bye, bye."

Chocolate cake, the breakfast of champions. Her nosy neighbor must've entered the house when they were gone. As unofficial caretaker of the home, Alexis was grateful for Mrs. Kelly's help. She replayed the message and realized her neighbor may have a point. Nothing inside the house had been changed or replaced since her grandmother's death six months ago. The actual house could use some upgrading. Her father had agreed to will it to her, that didn't mean she could do what she wanted to the property. She had to get him to sell it to her outright. Then she wouldn't have to worry about Gloria removing all the precious items that reminded Alexis of her grandmother in her desire to redecorate.

Alexis glanced at the sturdy ornate brass bed and baroque miss-matched furniture. Along with the ancient knickknacks and the lacy doilies, the items gave the room nineteenth century feel. Those she would keep. The pictures of long dead unknown family members had to go. She grabbed a handful of the stuff, shoved them into a storage container, and headed to the pull cord dangled overhead in the middle of the hallway. Easier to do some house cleaning than face the five ton gorilla waiting downstairs. A hard tug, and rusty hinges squealed as the stairs unfolded.

"Do you need my assistance?"

She looked over her shoulder at Reign, her gorgeous gorilla. The hunger and despair had left his features. His expression neutral, he seemed okay. "Thanks, I got it."

Alexis maneuvered up the squeaky stairs and plowed into a spider web. She yelped and the items clattered to the floor. Eyes shut, she swiped at her face.

"Cease." A hand landed on her shoulder. Gentle fingers moved across her forehead, cheeks and nose sending sparks through her bloodstream. When she opened her eyes, his deep ocean blue eyes block her view. "You are fine," he said much too close to her face.

No, she wasn't fine. She hated spiders and his nearness didn't help either. "Thanks." He picked up the container before she reached for it.

"Where would you like this placed?"

Alexis waved her hand in the direction of an already crowded shelf. "Over there, somewhere." She walked deeper in the attic. The warm appraisal of his gaze flustered her, made her head swim. *It's hunger, not him.* She thought as the room dipped. His hand landed on her shoulder again. He stepped closer. Her heart fluttered.

Annoyed with him, but more with herself, she slapped his hand away. "Can you leave, go downstairs, something, anything!" Alexis flung her hands in the air.

Spine stiff, he jerked around and left, his footsteps receding like rolling thunder on the wooden floors.

Alexis sank into a dusty rocking chair, irritated at the unexpected wave of guilt rushing through her. Since when did she begin to care about his feelings? No. She didn't care. She was just a nice person and being nasty never got anything accomplished. Now her stranded ghost—spirit—stalker—whatever hated her. Not a good thing if you wanted him to kill for you, and if you had to be haunted, one would prefer *Casper* rather than the ghostly apparitions from *Poltergeist*.

Besides, he was a liar. Not to be trusted.

Alexis huffed a heavy sigh and then noticed her grandmother's steamer trunk. The October nights had started turning cold. Plus, she could stick the pictures in there and retrieve some blankets. She moved the stack of books from the lid and released the latch. Rusty hinges fought the invasion of the box's privacy, but her strength prevailed.

Grandmother's patchwork quilt peeked out from the folds of tissue paper. She had forgotten how beautiful it was. Nana's lilac scent filled the stale room when she freed the king-sized multicolored quilt. When would she stop missing her lazy smile that had told everyone to slow down, her ample bosom that had pillowed Alexis's head when she didn't want to sleep in her own bed and the walnut brownies she made every Sunday after church for dessert? She wrapped the quilt around her shoulders and pretended the quilt was Nana's arms.

A very poor substitute, but she would take what little she could get and hold onto the memories of the rest. She started to close the lid when she spotted a black satin box sitting on top of a collection of brown leather books.

Nana had no jewelry so there couldn't be anything of value in the square container. Still, a quiver of excitement shook her hand when she reached for it. Alexis opened the box and gasped.

A triple coiled gold bracelet on a red velvet bed lay within. At both ends, the delicate head of a snake, one with ruby eyes, the other emerald. The thing had to be worth a fortune. She stroked a finger down its golden scales and found it slightly warm. Where did her grandmother, an elementary school teacher, get this? From every angle, the thing was exquisite. Even in the dim light of the attic, it glowed. Gloria always claimed they came from wealth, but any wealth originated from the paternal side of the family. Nana was as middle class as one could get.

How would it feel on her arm? Would it be heavy and weigh her down or light and hardly noticeable. She fought the temptation to wrap the bracelet around her wrist. Never one to wear jewelry of any kind, she shouldn't care, but she did, badly.

What's wrong with me? Now isn't the time for this. She had more on her plate than to obsess over a piece of gold. She snapped the lid closed. Once out of sight, the temptation eased. Her first instinct was to return it the trunk. If she wore it, she wouldn't be able to let it go.

She opened the satin box again and stared once more at the bracelet. The green and red eyes twinkled, clearly begging her—just once—to see it gleam on her skin. She snapped it closed again, her decision resolute.

Sell it and get out of debt, her inner voice argued. Maybe not all of her bills, but at least her credit cards, maybe even her car note. Instead, she peeked inside the trunk hoping for more hidden treasure, but the books were all that remained.

Alexis expected to find Reign waiting for her at the bottom of the attic stairs and ignored the thread of disappointment. The silent house didn't fool her. She walked into her bedroom, placed the jewelry box on the dresser, and tossed the books on the bed. One popped opened, showing faded yellow pages. She reached over to pick up the journal, but her eyes zeroed in on the second line.

January 1938,

I met him. He's the one. He doesn't know it, but I do. I'm going to marry that man and live happily ever after, just like Cinderella.

1938, her grandmother was sixteen years old. Did she mean Grandpa? No, they didn't marry until 1950. This had to be a teen crush before Grandpa came into her life. Alexis read on, hearing her Nana's imaginary teenage voice as she shared her distant longings for a man that didn't know she existed.

There was such hope and certainty in her words and voice. That was her Granny. She lived never doubting her life or the possibilities.

October 26, 1938

How do I explain what happened? John and I…well, I can't bring myself to put it on paper. He made me his. I love him so much. I want nothing more than to be with him. I'm so giddy, I can hardly think.

What? Whoa! John was not her grandfather. Robert Jameson was her grandfather's name. Her saintly grandmother wasn't a virgin on her wedding day? Alexis nearly closed the book.

It wasn't what I expected. Margie told me what would happen, but I didn't expect to feel like I did. I mean, it was okay, it hurt a little. John tried to make it nice, and it was, but the moment he started touching me, my parts, and such, something came over me. I no longer felt like myself. And I could hear John. His thoughts were inside my head.

Alexis plopped onto the bed. Her eyes scanned the paragraph again.

His thoughts scared me. They were dark. I wanted him to stop, but I didn't know how to say no. The word sat on my tongue, but just wouldn't come out. It wasn't bad, he was kind and gentle, but I felt like I was looking into his soul. How could I do that?

Francis.

Her thoughts tumbled. Nana had experienced the same thing as she had. The next few entries were filled with romantic details Alexis truly didn't need to know about her grandmother. Then the entries changed.

June 29, 1939

I confided in Margie. I just had to tell someone. I thought she would say I was crazy. But what she told me was simplyoutrageous. Some cockamamie story about Egyptian Gods and nulls. She even told me she was a null. What the heck is a null? I asked her what had she been sipping. Turpentine? Really, I thought she was my friend.

The journal shook violently in Alexis's hand as flipped to the last page.

September 3, 1940

I cannot breathe. I may never breathe again. John is dead. Will I ever have that connection again? The complete oneness I found with him. I pray not. To be that completely lost within someone again is not something I would chose to repeat. Margie came to the service with me. We stood in the back, away from the family. Margie's the best friend I could ever have. She held my hand. I wish I could feel her palm against mine. Maybe I wouldn't have felt so alone. But the gloves prevent that from happening, thank god.

Dear Lord, is this now my life?

Trembling, Alexis closed the book and tossed it on the bed. So many things clicked into place. Her grandmother always wore gloves outside the house. She was never without a pair. And Gloria was the same. She thought it was just a family eccentricity that thankfully skipped her. Now?

Alexis studied her palms and fingers and then curled them into fists. *I'm the problem, not him.*

The secret to so many things lay within her. Is that why she chafed at the constraints life had placed around her neck? The one person who had the answers was buried in Oakleaf Cemetery. Her headstone faced east to catch the rising sun. Good thing her grandmother's best friend was still above ground and living across the street, and still not minding her own business.

Alexis snatched up the journal and marched downstairs.

"Where are you going?" Reign demanded as she passed him in the living room.

She kept walking out the front door, down the steps, across the street, through the gate, to knock on the front door of her favorite neighbor and her grandmother's best friend.

"Coming," Mrs. Kelly called from somewhere in the house.

A lock clicked. The knob turned and Mrs. Kelly's wrinkled, smiling face appeared.

"Alexis! I have cookies cooling. I planned on bringing them over for you."

Alexis watched her slip on a pair of worn cotton gloves. "What am I?" she asked without preamble. She waved her grandmother's journal in front of her neighbor's face. Mrs. Kelly's eyes widened just enough for any doubt Alexis had to fade.

"I don't understand, dear. What do you mean?" Mrs. Kelly folded her gloved fingers in front of her.

Head to the side, a questioning grandmotherly stare didn't fool Alexis one bit. Reign's footsteps thundered up the steps and across the porch. She didn't have to turn around to know he stood directly behind her. Besides, Mrs. Kelly looked past Alexis's shoulder and her head tilted up, way up.

"Greetings, Mrs. Kelly," Reign said.

Alexis whipped around. "You know her?" She turned back to her neighbor. "You know him?"

"We met the night you were attacked." Reign moved around her and bowed to her neighbor.

"You lied to me." Alexis pointed a finger at the woman. "I asked you—"

"Yes, yes. I lied because you weren't ready for the truth. Now, you are."

Alexis stepped closer to Mrs. Kelly. Anger made her head throb in time with her racing heart. She needed to hit something...badly. "You're lucky someone taught me to respect my elders."

The old woman smiled and a twinkle sparked in her eyes. "You didn't come here to pummel me, Alexis. You came for answers."

She did and that's the only reason she didn't turn around and march back across the street. Alexis grabbed Reign's hand and braced herself against the flood of emotions. Puzzlement and worry overrode Reign's anger and desire. "I. Can. Feel. Him. Right now, he's worried about me, about my sanity. He thinks he's pushed me too hard and he thinks...I'm not real, I'm a lie?" She glanced up and looked into his startled eyes. "Why would you think I'm not real?"

His gaze skimmed her body, and more intimate emotions rushed from him, making her blush.

"Excuse me," Mrs. Kelly cleared her throat breaking their connection. "The question isn't what are you, Alexis. Rather, it's what is he?"

Aged brown eyes studied him. Still holding his hand, Alexis felt his rising tension. Suddenly, he released her and pulled her behind him. She elbowed him in the ribs to move, but all she received was a grunt.

She heard Mrs. Kelly sigh. "Both of you get in here. It's too cool to chat on the porch."

They stepped into foyer and followed their host into her living room. She sat in a padded rocking chair near the window. Alexis sat opposite her while Reign stood close by.

"Well, sir? What are you? Or don't you know what you are? Come here." She seemed to say all of her words at once.

"We came here to find out what I am, not him." Alexis stated.

"I know what you are. You're a null."

A strangled sound came from Reign.

"Ah, you know what a null is." Mrs. Kelly stripped off her gloves and waved a finger at him.

"Well would someone care to tell me?" Alexis tried to keep the anger out of her voice.

Her hostess's gaze landed on her, and her mouth opened to speak, but Reign's angry voice cut her off.

"A null is a slave of the Egyptian Gods. The first condemned souls of the underworld. They serve their masters forever, touching none but the one they service. How can she be a null? They are trapped, bonded forever to *Duat.*"

"True, but early on, a few escaped. I am a descendant...as is Alexis. Your family and mine descend from one of those nulls."

Alexis couldn't string the multitude of questions clogging her brain into words, much less sentences.

Mrs. Kelly turned her attention to Reign. "The question still remains, what are you, sir? Or shall I say what do you think you are?" Her fingers steepled under her double chin.

"I am a warrior, a mercenary," he answered cautiously.

"Oh, you're a lot more than that." Mrs. Kelly held out her hand. "Alexis doesn't know how to use her gift. I do. I can tell you exactly what you are."

Indecision crossed his features, but he took a step forward. Alexis wanted to pull him back to her side and protect this immense warrior from a little old lady. But if he was strong enough to know, then so was she.

CHAPTER TWENTY-ONE

Walking toward the woman reminded Reign of his first march on a Viking encampment. Roman was next to him. They were only fifteen summers and didn't think they would greet sixteen. And though neither dared show it, they were afraid.

Her steely gaze never wavered; neither did her extended hand or the strength of her convictions. She believed what she said. He didn't know whether to hope she was correct or pray she wasn't.

Too soon, he towered over her withered frame. Her white hair haloed her weathered features. His heart beat wildly in his chest when he placed his much larger hand in her palm. Gnarled, bony fingers gripped him tightly, surprising him with their strength, as did the subtle power shifting across his skin, sinking into his muscles, stripping through him layer by layer.

Alexis came to stand next to him. Not caring what she was or wasn't, he wrapped his free arm around her shoulders and pulled her against his side. Minutes passed before the old woman released him. Her once steady hands shook and she slumped in her chair.

"Well," Alexis said.

Aged, watery eyes landed on him. "You are a god."

"I am not. What you feel is borrowed from the goddess Nephythys." This old woman couldn't tell the difference.

"Little of her paltry energy flows through you. The *vis*'Ra you wield is yours. Yours alone. You, Reign Nicolis, are an Egyptian God." Her eyes narrowed and a grimace crossed her weathered face. "A powerful one too."

He dropped to his haunches. "What game do you play?" he murmured. "I have been her slave for two thousand years, bound against my will." He raised his voice. "If I were a god do you think I would have stayed!" The house rocked and dust circled the air.

She laughed. "Oh, so mere humans can shout and shake the foundation of my house." Merriment danced in her eyes. "Your powers were bound, they still are, but not as tightly as they once were."

"Who bound them?" Alexis asked.

"Another God. A parent of yours perhaps."

"My parents were not gods. My father was a warrior. My mother-" He never knew, but his father called her his goddess. He rose to his feet and marched from the house.

Alexis's steps raced behind him, but he couldn't slow down. His churning thoughts wouldn't let him. Thoughts of his mother crowded everything else.

A tiled mural of her decorated the wall in the dining hall of his childhood home so all could see her beauty. His father said she was Grecian. That is why her skin was a lovely tan, her hair an unusual brown, and her eyes, amber. They took after their father, in build, temperament, strength, and visage. Nothing from their mother, much to his father's regret. It was as if she bestowed miniature replicas upon him, then died.

She was not a god. Just a woman. Grecian, not Egyptian, he chanted.

The Vanquished roared in his head and yanked him to a halt. He pivoted. One hundred feet away, Alexis stood by the gate of the house. Damn the Vanquished, he didn't want to be near her. Near anyone. Sheer will enabled him to take five more steps, before he flashed back to her side.

Strong arms wrapped around his neck. Gentle fingers threaded through his hair and caressed his scalp. His heart unclenched and the voices calmed. Alexis tipped her head up. He brought his head down and rested his forehead against hers.

"Where did you think you were going?" she murmured.

Instead of answering, he sipped from her lips in a long, slow kiss that promised paradise. His hands tightened on her hips and he hauled her flush against him.

Alexis groaned and slanted her lips over his.

Nowhere—that's where he was going—without her. Reign peeled his lips away and drew a ragged breath. He guided her through the gate. Before entering the house, Reign looked over his shoulder and met the gaze of their neighbor. She stood on her porch watching them and waved seconds before he slammed the door closed.

***

Reign wouldn't talk to her. He stalked upstairs and paced like a newly captured tiger displayed for the first time. *Please* burned Alexis's tongue, but she wouldn't beg. He would share his feelings with her freely or not at all.

It surprised her that she wanted him to share, even though she knew it was a deep dark well which may drown her. How many layers could a man have? Touching Reign exposed her to many. They whirled around and through her so fast she couldn't count them all.

But she wanted to, needed to. Was this compulsion or something worse? Could she be falling for the man she swore she would use. Separate her heart from her genitals.

"I did say that less than twenty-four hours ago, right? That was me? And I was in my right mind," she murmured. "Can't blame it on him or being a null." *Shit!*

She couldn't fall for him. The man was an immortal, an Egyptian god according to Mrs. Kelly. He was also a fugitive. She risked everything by having him here in her home. Her stomach knotted.

Alexis grabbed her purse and left the house. Fresh air, a brisk walk, and a good meal always cleared her head. And her favorite diner was only five blocks away.

She brought a newspaper from the newsstand and found an empty table in the back, away from the crowded middle. It didn't take long for a cold wind to circulate around her. Maybe a brisk walk is what he also needed. She sighed and snatched up the menu.

"What to feed a god?" she mumbled. When the waitress arrived, she ordered two tall stacks of pancakes and two steak and eggs combo platters with bacon. She added a pot of coffee and a carafe of O.J. The waitress gave her a crazed look. "I'm expecting someone."

She flipped through the newspaper, pretending to read, but she couldn't concentrate. Not when she could feel him sitting opposite her.

The waitress returned with coffee and silverware. Alexis waited for the woman to walk away. A quick scan of the room confirmed no one watched. She glanced at the empty chair opposite her. "I know you're here. Can you appear, please?"

One second the chair was empty, the next his body filled her view. His placid face gave nothing away.

"My apologies for my behavior earlier. There was no reason for me to ignore you."

"Then why did you?" She fixed both of them a cup of coffee and mixed in a liberal amount of amaretto creamer.

"The Vanquished—"

"No. Don't blame your behavior on your ghosts. You did it, not them."

Alexis swore his eyes turned neon blue before he closed them. A muscle in his jaw flexed angrily, while his hands curled into meaty fists on the table. His frustration reached out to her. She stretched across the table and stroked the back of his hand until his palm opened. Then slid the coffee cup into his grasp. "Drink," she ordered, staring into his now clear eyes.

Reign studied the milky confection with suspicion.

"It's not poison." Alexis raised her mug and took a mouthful. He copied her and though he didn't smile, his scowl softened.

"It'll grow on you." The food arrived, along with toast, bacon, and a caddy of jam. Reign's ravenous expression halted her from digging in. "When was the last time you had a meal?"

"Two thousand years ago."

Ookaaay.

"I figured you were hungry by now." She picked up her fork and started to eat.

"I do not feel hunger when I am faded, however, I thank you." He studied everything in front of him.

"There's no special way to eat it. Just pick up your fork and start."

Reign picked up the utensils. He watched her and then mimicked her table manners. *So much for teaching the barbarian how to eat.* Like a parent forcing a picky child to sample all the food on their plate, she watched as he tried everything. When he looked up with a smile on his face, her heart lurched.

"Why don't you believe Mrs. Kelly?" she asked when he had nearly cleaned his plate.

He looked up from his food and nailed her with a hostile stare. "Because it is not possible."

"Why?" She pushed not letting him off the hook.

"I know who I am and what I am not."

"She said one of your parents—"

"My parents were human."

"Are you sure? Because parents lie." *Grandparents too.*

He shook his head. "My father would not lie."

"How do you know? It's not like you can ask him. Or maybe you can?"

"What did you say?" Tension deepened his voice. He leaned in.

"What if your father was like you and Roman? What if he's alive and living a quiet existence in some village in Thrace?" She shrugged and refilled her coffee cup.

Reign stood so fast his chair flipped over. Conversations stopped and all eyes turned to them.

"My father is dead. This I know because I saw the man who cut him down a second before I killed the bastard." He stomped from the diner, leaving her stunned, and the crowd whispering.

"Have you lost your damn mind?"

Alexis glanced up. Paul snatched Reign's chair off the floor and plopped down in front of her. Dumbstruck, she stared into his furious face.

"You're harboring a fugitive! I came in here for breakfast and find you and that criminal!"

"A-a-a." Her mouth opened, but no words escaped. She had none. What the hell was he doing here, on the opposite side of town where he lived? Paul glanced over his shoulder at a blond waiting impatiently for him by the exit.

Dick following pussy. She'd laugh at the irony if she wasn't wading neck deep in shit.

"Is he worth your career, huh? Worth losing everything you worked for?" Head cocked to the side, his livid features said more than his words.

Nothing was worth that, especially not a man. Her heart squeezed painfully. "No..." But what good would it do to hand him to the police again only to have him vanish from prison and end up on her doorstep once more. She wanted to explain, but no one would believe this situation.

"I don't want to know what the hell is going on with you two—"

Yeah he did. She could tell by the jealous glare sweeping over her.

"—you've got twenty-four hours to turn him in or I go to my captain." He left the restaurant with the blond and turned in the opposite direction Reign had taken.

Twenty-four hours. She had that long to sever the ties that kept Reign with her and arrest him. Oh, and somehow find a way to keep him locked in a two-by-four cell.

Alexis trekked back to the house alone, but she hadn't been there five minutes when the doorbell rang. Mrs. Kelly stood on her porch.

"I have a few quotes from some contractors to finish the work on your grandmother's house." She waved some paper in front of Alexis's face.

Alexis stepped aside. Mrs. Kelly glided past her. She removed her sweater and unwrapped the scarf from around her steel colored hair. "October feels colder this year. Mark my words, winter will come earlier and stay longer. I don't know how my bones will take it." She stopped to listen to the pacing upstairs.

Alexis didn't buy the gentile grandmother routine. "How old are you, Mrs. Kelly?"

"Old." She lowered herself onto the sofa. "Much older than I look, but not older than Reign. I came to ask when were you planning to leave for the Vineyard and if I could join you in the drive?"

The Vineyard? Crap! The anniversary dinner. "My mother sent you an invitation?" Alexis couldn't keep the surprise out of her voice.

"Yes, I received an invitation."

Why would Gloria send you an invitation?

"Hah! I can tell by that look on your face what you're thinking. I called her and told her to invite me. That woman can teach a class in stubbornness. It was her job, her right to tell you what you are, but she never believed. Stubborn and stupid. We warned her, your grandmother and I tried to tell her what she was. She didn't want to hear it. Nothing we said fit in with her plans to marry Martin."

"Why are you really here?" Alexis leaned against the archway and waited for Mrs. Kelly to answer.

The elder sighed. "I came here to tell you the truth. All of it. You are so much more than your mother. You can handle what she couldn't."

Alexis didn't want to hear this, but good manners prevented her from stopping her neighbor from continuing. "Then tell me and get the hell out."

"Before we were nulls, we were Eidos, Elementals not slaves. Our race was the first, here before the gods and man arrived. We were the spark of life in the primordial seas, the heat that made the volcanoes flow, and the oxygen in the air, until they came. All of them, Egyptian, Greeks, Romans, they came from the cosmos, saw what we could be and stole that energy from us. From rulers to slaves. Some of us escaped with our powers, stayed hidden within the changing landscape of earth until we were no longer hunted."

"Are my brothers nulls too?"

"No, all Elementals were women, as all nulls are females.

"Why now? All this time, I've never felt anyone's emotions when I've touched them. So why now?" She punctuated the last sentence with a fist pounding the air.

"There is always a trigger. Reign must've been yours." Mrs. Kelly shrugged.

That was easy enough to believe. "Are you done with the history lesson? Because all you've told me is what *we* once were."

A gleam sparkled in her eyes. "I will tell you what I know. A war is coming, Alexis. And there are more sides than the two presently on the battlefield."

"You come here with more tales." Reign appeared across from them.

"You call them tales. I know they're the truth. You would too if you just accept it."

"Accept?" He threw back his head and gave a single, abrasive laugh. "All my life I've accepted what the fates have decried. No longer."

Abruptly, he pivoted toward the door, his blade glowing in his hand. "Stay here," he ordered.

Alexis almost obeyed. She jumped up and followed him. Half way to the door, he paused. His sword vanished.

"It is Roman." He yanked opened the door and sure enough, Roman Nicolis stood on her porch. The two men were so similar yet so different. Roman with his short haircut, clean-shaven face, designer clothes, was slick and polished corporate America. While Reign with his long shaggy hair, whiskers shadowing his jaw, weathered jeans and faded tee was a rougher, harsher version. Slightly taller, a little bit brawnier, Reign was just more.

"We need to talk, alone." Roman stepped into the house.

Alexis's hands landed on her hips. "This is my house and I'm not going anywhere."

"Excuse me, gentlemen." Mrs. Kelly cut between the brothers. She gave Roman an appraising look before turning to Reign and Alexis. "I've said my peace, now it's time for me to return to my corner of the world." She took Alexis's hand. "I'm here when you need me, dear. No matter the time." The steel in her voice matched the strength in her hands and the determination in her gaze. Mrs. Kelly pulled Alexis into a tight embrace and then sailed through the open door.

"Say what you have to say, *brother,*" Reign sneered the second the door closed.

Alexis swore she could feel the frustrated hurt rolling off him. And the love he held for his twin. Simple emotions, but they confused and embarrassed her. She hated this window into his soul. It felt wrong, a violation. "I-I need to clean up the living room." She stepped away, rounded the corner into the living room, and stopped. She wasn't too embarrassed to eavesdrop.

***

"Talk," Reign said.

"Where did you get the sword?" Roman pushed.

Reign suspected it came from Nephythys. The power she endowed in him manifested in the sword when he needed it. "From the goddess, Nephythys."

"You said she sent you here to kill Alamut. Yet when you find him, you prop him up for a chitchat instead of sticking your special blade into every piece of him. Why?"

Reign gritted his teeth. "I have my reasons for keeping him alive. Why do you need him dead?"

Roman moved too close for comfort, but Reign didn't step back. "Because before he was Alamut, he was Daniel. A boy I took into my home, raised as one of my own and he turned, killed eleven people, and nearly killed my wife—twice! Once he was human, now he's an immortal jigsaw puzzle lounging in my vault, reanimated by your goddess's son, Anubis—yeah, I've been doing my homework. I've tried every way to kill him, but he won't die. Now you show up with your *sword*. You killed the others. I need you to kill him."

Doing that would send him back. No matter what he told Alexis about returning to Chemmis, the heat from her kiss still lingered in his mind. He wouldn't go back.

"No." Inches away from each other, he registered his brother's building rage and his own rising.

"You two are not going to destroy this house. Step away from each other." Alexis ordered a few feet away.

Inwardly, Reign groaned. Now was not the time for her to interfere. Still, he took a step back, but his gaze never left Roman.

"Okay! Let me get this straight," she said and moved between them. First, she faced Roman. "Alamut and Daniel are one and the same." She turned to Reign. "And you knew all of this and didn't tell me?" She held up three fingers and waved them in his face. "Strike three!"

The coldness in her voice couldn't compare to the frost in her eyes.

She whipped around to Roman. "Daniel is alive and you're hiding him in your vault until you can kill him? I should arrest you."

"Daniel doesn't exist anymore, Detective Lever, only Alamut remains. Explain the facts to your girlfriend, Reign. And explain to her why you saved her life, and won't do what's necessary now. I need you, Reign, tonight at RockGate." Roman slammed the door closed behind him. Alexis's coppery gaze burrowed into Reign.

"He has the same sentiment I do," she said.

Though he'd never run from any battle, this fight, he wished he could flee. At least fade until he could string the correct wordage together. By the tight stance of her body, her thin lips, and furious eyes, he didn't have that option.

"The man you know as Daniel is also Alamut, the beast that destroyed this home. I was sent here to slay Alamut."

"By whom, you mean the goddess you're brother mentioned?"

"Yes."

"So why won't you do it?"

"Because I will not be a tool she uses to shame her son." His jaw ground together as fury rippled through him. Never mind killing Alamut would send him back to *Duat*. That piece of information he would keep to himself a bit longer.

"How did she shame her son?"

"She never claimed him. Left him for his father, the God of All Evil, to raise. A motherless child in a matriarchal society is an abomination."

"Why does she use you?"

The truth clogged his throat. "For entertainment. Life holds no value to her. Only her enjoyment matters." She would question him more and the truth-could he tell her and watch the disgust on her face?

Shrewd, coppery eyes assessed him. Reign steeled himself for the coming interrogation. But her gaze lowered and she nodded slowly. "Okay—" She finally spoke and the breath he hadn't realized he held, released. "Because I don't give a rat's ass what Alamut is. If Daniel Nicolis is alive, he's going to jail and I'm getting my career back."

CHAPTER TWENTY-TWO

Daniel shot upright. The room, the colonial furnishings, the weak afternoon sun streaming through a part in the heavy curtains, and the comfortable four-poster bed, all confused him. Until Hector's voice filtered from downstairs. He was at the cottage on the grounds of RockGate. Bianca's and Hector's raised voices mixed from below.

Time to bail. He flashed from the cottage to the house opposite the factory. He approached from the rear, cautiously picking his way through the abandoned backyards of neighboring homes. Location, location, location. He didn't buy this house in his grandmother's name for the pleasure of owning a rundown piece of the American dream. First, he needed privacy away from the prying eyes and inquisitive minds of the family. When he began harvesting souls and transforming bodies for Anubis's army, the factory was the perfect place to hide them.

Before Anubis gave him more power, he had spent a summer digging the tunnel connecting the two structures. Back breaking work, even when he transformed into Alamut, but the benefit outweighed the risk.

Quick and quiet, Daniel entered the house. He paused inside the doorway while his eyes adjusted to the gloom. Passing through the house, his gaze darted to each shadowy corner, searching for an ambush. He went to the kitchen, dodged the yellow streetlight filtering through the dirty windows and eased open the basement door. The dark waited. Unafraid, he stepped on down the stairs, welcoming the inky darkness creeping up his body.

He made his way to the center of the room and dropped down into the tunnel. Motion sensors activated the lights hanging from the bedrock. Fueled by the need to be with his own kind, Daniel jogged the remaining distance and stepped onto the metal crosswalk.

Anubis's army fermented in a greenish, amniotic, gelatinous soup in the pit below him. He shed his clothes and dived from the crosswalk. Eyes closed, he allowed himself to sink beneath the surface. The slime cooled his fevered skin as the silent malevolence oozing from the quimaera seeped into his soul, calming him. These beasts were his true family. The only family he needed.

Sometime later, Daniel surfaced. Once again, Anubis's vis'Ra flowed through him. Rejuvenated, he rose from the pit. The slime sucked at him, unwilling to release its hold until the very last second.

As he rose, a pair of shapely legs came into view. A petite woman, shrouded in rags. Moonlight streaked from the damaged roof and dappled her skin, making her appear to be made of quicksilver. Though concerned, her presence didn't give him pause. The dozen quimaera standing behind her jerked him to a stop.

The pit from which he ascended had a full complement of quimaeras. The beasts guarding her must have come from another. Anubis was the only one who could activate the army, so how had she achieved the feat when Anubis refused to give him the power?

Daniel touched down on the rim of the pit. The change swept through him. Bones lengthened, ripping tendons and muscles, he grew. His face and clubbed tail extended from his body. Scaly, pearlescent skin replaced his own as he completed his transformation from Daniel into Alamut, the beast. He was bigger than the eight quimaera squaring off against him. His muscles, thicker. The spikes on his tail longer. His last fight hadn't exactly ended the way he'd planned. He would not lose again.

Alamut bellowed a challenge.

The woman studied him. Head slightly titled, questioning his presence. Unafraid, she walked around him in an arc. He maintained eye contact even as she left firm ground and floated over the pit. He swallowed his surprised.

"I am your new master." She pointed to the ground. "Kneel and submit to me."

Anubis is the only master he would answer to. Alamut lunged. This dark haired bitch would die beneath his claws.

A quimaera snagged Alamut's tail before he reached her. Inches short of digging his claws into her body, he slammed into the wall of the pit and was dragged backwards. With a flick of his tail, he freed himself and flung his opponent into the others. Alamut flipped around, caught the nearest quimaera in his jaws. He bit down on his prey's neck, grabbed the side of his head, and ripped. Head went to the left, body tossed to the right. The rest of the quimaera charged.

"Enough," the woman shouted behind him. The quimaera stopped.

Braced for attack, Alamut dare not turn his back on the horde still facing him to look at the woman.

She floated into view. "They will no longer harm you."

He couldn't grin in this form, but he didn't need to flash his bloody teeth. "I'm relieved," he barked.

"You doubt my words?"

He impaled a quimaera with his barbed tail. The beast didn't have a chance to scream before it expired. "Do you doubt my skill?"

"I could call more warriors to my aid. But I will not. Your skill has impressed me."

Alamut ignored the compliment. He was more interested in how she did what he couldn't. "How did you activate the quimaera?"

A smile flirted with her lips. "Which god calls you his bitch?"

It took everything in him not to leap across the distance and show her exactly which one of them owned that title. "I suspect the same one as you."

"I answer to SET. He granted me my freedom from Duat."

SET, the God of All Evil. The name alone sent a chill down Alamut's spine. By the way she spat the name, it must've tasted foul on her tongue.

"I stole the spirits of these beasts from Anubis." She smirked and the tattered rags of her clothing fluttered though no breeze circled the room.

Bound to SET and thieving from his son, this woman lived dangerously. He wasn't sure if he should make her his enemy or ally.

Wait! If SET sent her what did that mean? "Why are you here, Great Goddess?" The endearment rolled of his tongue. Better to curry favor with an unknown deity than end up dead or worse, in pieces again.

A quick spark of anger illuminated her jade eyes and the smile wiped from her face. "I am here to re-gain SET's honor." A chuckle burst from her, then delight crossed her features and she laughed again, this time a deep throaty sound that set his nerves further on edge.

She wasn't much to look at, not his type at all, but with all that spiky hair and night-of-the-living-dead theme, damn if she wasn't sexy.

SET's honor? That meant she knew about Reign. Who was this goddess?

"Who claims you, demon?" she asked again.

If she couldn't tell Anubis owned him, he wouldn't volunteer the info. "I am not a demon and I don't know which god claims me."

"Are you the leader of these beasts?"

Sometimes diplomacy was better than valor. At least until he discovered who this deity was and how much could she aid or fuck up his plans. "I was." He dropped one knee onto the concrete, but wouldn't bow his head.

"You are wise. Will you swear loyalty to me?"

If it will save my life. "Yes."

"I have no use for one such as you, a disloyal slave."

Rankled, Alamut rose. "And what are you if not the same?"

Her features twisted and dark waves peeled away from her floating body in arcing streams. "I am Khuket, Goddess of Ogdoad, the first and last of my kind—"

"—And slave to SET," he barked. "I am Alamut, a slave. But it's not where I'll stay." He shifted to his human form and returned to Daniel. "I hate the Egyptians for what they've done to me and what they've made me do."

Khuket floated closer to him. "Who owns you?"

Her eagerness to know seemed more than curiosity. "Anubis," he said.

Her eyes narrowed. "The father owns me while the son owns you." Calculation gleamed in her eyes. The deliberate assessment of a general planning a war. And he had to pick a side.

"What does SET want from you?"

"I am charged with killing his wife's lover and returning his body to SET."

And Anubis demands I kill him. Shit! "Let me help you. I would rather serve you than them."

"Why should I trust you?" Her pouty lips pursed. He wasn't fooled by the display. She was interested.

"You shouldn't. Neither should you trust the ones who enslave you." He turned toward the exit.

Daniel had made it to the door before her voice stopped him.

"Halt."

Hand on the knob, he opened the door and placed one foot over the threshold, before he pivoted.

"You know well this world." She drifted closer. Her gaze judged him.

He stiffened his spine and squared his shoulders. "Yeah."

"Then you may stay." She turned away.

So he had a value to her after all. "I need a better reason than that."

"Have you love for your master Anubis?"

"I love Anubis as much as you love SET." He stepped back into the room.

The tattered fringes of her clothes smoked and extended toward him. They quivered, as if agitated. He didn't move as they stroked up his back, around his waist, between his legs. They violated each crevice and seeped into each orifice. She sought his truth. He couldn't let her have it.

Rage, the ever-present companion, flooded his system and masked his true motivation. More powerful than any drug he had ever induced, rage placed him on the path to vengeance and immortality. This goddess was another hurdle to leap over in his sprint to the finish line.

Khuket withdrew. A smile flirted with her lips.

"Have I passed your examination?"

"Yes, you have."

He stretched his mouth into a smile. "Then we shall help each other."

"Your usefulness to me begins now. My pets hunger. They need to feed."

"F-feed?" It took less than a minute for her to reduce him to a high school lunch lady. "What do you feed them?"

"They have a taste for flesh."

Naturally. "Shouldn't be too hard to find an all-night buffet. After all, this is New York." The perfect place came to mind. The same place he had visited many times before when he was building his army. High Bridge.

***

After days of nesting in a cliff-side nook overlooking the shimmering sea, Nephythys's *Chu,* essence, caught a wind current, and allowed herself to be swept away. Above her, the universe waited. Though her *vis'*Ra came from the cosmos and—as with all things—would return, the vast expanse terrified her. The goddess, Nu, had ventured into the universe and purposely lost herself there to escape the dictates of the Pantheon. Nephythys would never be so lucky.

Tumbling on a salty breeze, this was as close to free as she would ever be. She enjoyed every second the wind buffeted her wispy form, pulling, pushing, and twisting each way. The jagged entrance to the underworld waited. She passed through the many layers of earth and arrived at her palace in the subterranean cavern.

In every direction, a bleak landscape greeted the eye. Mountains of ash shifted in increments on faint drafts of sulfuric air belched from vents on the cavern floor. Red and brown plants sprouted their lethal leaves enticing the new arrivals with their deadly beauty.

Perched on the highest peak, the gleaming ivory marble of her palace cast away the gloom clinging to everything in *Duat.*

Her balcony overlooked every being she had judged and if she desired, she could hear their pleas.

Eons spent judging the sins of others left little sympathy in her heart for the wretched humans. They were a pestilence on the Earth, a blight that needed to be trimmed, like a thinning of the herd at market time.

She needed to see him. Anticipation increased her pace to her palace. Can you call a man whom you have never touched or allowed to touch you, your lover? She pushed away the errant thought. Reign belonged to her, body and soul. Time was on her side. His anger would not last, could not. He would be grateful she allowed him a taste of freedom to save his brother and be a warrior once again.

Nothing mattered more than seeing him. She prayed to Ra Reign had accomplished his goal and waited to return to her. Maybe his time away made him appreciate what they had, their secret love. Treachery and danger filled the human realm. Their simple life together with simple pleasures was enough for her and after this excursion, enough for him.

Nephythys entered through the parted curtains of her balcony. She gasped. Her beautiful bedroom with all the lovely trinkets she had collected were smashed and scattered about. But worse, her body lay in a heap on the bed. The evidence of copulation smeared on her open thighs.

She quivered in rage. How dare her nulls leave her thus! She spun around to leave and met the glacial stare of her husband. Dressed in the black with blood red trim ceremonial robes of his station, SET waited in the doorway.

In his human form, he was a tall, thin man with sharp aquiline features, slick dark hair, and trimmed goatee. His black essence swirled beneath his translucent skin and matched his sunken coal eyes.

He never lingered after their joining. So why was he now?

"Wife, rejoin your body," he commanded.

Nephythys shimmered into a wavering female form. "Explain yourself! Why have you destroyed my bedroom?"

"I have destroyed much more than that." His whispered words stroked a building terror she failed to recognize until this moment. However, showing that fear would be a fatal mistake.

"Re-join your body, Wife." His voice boomed and lightning flickered in the depths of his eyes. Only once in all their time together had he used that voice with her; their wedding night when she refused to welcome him into her body...ever. That was the catalyst for their appalling...*compromise.* A bargain so terrible history recorded it.

She looked over at the filthy shell and couldn't contemplate stretching her senses to cleanse and heal what damage he had done to her. The way he left her, surely some broken bones and internal damage needed repair. A goddess, discarded like rubbish. Her condition infuriated her.

"After my nulls have removed your filth, then I will comply."

Before she could move, SET's vis'Ra engulfed her, caged and compressed her into a tight narrow space. Knowing that he couldn't kill her kept true panic at bay, but there were worse things than death in *Duat.* Certain things that left a god wide-eyed and afraid of the dark. Eternity imprisoned in the lowest level of the Underworld took on new meaning to an immortal. Nothing in the world, in any realm, was immune to loneliness.

Dear Ra, he couldn't mean to place me there? What have I done to deserve that?

Reign!

The image of his handsome face flashed into her mind. She met her husband's hostile eyes and feral grin.

Was Reign still living or nothing more than ash blowing on the wind?

Her strength faltered and SET shoved her essence back into her body. Immediately, she cast a spell to heal her flesh, but Set blocked her vis'Ra. Unable to fix the damage he caused, Nephythys braced herself for the pain. Her senses stretched and touched ever cell and nerve ending, and found nothing.

Her eyes fluttered open. Prone, all she saw were the crumpled damask sheets. She inhaled, drew in the heady, musky scent of two sweaty bodies. Is that what sex smelled like? She had never experienced that before. All trace of any activity with SET was erased and her flesh sanitized before she reclaimed her body after her husband exercised his rights. And Reign, their liaisons were an illusion created by her to keep him at her side.

She pushed away thoughts of Reign and shifted onto her side. As she drew her legs closed, ripples of pleasure cascade from her groin and tripped their way through her body until every follicle of hair on her head sighed in exquisite pleasure. And continued on for seconds, minutes, hours, time ceased as the sensation traipsed through her. Breathless, she opened her eyes and found her husband hovering over her, watching her quivering reaction with eyes that held a smug satisfaction she had never seen before.

"Rise," he commanded and moved away.

She swallowed the automatic 'No' that surfaced and rose slowly to a seated position. Muscles that she had never used, twitched sending smaller, but no less delightful waves from her core.

SET drank it in with greedy eyes that left her wondering exactly what had he done to her body. She could smell him on her, not the sulfurous stench he usually oozed, but a different smell emanated from between her thighs. Not completely unpleasant.

On unsteady feet, she stood and willed her robes to cover her body. Nothing happened. She raised an eyebrow at SET. He smiled.

"Too long I have been denied the pleasure of seeing life in your naked form. You are magnificent and I will enjoy this moment."

"Will you at least allow me to cleanse myself?" The indignity of the situation galled her.

He came close. The black and red of his robes a perfect contrast to his pasty skin. For the first time, in a long time, she *looked* at the god fate forced her to marry. Deep in the pit of his eyes, she found a man, angry and in pain, but still a man stared back at her. A smile stretched her face. It pleased her to see his anguish.

"I enjoy seeing my seed upon you. And it will remain as long as I will." He turned and as he swept away, a force pulled her behind him. She followed in his exact footsteps, marching behind him, passing rooms of utter destruction. Rubble lay everywhere.

Speechless, Nephythys couldn't appreciate her unscathed statues in the conservatory and the Scrying bowl upon the table, until the waters started to swirl and bubble. She stood next to SET, but didn't command a viewing of the sacred waters. She glanced at her husband. Serene, his dark eyes almost drowned her in the dark depth.

"Don't you want to see?" SET's wide grin showed jagged jackal teeth.

He mocked her. It was her duty to see, to judge. Whether she wanted to or not, she had to look into the sacred bowl. "What will the waters show me?"

"The fate of the human you harbored."

She swallowed the dry lump in her throat. SET's hands clamped around her arms and he grabbed her to him. Braced against his body, the hard length of him pressed against her hip. To her confused shame, her core quivered with unexpected need. She pushed, but he didn't budge.

"Afraid, Wife?" He released her. She stumbled and banged her hip on the edge of her table.

Instead of answering, she clasped the bowl between her hands and drew it closer to her. After a moment of hesitation, she looked into the ancient Nile waters, and regretted it.

CHAPTER TWENTY-THREE

A few hours after calling Judge Mitchell, Nicolis Grayfield and Senator Orley, Roman and Stella waited in the driveway of RockGate watching an ambulance roll up the driveway. Power did have its perks. Cutting through red tape was high on the list.

Stella fidgeted beside him. The waning sunlight bathed her in a warm glow. They should've been sailing the Mediterranean aboard a private yacht on the second day of their honeymoon. He didn't need to wonder whether she would've preferred sunbathing on the deck of a boat instead of waiting here listening to the beep of the ambulance backing up.

He took her hand to stop her from twisting her fingers and kissed her. Her delicious lips parted and drew his tongue inside. His breath caught and his body tightened with love and longing. He had to force himself to stop. "You're worried. Why?"

The EMT's hopped out of the cab and approached the back door of the ambulance.

"I-I don't know." Her chin dipped to her chest.

He hooked a finger under her chin and lifted until her anxious gaze met his. "This is where your sister belongs. Here, with people to care for her, love her. With you."

The techs had the doors open and were climbing into the ambulance.

"W-what if she doesn't wake, doesn't get better?" Tears streaked down her cheeks before he could wipe them away.

Once again, death stalked them. He could protect her from so much, but not this. Finding her sister after all these years was a mixed blessing. If the child died...

"We can't know what the future holds. All we can do is make Ember as comfortable as possible."

"You're right, I know." She nodded and dashed away another tear.

The stretcher wheeled by with Ember, EMT's and a nurse beside her. So peaceful, anyone would've thought she was sleeping, not in a coma.

Roman and Stella followed, watched as they moved her to the hospital bed in the room Stella once inhabited a few doors away from the master suite. A feeding pump, cardiac monitor and other monitors were hooked up. The entire procedure was completed within a half an hour. Just in time for his other guests to arrive.

Hector directed him to the solarium where Tyrone and his mother, Hathoria Gregory, waited. The jumbled story Avery and EJ gave him made limited sense. Better to get the true story from the source.

Roman entered the room only to find it empty with the door to the garden open. He joined Tyrone by the stone birdbath. Roman studied the man, searching for the hidden powers Avery and EJ had detailed. Tyrone appeared the same: tall, muscular, brown skinned, glistening bald head. But where was his mother?

Roman spotted movement by the naked rosebushes. He crossed the garden to greet his guest. Twenty years ago, he'd met Hathoria Gregory. She was a late in life mother, giving birth to her son at age forty-five. Though the natural movements of time had taken their toll, he thought she was beautiful. Widowed shortly after her only child's birth, she struggled as an artist, selling African art on the sidewalk, at street fairs, flea markets, where ever she could.

Brayden and Tyrone had met at The Dalton School. At forty thousand per year, he assumed Tyrone had a scholarship. When Tyrone became a permanent fixture at his dinner table, Roman did a cursory investigation and found a modest trust fund, which paid for Tyrone's education. His late father had provided for his family.

Christmas was the last time he saw Mrs. Gregory. Though frail and clearly starting to wither, she had a vibrancy that made him look at her twice and try to picture the woman she was 50 years ago. The beautiful woman coaxing a dormant bud to blossom on the rose bush couldn't be her.

The wrinkles at her eyes and laugh lines bracketing her mouth were gone, replaced by smooth, tight, perfect milk chocolate skin. The tight skin at her chin revealed a slender, elegant neck. Supple hands clasped the rose. Her swollen knuckles and misshaped fingers had vanished along with the age spots that once speckled her skin.

Roman looked into her eyes. Eyes that were milky from cataracts, now were bright, honey brown and staring right through him.

All of her was golden. She sparkled in the sunlight and seemed to hover above the grass. It had to be a trick of light. Suddenly, she was young and old at the same time. The husk of the woman Roman knew stood on terra firma, while the serene, beautiful young woman hovered above.

When the sun faded behind a cloud, the hovering form sunk into the old woman and the two merged. The youthful glow faded and the Hathoria Gregory that Roman knew, sighed. She breathed deeply and turned her milky gaze toward him.

"Mrs. Gregory." Roman greeted her with a small bow.

She smiled. "I've always liked you, Roman. Otherwise, I never would've allowed my only child to associate with this family."

"I would expect nothing less from any parent." He extended his arm and guided her back to the solarium.

Seated on the lounge, sipping a cup of tea, she stared at him over the rim. "We are here at your request. I am ready for you to ask your questions."

Roman glanced at Tyrone. His neutral expression gave nothing away. "What are you?"

She smiled and the familiar wrinkles moved in slow motion. "I am Hathor. You would know me as the Goddess of Love."

For the first time in his life, Roman had no answer.

Hathor sucked her teeth and muttered a curse. "Men." Like stepping from one plane to the next, she peeled the façade of the elder off as if it was a jacket she wore to keep the cold away.

Before Roman's eyes stood loveliness. Dressed in traditional Egyptian robes of a simple linen sheath and a collar made of turquoise, lapis, and gold, kohl lined her eyes in a supple face. She was regal. Power radiated from her body.

Roman fell to his knees in adoration. He loved this woman. This woman was his mother, lover, wife, child-

"Enough, Mother." Tyrone commanded.

She sighed heavily. "If felt so good to be me for a moment." She withdrew and again she was Hathoria Gregory, elderly, dignified matron.

It took him a moment to come to his senses again. To shake off the overwhelming love he felt and remember who, and where he was. He stood slowly and looked at the shrunken woman facing him. Roman's mind raced. After two thousand years, he'd seen a lot—but not this.

"Goddess." Wary, he honored her with another short bow, but never took his gaze from her.

A giggle escaped and behind her eyes, something stirred. "It is good to be me."

At present, she looked like anyone's mother, elderly, and slight in form, ready and able to care for her son with a meal and a tongue-lashing. It was all a deception. She was so much more. A goddess sat before him. He could never claim any psychic ability, but all of his senses told him this did not bode well.

"If I was younger, I would turn the intensity of your stare into something much more satisfying."

Roman blushed and looked away. Then he caught himself. He hadn't blushed since his initiation.

She gave a throaty laugh. "One is never too old to experience youth. Blush while you still can. Immortal or not, take the full measure of joy." She seemed younger again, stronger, straighter in the chair opposite him.

"Leave be, Mother." Tyrone snapped. "Stop expending energy you don't have."

Once more, she withered. "What do you know?" She grumbled like a cantankerous child. "Don't lecture me. I am still your mother and I out-rank you."

Roman gave Tyrone a quizzical look. "So what are you, Tyrone? If your mother is a goddess, what does that make you?"

"I am *niSf Al-laah,* a demi-god." Tyrone took a swig from his bottle of beer.

"My husband, his father, was human. My love sustained him for longer than a normal human would have lived but in the end, he left us."

"Forgive me for asking, but, how old are you?"

"So asks the two thousand year old man. Whose age are you asking? Hathoria's or Hathor's?"

"Both." He shrugged.

"This shell, this woman that is Hathoria Gregory, who loved and gave birth, she is 150 years old."

"Are you going to die?" Roman asked.

Tyrone gagged and beer trickled down his chin.

"How old are you, Tyrone?" Roman asked. "A hundred or so?"

"No, he's 27 years old." Hathoria took a sip of tea.

"And Hathor?" Roman persisted.

"The Goddess of Love? I have been here since the beginning, in one form or another. I am the peace after war, the healing after the hurt, the blessing after the curse, the baby after the birth. How long have I been here? I don't even know."

"Are you dying?" Roman repeated.

"Considering that this body is human, yes, eventually I will fail."

"And when that happens?"

"I'll return from whence I came. To Chemmis. To exile. I've been free for so long I won't know how to assimilate. I must though. I'll miss all that I have here." She looked toward her son. "But I'll never be far."

"And you, Tyrone?" Roman studied the man he welcomed into his family as a brother.

"I'm immortal. I'm gifted with *some* abilities." Tyrone shrugged.

"Obviously," Roman said dryly. "Brayden and the others told me what happened. I suspect you have more to add."

Tyrone sighed. He glanced at his mother and received a slight nod. "Your twin is corrupted—"

"I know that already." He sensed that from the moment he saw Reign. "Tell me something I don't know." Roman glared at Tyrone.

"By a god and something else." Tyrone finished.

Roman's shoulders fell.

"You already knew," Hathoria whispered.

"Not about the god part." Roman wished he had a glass of whiskey. "For so long, we were equals in all things, the best warriors Thrace had to offer. We fought for our country, our honor, and our family." Dead memories crawled into the sunlight. "Sometime around our twentieth year, I faltered, began to doubt our purpose. My conscience ate at me and I began to see the men I killed on the battlefield…apparitions. I tried to ignore them, but they wouldn't leave me. They tainted me with their hate."

"In the middle of a battle I succumbed, better to die beneath the blade than a crazed fool roaming the countryside. Reign saved me, not just from the battle. He took the souls that haunted me into himself. I don't know how he did it. He never spoke of it, but he shouldered the guilt for both of us. My brother saved my sanity." Roman shuddered. He scrubbed a hand over his face to chase the memories away. "We've always been able to sense each other."

"And now what do you sense?" Hathoria pushed.

"An endless pool of rage."

"Did you cost him his soul?" Hathoria leaned forward, her gaze unforgiving.

From the first, Roman had avoided that question. "Not at first, but yes. I'm first born. I should've accepted the responsibility for both of us—"

"Your brother did what you couldn't." Hathoria touched his forearm.

Roman pulled his arm away and stood. "You don't understand." His fist balled, needing to hit something. "He removed my conscience and with it went all my inhibitions. I became a person we both despised, until I met Elyssian and she gave me back part of what was missing." He paced like a caged animal. "My brother is haunted by the men we slew as mercenaries."

"Why just those men? You have soldiered in many wars since your brother was imprisoned. What was different about those men you've killed?" Tyrone questioned.

"Those wars were just and my reasons for fighting weren't about payment."

"Roman, we are mercenaries now." Tyrone stood. Aggression crackled from him.

"True. And every client or company we've protected has been just. I made sure," Roman stated. The conviction in his voice didn't waver.

Some of the tension eased from Tyrone. His shoulders relaxed and the heat left his eyes. "Reign is out of control. I'm the only thing that stopped him from killing everyone in the club. And he has the powers of a god," Tyrone said.

"I sensed Nephythys when I gifted you my vis'Ras, Tau," Hathoria said using her son's nickname.

"Who is Nephythys?" Roman asked.

"Goddess of the Dead. SET's wife. She sits in judgment of the souls condemned to the Underworld. She's often fair in her judgments, but always bitter toward her husband and her son, Anubis." Hathoria spat and shifted in her chair.

The pieces of the puzzle started to fit together. "Alamut said his master was Anubis."

"Who is Alamut?" Hathoria asked.

"Alamut is or was Daniel. A hybrid beast, part man, part cobra and part crocodile. Stella and I dismembered him in the woods outside of my cabin."

"Quimaera, they are called. Devils created by a petty child," she murmured with a distance gaze. They waited for her to continue. "Eons ago, an invading warrior promised his daughter in exchange for an army to defeat a pharaoh. The quimaera were the result."

"Three of those things attacked Reign." Tyrone stood next to Hathoria's chair.

"My men said he killed them without raising a sweat." *Yet it took half the night to kill one and only after Stella returned gifted with all the spirits Elyssian inhabited.* Roman wished his cup held more than tea.

"Not him, his sword. Mother, it spoke in your ancient tongue," Tyrone said.

"How did he kill them?" Roman leaned closer. Avery and EJ had told him their version of events, one more perspective could help.

"The sword turned crimson and the beast disappeared." Tyrone said. "He incinerated them."

"Crimson? Those are Nephythys's colors," Hathoria added.

"How many more of the animals are there?" Roman said.

"Depends on how many Anubis made. I doubt he stopped at four." Hathoria placed her cup back on the tray.

"But now we know how to kill them." Tyrone started to fill another cup for his mother, but she waved him away.

"No, Reign knows how to kill them. We know nothing." Roman looked at Hathoria. "Can you kill them?"

"I-I," Flustered, she rose. "I am the Goddess of Love. My vis'Ra cannot kill."

"Mother." Heads together, they mumbled in their own language.

"But what does it matter? They are all dead," she cried. Her hands trembled.

Roman sensed there was more at stake here than finally killing Alamut. "Not all. Alamut is dismembered, not dead. I have him stored in my vault." Roman stood. Grim, he was ready to plead his case to get her cooperation.

They whispered more until Hathoria nodded.

"Come with me." Roman escorted them from the solarium. As they passed the game room, Avery, EJ and Thane joined them.

Yet one person was missing.

They crossed the vestibule and the doorbell rang. Hector opened the door.

Tyrone leaped in front of his mother. "What is he doing here?" he shouted. Hathoria moved from behind her son's protective shield and approached Reign and Detective Lever with her son close on her heals.

"Hello, I'm Hathoria Gregory. You are Roman's missing twin." She spoke. "Yes, Nephythys' signature *vis*'Ra taints you…however, something else is there." She pressed a finger into the center of his chest. "A deep well of untapped power."

She glanced at Roman. By her raised brows and pursed lips, a question had formed.

"Why is he here?" Avery growled.

Tensions in the room took an upswing. "He killed three of the beasts. I invited him here to kill this one." Roman led the way to the cellar. He walked over to the barrel and pressed. The wall receded and slid to the right revealing the steel door of the vault. He punched in the code and the door hissed before it swung open. Interior lights automatically flickered on. Roman entered the vault.

The canisters which held Daniel were scattered on the floor, empty. Roman stormed back out. "What have you done?" He charged across the room.

The first punch slammed into Reign's chin, rocking his head back. He ducked the next, but Roman waited for Reign's head to snap around and landed a one-two jab, and an uppercut combo that dropped Reign to one knee.

In a boxer's stance, bouncing slightly on the balls of his feet, fists ready for more, Roman waited.

***

Alexis's heart lodged in her throat. Since watching her brothers, John and Thomas, beat each other daily in the backyard, boxing was not her favorite sport. She hated standing here watching Reign and his brother slug it out. Yet she couldn't help rooting for one particular man.

Reign exploded to his feet. His shoulder smashed into Roman's gut and lifted him. He flipped him over and tossed him into a wine rack. Bottles shattered and the heady bouquet of fermented grapes filled the air. Roman dropped down and aimed a kick at Reign's kneecap. A sickening crunch echoed. The unexpected shift caused Reign's other knee to give out and he fell into the glass-covered, wine-soaked floor.

He didn't stay there for long.

Roman hoisted Reign and slammed him into a row of barrels lining the wall. He clocked two jabs into Reign's face before his brother grabbed his fist and hauled him off balance. A head butt knocked Roman into the opposite rack.

Alexis couldn't take anymore. She took a step forward. Hathoria blocked her path and gently touched her arm.

"You're worried, yet he's in no danger. Look at him." Hathoria nodded at the men destroying the cellar. "They're doing more damage to the room than themselves. They're letting off steam, as only men can do."

"By beating each other to death?" She grimaced as Reign slipped in the spilled wine and cracked his skull against the side of a fallen rack. Jagged pieces of glass protruded from his thigh. He yanked them out and continued to fight.

"Yes, stupid I know, but alas, they are only men. Immortal men." The elderly woman pushed her back, out of harm's way, and smiled at her startled reaction.

"If they wanted to kill each other, they would have drawn weapons, yet neither have. Look around you at the men gathered. They're enjoying this because this isn't about death."

Alexis glanced around the room. Stationed near the vault, she had a bird's eye view of the night's entertainment and the other occupants. Roman and Reign were the center of attention, but those relegated to the sideline drew her attention. Avery and EJ shadow boxed, grinning wildly with each punch Roman landed and flinching with every bone numbing connection. So did the other men. With each blow Reign received, her refrain shattered a little bit more until she gasped every time he groaned and she clasped her hands together to keep from reaching for him.

Reign had his brother in a headlock, while Roman punished Reign's kidneys with blows to the back. But, by the delight on his bruised face, Reign enjoyed every second.

"It's about reconnecting." A smile spread across Alexis's face and Hathoria joined her.

"I'm taking you home, Mother." Tyrone took her arm.

Hathoria slapped his hand away. "No, you are not," she said without taking her eyes off the action. "This is the most fun

I've had in a while and I can take care of myself." She glanced at her son and giggled.

A piercing scream stopped the fight and everyone turned to the entrance. Hector tripped down the stairs and nearly face-planted on the concrete landing. The butler paused after his Cole Haans took the first step on the wine soaked floor and made his way over to a splintered rack. He lifted a fragment of a bottle.

"You've destroyed an entire rack of *Rothschilds!*" He cradled the label in the palm of his hand. He dropped it and ran over to another smashed rack. "The *Conti,*" he sobbed. "They're all gone." He turned to Avery and EJ and pointed a finger. "Move!" His voice boomed around the room and the two men scattered like chastised children.

Hector rushed over to one of the last intact racks and gently caressed each rare bottle. "Thank you, Jesus for sparing the *Latife* and the *Massandra.*"

"We protected them for you, Hector." EJ sucked up and Avery wisely stepped away from his sibling's side.

Standing at opposite ends of the room, both heaving in great gulps of air, Roman and Reign glared at each other...but prideful identical smirks crossed their faces. They enjoyed this stupid display of brawn. Hathoria caught Alexis's eye and both women shook their heads in disgust.

"Are you two idiots done, 'cause this trip and slugfest accomplished nothing." Alexis folded her arms under her breasts.

"You are correct, Alexis." Reign wiped the blood from his lip and plucked glass fragments from his arms. In front of their eyes, his wounds fused together.

"Damn, he heals faster than Roman," EJ mumbled to Avery.

"Come, Alexis. We go." He held out his hand for her.

He did *not* just use that master-slave tone with her.

"You're not leaving until you tell me where you hid Alamut's body," Roman growled.

Reign's hand dropped to his side. "I do not have his body."

"You broke into the vault the last time. You could have done it again and taken him." Thane jumped in.

Reign's gaze never wavered from Roman's. "You question my honor, *brother*?" Alexis heard the warning in Reign's voice and tensed.

"If you don't have him, then who?" Roman stated.

"I suspect another god." Hathoria's calm voice seemed to echo in the room.

"Anubis retrieved his slave?" Tyrone moved closer to his mother. "It's more than likely."

The two worked as a unit, Alexis noted.

"If it was Anubis, why did he wait so long to pick up his pet?" Roman demanded.

"Time moves different in Chemmis, Roman." Hathoria picked her way through the broken glass and wine-soaked floor without her son's help, and stood between the combatants. "An hour there is more like two to three days here."

"Do you detect the presence of another god here, Mother?" Tyrone asked.

Hathoria shook her head. "No, Anubis's trace has long since disappeared. Nothing remains, however, I believe Reign. I see no deception in him."

"When we find him, you will kill him," Roman commanded Reign.

Reign's face contorted in fury. His blade appeared, glowing crimson. "You, *brother*, have never ordered me to do anything and you will not now. You lead this gang of misfit lost boys, a false prophet promising salvation when you have never saved anyone or any—"

Alexis blinked and she and Reign were standing in the driveway, next to her car. "What just happened? Did you do that?"

"No, I did not. That old woman. I sensed there was more to her than at first glance."

"How could she?"

Then she thought of Mrs. Kelly and her hidden skill at sifting through people. She had to stop looking at things and only seeing the obvious. Otherwise, she wouldn't last long.

***

Mother, what did you do? Tyrone asked privately.

Hathoria Gregory shrugged her shoulders. *I returned them to their car. Another moment and true blood would've flowed. Brother shouldn't kill brother.*

Roman turned to her. "Did you do that?"

"Yes," Hathor answered.

Footsteps clicked on the cellar stairs. Stella stopped at the landing and gasped as she took in the damaged wine racks. "What the hell happened?"

"You must be Stella." Hathor threaded her way through the debris to the landing. "I'm Tyrone's mother. It's a pleasure to meet you. Your husband and his twin decided to use their brains to settle their disputes." She gestured to the chaos around them. "Unfortunately, the two half-wits didn't get far."

Roman joined them. He pulled his wife into his arms, but she pushed away and whipped the blood from his forehead and chin.

"Are you okay?" she asked.

He gave her a smile which she warily returned. The love between them was deep, lasting, forged through millennia of trials. Hathor was never able to puzzle who had cursed Roman Nicolis. His past was an enigma, which refused to be solved. Still, it was good to see a couple survive the whims of fate.

The goddess within her stirred and sent a blessing their way. A barrier flared, blocking her power. She recoiled. Wards—unseen until her blessing reached for them—surrounded the couple. The origins were somewhere in the house.

"Mother?" *Are you all right?"* Her son's voice filled her mind. His arms steadied her.

She ignored him and turned toward the stairs. The presence of another god resided in this mansion. She focused her energy and pinpointed its location. As she flashed, Hathoria Gregory melted away. The goddess, Hathor, swept through the house, passed through a closed door and into a bedroom.

A child lay in a sick bed surrounded by machines, which monitored her bodily functions. But illness wasn't what threatened the child's health. Waves of forest green tinted energy leaped from the body and suffused the room. Bright and healing, so many of its strands mimicked hers, but their vis'Ra eclipsed Hathor's paltry energy. She fell to her knees cowering, praying this unknown deity would only imprison her, and punish, not kill her son.

"How dare you," the voice hissed hovering above her.

Afraid to lift her head, Hathor mumbled, "Forgive me, Great Goddess." The light faded and she could see the hem of a brown gown trimmed in gold. Only one god wore those colors. Hathor raised her head and stared at the mother of the Egyptian Pantheon.

"Rise, Hathor."

She obeyed and considered Nu, while the Eldest Goddess, studied her.

"Why have you come here?" Nu demanded.

"I am an invited guest by Roman Nicolis and mother to one he claims as his own, though my child is not of his seed."

"I know of him. And you. Your time here is short, Hathor. The body you inhabit is close to its end. That is how you passed through my outer wards unencumbered." The goddess's eyebrows knit together in deep thought.

"The body you inhabit, Great Goddess, withers from your infestation." She noted, purposely looking at the declining child.

Anger sparked in Nu's eyes. Hathor lowered her gaze.

"My weaves protect this family from harm. What are your intentions, Hathor?"

"I have no intentions other than to be of help to my son and those who have always been a friend and ally to me and my offspring." Hathor bowed low.

Running feet pounded down the hallway.

"You will tell them nothing of my presence," Nu commanded.

My son will question me. How to deceive him? They had never lied to each other.

Nu vanished. The door flew open and rebounded from the wall. Hathor spun around as the room filled with Tyrone, Roman, and Stella.

Stella rushed to the child.

"Everything is fine. The child's ill spirit called to me. I came to heal her." The lie twisted her gut and Tyrone looked at her sharply. So in tune with each other, she saw the suspicion in his amber eyes.

"Did you heal her, will my sister be okay?" Stella held onto the child's hand.

Feeling courageous, she extended another strand of energy and skimmed the little girl. The body was well-formed and strong, but she couldn't handle the essence contained within. Nu used the girl like a parasite to hold her spirit and every time she used her vis'Ra, the child's life force drained, thus limiting the goddess. That potent display of power would cost her.

"Yes. She will be fine and eventually she will awaken." Hathor faded and Hathoria replaced her. "I tire. I shall leave you now." She retreated from the room.

Back in the hallway, Tyrone touched her arm. "What was that all about?"

"Leave be, Tau. There is more here at work than Anubis and Nephythys," Hathoria whispered.

"Tell me."

She shook her head and felt her abnormally long years weighing on her body. "No. On this you will have to trust and not question."

His features shuttered. He gave her a stiff half-bow, then pivoted and stormed down the hall. She wanted to order him to stay away, but that would only spur him to action. On this, she must remain silent and pray whatever plans Nu had for this Nicolis family, didn't involve her or her only child.

CHAPTER TWENTY-FOUR

The long drive home didn't help Alexis's frayed nerves. Especially with Reign sitting next to her. He stared straight ahead, focusing on nothing. Still bloody from his recent brawl, his brooding silence didn't answer the questions pounding against her temple. And it annoyed the hell out of her. Alexis swore she didn't want to speak to him, but his complete ignorance of her presence grated her resolve.

"You enjoyed that, didn't you?" she snapped. "Had a grand time beating Roman to a pulp?"

A wicked grin tugged at the corner of his sensual mouth causing a responding tug low in her groin. A horn blared.

"Shit!" Alexis jerked the wheel and corrected her drifting car.

"I could get us home in an instant." He offered.

Even though her head pounded and exhaustion tugged on her senses, she didn't like the whole '*Beam Me Up*' thing. She needed all her atoms in one fixed location, thank you. And since when did *her* home become *his* home.

"Just answer the question, Reign." Her gaze darted between him and the road.

"Yes, I should have beaten him before." His hands balled up. "It felt…" he paused, searching for a word, "good." A wide smile transformed his harsh face. The cuts on his lip and cheek had vanished, leaving nothing but perfect skin.

"Would you have killed him?"

His brows furrowed and his gaze turned distant, unfocused. "No. Never would I harm my brother."

"Then why did your sword appear?"

"Did it?" He shook his head. "No. It did not appear."

"Yes, Reign. If that *woman* hadn't flashed us out of there, I think you would've stabbed him." How could he not remember clutching it in his hand?

"I do not remember the sword." He scrubbed a shaky hand across his forehead.

"So, what about you and that goddess your brother mentioned?" She tried to change the subject and ended up sounding like a needy girlfriend. Damn, that was the last thing she wanted.

He paused so long she thought he wouldn't answer. "She and I have a pact."

Jealousy shriveled her tongue. What type of pact could he have with a goddess? Her mind raced through the endless possibilities, each one worse than the other. She had no right to ask and he had no obligation to answer. That didn't stop her heart from wanting an explanation. She was a detective, damn it! Questioning people for a living was what she did.

"Is she pretty?" Alexis blurted at a red light. *Oh, God.* She groaned and wanted to bury her head in the steering wheel. Humiliated, she couldn't look at him.

"Yes. She is beautiful." His frigid voice matched the icy waves rolling off him. Her breath curled in the air.

Alexis looked at him and nearly drowned in the depth of his eyes. Those eyes did something to her. They made her think of long nights surrounded by his naked body and orgasms that didn't come from Duracell. A ripple cascaded through her core.

But that steamy look wasn't for her.

She turned away and focused on the red light. Traipsing down this path would lead nowhere. Better to think of the investigation than the man sitting next to her.

Daniel Nicolis had more lives than a cat, she thought. This was the third time he had been resurrected and vanished. The blare of a train drew her attention to the station on her left. Brakes hissed as the train rolled in and lined up with the platform. Doors snapped opened and people tumbled out. The commuters disembarked and streaked in front of her car to the parking lot on the opposite side of the street. Mainly business people comprised the lot, with a few college kids thrown into the mix. A commuter tossed a greasy bag and drink into the trash. Not five seconds later, a homeless man snatched both items from the bin and shuffled away.

Alexis couldn't take her eyes from him as he entered the train station. A car horn beeped behind her, but she couldn't move. Her mind had stuck at the crossroad where the businessmen, the college kids, and the homeless man intersected.

"Alexis."

Reign's voice snapped her out of her reverie. She glanced in her rearview mirror at the line of angry drivers and hit the gas a second before the yellow light turned red. She made an illegal U-turn at the next light and raced back to the station.

She parked and jumped out of the car. The few remaining stragglers gave her a wide berth as she ran inside the station searching for a map. She found it framed in a dim corner. A layer of dust coated the commuter railroad map with its listings of stations extending through New York, Long Island and parts of New Jersey. Mario's words came back to her. Tarrytown was where the businesses were found. Her index finger landed on the station.

Riverdale—where the students were found. Another finger, another station.

Downtown covered a wide area. She didn't know where they found the homeless, but she'd bet her paycheck it was near Grand Central Station. A shadow cut the glare of the overhead fluorescent bulbs.

Alexis glanced up. She was surprised Reign hadn't interrupted her thoughts with demands for answers. His inquisitive eyes searched her face, but he waited for her to speak as if he respected her opinion.

She turned back to the map. "I think the unaccounted beasts are feeding." The word stuck in her throat. She opened her phone and googled the information. "The businessmen were killed first, the students next and then the homeless, here in the Bronx. A station was near each scene, leading away from the factory. "I think they're following the railroad tracks."

"Why?"

"It's an easy way to travel. Access in and out of the city."

"Again, I ask why."

She had no answer for a good question. "A better question is what if Daniel has met up with the missing animals and he's leading this merry band."

That shut Mr. Twenty Questions up.

"We have to find him," Reign said.

Again with the 'we'. She studied the map. *If they were feeding, where would they go next?* No matter how hard she studied the map, it offered no clues.

"May I make a suggestion, Detective?"

He'd never called her that before. Did he just mock her? Alexis whipped around, ready to take an inch off his height and a yard of skin off his ass. Concern, not arrogance, graced his face. She didn't trust him or the concern, at least she shouldn't have. But some of the fight went out of her. "What?"

Another train pulled into the station. The doors dinged and opened, releasing a stream of commuters. Like a boulder embedded in a riverbed, people swept around Reign and Alexis.

He pointed to the train. "Do these machines rest at night?"

Alexis stifled a laugh and shook her head. "Machines don't need rest, Reign. They need—"

Maintenance! She searched the map again and pleaded with God for it to be there.

Yes!

She found it. And only twenty miles from south of the factory, in The Bronx.

The High Bridge Train Depot was situated yards away from a homeless settlement living under the stone arch of High Bridge.

One mile from Yankee stadium.

And the opening game of The World Series.

CHAPTER TWENTY-FIVE

The train yard was easy to find once you knew where to look. Alexis parked her car on Sedgwick Ave. She glanced at the time on her cell phone. The game had started an hour ago. And give or take ninety minutes the stadium would empty, sending seventy thousand fans into the street at one time.

Somewhere out there a dinner bell would ring.

The access road to the train yard was straight ahead, however, after crossing the overpass Alexis and Reign made a sharp left. The street-lights failed to illuminate this dark strip of land between the street and the chain link fence. The tall brush on the embankment snagged Alexis's hair and coat. She stifled a yelp, but couldn't stop the grunt of pain. Strong hands grasped her shoulders. Fingers spread through her hair, freeing the tresses.

"Better?" Reign asked when she turned around. His deep, soothing voice came out of the darkness. Calloused fingers stroked her cheek.

She couldn't help turning her head into his palm. "Yeah." How had this happened? How had he wormed his way into her heart in a few short days? The wind kicked up, whipping her hair and sending a chill down her spine. Yanked away from her thoughts, she wrapped her arms around her body and shivered while Reign stood coatless next to her.

"Aren't you cold?" she asked.

"Yes, but I have fought in worse climes, dressed in less."

Okay. If ever there was an image to post on Facebook. Nope. That image will forever remain in my personal file.

Reign walked ahead of her, his sword clasped in his hand. He cut a path through the brush. She had to admit they worked well together. He listened to her, actually looked her in the eyes, and paid attention. Even followed her lead.

She didn't complain when he sliced an opening in the barbed wire fence surrounding the train yard, which saved her from crawling under. Weak sodium vapor lights cast rows of boxcars and tracks in a yellowish glow. The pungent scents of gasoline, tar, and manure, overlaid with decaying wood, assaulted her nostrils.

Their feet crunched the gravel lining the track bed. So much for the silent approach, yet nothing unexpected leaped out at them as they walked the perimeter. She grabbed a handhold on the side of a railcar, hauled herself up onto a ladder, and crossed between the cars. Reign waited on the other side. Firm hands grabbed her waist and he lifted. Her breasts and belly skimmed his hard torso.

Now wasn't the time for this. And never was perfect. Whatever she thought she felt was futile. This relationship— scratch that—this temporary partnership would end as soon as the quimaera were defeated and he returns to, *her*...his goddess. That should have quelled her libido.

Her feet touched the ground, but he didn't release her. His hands slid to her hips and settled. He pulled her closer against his hard shaft.

Her body wanted this, craved a spark, any attention he could throw her way. She wouldn't give in.

"Must be nice having a goddess so lovesick she loans you her powers." She wanted to sound angry. Instead, she ended up breathless and needy.

His hands tightened on her hips. "It was not nice."

His rough voice dragged over her. She looked into his shadowed face even though she didn't need to see his expression when she could feel his anger in the hands clutching her.

"Nothing about it was nice," he said.

"Really? Is that why you hung around so long? I find it hard to believe a big strong capable warrior such as you couldn't find a way to escape in two thousand years, if he wanted to. Or die trying."

His hands dropped and balled into meaty fists. She'd struck a nerve, yet he didn't move away.

"You loved her, didn't you," Alexis whispered.

His chest heaved and a long sigh passed between them. "Once. So long ago, I no longer remember the emotion. All that's left is hate." He turned away.

Alexis touched his arm, halting him. "The opposite of love isn't hate, Reign. Hate is just love gone bad."

A faint scream drifted on the wind.

Reign and Alexis both spun.

"Where did that come from?" Alexis scanned every direction, hoping to catch the sound again.

"I do not know." Reign studied their surroundings.

"We should split up. You go in that direction." Alexis pointed south. "And I'll go this way." She didn't wait for his approval to start walking north along the tracks.

"Have you forgotten I cannot leave your side? And even if we could 'split up', I would not leave you." He strode ahead of her.

Fine. If he wanted to be Mr. Bulletproof, she wouldn't stop him. They jogged between the rows of boxcars until one row ended and the yard opened up showing a few brick houses and five rows of empty tracks. Up ahead were more trains and High Bridge, the oldest standing and only pedestrian bridge in New York City.

"I see light." Reign pointed toward an arch of the stone and steel structure.

With his height, of course he did. She couldn't see anything but train cars. They started in that direction. A breeze brought a mixture of scents to her: wet decay from The Harlem River, machine oil, a hint of smoke from burning wood…and *That Smell!*

A scream shattered the silence and abruptly ended on a gurgle.

She pulled her phone from her pocket and pressed 911. "I need an ambulance at the High Bridge train yard. Under the bridge. Multiple people injured." Alexis ran, but the crunch of their feet didn't drown out the sounds of flesh hitting flesh or the snap of bones breaking.

Reign's big body darted in front of her. She struggled to catch up as he outpaced her stride. He shouted what sounded like a curse and skidded to a halt. Alexis swerved and stopped beside him.

The boxcars had ended but the yard had widened in a work area then narrowed to a single track under the bridge, which passed a homeless encampment.

Quimaera, too many to count, swarmed the encampment.

"Holy—" Alexis pulled out her gun. She steadied her shaking hand, aimed and fired. Shell casings plinked as they ejected and hit the gravel. By the time she emptied her clip, she had all of the quimaera's attention.

"What now?" She looked at Reign.

His glowing eyes pulsed in time with the jagged, crimson sword in his hand. He glanced between her and the advancing animals.

"Run."

Reign grabbed her hand. Breathing hard, Alexis kept pace. She could hear them; their claws scraped the loose gravel as they gained ground. Their rancid odor filled the air. Reign scooped her up and continued to run.

"Where are we going?" She wheezed, breathless.

He stopped at a boxcar. One slice from his blade and the handle fell to the roadbed. He pushed the door open and flashed them inside. The car smelled of stale air and rotted food.

"Why didn't you do that before?" she asked as Reign backed her into a corner.

"I needed them to follow."

One beast leaped into the car. Others followed. Eager to join the party, they filled the interior.

"B-b-but, you've trapped us in here."

"No, I have trapped me in here." Reign stabbed his sword into the roof of the stock car. One circular swept opened a hole. He hoisted Alexis up and shoved her through.

"Go," he shouted and the rest of his words were lost in a cacophony of snarls. One second he was there, the next gone.

"Reign!" She almost jumped back into the car.

"Go."

The muffled word halted her *Wonder Woman* instincts. He didn't need her in there distracting him from surviving.

Alexis jogged across the curved roof and descended the ladder. She heard a shout, a deep guttural sound that wrenched her soul and nearly made her return to the opening and throw herself into the fight. She didn't, because conventional weapons were useless against these things. That didn't mean she couldn't help. One hundred feet, not a great distance. That's all she needed to yank him out of there.

The tip of his sword shot through the side of the car, near the handhold. Blood trailed from the edge and dripped down the wood before he—or something—yanked it out.

She stared at the wet wood.

It's not Reign. It's not Reign.

The words became a litany in her head until the warble of a siren caught her attention. She jumped and rolled to her feet. From a jog to a run, one hundred feet became a marathon as she ran toward the growing wails and flashing lights.

CHAPTER TWENTY-SIX

Reign backed up as the quimaera piled into the tight quarters inside the stock car. Five became eight, then ten as more continued to enter, including Alamut. Reign couldn't see him in the mass of beasts but knew by the humming of his senses that Anubis's champion was here.

He flexed his shoulders, widened his stance, and braced for the coming battle. His sword throbbed in time with his increasing heartbeat, which drowned out the snarling animals.

The first one lunged. Reign planted his sword deep in its gut. The blade incinerated the beast from the inside out as he kicked another back into the pack.

He yanked his sword free and flashed to the doorway. A hard tug slammed it closed. He faded and passed through the crowd before the beasts reached him. The darkness of their combined souls amplified the churning pit within him. The Vanquished howled. They wanted blood and wouldn't be denied.

"We meet again, Reign," Alamut barked.

"I remember. You tormented my brother and his wife. She stopped you. Twice. Fallen by a slip of a woman. Now you challenge me?" The blade dimmed a notch, losing its ability to incinerate. No quick death for Alamut. The Vanquished wanted sport. They craved Alamut's blood.

No! Reign shook his head to clear the rage-induced haze clouding his mind. He couldn't kill him. No matter what the cost Alamut had to survive.

Reign evaded, buying time for his need to kill his enemy to subside. Alamut charged. But the blade would not be denied.

Two swipes, a duck and fade, left two beasts armless and the blade piercing the chest of his enemy with a knee pressed to his neck. Behind Reign, the remaining pack of quimaera closed in.

"Order your minions to cease," Reign roared.

"Kill me and be free to return to your slavery."

Reign faded and passed through Alamut. He wrapped his arm around Alamut's throat. His other hand grabbed the beast's snout and yanked in the opposite direction. He knew it wouldn't kill him. But the satisfying snap appeased his personal demons. He jerked his sword free as Alamut fell and returned his knee in the center of Alamut's chest.

"What? No flaming death?" Head at an abnormal angle, the beast's words slurred.

"If you want to continue drawing breath, never cross my path again." Reign crouched close to Alamut's head.

"You don't want to kill?" A crooked smile further warped his face. "Don't like being a goddess's bitch? Can't blame you. So you and I need to come to an agreement—"

"I let you live and you disappear. That is our agreement." Reign growled.

"Why? When you are bound by Nephythys to kill me? As I am bound by Anubis to bring you to him. We need to have an exchange."

"You have nothing I desire."

"Not even Alexis's life?"

A cold knot formed in Reign's chest. He grabbed Alamut's throat. Crimson light bled from his hand. Alamut's skin smoked beneath Reign's palm. Alamut vanished. His true form—Daniel Nicolis—returned.

Reign hauled Daniel up and dangled him in the air. "Touch Alexis and you will never know a day without agony. You live at my discretion. You live because I choose the timing of your death."

Daniel's face tightened, but he didn't struggle as Reign expected a warrior would. A warrior would fight to the end; die with honor cloaked around him. Even in defeat, he would leave his heart, along with his body on the battlefield knowing that with his final breath, he gave all for his cause. He refused to believe this pile of dung descended from his father's bloodline.

Reign flung Daniel to the ground. The blade to his neck stopped Daniel from moving. "How could Anubis think you worthy to be a champion? You are a poor excuse of a man."

"Yeah, but you keep talking of killing me. So, you want something."

Reign warred with the Vanquished before he managed to ease the blade from taking Daniel's head. Reign stepped back and allowed Daniel to rise.

Reign's pulsating blade touched his enemy's gut. It glowed brightly, prepared to incinerate as Daniel transformed into Alamut. The beast towered over Reign and the hostile crowd at his back bristled. "You will leave this place, this land and never return."

"Ah, now, we bargain. Well, bargains are made with blood," Alamut snarled.

Reign ran his hand along the edge of his blade, slicing his palm open. He flicked his wrist and the tip of his sword parted the skin over Alamut's heart. Reign slapped his hand against Alamut's wound. "There. You have my blood promise."

"That's not whose blood I'm talking about." Alamut face stretched into a horrific grin. Before Reign could move, Alamut's jaw unhinged. He seized Reign by the shoulder. Muscles shredded. Bones snapped. Reign's howl of pain drowned in the yapping and barking of the beasts as Alamut tossed him to them.

Claws and teeth tore into his flesh as they fought over the right to devour him. Fury burned through the pain, leaving unquenchable rage. His barriers dropped. Reign became the thing he most despised, *el Mortem*.

Cold fury singed his nerve endings. He drew on it, poured the energy into his sword arm, and channeled it into the blade. The quimaera fell like wheat at harvest. Some tried to escape, but Reign shielded the car, trapping them inside.

Flames consumed them before their bodies hit the floor. Death came quickly with nary a scream to mark the end, leaving none standing. But their souls attached themselves to Reign, weighing him down, dragging him to the lip of the precipice. Only thoughts of Alexis kept him from succumbing to the waiting abyss. He held on, focused on her beautiful face, and what lay in his heart.

A scream echoed in the night.

Alexis! While he allowed The Vanquished their pleasure, she was hurt.

What had he done?

***

The damn train yard was a maze. Alexis could hear the sirens and see the strobe lights, but couldn't get to the police. She had to save Reign and the victims. One hundred feet would accomplish one of those goals, but damn it! She was lost. The train yard didn't seem so complicated when they entered.

Alexis doubled back and skidded on the gravel. Daniel blocked her way.

"Halt! You're under arrest. Put your hands above your head and get on the ground." She aimed her weapon at the center of his chest. One move and his heart would add a fifth chamber. She couldn't believe it. She'd caught the Village Strangler and redeemed her career.

Sweat trickled into her eyes. She blinked the sting away. The wind kicked up, bringing that awful odor. Quimaera. Somewhere near. They had to get out of here.

"Turn around." She'd walk him to the police.

A snap echoed, but neither of them had moved. Daniel groaned and in the dim light, his body leaned awkwardly to the right. He jerked, twitched and before her startled eyes, his body changed. Bones snapped and elongated. Muscles ripped and grew, bulged, ripped again, and bulged more. Fingers turned into claws, a tail sprouted from his lower back. His neck thickened. His shoulders widened. A broad snout morphed from his nose and mouth, and pushed his eyes to the side of his head. Those protruding orbs rotated and locked on her.

A tremble started in her gut and spread to each limb. *I don't want to die. Not now. Not like this.*

She dove beneath the nearest train car. Pebbles dug into her skin, cutting her hands and scratching her face. She shimmied to the center. The beast bellowed and slammed into the car. Metal screeched. The train rocked and then settled back on its wheels.

Alexis didn't move, didn't breath. Above her, wood creaked and cracked. Pieces were torn free and littered the ground. She screamed, couldn't stop if she wanted to. Terror had stripped her mind of reason. Alexis prayed, hard and fast. Eyes squeezed closed, she babbled to God, promised him everything if he would just—Silence. The sudden quiet confused and hurt her ears.

A puff of air ruffled her hair. *Dear God.* She angled her head to the right.

Crouched on all fours, it peered beneath the car. Razor sharp teeth showed through a hungry smile. Its pinpoint eyes ran from her face down her body. She reached for her weapon. She may not be able to kill Daniel, but a bullet to this creature's eye would give him something to consider. Her hand slipped into an empty holster. The gun was gone.

Claws stretched beneath the car and raked down her side. Fire laced up her flank. She screamed again. The beast gripped the undercarriage and lifted.

Metal wheels left the track. The train tilted. Then crashed on its side. Alexis tried to scurry away. But the beast loomed. And she bled. Its huge body blocked the dim light cast from the street. It dropped to all fours again and covered her, pinned her to the ground. Sharp pebbles pierced her back. Inches from her face, rows of bloody teeth gleamed, comically white. Noxious breath and drool fanned and coated her skin.

Jaws unhinged and opened wide.

Alexis closed her eyes.

***

Reign scattered his atoms and sent them across the distance separating him from Alexis. He found her lying across the tracks, her fingers splayed to her abdomen, blood seeping between them. Equal parts of terror and defiance plastered her face. Alamut hovered over her, ready to cleave her head from her shoulders.

Reason vanished, leaving undiluted violence. One swipe cleaved Alamut's head from his body. He thrust his blade into his enemy's torso. The sword illuminated the beast from within and turned the pasty skin robin's egg blue. Before he could wrench the blade upward and separated the body into equal halves, Alamut vanished. Only a fine mist remained, which dissipated in the shifting breeze. A hollow chuckle echoed and drifted away.

"Over here!" Someone shouted.

Reign dropped to Alexis's side.

"You have to go. The police are here." Her words hitched on a ragged breath.

Blood had drained from her face, leaving her skin gray and her lips tinged blue. Gently, he moved her hand from the wound.

"No, please leave. They're going to arrest you." She winced with each word.

"Shhh." He pressed his hand over the wound and leaned close.

She bit her bottom lip, but a whimper slipped through. Tears glistened in her wide, glassy eyes.

"I will never leave you," he said.

Her trembling hand reached for him. He grabbed it with his free hand and pressed kisses to her bloody knuckles while he concentrated on healing her torn flesh. Without her to balance him, the Vanquished would win and he would cease to exist. Even if he could survive without Alexis, he didn't want to.

He glanced down. Light emanated from between his fingers and streamed into her side. A cry slid from between her compressed lips. "Forgive my clumsiness."

Alexis shook her head, but she wasn't looking at him. She stared over his shoulder.

"Police! Get away from her!" Someone shouted behind him.

"No, stop." Alexis struggled to push him away, but Reign pinned her shoulder to the ground. He forced more power into her wound. She grabbed his wrist. A backwash of fear flooded his senses. But she didn't fear him. She was afraid *for* him.

Thunder rolled as guns fired.

Reign jerked. Pinpoints of fire bloomed on his back. But he wouldn't let go of her wound. He couldn't stop. With her life in the balance, stopping meant losing them both. Somehow, the tether hadn't just tied his body to her, but also his heart and soul.

A shimmering light enveloped her. Alexis gasped and her breathing eased. Color returned to her face and pain faded from her features. As the light soaked into her, she relaxed and sighed.

Someone tackled him from behind. He tucked and rolled, stopping only when he was on top. His arm cocked, fist clenched to deliver a bone-crunching blow to the man's face. Alexis's shout whipped his head about.

She'd wobbled to her feet and took a careful step toward him. A policeman pushed her back to the ground. She fell hard across the metal tracks, clutching her still tender side. She looked at the officer standing over her, gun pointed at her head.

"I'm a cop," she yelled, her hands raised about her head. That didn't stop the officer from shoving her onto her belly with his boot.

Crazed, Reign leaped to her side and knocked the officer off his feet. Shouted commands came at him. Meaningless words drowned out by the Vanquished screeching for carnage. His palm welcomed the heavy weight of his sword. Its glowing blade a beacon that parted the darkness and called for their deaths.

He crouched. Muscles tight, power humming, Reign braced for attack.

A soft hand touched his bicep and jarred him from his deadly path. His gaze shifted to Alexis. She was on her feet. He shifted to protect her, but she countered his move. She faced him, her unguarded back to the crowd of armed men.

"Please don't kill them. We both know you can." *I'm begging you not to.*

The last five words filled his head. Through their connection, she'd pushed her thoughts into his mind and silenced his ghost. The acrid taste of her fear choked him. She worried more for his safety than those of her fellow officers. Reign swallowed the sudden lump in his throat and glared over her head at the waiting officers.

"They're only doing their jobs. They don't know what really happened here." *But we do.*

He gazed into her eyes. Her intense confidence speared his soul. He couldn't remember the last time anyone had given him their trust. He gave a single nod. Her hand slid from his arm down to thread her fingers between his. Mrs. Kelly sifting through him flashed into his mind. He submerged his longings, buried them deep because he shouldn't want what he would never have. And her knowing would serve no purpose.

Together they sank to their knees. It didn't take long for the men to rush them. Jerked apart. They slammed him to the ground and piled on top. He didn't respond or return the punches to his ribs, gut, and head. And he didn't resist when they spread his limbs. A knee pinned each wrist to the ground and a man held each leg while they searched his clothing.

The Vanquished were strangely quiet. Their anger banked as never before. Docile, as if waiting for further instruction. For the first time since arriving here, he could think clearly without their intrusion.

He ignored the questions fielded at him and focused on Alexis who was surrounded by three uniformed men. They shouted and pointed fingers at her, and at the bloody scene left by the quimaera. She shouted back, but he couldn't hear her words.

Then they pointed at him.

Her head swung in his direction.

Dragged to his knees and handcuffed, Reign studied her drawn eyebrows and the grim line of her lips. Wisps of hair haloed her face and for a moment, she seemed lost to him. Then she closed her eyes, took a deep breath, and turned to her accusers. She gave a single nod and stretched out her hands. One removed a pair of handcuffs from his pocket and snapped the metal around her wrists.

No! They could have him. Not her. Reign lunged to his feet and dragged a few men along.

Alexis whipped around. She shook her head and mouthed "No" before they led her away. Her plea not to harm these men corralled his instinct to kill. By her grace, they live and they had arrested her. They should know she had saved their worthless lives.

Reign gritted his teeth. His body strained to follow. Then he stopped. He didn't need to fight these men. A silent count started in his head. One, two, three…One hundred feet is all he needed.

He allowed the officers to shove him into a patrol car. They thought they had caged and conquered him, won the battle. Thirty seconds later, the tug on his atoms began. He welcomed the hard yank, thankful fate had shacked him to a fiery redhead that had captured his heart.

CHAPTER TWENTY-SEVEN

Once more, Alexis shifted her butt, this time a little to the right. Blood returned to the numb cheek with a stabbing awareness, which would've made her wince if it wasn't for the two detectives sitting across the table staring at her. She'd never been to this precinct and didn't know these men. Standing and stretching was out of the question. They would see it as a weakness to exploit. They'd offered her something to eat, drink, another bathroom break, anything to get her to talk.

She almost laughed at their frustration. Then she'd looked down at her orange, correctional institute jumpsuit and realized she had nothing to laugh about. Twelve hours by the clock on the wall, that's how long she'd been in this gray room with a mirror on one wall, a barred window on the other, and steel door guarding her from escape. They didn't realize she'd let them shove her into a police car and haul her to the precinct in order to save their lives. One hundred feet and she felt Reign's presence in the enclosed rear of the police car. She wasn't concerned for herself.

A knock sounded at the door and McCabe entered. He nodded to the two detectives who gathered their note pads and shuffled from the room. McCabe shrugged out of his jacket and draped it on the back of the chair. She noticed his empty holster dangling under his armpit. He unbuttoned his sleeves and rolled them up his beefy forearms.

Alexis glanced at the mirror, certain his performance was for the audience gathered behind the two-way. They must've invited him to grill her when their men failed to deliver a confession. She estimated the two detectives, a prosecutor, and the captain of the precinct watched. Everyone wanted to watch the show when a cop was in the crosshairs.

McCabe slammed his palms on the table. She didn't flinch.

"Glad to have your attention, Detective Lever."

He used her title not as a show of respect, but to remind her of what she'd lost. Maybe what she never was.

"Let's start at the beginning." He braced his elbows on the table and leaned forward. His big, round, florid face hung in front of her.

God no. She sent a silent plea to the heavenly father, which he ignored. McCabe started where he thought the beginning was, at the arrest of Reign Nicolis by the New City PD. He proceeded to lay out a similar scenario the previous detectives pursued. She and her fugitive lover went on a rampage under High Bridge, killing eight homeless victims. He didn't mention the bloody crime scene or the scraps of human remains as if she and Reign had stopped for a take-out snack of homeless tartare. She blinked hard, but images of the quimaera feeding frenzy would never leave her mind.

And Daniel. His transformation into that huge beast left her trembling. Never in her wildest imagination could she have envisioned something so—

"Where is he, Lever? Where's your partner?" McCabe's hard stare bore into her.

The image of Daniel's morphing body clung to her, refusing to be pushed away. "I don't have a partner."

"The man you were with. Reign, no last name. The same guy New City PD is searching for. The guy who was with you at the train yard. That partner."

A cool breeze fluttered her hair and lifted her heart. *He's closer than you think.* "Am I under arrest, McCabe?"

"That's all you have to say after your lover left you holding the bag for murdering people? I never thought you'd be one of those women who throw away everything for a stiff one."

That stuck in her craw. "It never occurred to you to give me the benefit of the doubt? It never crossed your mind I could be innocent?"

His hollow smile gutted her. "You're not innocent, Lever. You're standing by a killer instead of your oath to serve and protect."

The door opened and a detective entered. He waved for McCabe to follow him. McCabe stood and slipped back into his jacket. "You're chin deep in shit and soon to go under. And I'm gonna be the one to give you that final push." He exited.

Alexis sucked in a sigh that flipped into a sob that burned its way up the back of her throat. She tried to swallow it back down and ended up choking when the other sobs crawled up. McCabe's words planted the image of her drowning in a sewage tank. She'd worked so damn hard at her job only to lose it all in a few days.

Maybe all isn't lost?

Yeah, because there was a great record of cops returning to work after being implicated in a mass murder. The department would never stop investigating her. Everyone ever associated with her would be scrutinized. No one would ever want to work with her again.

And her father! God, how could she explain this? She couldn't, not without a massive amount of lying because the truth would get her committed.

'There's a hybrid army of Egyptian beasts devouring innocent people in New York. Oh, and the serial killer your trolling New York for, he's one of them.' The second the words left her mouth, she'd be in a straitjacket.

Alexis jumped to her feet and paced the small room. She ignored the two-way mirror and the steady red light on the surveillance camera in the corner of the ceiling. Too many questions circled in her head, spinning like a haywire top. Her side throbbed at the site where the beast clawed her flesh. She remembered Reign, pouring his power into her wound, connecting them. Through this bond, she shared his anguish when the first bullet ripped into his shoulder. More bullets riddled his body. For precious seconds she couldn't think as their joint suffering magnified and reverberated. Then all her anguish ceased. She floated in a tranquil sea. *Reign.* His presence surrounded her, healed her.

How many times had he saved her? The house. The shooting at the bodega. The train yard. He'd taken bullets for her. No one had ever put their life on the line for her. Done so much to protect her without asking for anything in return.

The door opened and yanked her back to the present. McCabe barreled through. "Your apartment and grandmother's house checked out clean. We've got nothing else to hold you. You're free to go." He stomped from the room.

They kept her clothes for DNA processing and her gun, but returned her badge, keys, phone, and wallet. Alexis stepped out of the precinct in an oversized zippered cardigan and baggy jeans donated from the Salvation Army. She inhaled a comforting breath of stale, exhaust-filled New York City air and smiled. Freedom smelled like sweaty gym shorts left in a locker over the summer, but nothing had ever smelled so sweet.

As she walked, the night replayed in her mind. She remembered lying on the hard gravel with the wreckage of a train nearby and the police closing in. Reign pressed his hand against her wounds and light filled her. His radiance bathed her soul and then the link had been severed.

He had climbed to his feet and faced at least twenty armed officers, his features feral with flared nostrils and bared teeth. His blue eyes glowed. She had no doubt he'd killed all the quimaera he'd led into the stock car. And if he had to, he'd kill all the officers there. She wouldn't allow that. She'd do whatever was necessary to stop him from taking innocent lives.

Alexis had grabbed his arm. Ripples of awareness leaped from her palm and tore into Reign. She swept passed his defenses, seeking his radiance. Memories slammed into her. The wars, the battles, death, destruction, and loss. His deal with Daniel to stay here, and...Nephythys. Profound loneliness had encased his heart. His gaze had lurched to her. Fury and confusion had swirled wildly in the depths of his eyes. A foul churning darkness had replaced the light that filled his soul moments ago. His tense body had braced for attack from her and from the officers waiting outside of their private circle.

She couldn't believe he listened to her plea for mercy and didn't kill every officer there.

A block away from the precinct, coffee scented the air and propelled her to a sidewalk vendor for a mocha latte and muffin. She thought she'd blended in with the lunch crowd until a subtle movement on her peripheral caught her attention.

It was the way the man looked at her, and then didn't. She studied his stance, his athletic build, and the slight bulge under his arm. She tagged him for a cop.

A growl sounded close to her ear and the temperature surrounding her plummeted. She jerked around, praying Reign hadn't chosen now to appear. A lump formed in her throat. After everything they'd been through, she couldn't lose him now.

She closed her eyes and reached out to him. He was there, in her mind, an angry bundle of leashed energy waiting for an opportunity to strike.

"Hey? You okay?" the vendor asked.

Alexis snapped out of her trance. Customers gave her a questioning stare, but a tad crazy was the norm in NYC. At the back of the line, the undercover cop watched.

Nibbling on her muffin and sipping her coffee, Alexis strolled down the street. Every so often, she studied her reflection in the store windows and the man yards away who kept pace.

"What a freakin' waste of time," she mumbled.

The police hadn't a clue what they faced. Or who. The public had no idea they'd dropped a rung on the food chain. And the only thing stopping the human race from being the main course on the breakfast, lunch, and dinner menu was one warrior with a neon sword. Not the NYPD, not Seal Team Six, and certainly not her with just a nine millimeter and an attitude. And Daniel Nicolis. The food in her stomach threatened to crawl back up her throat. Nothing could've prepared her for the horror of seeing him.

Though Roman Nicolis hadn't killed Daniel, he did manage to stop him with an ordinary sword. The quimaera were hard to kill, not invulnerable. With Roman's help and the rest of the Nicolis clan, they could find Daniel and finally put him six feet under. No trial. No jury. No appeal. Straight to a death sentence.

Alexis forced herself to keep up her nonchalant appearance and continued eating. By the time she'd finished her food, she'd strolled into a shopping district. She entered one of those department stores which catered to teens and grabbed a pair of jeans and a graphic tee from the first table. A wave at a sales lady got the woman to unlock a changing room stall just as her stalker entered the store.

She tossed the clothes on the bench and took a cleansing breath to steady her racing heart. She could do this. She had to. Adrenalin bled from her system making her weak. The weight of her decision threatened to swamp her. Her career, family, friends, she had to walk away from all of it because once she crossed that bridge, she'd have to burn it to the ground and never look back. When the fate of the world lands in your lap, you draw an 'S' on your chest, tie a cape around your neck and snap on your bulletproof bracelets.

She plopped her butt on the bench. Her chin hit her chest and stayed there. To Serve and Protect, that's what she signed up for when she joined the police force. And that is exactly what she would continue to do.

"Reign, I need you," she whispered.

When she finally lifted her head, he was crouched in front of her, squeezed into the small space. His worried gaze didn't waver as he drew her to her feet. She laid her head on his hard pecs and listened to the beat of his heart. A comforting silence stretched between them.

"I'm ready to go."

"Where?" He stroked her back.

"The factory first."

Reign folded her in his arms. The tug on her atoms didn't frighten her. This time she welcomed the unraveling and opened herself to him. Mingled together, he surrounded every fiber of her being. They were one entity, shooting through space in the blink of an eye.

Pain faded, anxiety disappeared, leaving a freedom she had never known before. Too soon, it ended. They flashed into the abandoned factory and took a head count. The same number of quimaera were missing and dormant. She'd take this as a good omen.

A low-pitched keening spun her. Reign stood over a pit. His sword pulsed, turning the open space into a macabre dance club. His face was set with the same hard expression she had seen when he faced the police. At the edge of a pit, he leaned forward, ready to jump.

"Don't!" She raced over and grabbed his arm. "What are you doing?"

He wrenched free and didn't look at her. "It's time we eliminate the threat."

"We can't. Not yet."

"They hunted and killed. You and I are blamed for their destruction—"

"I know, but we can't kill them. Not until we discover who leads them."

"Alamut leads them." He met her gaze.

"We don't know that for sure."

He whipped his hair back. His hard features slapped her. "We kill these and deal with Alamut later." He leaped into the pit.

"Damn it! Killing one may awaken all of them. You said that, not me. And even if you can kill all of them, we don't know if this is the only factory." She climbed down the ladder, jumped into the greenish goop and stalked over to him. "You can't kill and ask questions later."

"I almost lost you, Alexis!" Nostril flaring, he vibrated from anger.

Speechless at the desperation in his voice, Alexis stared into his eyes. Loneliness and longing tore at her. Every fiber of her being sobbed in response. She held him tight. "You haven't lost me. I'm right here," she whispered.

"It was my fault. Mine," he mumbled into the crook of her neck. "I had him, could have ended it. But I did not. If anything happens to you because of my actions…"

One of them trembled, but she couldn't tell which. She brushed strands of his hair behind his ear and guided him to her lips. A shudder ran through him the moment they touched.

"Let's go home," she murmured.

The next moment they were dripping goop onto the carpet in her grandmother's living room. And she didn't care because

Reign still held her close. The intensity of his gaze made all of her blush, and then run hot. His hands slid slowly from her body, leaving her aching for their possessive touch. There was a denied urgency to him that made her want to see him unrestrained, his passions unleashed.

Reign stepped away, creating daylight between them. May as well have been the Grand Canyon.

She took his hand.

A war raged inside her. Fugitives didn't have time for foreplay—but they needed this. She needed him. She could admit that now. From the moment their lives collided, he'd been in her corner, driving her nuts, but also supporting her, following her lead, listening. An ancient warrior from an uncivilized time listened to her when the men in her own time period wouldn't. From the moment he set foot in New York, he saved her. Not just her body, also her heart.

Alexis led the way upstairs.

Inside her bedroom, she guided him to a rattan chair, which groaned under his weight. She backed away and toed off the soggy sneakers, then grabbed the tab of the zipper on her sweater. Slow and steady, the whiz of the descending tab was the only sound in the room. His hands gripping the arms the chair, Reign leaned forward, lips parted, eyes glazed. His gaze traveled with the zipper and then shot to her face.

A wicked smile answered his unasked question. She turned, showing him her back. She shrugged one shoulder free and peeked over it, making sure she had his full attention. His gaze hadn't left her. Another shrug and the sweater slid to the middle of her back.

The chair creaked.

She didn't turn around. She let the sweater fall. The pants followed, pooling at her ankles. Maybe she should thank the NYPD for not confiscating her lacy underwear. Bending over, she stepped from the pile of clothing. When she straightened, she knew Reign no longer sat in the chair on the other side of the room.

Heat radiated from him, warming her back. The straps of her bra dangled. She reached behind and with a pinch and twist; the bra fell to the floor. She hooked her thumbs into the sides of her string bikini and shimmied out of them.

Heavy footsteps followed her into the bathroom and stopped when she entered the shower stall. The strip of frosted glass on the shower door hid enough to let the imagination run wild. By Reign's strained stare, tense body, and the vein pulsing in his neck, he imagined a lot.

Alexis crooked a finger and invited him inside. She didn't want him to imagine. She wanted him to see.

***

Transfixed, Reign couldn't take his gaze from her pert, coral-tipped ample breasts, which balanced above a narrow waist that flared to voluptuous hips and a fiery strip of hair shielding her core. Everywhere his gaze traveled, her curvaceous body took his control on a dangerous trip.

Water cascaded from an overhead spout, plastering her hair into coppery waves, and streaked down a body built for pleasure. She plucked a container off a shelf and poured a substance into her palms. Whimsical jasmine scented bubbles erupted wherever she touched. They glided down her breasts, playfully peek-a-booed with her rigid nipples, dipped into her belly button, curved over her hips, tangled in her nest, and finished the marathon by racing down her long, graceful legs. Gossamer suds clung to places he wanted to taste and touch, linger over, revere.

She lathered her rear, cupped, and caressed her flesh. Foam cloaked her, then sluiced off leaving behind perfect skin. He tried to close his eyes to keep from lunging forward and claiming what his body demanded, but he couldn't deny himself this pleasure. He had to see.

Alexis stared at him. Beads of water clung to her lashes, making her eyes sparkle. He waited for her to order him away, something Nephythys would do. A sultry smile graced her pouty lips as she crooked a finger and ordered him near. Fully clothed, he stepped under the spray.

She giggled and laughed...at him. A tinkling sound filled with mirth that carved out a hollow space in his heart. He was about to escape as far away as the tether would allow when she plucked the soaked shirt from his chest and slipped her hand beneath. His skin sizzled where she caressed. Her other hand skimmed down to his crotch.

His world shifted from a dismal abyss to a carnival filled with carnal delights all centered on one woman.

"I want you naked. Now." She ordered.

His throat dried and the clothing keeping her hand from his hard cock vanished. Her soft palm gripped him hard. Her thumb slid over the tip and spread his juices. Slack-jawed, the back of his head slammed into the wall. Ripples of pent-up passion spread from his cock outward to every part of his being. She cupped his tight balls. His breath became ragged, wheezing through his lungs, whistling through his clenched teeth. She stroked him; up, down, around. Pumping with a steady rhythm until thought ceased and his hips took over.

She stopped, though her hand still fisted around the base of his shaft. He throbbed.

Do not cease!

She stepped away leaving him bobbing in the air and desperate for her touch. Water dripped from the tip of her nose to her cleavage and trailed down her abdomen.

"Turn around," she ordered.

As he turned, she squeezed a handful of thick liquid into her palm from the same container. Jasmine and honey filled the air and he recognized it as the unique smell he always associated with her.

"Arms up and on the wall, please."

Curiosity aroused as much as his body, he leaned forward and complied. Soapy hands shocked his nerve endings as she glided up the center of his back, over his shoulders and up his arms as far as her hands could reach, then scratched her way back down. A groan rumbled from his throat and he arched into the sensation.

"You like?" Her breath fanned his skin.

"Yes." He panted.

Alexis soaped his buttocks. She slipped a hand between his legs and stroked from his thigh to his ankle, switched to his other leg and slid back up.

Torture.

Never had a woman touched him so boldly.

"Now for your front." She stepped back as he turned. Her gaze traveled over his body. Heat ignited in her eyes. "Damn, you're beautiful."

Reign couldn't move, couldn't breathe. He'd been called many things in his long life, beautiful wasn't on the list. For the first time, he was afraid. A woman had brought him low before, he couldn't chance it, not again.

Fingers roamed his chest, teased his nipples, and eased down his abs. She took his hand and pulled him beneath the spray. On tiptoes, she leaned into him, her nipples teased and her breasts pillowed against his chest. Millimeters away from his lips, her tongue flicked out and licked his bottom lip.

"What are you waiting for?" Her belly brushed his arousal.

"You tease." He didn't recognize the strained voice that exited his mouth.

"Never about this."

"You dangle what I want only to snatch it away the moment I reach for it."

She grabbed his hands and forced him to her breasts. Her nipples pressed into his palms. Every muscle in him turned rigid. He crushed his lips to hers. She slid her hand up the back of his neck, slanted her lips across his, and drew his tongue into her mouth. Lost in the feel of her lush body and heady scent he wanted to lose himself in all she had to offer.

Reign yanked away. Rational thought was moments away from crumbling. "You don't want this."

"I do. I want you." She rubbed against him.

Her slippery body drove him insane. And he adored it, loved that she made him want to commit a crime just to be near her, never wanted it end.

Damnation. "I won't be gentle. I can't. Not this time." He hated that his voice trembled along with his body.

"I'm a big girl. I can handle you." She shifted so that her curls teased his shaft.

His fragile control snapped.

Reign scooped her up and pinned her to the back of the shower stall. Alexis braced her feet on his hips and opened herself to him. He cupped her ass and slid home. He buried himself inside her tight, slick heat. Hot, wet, and so damn good, his seed boiled. He quivered from the strain.

Alexis gasped. Her eyelids fluttered closed as her hips bucked and her nails dug into his shoulders.

He hurt her.

He started to pull out, but she locked her long legs and arms around him.

"Don't. Stop." Her body clenched.

Locking him inside heaven.

She rolled her hips and her sheath glided up and slowly down his rigid shaft. Spurred by a frantic need, Reign thrust into her, long deep strokes that rocked her body. Her taut nipples scoured his chest. Her fingers gripped his hair and twisted, leaving his neck vulnerable to her wet tongue. Down the column of his throat, she licked, sucked, bit.

His heart slammed in his chest. His blood roared through his veins as he came. Millennia of celibacy ended with a woman he could touch, kiss, love.

Her breath caught on a sharp inhale. She groaned and writhed in his arms as her sheath seized his flesh and milked him. His knees threatened to buckle from the consuming pleasure.

Soft breath tickled his chest. It was then he became aware of Alexis crushed between him and the cold tiles of the stall. He cringed, realizing he had treated her like a whore and took her like animal in heat.

"That was fun," she murmured in a throaty voice and trailed tiny kisses along his collarbone and chest.

She lied. No woman would enjoy how he used her. He tilted her chin to look into her face. A shameless grin curved her lips and mischief filled her eyes. Her head dipped to his nipple and she suckled. His cock jerked.

Damnation! Still hard. Her low moan rumbled through him and ended on a sigh.

"Are you real?" He breathed. "Tell me this is not a dream and I am going to wake up back in—"

"Shhh." A finger silenced him. "You're as real as I am," she murmured and brushed those sexy lips back and forth, barely touching him. "I wish we had time for more, but we gotta go."

Alexis slid down his body and stepped back under the spraying water. He gaped at her, fascinated by her sensuous movements. The desolate ache, which had long settled in his heart, dissolved. A glimmer of hope sputtered to life in its place. Followed by the sweet rush of an emotion he dared not name. Not if he wanted to keep her alive. He didn't love her. He couldn't. But as he faded away and left her alone, he damned himself for being a liar.

CHAPTER TWENTY-EIGHT

Alexis peered over her shoulder to request some help washing her back. White tiles faced her instead of a sexy wet man at her command. She turned the water off, pulled open the sliding door, and stepped out of the shower. Everything seemed normal; the drip of her bathroom sink, the drone of her heating unit. Then why had a knot wedged itself into her heart. Water dripped from her body onto the bath rug as she strained to feel Reign's presence.

Nothing.

She shivered and cold dread settled around her. Alexis twisted a towel around her hair and wrapped another one around her body. She opened the bedroom door and paused to listen. The quiet house unnerved her. Where was Reign?

She made it halfway down the hallway when his heavy tread sounded downstairs in the kitchen. Relief jellied her knees and she sank onto the top stair. Her thoughts tumbled around three words that had settled in her heart.

Don't do this, Alexis. Now is not the time to get gooey about a guy. Keep it simple. You need each other to deal with the quimaera. Dangerous men and dangerous situations lead to mind-blowing sex. But afterwards, you put your panties back on and deal with reality.

And reality is?

"Once this is over, he's leaving."

An ache seized her, but she stood and marched back to the bedroom. With cold determination, she yanked on dark jeans and a black thermal tee. She pulled her hair back in a tight damp bun, grabbed a duffel bag, and started packing key items:

toiletries, underwear, socks, another pair of jeans, a heavy sweater, and her Glock .357. The journals were on the dressing table along with the jewelry box containing the gold bracelet. They were the only things of her grandmother's she could take.

She walked back into the closet for a final look when her eyes caught on the blue formal gown Gloria had shipped to her for the anniversary party tonight. Her lips curled and she gingerly grabbed the satin material between the tips of her thumb and forefinger. As if she would actually wear the long-sleeved, boat neck, satin contraption.

Had they heard the news yet and already condemned her without a trial or jury?

The rumble of an engine caught her attention. She ran to the window and peeked through a part in the curtain. The sun had set a few hours ago. The Martins' SUV was parked in their driveway. She spied the couple and their two kids sitting at the dinner table through their side window, otherwise the cul-de-sac was empty. Quickly, she finished packing and jogged down stairs. Reign, bare-chested in the kitchen, was hunched over the remains of Mrs. Kelly's chocolate cake.

"What in the name of the gods is this?" He shoveled in another mouthful.

She'd planned to be distant, but how could she when he was shirtless in her kitchen, licking chocolate from his fingers with the glee of a five year old? "It's called chocolate cake. You like it?"

His eyes rolled back in his head. He nodded. Smudges of cake were on his lips and crumbs littered his chest. How could you not adore a man who loved chocolate?

"You have food." She pointed to the corner of his lips. His tongue flicked out and licked the crumbs away.

Reign sighed, causing his pecs to heave and his six-pack to ripple. Alexis remembered his lips and tongue on her breasts. Him moving inside her body and her needing so much more of him. He filled her, completed the puzzle missing from her heart.

He's leaving you.

But right now, he's here.

She brushed the crumbs away and laid a hand on his chest. Sensual thoughts, filled with tenderness swirled between them. Warmth glazed over her, tightening her nipples and clenching her core.

His gaze traveled down her body and a wolfish grin crossed his face. Lost, she couldn't resist when his mouth devoured her. He tasted decadent. His sinfully hard body felt like heaven. He picked her up and sat her on the kitchen island. Her legs draped around him. He released her hair, pulled her tresses to the side, and nuzzled her neck, tickling her with his whiskers before his tiny kisses trailed to her earlobe.

A palm cupped her breast through her shirt. She gripped his biceps and let her head drop back, exposing all of her to him.

He stilled. His hands dropped from her body.

"Reign?"

His lips had drawn back in a silent snarl, replacing his playful smile. In his hand, he clutched his blade. "They're here."

Alexis slid off the island. She raced up the stairs with his heavy footsteps thudding behind her. She grabbed the duffel and peeked out of the window. A police cruiser had parked out front and two officers approached the house.

She was about to turn away when she glanced at her neighbor's home. Mrs. Kelly stared out of a bedroom window, directly at Alexis.

The front door creaked. She whipped around.

Reign faced the bedroom door. His black blade clasped between both hands. The corded muscles in his back were tense, ready.

"Take us to Mrs. Kelly's," she whispered. He shook his head. She stepped in from of him and forced him to look at her. It took most of her strength to jerk his head down. His unfocused eyes wouldn't meet hers. Cupping his face, she stared into their bottomless pits. His raging emotions cascaded into her, turning her thoughts toward death. For her sanity, she needed to let go. Instead, she clung to him.

Again, she registered nothing, no ghosts haunting him. Only an abiding anger.

She molded her body to his hard length. An arm banded around her waist and drew her even closer. "Please, Reign. We have to go."

His eyes lost some of the distance, as if he pulled back from the edge to hear her. He shuddered. For a brief second, his grip hurt, but he released her and shouldered her bag. Then he flashed them across the street into Mrs. Kelly's living room.

"Get up here." Mrs. Kelly ordered from the stairs.

They gathered with her in the master bedroom at the window. Police cars filled the cul-de-sac outside her grandmother's house. Headlights turned the evening to day, which drew the Martin's and the other neighbors from their homes. The police ushered them back inside.

"At least they're not sneaking around anymore." Mrs. Kelly stepped away from the window.

"What?" Alexis moved toward the window.

"Alexis, you have untapped gifts that you must start utilizing." Mrs. Kelly lectured and pulled her away. "I sensed their presence long before I saw them. Just as I sensed your presence in the house. I would've called but didn't want to leave a record for them to harass me." She glanced at Reign. "I'm surprised you didn't sense them, but perhaps your attentions were otherwise occupied." She pointed to Reign's bare chest.

Alexis tried not to blush and failed while Reign magically created a shirt. She didn't have time to question her neighbor on the untapped gifts at her disposal. "Thanks for all you've done, Mrs. Kelly, but we don't want to put you in further danger."

"I saw the news. I know why they're here, ransacking your grandmother's home. This room is shielded. They can't see us from the street. I would ask if this is the right path for you, but I see you've already made your decision. So, how can I help?"

This woman, who only knew her by proxy through her grandmother, embraced her. She smelled of a mix of chocolate, vanilla, and coconut. An image of her grandmother's homemade coconut macaroon came to Alexis's mind. A sob tore through her with tears close on its heels.

"It's okay, dear." Mrs. Kelly hugged her. "You've been through a lot, but I'd say you're stronger for it."

Stronger? She didn't feel stronger. Her life was wrecked. There was nothing to salvage. A heavy hand landed on her shoulder. Alexis inhaled a slow breath.

Reign stood behind her. She leaned back and let him catch her, his strength was her fortress.

"We're leaving." Even though she had no idea where they were going, saying the words made it real. But there was one thing she had to do before she kissed it all goodbye.

CHAPTER TWENTY-NINE

Alexis stared at the front door to her parents' McMansion, her finger centimeters away from the doorbell. She had no idea what she would say to them. How do you say goodbye to your family when you can't explain why you have to leave?

She glanced over her shoulder at her entourage, Reign and Mrs. Kelly. Her neighbor insisted on tagging along. Reign hadn't been certain he could transport both of them, but she assured him he could. He didn't seem worse for wear after scattering their atoms and transporting them here. He looked exhausted from having to listen to Mrs. Kelly's incessant chatter.

Alexis had never brought a man home and wasn't about to break that pattern now. The argument with Gloria would be bad enough without having to deal with introducing a man to her father and brothers. Should she tell him to remain hidden or trust that he'd figure it out?

Leave a man to figure something out? Yep, that would not work. Besides, they wouldn't be here long and as soon as they were out of here, it was back to the factory to start her new fugitive detective career.

"Why do we linger?" He scanned the area.

"I want you to remain invisible."

His gaze landed on her. A muscle flexed in his jaw and his eyes seemed to darken in the porch lighting. She'd hurt him and didn't mean to.

"As you wish." He faded before she could explain.

She entered the house with her arctic front following close behind. A servant met her in the atrium. "Where is everyone?"

she asked Louisa, the latest live in maid. Her mother went through servants like water to a colander.

"They've already left for the pavilion, ma'am," Louisa answered.

Anger made her cheeks burn, until she glanced at herself in the hallway mirror. Wild hair, dressed in jeans and a leather jacket. She didn't even have makeup on to give her some color and hide her freckles. There was no way she could whip herself together to attend a formal function and not embarrass her father. So much for saying goodbye. She'd come all this way for nothing.

Alexis sat in the living room. Shoulders slumped forward, chin buried in her chest. Any minute, she would figure out what to do next. She hid her trembling lips behind her hand.

"Ma'am, the hair stylist, and make-up artist are still here. I can ask them to wait," Louisa said.

If the party was tonight, there's a good chance her family knew nothing about what happened. Alexis lifted her chin and her blurry vision met Mrs. Kelly. Her gray head bobbed once.

"Do you think they would?" Alexis asked Louisa.

"I'll ask right now." Louisa hurried away.

"Think they can make me pretty, too?" Mrs. Kelly smiled at her, then grabbed her hand and pulled her to her feet. "Shower, then the professionals will make us beautiful, though, you already are."

It's something her grandmother would've said. God she missed her.

Reign materialized, his face brooding and pensive. She wanted to explain the complicated relationship she had with Gloria and her family, but they didn't have time. Mrs. Kelly gave her a push toward the bathroom and she went, grateful to get away.

Fifteen minutes later, she marched downstairs wrapped in a plush robe to find her neighbor sitting under the dryer. Alexis looked around the room at the extensive set up and remembered why she avoided all this. Since the time she gave up diapers, she had a standing appointment at the best salon, in whatever town the military had shipped the family. All this primping never made her beautiful. Never helped her win a pageant. Never made Gloria look at her with love instead of a project to correct.

And in the short amount of time she had to say goodbye, she had no idea how to change it.

***

As long as the tether allowed, Reign wandered around the house, searching for any threat. He stayed away from Alexis. He shouldn't be surprised she didn't want her family to see him. What woman would? He had nothing to offer but his blade and a curse. Alexis deserved more. And he had nothing to give.

For a few minutes, he watched her flinch and wince while one woman attacked her hair. He was about to appear and order them away from her when she sighed and smiled dreamily.

"This is absolutely wonderful." A woman soaped Alexis's hair. Her eyelids slid closed and a look of ecstasy settled over her face.

"I used to hate all this stuff," she murmured. "It's been so long since I did this; I guess I can appreciate it now."

He hardened and had to turn away. The gods knew how much he wanted her. Being tied to her was equal parts heaven and hell.

She seemed to care. When that silly old woman said his mother was a god, Alexis had pulled him back to her, wrapped her arms around him, and held him as if he mattered. He felt her. The curves of her body had molded to him. Nephythys never did that, touched him of her own free will. Never allowed him to touch her.

Two thousand years without the touch of another being and Alexis had stumbled across his path, into his arms. The slippery feel of her had surrounded him... His heart twisted viciously in his chest. It was good she didn't want him to meet her family. They didn't need to meet the man who had brought ruin to their daughter. Time was his adversary. God, he had to find a way to leave Alexis before Nephythys discovered her.

Mrs. Kelly blocked his path and glanced left and right at both entrances into the spacious living room. Could she see him?

"Come with me," she whispered.

Curious, he followed her into a bedroom and materialized when she closed the door. The Vanquished whispered as the tether drew taut. An uneasy knot began in his stomach as she walked around him. Her shrewd eyes scanned from his head to his toes much like a buyer studying a slave.

"How may I help, Mrs. Kelly?"

"Oh, I don't need your help. Alexis does. She needs an escort to this shindig, and you just volunteered."

CHAPTER THIRTY

Unseen, Khuket hovered near the ceiling of the bar. Below, four men slung back beers while playing pool. Intricate, colorful chaos bands pulsed around them. Each had their own personal demons clinging to their souls, making them exploitable. She'd learned their names: Thane, Quin, EJ, and delicious Avery. The disfigured one.

Nothing more than a wisp of smoke, she dropped from the corner of the ceiling of the bar and closed the distance between her and her prey. She didn't need to touch him. Just being near to his latent and manifested turmoil stoked her appetite. His chaos was an unending banquet she could feed on forever.

"You are strong," she whispered into his subconscious, bolstering his flagging will. Having him succumb too soon would not satisfy her purpose. As she supped, parts of the men's conversations drifted to her. They were concerned about her army and Alamut. They needn't have worried. Most of the canopic jars were secreted away in the factory. The rest were trapped within her cloak, present only when she desired. Until she released the souls within the jars, her army would remain dormant. Hopefully, Alamut would prove capable and lead her soldiers.

Her dinner trembled. He fought her control. It was odd watching such a large, formidable male become noticeably shaken, but she enjoyed his awareness of her presence. She molded herself to his body and slurped at the chaos bleeding off him in abundant waves until he fought the havoc gnawing at his senses. To her shock, the chaos within him calmed when it should've escalated in her presence. He controlled the chaos instead of succumbing.

"Hey, you okay?" EJ said to her prey.

Avery pushed EJ out of the way and stormed from the bar. She peeled away and allowed him to flee. After ingesting his succulent aura, he could never hide. She would never hunger again.

She returned to the factory moments before Alamut materialized in his human form. Wet and badly bruised, he collapsed on the floor. Unimpressed, she glanced behind him. "Where is my army?"

"Dead."

Her essence bristled and roiled, and her true state threatened to break free. She couldn't allow that destructive force to conquer the reasoning and control she had gained after millennia of solitude. "I sent you to feed my minions, not get them slaughtered. How did this happen?"

"Reign."

Rage swept through her. Her army dead at the hands of the man she needed to kill to ensure her freedom. An opportunity wasted by a worthless hybrid. Now she understood SET's contempt for Anubis. Bands of chaos unfurled from her body. Layers peeled away, revealing the pure chaos that lay beneath. They stretched, and filled the space.

"You should not kill me." His mouth stretched into a bloody grin.

"Why?" She leaned closer, enjoying the fear on his face.

"Because I can track him." He held up his hand. Blood coated his palm. A smile curled the corners of his lips.

Khuket swept a finger across his palm and rubbed the vital liquid between her thumb and forefinger. Tinged with chaos, the acrid aroma wafted in the air and pointed her in the direction of her enemy.

She lifted her gaze to Alamut and mimicked his smile. "You have done well, my slave."

***

What was it about that woman? Reign groused. In his faded state, he sat in the passenger seat of the car while his tormentor hummed in the back.

It must have been the look in her eye, a parental glare that compelled a grown man to comply regardless of his inclination to run. He should have run, but then she added Alexis to the equation. So he let the old woman have her way with him, but that didn't mean he had to appear like an obedient child. He could protect Alexis just as well faded. He glanced at her seated next to him as she drove the car.

A velvet cloak completely shielded her body and hair from the fine rain that had started moments before their departure. All he could see were her kohl-lined coppery eyes framed by long lashes that were no longer reddish, but now black, making them even more alluring. Her pink lips were tinted red and parted as she breathed. Her tongue flicked out and swept across her top lip, leaving it glistening—and so damn tempting. He wanted to taste her, pull her into his arms, and lose himself in her eyes, her lips, her body. He would never get enough of her.

She didn't want him, had made that clear when she asked him to fade rather than meet her family. She was right to do so. Alexis wasn't safe with him. Not only because of Nephythys. Something was wrong.

His control was slipping. He couldn't blame it on the souls of the dead quimaera. It started before the battle under the bridge. And this time, the Vanquished weren't involved. Whether they raged or remained silent, his thoughts were not his own. Even with Alexis in close proximity, chaotic impulses pressed him. Never one to have a hair trigger, now nothing would please part of him more than to kill everything.

After tonight, he had to leave Alexis before he hurt her.

The car stopped and a young man opened her door. Faint strains of music swelling over muffled voices reached him. Alexis's breath hitched. Instead of leaving the car, she paused. Her hands nervously clutched the steering wheel. A bead of sweat trickled from her hairline down the side of her face.

"It's going to be all right, dear." Mrs. Kelly handed her a handkerchief. "We'll both be with you."

Her eyes widened, she glanced in his general direction. Then her eyebrows drew together. "Oh, yeah...Reign, I think it'd be best if you stayed invisible. This won't take long." She slipped out of the car and walked up the stairs alone.

Her words stabbed his heart. He couldn't blame her. He brought misery since he entered her life. And he would bring much more when he left her alone to face this world's justice.

"You don't listen to her. She doesn't mean it. You listen to me! That girl has no idea what she's walking into. She needs you by her side tonight." Mrs. Kelly insisted as she exited the car. A couple paused to stare at the elderly lady chattering to herself. She gave them that same parental glare until they continued on their way.

"Reign Nicolis, you appear right now," she whispered furiously through pursed lips. When he didn't do as she commanded, she huffed and marched up the stairs. "She didn't mean what she said, Reign. The girl is stressed, under pressure. Between the discovery of her true nature and that mother of hers—"

"Enough," he barked and appeared. "Excuses are unnecessary. Alexis does not want me by her side. I will honor her request and not shame her with my presence."

Five feet and four inches, younger than him, but older than the average human, Mrs. Kelly ripped off her gloves. Her gnarled hands stretched up, grabbed hold of his lapels and pulled him to her. Aged, milky eyes looked deep into his core. "She *needs* you, in there by her side. Can you do that? Or will your doubt end you before you've even begun?"

She took his hand, but didn't sift him or use her gifts to force him to her will. She held him. Her warm hands were soft as worn leather, but strong. Their heat and strength seeped into him, staving off the ice coating his heart. Chaos receded as he focused on her words.

The old woman was right. He needed to do this final act. But the longer he stayed, the more danger Alexis faced. Killing Alamut would solve the problem, make everyone happy, and keep her safe.

Even though it meant returning to Nephythys.

"I will do what you ask. Then I will find Alamut." Tonight, he would stand by her side—if you could call one hundred feet away at someone's side—whether she liked it or not. *And never see her again.*

"Care to escort an old lady inside?" She grabbed his arm. Together, they walked up the remaining stairs and into the spotlight.

***

Alexis peeled the cloak from her and handed it to an attendant. She paused in the entrance of the ballroom, scanning the room for her family. She wondered if they'd missed her, ask why she hadn't attended a mandatory family function. Probably not. Whatever lie her mother concocted would have been accepted without discussion.

Where was the unconditional love? Hell, nothing was unconditional about Gloria Lever. Everything she did, wanted, loved, came with conditions. Lots of them. *Either way, it ends tonight.* She strode into the room.

A few appreciative glances came her way from a nearby group of men. Nervous, she smoothed a hand over the lacy strapless dress. A black sheath underneath the intricate lace stopped mid-thigh while the lace skimmed her knees. This was the dress she had sent for her mother's approval a month ago. Gloria's response was to send that horrible blue gown still hanging in her closet. Luckily, Gloria hadn't tossed it out.

People milled about, gossiping in the guise of networking, foreplay in the guise of dancing. She spotted her brothers in their dress uniforms exactly where she thought they would be, tossing back drinks at the bar, not at the center table with their wives, rowdy children and their parents, who were missing. She scanned the crowd again, looking for Gloria's telltale upswept hairdo, but didn't spot her.

She skirted the edge of the room and made her way to the bar. George, John, and Thomas, so named after the first three presidents of the USA. She would've been James if God hadn't intervened and made her a girl. Their buzz cuts left just a hint of brown hair, bushy eyebrows, no neck, and thick shoulders. Scowls clung to the arrogant features, so close in appearance they could pass for triplets. Army, Navy, and Marines, the armed services were well-represented in her family. Twenty-four months separated each of them. Dad loved deployment and didn't believe in withdrawal. Thank God for birth control, yet ten years after Thomas, she showed up.

"Hey." She gave her brothers a quick glance, then pushed Thomas out of the way and waved at the bartender. The only woman at the bar, he spotted her and glided over. A week ago, his boyish grin and weak chin would've been enough to pique her libido. Now...

She noticed the absence of her cold companion. Maybe she shouldn't have asked him to stay invisible, but what else was she supposed to do, have him escort her here dressed in leather pants and work boots? Bad enough she bucked tradition and showed up in a mini-dress instead of the long flowing gowns her mother preferred.

"A-Alexis?" George stuttered.

She waited for the accusations to begin. None of them would bite their tongues to spare her feelings. If they knew of her predicament, they'd drag her over the coals and hang her by her entrails for the enjoyment of the rest of the Lever clan. When the tirade didn't come, she ordered a drink.

"Bourbon, please." In the mirror behind the bar, a stylish woman met her stare. Her tamed fiery mane was swept to the side and coiled on one bare shoulder. Her grandmother's diamonds glittered in her ears and the gold snake bracelet wrapped twice around her gloved wrist. With her drink in hand, Alexis saluted the woman in the mirror before turning around. Three pairs of stunned eyes glared at her.

She wanted to toss her bourbon to the back of her throat and let the smooth liquid slide down and pool in her stomach.

"Yes, George. It's me." She took a very ladylike sip. Though they had seen pictures, none of her siblings had ever seen her in anything but slacks, jeans, and a tee. By the time Gloria started her on her pageant quest, the boys were gone, George and John in the military, Thomas in college. They left their tomboy sister at home.

"You look—" John started.

"Fucking hot," Thomas finished. "I was about to hit on you."

"You'd hit on anything," George said.

"Including my sister." Thomas grimaced.

She gulped the rest of her drink and slammed the upturned glass onto the bar.

"I thought you weren't coming," John's eyebrows knit together, confused.

"Why are you dressed like that?" Thomas still stared.

"Like what?" she snapped and looked down at herself. "A grown up? A dress and some heels, a little makeup. You three act like you didn't know I was a girl."

All three blinked stupidly at her until George finally said, "We knew you were a girl, we didn't know you were…feminine."

Her fists clenched. God, she'd give anything to slug all three of them. Was that a compliment or an insult? She couldn't quite tell which one. Ten light years separated them from her. Why was it so hard to say she was pretty?

"Alexis? Is that you?" With a southern twang, Kimberly, George's second wife, a petite blond with store-bought boobs and lipo-ed abs, led the other two wives to join them. "Wow, I mean, wow, you look…uhm—"

"Beautiful, she looks absolutely beautiful." A few feet away, her father stood outside the family circle.

"Daddy." It took everything she had to walk up to him and dutifully brush her cheek against his when all she wanted was to throw herself into his arms and bury her head in his broad chest. He smelled of whiskey, cigars, and cologne. More salt glinted in his hair and more wrinkles lined his face. His stocky frame had thinned a bit since the last time they were together. Still, the hand patting her back felt strong. How could her dad be anything but strong?

He tilted her chin up. "I'm happy you made it, though you're a little late. You've missed dinner."

Not my fault. "Work kept me busy."

"You're still a cop?" Kimberly giggled, her shoulders shaking.

"She's a detective." The proud note in her father's voice caused her eyes to well. "And a good one from what I hear."

"Thanks, Dad." The lump in her throat prevented her from saying more.

"Now, where is your Mother?"

They both scanned the room, but her gaze didn't land on Gloria. A man filled the doorway. Conversation abruptly ended as both men and women paused to appreciate the predator in their midst. He studied the room until his gaze leveled on her. Desire flared in his blue eyes, turning his hard impersonal stare into a smoldering caress that left her charred. Everyone and everything faded, leaving only him.

He bent and whispered something to Mrs. Kelly. Her neighbor smiled and went in the opposite direction while he approached Alexis. Crowds parted. Men pulled their women closer while other women gawked, whispered to their girlfriends, and tried to intercept him. He paid them no attention. His gaze never wavered as he threaded his way to her.

He stalked her, moving smoothly between the tables and the dance floor until he stopped inches away. The tuxedo didn't hide the perfection of his body. Clean-shaven, his chiseled face held no softness except for his newly cropped, wavy hair curling around his ears and nape, tempting her. Different clothes, different hair, same eyes. They were still deep, ocean blue. Those orbs drained her will and left her remembering their only night together.

"Apologies for my delay. Mrs. Kelly needed my help." He held out his hand to her and without a thought, she took it and he pulled her closer. "You are the most stunning woman I have ever seen. You steal my breath, *Amori*. If I knew you shielded this," his gaze swept her from head to toe "beneath that cloak, I would have held you captive in your bedroom."

"Y-you cut your hair," she stuttered and couldn't resist reaching up and threading her fingers through the waves. "And your beard. I liked your beard," she breathed. Especially when he brushed his chin across her nipples right before taking them into his mouth.

"For you, *Amori,* I will grow it back." His lips were inches from her. All she had to do was lean in to taste him.

"And your clothes? What happened to your jeans and boots?" She fingered the lapel. Dangerously delicious in regular clothes, in a tux, Reign was a thousand sins to anyone with an ounce of estrogen.

"Mrs. Kelly. She showed me a picture in something called a magazine, *Vogue.*"

The word sounded strange on his tongue and made a laugh bubble in her chest.

"That woman was a warrior in another life." A smile teased the corner of his mouth. She leaned closer to his hovering lips.

"You did this for me?" She couldn't hide the hope in her voice.

Reign nodded. "I would do anything for you."

A tingling awareness spread from her chest to her limbs and shot up to her brain, leaving her lightheaded and swaying toward him. His hand rested on her waist and drew her into the shelter of his body. She didn't resist the craving need to feel his heat, share it, and share hers. She didn't suffocate beneath the glare of his smoldering blue eyes. She breathed, she lived, she— *Oh...shit!* She couldn't bring herself to even *think* the word.

Her throat had dried to sand, but she swallowed the dry lump and opened her mouth to speak, though she had no idea what words were about to leap out.

Someone cleared their throat, ending her trance and reminding her they weren't alone. Behind her, her father and brothers glared at Reign while her sisters-in-law struggled to hide their interest.

"Everyone, this is—" *Oh God, what can I say?* "Reign Nicolis, my..." *lover* "escort," she said, and refocused on Reign. His eyes darkened and his lips compressed into a tight, grim line. She tried to pull her hand away, but he had placed her hand in the crook of his arm and pulled her against his side. She went around the semi-circle introducing everyone and cut the group off before the interrogation began.

"I haven't seen Mom yet. Anyone know where she is?"

"She went outside to get some air," her father said before being distracted by an Army buddy calling his name.

Questions came from every direction, bombarding Alexis. Who was he, where did he work, how did they meet, were they a couple? A quick and ready answer for each didn't relieve the growing tension she felt radiating from Reign. She ran her hand down the inside of his arm and ended by lacing her fingers through his and squeezing tightly.

She didn't need the skin on skin contact to feel his uncertainty. Facing her family was a daunting prospect, even for a two thousand year old man. He wanted their approval. But why? Why would he care?

His fingers grazed her elbow and instinctively she used her power and sifted through his emotions. When she found the answer, her body jerked. Her gaze shot up to his and found his eyes had turned molten with need. A need she couldn't possibly fill. Maybe another woman could, but not her. She wasn't capable of that kind of commitment. That's what loving Reign meant. And she couldn't do it. It would take more than she was willing to give.

Her gaze skated to her dad. After all this time, she still sought his approval. By the set of his chin, she could tell he was slightly impressed with the polished package Reign displayed. What would he think when he knew the truth that she, an officer of the law, aided and abetted a criminal. Her career was over. He'd never forgive her.

Alexis tried to pull away again. Reign's hand tightened around her and a wave of hurt slammed into her before he released her arm.

"Your mother, we need to find her now," he prompted, cold and precise. The unspoken passion between them had vanished, leaving her twisted and sorry for not saying the words burning her throat.

"Uhm, yeah." She glanced at her brothers. "We'll be back, guys." She swept past Reign and led the way through the gallery to the veranda. The palpable tension between them, not the cold, made her shiver as they walked the length of the porch, darting between smokers and lovers until they reached the end.

"Could she be out there?" He nodded toward the golf course. Orange and red leaves tumbled along the greens and fairways, propelled by a stiff, October breeze. Winter wasn't far.

Reign shrugged off his jacket and draped the silk over her shoulders. She couldn't help burying her nose in the collar and drawing a bit of him into her.

"No, but the pro shop and clubhouse are just down the path." She struggled down the walkway and wobbled a little in her four inch heels. Reign's hand landed on the small of her back, steadying her. He matched his stride to hers and she moved closer to his side.

"Thank you," she murmured. Warmth from his hand stole up her back, making her limbs languid. She had to say something, anything to stop the growing void between them. She could tell him how much she wanted him, but feared that wouldn't satisfy him. Most men would settle for a woman wanting them. Reign's emotions ran way deeper than that. They ran Marianas Trench deep. A girl could find herself smothered by those emotions and tossed up against a rocky shore afterwards. Or, she could find herself the most loved woman in the world. She started to speak when she heard Mrs. Kelly's sharp voice.

"How could you, Gloria? You have failed your daughter miserably," Mrs. Kelly yelled.

"I did what was best," Gloria said.

Reign and Alexis found them arguing near the pro shop.

"For you, not for Alexis!" Sixty-two inches of fury, Mrs. Kelly had a finger pointed in Gloria's face.

"How dare you. You didn't have to raise her, be terrified every day of her."

"You selfish woman. Fate blessed you with a daughter. Not a handbag you waited too long to return and now you're stuck with."

"I never wanted a daughter. I had sons." Her mother answered with that haughty tone she used when dealing with anyone she deemed beneath her.

The air whooshed from Alexis's lungs. It wasn't as if she hadn't already known, but hearing it aloud still stunned her.

"And with sons you didn't have to worry about your lineage," Mrs. Kelly added.

"I believe we should leave, Alexis." Reign took her arm and pulled, but she wouldn't budge.

"Gloria? What are you two talking about?" Alexis stepped forward.

Gloria spun, her face startled.

"Only females are Eidos or nulls. The gift is passed from mother to daughter, though in her case," Mrs. Kelly pointed a thumb in Gloria's direction, "it didn't take, and until Reign came along, I thought it had passed you too. I thought your lineage had died with your grandmother."

"It should have died—it would have died—"

"—if I hadn't been born." Alexis finished her mother's sentence. "I'm living proof of what you don't want to be." All the questions she had her entire life settled and brought a cold clarity she'd always lacked.

Gloria glanced at Reign. "I had hoped you would've had enough sense not to come and especially not to bring your fugitive lover with you."

Alexis's shoulders stiffened. "You heard."

"It's all over the news, though they haven't released your name yet. Chief Roberts called your father. Luckily, I answered his phone. Do you know what you've done to the family?"

Explaining would do nothing but make her seem nuts, but still, she tried. "It's not what you think."

"I think you've thrown away your freedom and respect for a man you don't know. And dragged the family into the gutter with you. Have you thought about how any of this sordid business will affect your brothers' careers and their families? Representatives from the RNC are here to speak to your father about a possible run for state senator, maybe something bigger. Now all of that is ruined."

"Is that all you care about? Your daughter is in trouble and you're worried about politics?" Mrs. Kelly shook her head.

"Mrs. Kelly, please!" Alexis had enough. "My mother's right. I've let her and my family down. If there was a way I could make this up to you—to Dad—I would—" she pleaded.

"The only way you could make this up is by leaving. Right now, before anyone else sees you and him, and calls the police. Really, Alexis! What were you thinking?" She glanced at Reign. "Then again, I don't think much thought occurred between your ears at all."

"I—I wanted to say goodbye to Dad," she whispered. This would be the last time she would ever see him, all of them.

"No, absolutely not. Do not drag him into your mess. He must stay above this. By tonight, we'll have formulated a story to give to the press and RNC. Now, leave and do not go through the clubhouse."

Alexis spun and took off across the golf course. Her heels flew off after the first few steps and she dashed across the grass. Directionless, she ran until her lungs burned and pain stitched her side. She ran until her legs ached and her knees buckled.

Strong arms scooped her up before she hit the ground. He took the brunt of the fall, skidding on the grass, while sheltering her with his body. One hand held her waist. The other palmed the back of her head as she gazed down at him.

"I'm sorry, Alexis." His hand trailed from her nape to cup her face. His thumb brushed away the tears coating her cheeks. She rolled off him and sprang to her feet. She wanted to run again, but only made it to a lonely tree standing nearby. Hugging the rough bark, she wept, sharing her despair with the night. The tears were more than from the caustic words of her mother. They stemmed from a culmination of all the events in the past few weeks. All the emotions she'd bottled up since putting on her detective shield, she released in a torrid stream.

"That's enough," he said close to her ear. She turned her head a fraction and saw him inches away. He grabbed her shoulders and turned her toward him. She tried to listen to him, but her tear ducts had decided to throw a pity party. The tears kept coming regardless of his order.

"I just wanted to say goodbye."

He kissed her. Hard. He molded his lips to hers, his body to hers, until her tears, her mother, and her former life were the last thing on her mind. Desire replaced the hurt, leaving Reign with his calloused hands, wicked tongue, and sinful body. He blotted out everything, but him. Burned away the hurt until she burned for him alone. More than she could ever have guessed, she needed him. Just him to help her bury her past and move into their future. She reached for him, cupped the bulge in his pants, and slid the zipper down.

He yanked away. She followed, desperate for his mouth on hers. Reign pushed her against the tree and held her there with one hand. She opened her mouth to question why.

"No." He shook his head. His chest heaved. Anguish lined his tight face. He wanted her, as she wanted him. Alexis grabbed a fistful of his crisp white shirt and pulled. He didn't budge.

"You will regret it later, when it's over and your tears have dried." His eyes were hard, his voice glacial.

Regret? She shook her head. "I won't regret us."

"You say that now," he said, so low she almost missed it. "You only want me to temporarily soothe the pain. It will not work. Though I wish I could, I cannot fix this hurt."

She couldn't deny what Reign said. Instead of breaking her, his un-sugarcoated truth strengthened her and clarified her resolve. Yeah, she needed him to soothe the hurt away. But not only for this moment.

She wanted a lifetime.

Oh...God. She inhaled a slow breath. "I want you. Hell, I seduced you." She glanced at her upturned hands and then rolled them into fists. "I felt everything you were feeling. It was the most intimate, intense experience of my life." He moved closer to her, his hand gripped her hip and tugged her to him. Every inch of him was hard. "I want to feel that again and not be afraid. I want to feel you again, moving inside me. To be a part of you."

She ripped off her gloves and the bracelet slipped off her wrist. She touched his abdomen. The muscles clenched beneath the crisp shirt. Alexis slid her hand up to his pecs, slipped her fingers along the open collar onto his warm skin and up the strong column of his neck. Yearning, abrupt and intense, stoked her. A corresponding echo built in her body and vibrated between them.

Reign picked her up and covered her mouth with his. Her tongue thrust wildly inside his mouth, mimicking exactly what she wanted him to do to her. She wrapped her legs around his waist and fit her core intimately against him. He palmed her ass and while his hips did a slow grind into her, his fingers slid beneath the edge of her mini. His hands were warm, just like his eager mouth. He squeezed the globes and one finger followed her thong.

Through her panties, he traced her lips, making her crazy. Alexis nipped his lip, urging him to slide the slip of fabric to the side and touch her. His slow fingers toyed with the lacy edge until she growled. She pulled his shirt from his pants and dove her hand beneath. The hard muscles of his broad back became her scratching post.

He hissed and then laughed when he yanked the lace to the side and delved into her liquid heat. Head thrown back, she rode his hand, crying out as he ground his palm against her clit.

Pleasure rippled through her. Alexis dragged her fingernails from his back, around his waist to his abs and squeezed them between their straining bodies.

One second they were dressed, and then they weren't.

"Reign," she yelped. Though the lighting so near the rough was dim, a passerby could still spot them.

"Shhh." He stroked from her nape to her rear. "No one can hear or see us."

A shimmering aura enveloped them. The barrier muted the starry night and cold evening air. Alexis didn't care about the hows, whys, or buts, only about the warm iron pressed against her.

Her hand slid over and around, circling until he moaned, "Alexis." Sensual words passed from his lips to hers, words that had no meaning to her ears, yet their sincerity touched her heart and opened her soul to him.

Reign shifted, placed his broad back against the tree. Alexis leaned back, tipped her hips, and guided him into her wetness. He stretched her, filling her so completely she purred when he nudged her womb. She gripped his shoulders, let her head drop back, clenched, and released her muscles around his shaft.

Reign's eyes crossed. A guttural moan ripped from his throat. She dipped dangerously close to the ground before he recovered and banded his arms around her.

"Don't do that again." He kissed her roughly.

So—she did it again, this time accentuating each part of the move and felt him throb within her body. He lifted her until the head poised to slip free and a sense of loss enveloped her. Then plunged into her. A jolt of ecstasy swept through each cell in her body, leaving her aching.

"More." She demanded and licked a trail from his ear to his flat nipple. Her nails flicked over his sensitive tip, causing his body to jerk. Frustration and pleasure mixed together in his throaty groan. She tweaked and laved each nipple while tilting her hips back and forth, clenching and releasing her muscles around him. He closed his eyes. His head fell back. Palms flat on his hot skin, his overwhelming need flowed into her. The need to belong. To be loved. The same need driving her.

Alexis braced her hands on Reign's heaving chest as his breath whistled through his gritted teeth. Mercilessly, her hips rose and fell in a steady rhythm. She rocked her body into his, taking him to the edge. Then slowed and leaned back so she had better leverage to grind her pelvis into him.

"Enough," he pleaded and wrapped his arms around her, stilling her movements. Effortlessly, he held her while his chest heaved. Pleasure rolled through her in successive waves and left no room for thought or reason. She wiggled a little, but one hand slid down her back and cupped her rear. He kissed her slowly, exploring her mouth as if nothing else in the world mattered. Then he lifted her bottom.

The loss of his thickness left her desperate until he eased her back down onto him again, and again. Faster, he thrust up into her body. Tiny orgasms racked her. Nothing had ever felt this good. A shock wave of ecstasy radiated from her core to every nail and hair follicle. She climaxed in a bright blaze of passion. Her cries, his shout, were for their ears only. Dazed, she felt Reign touch her womb and release a torrid stream, groaning her name in sweet relief.

CHAPTER THIRTY-ONE

Reign didn't want to let her go, but she slid down his body as he slowly released her. She leaned against him, her softness stirring him again. She gave him a lazy, sated smile. He buried his emotions and smoothed the hair off her face, and then kissed her swollen lips goodbye.

When they parted, they were dressed again; her hair and makeup were perfectly arrayed. No visible trace of the passion they'd shared lingered.

Space. The more, the better. He moved a few feet away from his Achilles Heel, yet he couldn't evade her gaze. Questions filled her coppery eyes. He had only one answer. Kill Alamut and return to Chemmis. That would please Roman and Nephythys, and safeguard Alexis.

Simple. Then why couldn't he tell her?

She stretched out her hand and touched his cheek. He didn't move. Her gaze stayed locked on his as she sifted through him. Thankfully, she didn't dig deep like Mrs. Kelly, only skimming the surface of his emotional grid.

He drew on his battle skills and submerged what his heart wanted, leaving the cold hatred of the Vanquished. A wave of fury surfed through him, banked by her palm and startled expression.

Alexis jerked her hand away and stumbled back. Her eyes wide and confused.

"Tonight hasn't ended the way you planned. Your mother doesn't deserve you." The Vanquished urged him to find the bitch and gut her. Finally, he wanted to comply with their wishes. "I know you want to bring Alamut to your kind of justice. Mine will have to suffice. I will take you back to your family and leave you in their care."

"You're leaving? Just like that? After..." Her eyes blazed with hurt and then darkened to a cold, flat glare. She marched away from him and snatched up her gloves and bracelet.

Immediately, the protective aura surrounding them ended. Sounds of the night, cold air, and the scent of fresh cut grass assaulted them. She shivered and wrapped her arms tightly around herself.

"Alexis."

Instead of stopping, she moved faster. He tried to flash and intercept her, but nothing happened. His atoms didn't separate and flow through space and time. He was still in the same spot with Alexis striding further away from him. He tried to fade. Nothing. Nephythys's vis'Ra was gone. Had she taken it back or had he used up his allotment? More importantly, did she know about Alexis?

"Alexis!"

She continued. He raced toward her, overtaking her quickly and grabbing her arm.

"Don't touch me." She yanked her arm away. "I thought you were leaving."

"I am—"

"Then leave!" she shouted and stepped close to him. "I don't need you to take me back to the car. I can get there without your damn help." Thin-lipped and tight-jawed, her body vibrated and her eyes buried daggers in his chest.

"Why are you angry?"

Her mouth dropped opened and her eyes narrowed dangerously before she growled, balled a hand, and struck him in the jaw. The surprise stung more than the blow.

"You. Are. An. Ass," she hissed. Toe to toe with him, her special scent mixed with his, filling his nostrils. He'd marked her. She stalked away, stumbled over her purse, and snatched it up. "You know, you almost had me fooled. But a man is a man, whether you're fourteen or two thousand years old. So, go, flash, fade, shift, disappear, whatever. I really don't care."

He tried again to shift and again, nothing happened. "I can't leave you. I tried."

"Bullshit. You're a god—wait, you've tried to leave already," she whispered.

"Yes, a moment ago."

She threw her purse. He caught it a second before she launched into him. Wrestling a woman wasn't something a warrior ever prepared for, especially when she fought dirty. She scratched, pulled his hair, and elbowed his ribs. When she kneed him and missed, he flashed behind her and scooped her flailing body into his arms.

"You lied!" she shrieked.

"I didn't lie. I don't know why I was able to shift a moment ago."

"Put me down." She pushed at his chest.

"No, not while you continue to fight me. I will not allow our last moments together to end with bitterness."

She stilled and the anger drained out of her body. Her face turned into his chest and for a moment she clung, her arms embracing him. She murmured, "Please, put me down."

He released her and regretted the emptiness when she stepped away. Wisps of wayward hair fluttered in the chilly breeze. In the weak lighting, her eyes were chocolate pools. Any man would die to erase the pain wallowing in their depths.

"Alexis." His sigh matched his desperation. He cupped her cheek, hoping his touch would convey how deeply he loved her.

"Don't," she pleaded, squaring her shoulders and stiffening her spine. "You told me you couldn't leave. You're tethered to me."

Her soft gaze threatened to unman him. "There is a way to break it."

Her shoulders slumped. "Why didn't you use it before?"

"I wanted to stay."

"And now you don't?" Sarcasm dripped from each word. Her nostrils flared and she folded her arms beneath her breasts.

"I cannot!" he yelled, frustrated at the universe.

"Then go!" She pointed off in the distance toward the dim recesses of the golf course. "You're not the first man to leave me and you probably won't be the last."

The thought of her with another man, touching where he just touched, filling her as he just did, made his blood pound in his ears. His vision dimmed until all he saw was her, with a phantom lover, stroking her lush body, making her slick channel clench and release as she moaned his name. Vicious thoughts crowded out common sense and good intentions.

"You are mine." He captured her lips with a fierce kiss meant to brand her soul. Too bad it had the opposite effect.

Alexis pushed away. Her face inscrutable, as her hair whipped about. "Then stay."

He drew her roughly into his arms and smoothed her wild tresses over her shoulders. "To save you, I must go," he breathed against her cheek.

"Save me? What do you have to save me from? What aren't you telling me?"

A thick fog gathered and rolled across the golf course. The Vanquished roared. Reign's blood quickened. Quimaera were near. He sensed two, then five, then more. His battle instincts merged with the Vanquished, turning him into *de Mortem, the Scourge*. His jagged blade materialized in his palm, ready to taste the enemy's blood.

The fog shrouded their bodies, but not their existence. They came from the fringes of the course, past the fairways and roughs, leaving only one escape route, the path back to the party.

"Run, Alexis. Get in your car and drive away."

Fright bled the color from her face. "They're here, aren't they?"

He nodded once.

"We led them here." She accused, her eyes impossibly wide.

"Get in your car and go." He shoved her toward the path, away from the encroaching mist.

"No!" She returned to his side. "My family is here. And I'm not leaving you." Alexis pulled away from him and ran to her purse. She snatched the evening clutch up and pulled out a small gun.

"That won't stop them." He studied the fog, aware of the danger to Alexis.

Her gaze met his. In her eyes, he could see the worry and the unasked question. How many were out there and could his soul afford the tally?

"It's better than nothing," she snapped.

A throaty bark echoed in the fog. Alexis raced back to his side and her foot slipped. She went down to one knee.

Reign knelt on the damp grass beside her. "Are you all right?"

"Yes." She pushed herself up. He grabbed her arm to steady her and caught a glint of gold in the mist.

"What is that?" He pointed to the object.

"My grandmother's bracelet." She picked it up and wrapped it around her wrist.

"Damnation!" Reign swore. His blade, the only weapon that could kill the quimaera was gone.

CHAPTER THIRTY-TWO

Khuket streaked through the sky, leaving the city behind. Beneath her, open fields bracketed by small towns illuminating the night. Her direction didn't waver as she zeroed in on her prey. With her traveled Alamut and more of her army. Anubis's slave had served her well. Soon she'd have the means to secure her freedom. Never would she be imprisoned. Never would she be at the mercy of another. The next time she returned to *Duat*, it wouldn't be as a slave, but as master. The end of the Egyptian Gods neared. Her pantheon would rule again. Neith had disappeared. Khuket's would be friend had left her at the first opportunity. She would pay, with blood and flesh.

The glow from Reign's protective shields pinpointed his location. Khuket moved forward, floating over the field. SET's command came to her again. '*Destroy him. Then bring him to me.*' '*Make him love you*'.

It should have been easy, but she had miscalculated. After the battle at the club, she'd sought to infect Reign's mind with chaos. His mental barriers offered no challenge; they tumbled, allowing her access to his dreams, nightmares, and guilt. She thought subtle manipulation, an infection of chaos into his already fractured mental processes, would push him over the edge. She didn't count on the woman's stabilizing presence. A counterweight to all Khuket's plans, the woman was the key to his fall.

And as far as making him love her, from the moment she met Reign, she was too late. His heart already belonged to the woman. And though chaos could bring ruin to their union, once a soul bound itself to another, it would never truly be free to love again.

Yards away, the object of the god's wrath copulated with his woman. An interesting act they both seemed to enjoy. She studied them. The joining of two bodies. The sliding motion and the sounds of flesh meeting flesh. The grunts and groans, the long sighs. The lips.

Strange. Parts of her tingled at the sight of them. Her species didn't mate. They simply came into being. After the Egyptians arrived and conquered, they forced their new slaves to change. No longer could they roam the world. They trapped them in strange forms.

The quimaera waited behind her, linked to her mind. She shrouded the field in fog, and then gave the command to attack. Her army loped across the field and vanished in the dense cloud. If possible she wanted them both alive. If not, SET would have to accept their carcasses. The need for delay was over. Her freedom waited.

***

"Where's your sword?" Alexis pointed to his empty hand.

Reign shrugged and his shoulders lifted and seemed to drop a foot. He hauled her to her feet and swept her into his arms.

"I can't see anything," she said as he carried her through the mist.

"I can. We're almost there."

The faint glow of the lanterns hanging from the back veranda came into view. People milled about the wide glass doors and windows, staring out at the thick fog. Reign entered and sat her in the nearest chair. Her family swarmed when Reign stepped back and retreated.

"Wait," she cried as the door closed behind him. She jumped up and hobbled forward. Reign stood on the other side of the glass, one hand pressed to it, his expression—unreadable.

"No!" She tugged the handle. It didn't budge. "Open the door."

He shook his head and mouthed. "Stay here." Then he was gone, swallowed by the mist.

"Alexis." Her father stalked across the room. "What's going on?" He used the same tone on his troops.

A crash sounded outside and the crowd pressed closer. The heavy smack of flesh hitting flesh reaching them and an excited gasp raced around the finely clad guests, sickening her. This wasn't a prizefight.

"Help me." She pounded on the glass. Thomas gripped her shoulders and tried to pull her away. She jerked out of his grasp and bumped into George.

"Let go of me!" They wrestled her away. She slammed her elbow into George's gut.

George grunted. "You don't know what's out there."

Alexis knew exactly what was out there. The lights blinked twice and then winked out. Panic circled the room and the murmured questions turned into angry demands as voices escalated. A bellow echoed outside. The crowd went silent. Another bellow—this time closer to the building—answered. A woman's scream ended abruptly, replaced by smothered sobs.

Alexis crept closer to the glass. Thick mist whited out the landscape. Still, her eyes strained to catch a glimpse of Reign.

A patio chair crashed into a window, splintering the glass. The crowd rushed to the exit, but another bellow echoed in the shrouded night. This time, right outside the front of the building.

"We're surrounded," her father whispered.

"By what?" George glanced at his wife and children.

Footsteps sounded on the roof. Everyone's head tilted upward.

Reign. She could tell by the tread.

Chandeliers swayed as he passed overhead. Alexis tracked him from left to right, until he stopped at the edge of the roof. A heavy thud landed on the other side and everyone's head turned left. Footsteps, heavier than Reign's, rushed across. Chunks of plaster fell and chandeliers rumbaed. The panicked crowd ran to the exits.

Alexis dove under a table and bumped into Gloria. Huddled together, Alexis couldn't remember the last time she was this close to her parent. Frown lines framed her mother's mouth and marred her forehead as her eyes widened in fear. Around them people screamed. George and his family were under the table across from her. Thomas and her father, another one. She peered around for John but couldn't find him.

A chandelier broke free and crashed, striking the edge of the table, tilting it.

"What's happening?" Gloria cried. Her fingers dug into Alexis's arm.

She didn't pry her mother's gloved fingers from her and push her away, though she wanted to. Instead, she stared at her with ill-concealed anger. An equal amount flared in Gloria's eyes. Somehow, her mother had the same cold, condescending glare she used from the moment Alexis escaped her womb. That one look would quell any rebellious outburst, wayward impulse, and unladylike behavior immediately.

Gloria lowered her eyes and dipped her chin. The hand gripping her arm softened and almost caressed her when the silk covered fingers slid from her skin. Her lips trembled, betraying an emotion her mother—Gloria—never showed. Her watery gaze rose. Alexis's chest tightened. She steeled herself against the response.

This display wasn't new, didn't reveal anything different about the woman. Practice. Makes. Perfect. How many times had she stood before the mirror with Gloria inches away, instructing on how to achieve the perfect visage?

Smile brightly, Alexis. No, not like that! Too many teeth and you resemble a shark. Now you look like a horse. Close your mouth, no one wants to see your tongue. Eyes wider. Did someone poke you in them? No, don't glare like that. You'll frighten the judges.

"Alexis, if what I said seemed harsh…"

Gloria's voice drifted away on a wistful note, as if the bitterness she spewed thirty minutes ago had evaporated on a different breeze and was nothing more than a disagreement over the dress Alexis chose to wear. Her mother wanted Alexis to finish the sentence, supply the apology, save her from having to admit anything. From saying two fucking words.

I'm sorry. She had never heard those words emerge from her mother's mouth. And at twenty-five, she'd no longer wait for them.

Enough of this. She had to help Reign. She scooted out from under the table when something heavy hit the surface. The table tilted and the edge banged into her head. Dazed, she slumped.

"Alexis!" Gloria caught her. Her mother shook her and tapped her face.

"I'm okay." Alexis touched the tender spot above her hairline and winced. Her fingers came back red. She tried to sit up, but Gloria pushed her down, examining her scalp.

"Are you sure?" Gloria asked.

Now she's concerned? "I'm good." The swimming sensation between Alexis's ears called her a liar. She paused and beat back the urge to hurl. On all fours, a full minute passed before all her senses re-aligned and were in compliance again. That's when she realized she was missing something.

Her gun.

Her purse and weapon were missing. She scrambled from beneath the table. Chaos surrounded her. Muted cries mixed with the crowd rushing from one end of the room to the other, trying to guess where the battle wasn't. A couple pushed her out of their way and she bumped into Mrs. Kelly.

"There you are!" Mrs. Kelly yelled above the din of falling plaster and screams. "Where's Reign?"

"Out there." Alexis pointed to the shrouded golf course. "We ran here. Then he left and did something to the door so I couldn't follow him. Now I can't find my gun and I have to get back out there to help him." She ignored the skeptical glare on the elderly woman's face.

"Help me!" Alexis grabbed Mrs. Kelly's thin shoulders.

Mrs. Kelly nodded and searched the floor.

"Alexis, get back under here," Gloria called.

A woman dodged a chunk of plaster and plowed into Alexis's side. Alexis spun, lost her footing on a piece of ceiling, and fell to her knees, bruising herself on a piece of rubble. Wincing, she lifted her knee and saw her grandmother's gold bracelet. Green eyes in one head, red eyes in the other, both twinkled at her.

Alexis forgot about her missing gun and the pandemonium surrounding her. She forgot about Reign, fighting for his life outside on his own. She forgot about the monsters, Egyptian Gods, Eidos, and everything else.

Compelled, she reached for her grandmother's bracelet—and blinked.

Did the jewelry leap into her hand and snake its warm body around her wrist, metal against flesh, snug and secure? Or, did she do it and didn't remember. Maybe the knock to her head did more than split skin. Hand aloft, stretched out as if her lower arm belonged to someone else, Alexis examined the antique.

"Where did you get that?" Gloria grabbed her hand, breaking the trance.

"I found it at Grandmother's." She attempted to pull her hand out of her mother's grasp.

"Give it to me." Gloria pried her fingers around one of the head and tried to uncoil the body.

The bracelet's grip tightened.

"I found your purse!" Mrs. Kelly rushed up, holding out the clutch.

Alexis snatched her hand away from Gloria. She opened her purse and gripped the cold metal of her Glock. Being armed should have comforted her, it didn't. The bracelet on her wrist gave her more confidence than the gleaming black metal and the full clip.

Mrs. Kelly pointed to the bracelet. "Oh, dear. Where did you get that?"

The building shook like someone had taken a wrecking ball to it. Everyone ducked but Alexis. Though she had her gun, Reign's words rang true. Bullets wouldn't stop what was out there. Frustrated, she searched the room again for anything that would help.

Crossed cutlasses hung above the fireplace. Retro Civil War relics, she didn't have the luxury of wondering the state of their condition.

Alexis dodged decorative molding and plaster raining from the ceiling, and screaming people as she made her way to the fireplace. On tiptoes she stretched, yet still couldn't reach her goal. She moved the grill out of the way and dragged a chair over. As her hand closed over the hilt of the first sword, a beast crashed through the glass.

She ripped both blades off the wall, made sure the safety was on before stuffing her weapon—barrel first—into the bodice of her dress, and jumped to the ground. The beast had already leaped to his feet and rushed out to the fairway. Mrs. Kelly called to her, as did mother and father. She spotted her brothers herding their families.

"Alexis! What are you doing?" George, the closest to her yelled.

"My job," she ground out. Why was it so easy for them to forget what she was? Carefully, she stepped bare-footed around the minefield of broken glass littering the floor.

"You can't go out there," her father called to her.

"I have to. Get everyone out of here to safety and wait for the police. Please, Dad." Not waiting for an answer, Alexis stepped outside.

The cold bricks from the patio stabbed the soles of her feet. Five steps and the fog smothered her so thoroughly, her heartbeat could've been the drum leading the troops into battle. Dry grass crunched beneath her feet, announcing her presence. She stumbled along, favoring her ankle, all the while biting her tongue to keep from calling his name.

Smacking and grunting echoed around her. Alexis skidded to a halt. Frantic, she spun, straining her senses for a direction. Damn, he could be inches in front of her or yards away.

"Alexis," Mrs. Kelly hissed closed by.

What the hell was she doing out here?

"Alexis," Mrs. Kelly called louder and then ran right into her.

Only God kept Alexis from skewering the woman. "Get back in the building!" she whispered furiously and turned Mrs. Kelly around in what she hoped was the correct direction.

"I can help." Mrs. Kelly gripped Alexis's arm and tried to do the same thing Gloria did, pry the bracelet off her arm.

"Let go of me." Alexis yanked her arm away and ran into the mist. She didn't get far before tripping. She swallowed a yelp and braced for impact, sure that the grass would offer some comfort.

A body cushioned her fall. She couldn't help the scream that ripped from her throat or her scramble to get away. The last thing she wanted was to be anywhere near one of those things much less laying on top of one, but it wasn't a hybrid thingamajig.

It was a man.

He was older, mid-fifties with a paunch. Too much sun had turned his limbs, head, and neck leathery while his belly gleamed comically white. Only it wasn't funny seeing his body sprawled on the greens with a jagged abdominal wound.

Caught in the crosshairs between Reign and the quimaera? How many more victims were out there? Indecision tore at her. She debated returning to the clubhouse or continuing her search for Reign. She'd asked her father and brothers to protect the guests and get them to safety. She had to trust that they wouldn't fail her.

Something gurgled—followed by a wet, sucking sound.

It's close.

Tremors spread along her nervous system, turning her insides soupy. Chest tight, she peered into the mist, willing the shroud to dissipate and allow her to see. She backed away and into something sharp.

With her weapons raised, she spun, ready to annihilate a spike from the decorative iron railing surrounding the clubhouse. Her gaze drifted down the length of the pole. The tip rested in the chest of a twenty-something year old man. No, not just a man, it was Dorian—Ruthless. The conversation days ago with his little brother, Dougie in the parking garage, crashed into her. Dorian's clammy hand clamped onto her ankle. Broken wet words bubbled through the blood clogging his throat.

Alexis dropped to her knees and grasped his quivering hand. "It's gonna be all right," she told him, knowing nothing would ever be right for him again. She looked at the spike and it was a short debate on whether to remove it. She wouldn't snatch the few seconds he had left on Earth away. He would die, pierced through the chest, on a country club golf course. Poor Dougie. Her heart ached for the little boy.

"Help." The single word gurgled from Ruthless's throat.

"Yes," she nodded. "Help is coming. You're going to be fine." This was one lie she would proudly defend on Judgment Day.

His eyes rolled up, as if he was looking at someone. *This is it. He's gonna die right here in front of me.* Instead of his lids slowly lowering and his chest heaving a sigh, the boy seemed to stare at a fixed point in the distance.

The mist shifted and she spotted Reign swinging for the upper deck with a pole from one of the patio umbrellas. The suit and tie were gone, replaced by his usual jeans and tee. He connected with the skull of a quimaera. The resulting shock wave reverberated in the mist. The beast flew and landed like a meteor striking the ground.

"M-my b-b-brother. Help him. M-my fault," the boy mumbled through the blood clogging his throat.

Sudden realization exploded within her head. *They're men. He's killing PEOPLE. But they're animals. Why didn't I make the connection?*

"That's your brother?" Immediately, her thoughts leaped to Dougie. She shook his shoulder when his eyes started to close. "Which brother!"

"My f-fault Dante is h-h-here. Tell Mom I'm s-s-sorry," he whispered as his grip weakened.

She held on tighter, willing strength into him. "What happened? How did this happen? How did you get here?"

"Promises...he p-promised so much...and w-we f-fell for it. T-tell my Mom—" His voice stopped in mid-sentence. The bit of life left in his eyes fled, chased off by death.

Alexis stopped breathing with him. Suspended in that fraction of time between life and death, a part of her wanted to grab him and somehow drag him back to the living. Not for his sake, but for the mother who would have to bury her child and the brother left behind.

Air rushed into her lungs, painful yet sweet. She had to save Dante. Give him a second chance, hopefully to make amends, right wrongs, and live a better life. Maybe he had learned his lesson and this foray into the darkness would be his last. She would never know and she'd scant time to wonder. Reign had reached his prey. He'd lifted the pole above his head, his intention clear.

She raised her gun and fired a single shot in the air. "Reign, stop!" she yelled.

His head jerked around. The spiked tail of the quimaera flicked and embedded deep in Reign's chest. Lifted off the ground, Reign dangled in the air, waving like a flag in a stiff breeze before being slammed to the ground. With another flick, the tail yanked free and the beast limped away, leaving Reign motionless on the grass.

    ***

Nephythys held the bowl, her gaze fixated on the muddy waters. She saw him, the object of her obsession, walking with, talking to, kissing, touching, lusting, f-f-fornicating with a woman.

"Careful, wife." SET pried her fingers from the bowl. "Do not damage the sacred relic." He moved it a safe distance away.

She couldn't breathe. Images of them together clashed in her head until she braced against the table for support. All the while her husband's rabid eyes glared, his thoughts fermenting behind his red-rimmed stare. Nephythys forced herself to turn and face him. An iron will kept her from glancing at the bowl.

"How long had the human lingered in your home?" SET asked.

That was not the question he wanted answered. She could tell him the truth. But by the destruction of every room they'd passed through, she doubted the wisdom of volunteering that piece of information. Unfortunately, she couldn't lie. The Goddess of Judgment must be truthful lest she be judged unworthy of her post. "Two centuries."

Darkness churned beneath his translucent skin much like a tornado destroying a placid landscape. "Know this wife. Our bargain is at an end. Every night you will appear in my chambers. Unclothed, nimble, and wet."

Nephythys stifled a cry of outrage. SET could do much worse to her. Besides, once she deposited her body in SET's bedroom, her essence would depart as it always had.

"Essence intact, wife."

"What?" She could not have heard him correctly.

SET crowded her, loomed over her until his brittle features filled her vision. "I will have you every night into perpetuity with your essence wedged inside this form." His gaze traveled down her body followed by the tip of a single claw. From her cheek to her neck, down to the curve of her breast to circle a puckered nipple, her flesh flamed in angry response.

"Starting tonight."

Nephythys blinked and he was gone without even a stray tendril trailing behind. She reached for something to destroy, then thought better of it. So many of her precious items were already broken she had little left to vent her anger upon.

Freedom. That precious commodity she had so little of, now she had even less. Every night to lay beneath SET, staring into his soulless eyes while he rutted above her, completely aware, feeling each thrust.

In a hot wave, her returning *vis*'Ra rolled through her. Immediately, she cleansed and clothed herself. It was barely enough. If she could shed her skin and burn it in the lava pits, she would. What joy she had in this existence ended the moment she stared into the sacred Nile waters.

Reign. Once revered, his name was now a bitter wedge in her heart. The Scrying bowl waited. Reign waited. His punishment would not be a simple banishment to the lowest levels of *Duat*.

She would take from him what he took from her. Then give him the judgment he truly deserved.

CHAPTER THIRTY-THREE

Something wasn't right. A moment ago, he was about to kill the final quimaera. Then, Alexis distracted him. Now, his body wouldn't cooperate. His legs wouldn't move and his breathing labored. How did this injury happen? The battle was won. All the beasts lay dead at his hands. No power other than his could claim victory this night. Neither the goddess nor the Vanquished. He alone defended what belonged to him. *Alexis.* His skill and ingenuity saved her and her family from extinction.

When the quimaera first came, the powers Nephythys had gifted him surged forth. His sword manifested, ready for combat. Then it disappeared, leaving him defenseless against the coming onslaught. Lessons from his father, Thrace's greatest warrior, resurfaced after so many lost centuries. Improvise, he had often lectured after stripping his sons of their weapons and then attacking both of them, first together, and then individually when they had grown.

Finding the spikes and poles he'd used to kill five of them was a blessing. Two died from broken necks and the last one he was about to finish off when something pierced his side, dropping him to the grass. He touched the area and felt warm, sticky blood leaving his body. Pain sliced into his chest when he tried to rise. But below his waist, numb, as if nothing ever existed.

Alexis's frantic voice came to him from a distance. Was she hurt? Why hadn't she stayed where he left her? The last beast had to be finished off before it regained its strength and returned to kill.

He tried again to rise, only to groan and cough in agony. Warm blood flowed freely and pooled beneath him. His lungs ached. If he could catch his breath, all would be well. Each struggle resulted with less air entering and more blood exiting.

Is this how an immortal died on a cold battlefield, leaving his love behind to bury his body? *No.* A warrior died this way, only he never thought he would leave anyone behind.

"Reign?"

Her voice bathed his soul and her hands touched his face, shoulders, and chest, soothing him. Now that he had someone to live for he couldn't die. He dug deep and willed himself to heal. He threw what energy he had into the effort, but in the end, he still lay in a growing puddle of blood.

Alexis grabbed his shoulders and pulled. Her image swam in his vision.

"Reign!" She stared at her red palm.

Strange how her hair looked like a river of blood flowing in the misty moonlight. Her face was ghostly and haunting. This wasn't the last memory he wanted of her.

"You said you were immortal. Couldn't die. Why'd you lie?" Her voice was shrill and accusatory.

"Did not lie," he managed to whisper, using what little strength he had left to raise a hand and stroke her cheek.

"Why aren't you healing? You have to heal." She grabbed a fistful of his shirt and shook him.

If only I could.

His entire time here he spent trying to leave her. Finally, he would succeed. Not quite what he expected, but fate would have its way. The irony twisting his insides had nothing to do with his injury. She'd shot at him. Likely helped kill him, yet he felt no bitterness. His death ensured her safety. Nothing else mattered. He stared deep into her teary eyes and was grateful he had met her, loved her.

Thank you, God, for this respite. The centuries of torture were worth every moment.

He had to tell her. In these last seconds, he would bare his soul and lay his heart at her feet. Reign opened his mouth to speak.

"Alexis!" Mrs. Kelly hissed, lost somewhere in the mist.

"Over here," Alexis screamed, her tears pelted his face. "She's going to get help. You'll be fine! Fine, you hear!" She stroked his face. "I-I'm ssso s-s-sorry."

He couldn't die with her feeling responsible.

"Alexis, what happened?" Mrs. Kelly kneeled beside him.

"I distracted him. I didn't mean to," she sobbed. "I-I had to stop him. He was killing them. They're not animals. They're human beings. Real people trapped inside those things. But now he should heal, but he hasn't. Why won't he heal?"

Human? The quimaera weren't human. Whatever humanity they claimed ended long ago. They deserved none of her guilt and neither did he. But his reserves were gone. He wouldn't be long for this existence. He wondered if he would return to *Duat,* to Nephythys. If he knew which gods would answer his prayers, he would pledge his fealty.

"Impossible, he can't die. He's a god. Well, demi-god, still..." Suddenly, Mrs. Kelly whipped a glove off her hand and pointed to Alexis's wrist. "Take that off!" She commanded.

"What?" Puzzlement contorted Alexis's face as she looked around.

"The bracelet, fool! Take it off and place it here!" She pointed to the opening of her white satin glove.

"Why?" Alexis demanded.

"It's the Serpent! One of the greatest relics of the Egyptian Gods. It nullifies a god's *vis* 'Ra, turning them mortal. That's why he won't heal."

Alexis held out her hand. "Take it off!"

Mrs. Kelly shook her head. "I can't. Only the wearer can remove a relic."

"This is bullshit!" Alexis said.

He watched as she uncoiled the bracelet from her wrist and dropped it into the glove.

"What now?" Alexis said.

A fire ignited in his bloodstream, burned away his paralysis, and flooded his system with more power than he ever felt before. Every muscle in Reign's chest seized, his heart kicked into overdrive while his lungs contracted, squeezing a harsh groan from his throat. Excruciating pain raced up his spine. A tingle turned into a thousand stabs attacking every muscle from his waist down. His muscles contorted and seized in one violent spasm. Alexis threw herself on top of him, trying to hold him down. He pushed her off and rolled away from the women. Seconds later, he surged to his feet with his sword singing in his clenched fist. Awareness singed him, fundamentally changing him down to his soul.

He peered at his surroundings with different insight. The night faded away, revealing the landscape in brilliant colors and vivid details.

Especially Alexis. Not only did he see her, but also her essence coursing through her body. The purity of her soul stunned him. This was what captured his heart. Not just the beautiful outer shell. Her strength, honesty and bravery, her true self made him fall.

Alexis wrapped her arms around him. She buried her face in his chest, sobbing, wetting his shirt as she trembled against him. He held her close, reveled in her curves while stroking her back with his free hand.

Her swollen eyes and blotchy face threatened his resolve, but nothing had changed. He still had to leave.

Reign wiped her tears with his calloused thumb and brushed her wild hair behind her ears. His fingers swept along her wet cheeks. He kissed her, wanting to brand his memory into her. Her lips opened for him, welcomed him inside. She sank into him, molded her body to his, and instead, seared her memory into his heart. To the end of time, in his darkest hour, he would remember her touch, the jasmine scent of her skin, her soft lips pressed against his and the passion between them. Regret flooded him as he ended their embrace with a kiss across her salty cheeks. Leaving her would break his heart.

"Alexis...I—"

"Don't you ever do that to me again!" she hissed and pushed him away.

To her? "Explain to me what I have done to you when you nearly ended my life?" One moment she was crying, the next she wanted his blood.

Her eyes narrowed and her lips compressed into an angry line. A dangerous finger pointed toward his chest and he wondered what she planned on doing with it. "You. Died…almost."

"You almost killed me."

"You left me no choice!" She stomped away and picked up her gun and the glove carrying the bracelet. "I couldn't let you kill any more of them. They're not animals." She stuffed the glove carrying the bracelet into her bosom, and then checked her gun and clip.

Was she still blind to their presence? "That is precisely what they are."

"No, look." The mist parted as she marched toward where the beast lay. Reign cut her off and wouldn't allow her to circumvent him. "Let me show you."

She grasped his free hand and tugged. He moved in front of her and led the way. The mist swirled and parted for them, revealing what he didn't expect.

A boy lay on the grass. Bruises covered his chest and abdomen from the pummeling Reign delivered. His eyes were dulled with pain, but didn't veer away from his gaze.

"It's Dante Woodard, the brother of the boy in the garage."

The conversation returned to Reign.

"Can you heal him?" She kneeled next to the man.

Heal the enemy? To return and attack again? He yanked her away and raised his sword to finish his opponent. The Vanquished screamed their opinion between his ears. Their alternating seductive whispers and braying voices would allow nothing less than complete annihilation of all foes. And neither would he.

"No!" She threw herself at him.

He caught her. The feel of her body thrashing against him, her voice pleading for the life of another when their lives hung in the balance, angered him. He faded and she passed through him. His sword turned crimson as he raised it for the killing blow.

"Reign, don't, please!" She pounded on his back and tried to throw him off balance. Part of him wanted to humor her, give her all of her desires, but this was too dangerous to indulge.

Kill it. Kill the beast. Let none live. The Vanquished chanted and goaded him. Their urgings more in control than his will.

He pictured Alexis immobile and watched as her hands dropped to her sides. Her astonishment didn't last as her tongue lashed him with angry words.

He stood over the wounded quimaera, watching the animal shift from human to beast. His blade slid smoothly into the scaly abdomen and ignited everything it touched. When the flames ended nothing remained, not even crushed grass.

The weight of all the souls slammed into him. Reign dropped to his knees. His sanity clung to the edge of a precipice. Above him, black earth, dead grass, and ash filled skies. Below, nothing. A ledge appeared on the side of the cliff and somehow his soul climbed onto it. The ledge gave him a slight reprieve from madness.

"You killed him." Her ragged whisper reached him louder than the hurled words a moment ago.

"I did what needed to be done. Protect you," he snarled. Fury hummed through him. Anger, sweet and hot burned through all reason.

"I don't need you to protect me."

"Alexis, Reign is correct. That thing was no longer a man, no humanity remained in him. He had to die." Mrs. Kelly joined them.

"You don't know that! He, he had family, a brother who needed him. He shouldn't have died like this on a fucking golf course in the suburbs without even a bloodstain to say he was here. They don't even have a body to bury." She closed her eyes and hung her head. Hair cascaded forward, shielding her from him. But then she lifted her head. Her eyes, so dark in the moonlight, sent a chill through his blood right down to his core.

"Release me," she ordered.

"No." He labored to his feet, staggering under the weight of the Vanquished. The collective fury spiked his blood. Instead of finding solace with Alexis, her anger fed his. A cold fury settled around him. He was a warrior. He answered to none and tolerated no one opposing his will. He would not bow to a woman.

"Stay with her," he commanded Mrs. Kelly, and flashed to the remaining corpses. He wouldn't leave them where they lay.

This world had many rules. The first: leave no body behind for the authorities to find.

He found each one in their human form, sprawled on the golf course. In death, one would never guess they were quimaera, aberrations stalking the earth. Perhaps Alexis was correct. His thoughts clouded, stoking his anger.

When he returned, her cold demeanor and hate-filled eyes hadn't changed. Mrs. Kelly waited a few steps away, out of the line of fire. Wise woman. He recalled the energy binding Alexis and prepared himself for the onslaught. She didn't look at him or acknowledge his presence. Alexis marched past him and headed toward the clubhouse.

"Alexis," he called to her retreating back, though he didn't chase her. They both knew exactly how far she would get. At one hundred feet, the tether yanked him in front of her, blocking her way. He reached for her.

"Don't!" She slapped his hand and moved away.

"I will not apologize for doing what is necessary."

"You enjoyed it." Finally, she looked at him, though he almost rather she didn't. Grim-faced, her flat, dead eyes accused him while her sensuous lips curled with disgust.

"The killing, you loved every second. Here I was worried, thinking you needed me, when the only thing you needed was your shiny sword. But not having that didn't stop you. Stripped of your powers, even an Egyptian relic didn't stop you. You weren't even angry. You were...efficient. Mechanical. It didn't cross your mind what you were doing, only that it get done. However they ended up, they were once human. Maybe there was another way."

"There was no other way. I did what was necessary to save you and your family from a rampaging army. Now you accuse me of murder," he snarled. His vision tunneled until all he saw was Alexis. "Would you accuse me still if your father had died defending you family against these beasts? Or would your spilled blood be your requirement for justice?"

The hardness in her eyes softened a bit and she sucked in a slow breath. "Justice against one, not wholesale slaughter. But that's what a warrior does, right? In the end, they were still human and didn't deserve to be slaughtered." She inhaled sharply and continued. "No jail can keep you, so I can't even arrest you, keep you from killing anyone else. You're indestructible." Wearily, her shoulders slumped and she raised her lowered gaze to his. "They're all dead and every trace is gone. But the wreckage caused here will remain. Go. I don't want you near me."

Could she be correct? ...No, she wasn't. They were monsters to be destroyed—but even if she were right—even if something human remained, they couldn't be controlled. Anger he could accept, but the regret in her eyes, with revulsion and horror mixed in, scared him. Maybe he should have listened to her and not let the Vanquished goad him into this.

Was it the Vanquished? Or did he do this of his own accord? Could she be right? Once again his thoughts twisted. An ache throbbed in his head.

"I said go, Reign."

Leave? Not until every quimaera lay dead would he go. "There are more of them out there in the warehouse, waiting to be activated and killed."

"I know. I'll contact Roman. Maybe after I explain the situation he'll help me save them, instead of butchering human beings."

"You turn to my brother for help?" He laughed, a harsh sound even to his own ears. "You foolish woman. He will do the same as I would," he sneered and leaned closer to her. "You will obey me."

"Or what?" she whispered. "What will you do when I don't? Kill me?"

Reign shuddered at the thought, some of his anger drained. "I would *never* harm you."

A sad smile curled her lips. "I don't know that. Worse, you don't know that." She sucked in a deep breath. "The police should be here any second. You've cleaned up your handiwork. No trace of evidence left. But there are witnesses. Maybe they'll believe some of what I tell them. Maybe I won't spend the rest of my life in jail. So you can leave. Go back to your goddess." She turned and walked away from him. Her shoulders tight, her back stiff. Mrs. Kelly gave him a sorrowful glance before following Alexis.

Her words ripped a hole in his chest. Moments ago, he was about to lay his soul bare, tell her everything that his heart felt. Now, bitterness marinated in his blood, polluting his heart. He'd been a lackey to one woman for two thousand years. He wasn't about to do it again. So why couldn't he take his eyes from her rigid back? Why couldn't he turn away, as she had done, and leave? He should rejoice. This was what he needed to keep her safe. Instead, with each step she took away from him, the hole in his heart widened.

He accepted the torment. Let its razor edge cut into him until nothing remained but the widening ache.

Darkness called, wanting its due. His thoughts turned muddy, chaotic.

If I cannot have her...

Reign blinked. For a precious second he didn't know where he was or why he had faded. His tumbled thoughts refused to allow him to focus on anything but his sword, clasped in a bruising grip, raised above his head, poised to strike. The blade screeched a woeful song between his ears.

His confusion melted, leaving stark clarity. He was about to slay the only good thing in his life. Why, when he'd never hurt a woman in his entire life? Why now would violence override his protective instinct toward the one person he would protect at all cost?

Yards away, Alexis marched, steadily increasing the distance between them. He thanked the gods she hadn't turned and seen him. Not that it mattered. After how he treated her, she had every right to leave.

"Alexis, please..." He scrubbed a trembling hand across the back of his neck and prayed she would give him a chance to apologize.

Mrs. Kelly kept walking while Alexis stopped. Half turned, her profile showed a single wet cheek.

A flash of light illuminated the night. A shock wave slammed into him, lifted, and flung him across the field. He tumbled, feet over head and face planted in the grass. He sprung to his feet. Fury washed over him, bringing the unmistakable aura that always encompassed the Goddess of the Dead.

Panic gripped him. *She could not be here!* Reign squinted into the receding light to where Alexis last stood. He spotted her on her knees, doubled over, and grasping her head. Her face contorted in agony. He shouted her name. She turned to him. Her eyes were thin slits, her features twisted. He stepped toward her and was flattened onto the grass. Energy hummed around him.

Get. Up. The blade sang. The Vanquished roared, but he couldn't budge, though he quivered and strained against an unseen power. Time stretched while he fought a silent battle to move one muscle, then ten, then one hundred. Finally, he pushed back the energy pinning him and climbed to his knees. He raised his head and saw a whirling vortex between him and Alexis, who was sprawled unconscious on the grass. At the other end, Nephythys waited in all her regal glory. Her lips moved in a silent chant while her frigid gaze pinned him. Alexis rose and floated toward the swirling opening—and doom.

"No!" The bonds restraining him snapped. Reign flashed across the distance separating them. He dove, hands outstretched, reaching for Alexis. He almost had her. *Just a little bit more.* The ends of her hair brushed his fingers and escaped his grasp.

Reign skidded across the grass. By the time he gained his footing, Alexis was gone. The vortex had swallowed her. Only Nephythys remained, glaring at him from the other side. He leaped into the vortex only to be repulsed with equal force.

Nephythys's voice filled his head. "Fulfill your vow, Reign, and she will live. Fail and her life is forfeit."

"Touch her and die." His heart didn't race. His palm didn't itch for his blade. The Vanquished were coffin quiet.

"Kill Anubis's champion and return."

"As. Your. Slave." He glowered.

"So it shall remain. You stand judged."

The ethereal beauty that had once captivated him was gone, stripped away. Never had he seen her true essence, the stark power that ordained her to judge all who passed through her temple. Lesser men trembled, bowed, scraped to find her favor or gain clemency. If he thought doing any of those would sway her, he'd gladly do them all. He knew Nephythys would have none of it. Except her revenge.

The vortex winked closed, leaving the woman he loved at the mercy of the woman he despised.

CHAPTER THIRTY-FOUR

"Nephythys!" Reign bellowed into the night sky. His knees buckled and his body caved.

The tether binding him to Alexis severed the moment the vortex closed. Crushing pain bit into him and yanked him into the abyss filling his soul. Reign drank in the pitch, welcomed the encompassing hate. The darkness in him fractured what was left of his soul. Power leaped through his arteries and swept to every part of his body.

ALEXIS.

The Vanquished faced him. All of the men he'd conquered gathered in rows, fanning out. Their phantom shapes wavered in the gentle breeze. Their words hummed in his brain. Tempting him. For the first time, he didn't fight them. He hailed their collective rage, fed off the blinding fury sweeping away the protective resistance he had forged for two millennia.

Each kill he remembered, relived, and felt weighing on his soul. Most were righteous, though there was nothing righteous in warfare. There were tasks and goals, lands to conquer and foes to crush. Alexis was wrong. Never did he find any enjoyment in the killing. He used his skill to kill quickly, efficiently, and shouldered the remorse he buried with each swing of his blade. He carried on, collecting this army only he could see. And his recent kills had joined the Vanquished and added more weight to his soul. Once the precipice had seemed so far away, now only a hairs breath separated him from the yawning cavern.

Yet he didn't feel crazed. His fury, and that of the Vanquished, buffeted him, not with madness but with determination to retrieve what they'd lost, what belonged with them.

KILL.

The word whispered in his ear. Reign nodded in agreement. To save Alexis he would kill anything, anyone. Damn the consequences.

Instinct led him to raise his sword in the air and command the vortex to appear. Undulating waves appeared, but no whirling portal to the Egyptian Pantheon. Precious moments ticked by as he tried, finally bellowing in frustration.

His gut churned, imagining what Nephythys was doing to her. Would she house her in the palace or in the bowels of Duat—Hell? Or worse, Judgment and eternal damnation. He had to get her out! *Now.*

Their last words to each other haunted him. '*Go back to your goddess,*' Alexis had told him. He'd saved her only to lose her. Never would he have thought Nephythys could be so devious. There was no way out of this trap.

Reign pivoted toward a copse of trees.

Alamut!

He sensed the beast shrouded in the mist still covering the golf course. His knees locked, body thrumming. Killing Alamut gained him access to Chemmis and Alexis. Enslavement was the price he'd willingly pay.

Alamut charged from his lair, racing on all fours. Reign met him head on without his blade clutched in his hand. He wanted to feel the life ebb from Alamut's body. He dodged a swipe, claws grazing his head, and took the fight inside, close to the body.

A right jab knocked its head to the side. Hands balled, Reign punched the scaly armor protecting the beast's chest and belly. His fist bounced back, stinging from the impact.

"Is that your best?" It chuckled, a barking sound that was alien to the ears.

Reign ducked, narrowly missing being impaled by a barbed tail, but failed to dodge the dagger-like claws. They ripped through his tee shirt and opened the flesh over his ribs. The beast flashed. Reign followed.

He appeared in the woods at the rear of RockGate. In the distance, the mansion was a jewel twinkling in the night. Roman was inside, along with his wife and the men he called brothers. Family, something Reign once had, lost, and longed for with Alexis. Now, he would never have.

"It's so good to come home," the beast hissed a few yards away. "This is a good place to die. I'll leave your body on Roman's doorstep."

"This battle will not differ from the last. This time, you die." A left hook to the body lifted Alamut off his feet. A distinct snap of a rib sounded. He stumbled back. His grunt and gasp satisfied Reign, as did the energy surging through his veins.

Two quick jabs, followed by a round of body shots and Alamut's armor plating fractured, then cracked under the onslaught. Fire streaked over Reign's flanks and back. He ignored his injuries and focused on beating his way to Alamut's spine.

Alamut's mass began to dissipate. No longer completely solid, Reign's fist passed through the center of him.

He couldn't let him dematerialize again. Reign grabbed Alamut's hands. His claws dripped blood, Reign's blood. He didn't know how to be a god, part of him still didn't truly believe he was. But deep red waves bled from his hands and into Alamut. For the first time he recognized the source. His vis'Ra, not Nephythys's, flowed through him.

The beast's flickering form solidified. Reign looked into Alamut's slitted eyes, triumphant.

The smile slid from Reign's face, replaced by a growing numbness. His hands dropped from Alamut's wrists and dangled at Reign's sides. It was Alamut's turn to grin.

Reign looked down. His eyes-widened at the spike protruding from the right of his chest. With a flick of Alamut's tail, Reign was airborne.

Launched into the night air, he scattered his atoms and coalesced yards away, whole, healthy, sword in hand, crouched in attack stance.

Before Alamut could move, Reign was upon him. He feinted left, parried a blow while he brought his sword around, and sliced into the armored chest. Flames swept the edges, turning the blade neon. The sword cut deep. Alamut tried again to flash. He sputtered like a flickering candle. Reign couldn't tell whether he or the blade held Alamut to the spot.

The tail skimmed the ground, inching his way. Like a snake about to strike, it rose from the ground and crashed into Reign's shields.

"Did you expect the same attack to work again?" Reign yanked his sword free and dropped down. A slash to the lateral tendon followed by a punch to the kneecap pitched Alamut forward. Just before he would've toppled, Reign flashed behind him. His blade pressed inches into Alamut's throat, ready to cleave his head from his shoulders.

"Wait," Alamut shouted. Flames and the sharp edge licked his skin. "I can get you to Chemmis."

"Your death will achieve that goal."

"I can get you there without you selling yourself to Nephythys."

Was it possible? He dared not hope. "How?" He eased the blade a fraction off Alamut's thick neck.

Crocodiles couldn't grin, but that didn't stop Alamut from making an attempt. "I will show you, but first you have to do something for me."

CHAPTER THIRTY-FIVE

No.

The word exploded inside Reign's head. Alamut thrashed and tried to shake him off. Reign held firm and heard the satisfying sound of tendons ripping. He wanted to tear the beast's head from his shoulders for what he had suggested.

Reign had a choice. He could still kill Alamut and accept his fate. Yet, he couldn't trust Nephythys to honor her word. She might not be able to lie, but she would manipulate events to serve her purpose.

Alexis's face jumped to the forefront of his mind. Her warm coppery eyes set like gems in her freckled face, framed by her curly red hair. Despair ripped through him. He couldn't chance it and leave her to a fate no one deserved. She'd have an eternity of suffering. He had to save her even if it meant returning as Nephythys's slave and giving up the only rays of light he had in his entire existence.

He pushed Alamut away and watched him stumble. "Get up."

Alamut dissolved and the man he had met in Roman's vault appeared. "Daniel."

"I guess you've seen the wisdom in my words. And that you have no choice." Daniel climbed to his feet, clothed.

There's always a choice, Reign remembered his father saying as he stared at their mother's image. Frantic his mind searched every angle of this impregnable prison. "I could kill you and end this," he said, buying precious time to think.

"You had your chance. But you didn't. You let me go so you could have your happily ever after." Daniel flexed his neck.

"Without me still breathing you'd get life with the goddess as her slave."

"I regret not ending your life in the boxcar." Impotent fury pumped through his veins. The Vanquished howled. They wanted to carve the flesh from Daniel's bones in slow chunks.

"But ya didn't. Now you get to wallow in regret as my bitch." Daniel tipped over laughing. "I listened to you pleading with her on the golf course. Exactly what kind of slave were you?" He leered. "Doesn't seem bad to me, better than serving her fucking son, but to each his own."

Reign didn't answer, he couldn't. His one selfish action had led him to the ultimate betrayal. He did the only thing he could, he trailed behind Daniel as the shape-shifter led the way to the mansion.

"I'll wait here." Daniel stopped at the edge of the woods. "Bring Roman out here. I want to see you do it." A smug grin covered his face.

Reign clenched his fist to keep from burying his knuckles deep inside Daniel's face. He was tempted to ask why, but feared his control would fail if he had to endure any more of Daniel's voice. Instead of flashing, Reign walked and used the extra few minutes to wallow in his nightmare.

A thought struck him, momentarily blinding him. *There's a way!* He could do it. Save Alexis, and Roman.

No. It was too dangerous.

One wrong move and the two people he loved would be lost. Damnation.

His brain scrambled for another alternative only to return to the same conclusion. He had a single option, and if it didn't work—

Reign shoved the horrific thought away.

Half way to RockGate, a wavering barrier of energy barred the way. Tightly woven ethereal strands shimmered, similar to the barrier he'd encountered at the factory. He paused a moment and then barged through.

Faded, he passed through the brick walls and walked through the house. The mansion was quiet with only a few people about and only one of Roman's men present. Good. For now, avoidance was best since he'd have to face them soon enough. Especially if...

No if. Can't think about 'if'.

In war, *if* was a lesson in what could have been. Guarding his emotions from Roman, he stretched his *vis 'Ra* and searched for his brother.

Reign found Roman in his study, sitting behind a desk with his wife on his lap. He was embarrassed to interrupt what was clearly about to happen, but grateful he hadn't arrived a few moments later.

"Ahem," Reign cleared his throat with his back to the couple. His brother's wife shrieked and there was the frantic rustle of clothing while his sibling cursed.

"Heard of knocking?" Roman demanded.

Reign guessed they were decent and turned. Redness colored Stella's cheeks. She was a beautiful woman, delicate and dainty. Once he had favored the same type of female. Now his taste ran toward a redheaded, freckle-faced Amazon with a weapon tucked to her side.

"Brother, my apologies. I need you to come with me." He waited while Roman assessed him.

"Why, and where?"

Reign banked his emotions behind a neutral façade. "I need to speak to you." This was as close as he would come to begging. Any more and Roman would waver and unnecessary blood would be spilled.

Roman turned to his wife and tenderly kissed her. He whispered in her ear, causing a seductive smile and a twinkle in her eyes. She gave her husband a nod and walked away, but stopped in front of Reign.

"It's good to see you again, Reign. You've cut your hair and beard. Identical Nicolis', I can only imagine you two fighting together."

He didn't have to imagine. The memories were still vivid.

"You and Alexis are always welcome here." She graced him with a kind smile.

"Your hospitality is most gracious. My brother has found a jewel to treasure." He placed his palm over his heart and bowed.

She glanced over her shoulder at Roman and smiled. "So have I." The soft swish of her dress and subtle fragrance of her perfume lingered, hammering home all that lay at stake. The door clicked behind her, signaling the beginning, or his end. One chance is all he would have at this. One chance to save them all or lose everything.

"Though your timing sucks, I'm glad to see you," Roman started. "I apologize for my behavior the last time you were here. The greeting I gave you was not the one I envisioned."

"Roman—"

"Let me finish. All of our time together, through all the battles and journeys, I never doubted you. And you've done nothing to make me doubt you now. You're my brother, Reign, and I'm apologizing for treating you as anything less than my twin. My home is your home and I'd like you here with me." He came from behind the desk.

Reign couldn't speak over the lump lodged in his throat. For centuries, he wanted nothing more than to be rejoined with his sibling. Only his will and his last image of Alexis kept his emotions under tight control.

"Now, what do you need?" Roman clapped a hand on Reign's shoulder.

"Remember the last time we were together at the Villa?"

"Of course, I met Elyssian and you—"

"Disappeared." *And ended up at the mercy of Nephythys.* "We trusted each other. Can you trust me, brother, one last time?"

Roman studied his face before he nodded. "What do you need from me?"

Where to start? Yet he couldn't explain. The only way to ensure success was by surprise. Beside, even if he explained, Reign was certain Roman wouldn't believe him. The trust between them was to new. "Brother, there is something I must do." Reign didn't mean to whisper, but the words almost refused to leave his mouth.

Roman's brow lowered. Reign didn't move as his brother's gaze burrowed into him. Roman searched for truth while Reign searched for something else. He found it in a faint glow illuminating the depths of Roman's eyes.

Footsteps pounded down the hall and the door burst open. Thane raced in and skidded to a halt. "Roman! Daniel's on the back lawn by the woods."

CHAPTER THIRTY-SIX

Failure! Impotent fury raged within Khuket. What would it take her to finally be free? Every force in the universe had aligned against her. But she would thwart them all. First, she would stop leaving her fate in the hands of incompetent sub-creatures. But she wasn't powerful enough to kill Reign herself. And now with the woman gone, Khuket couldn't use her as a pawn. None of that would change the inevitable.

Ever watchful, Khuket followed Reign and Alamut from the golf course. When Alamut hid in the woods, Khuket shadowed Reign as he walked towards the large dwelling. She saw the shimmering wards, and so did he. He paused and tentatively stretched out his hand.

She did the same.

His fingers passed through. Her fingers sizzled as if placed on a pyre. The sensation raced through her essence, nearly debilitating her. The signature was familiar, undeniable. Shock numbed the burn. She shook off her momentary paralysis in time to attach herself to the man. Not inside him, because he would know she invaded him. She compressed her form and fit against his skin, under his layer of clothing.

The warmth of his flesh surprised her, along with the smoothness and the ripples of muscles underneath. As he passed through the wards, Khuket pressed herself more firmly to the contours of his body. She still sizzled, but clinging to him, she passed through intact. Immediately, she separated and streaked toward the house.

Subtle energy washed over Khuket when she entered the dwelling, setting her aflame. The author of her race's destruction resided here. Revenge would wait no longer. She sped through the structure, searching for the source of the faint signature that seemed to be everywhere. It permeated the house, confusing her efforts. Tonight, nothing would gainsay her. Tonight, she would dine on the blood of her enemy.

Up the stairs and down a long hallway, her essence sped until she jerked to a stop at a door protected by weaves similar to those shielding the house. Cautiously, she approached. Though comparable, these threads were dull, unbalanced, and ragged.

Khuket grinned. The barrier would not keep their maker safe. A slight singe jolted her hand when she forced it through the weaves. She didn't stop until she gripped the knob and moved into the room.

Not what she expected lay on the other side. In dim lighting, under layers of covers, a child slept...but the Egyptians were deceivers. Trust none and question everything your eyes see. Raised voices filtered through the walls, shouts and a scream.

A sudden spark of energy surged from the sleeping child. Khuket extended her power and gathered the unseen chaotic waves flowing through every being she could reach—even hers—into a tight ball. One chance is all she would have to slay her greatest nemesis.

***

Deep in her meditative state, Nu rebuilt her energy and healed the body of her host. It was a slow process. The child could barely contain her and each time she used her vis'Ra the child slipped further into the darkness. There was no biological reason for it.

Yes, her vis'Ras could be destructive, but foremost she was a healer, a grower, nurturer of all things, and mother of the Pantheon. The energy she fed the child was pure. So why did her spirit falter and split into darkness, taking Nu along with her? Each day they grew weaker. Only strict conservation of her energy had saved her from leaving this realm and being forced to return to Chemmis.

Days had passed since she last expended any energy to check on her children. She could sense them, knew they were alive and on this plane of existence. Sometimes their emotions filtered to her. Mostly anger and sometimes passion. She blocked the latter emotion and focused on their patterns.

If her sons were stronger, they could sense her like the Gods of the Pantheon. But they were half gods and thus limited. She did the best that she could for them by binding their *vis'*Ras at birth—and though it broke her heart—leaving them soon after to safeguard their presence. Those acts allowed them to mature. Now, they weren't just formidable men. Already Reign showed signs of a breach in the psychic fortress she'd locked his vis'Ra behind. If Roman would do the same, nothing could harm them. Together they were—

A backlash of energy pummeled her through the link to her sons. One was in pain, no…agony and rage, but why? Nu expended what energy she could and easily found Roman inside the house, happy and content. Frantic, she turned her attention to Reign, but the link abruptly severed. Using the secret pathways she always used into his mind, she tried again and found a smooth steel door. She couldn't reach him. Did he know of her?

She tried again, beating against the mental barricade to no avail and in the process, exhausting her host. Then she felt him pass through the wards she had created to protect the house. A moment of relief flooded her until she read his patterns through the weaves of the wards.

Altered.

The Reign she watched—even when he was in *Duat* enslaved by Nephythys—was not the same entity that now entered the house. She tried another pathway and another, flitting around the edges of the steel trap of his core, searching for any entrance.

When he flashed to the back lawn and passed through the next barrier to the house, she discovered a sliver of an opening and slipped inside. Her soul ran cold.

NO! This I will not allow.

Regardless of the consequences, she had to stop him.
***

Khuket paused, ready. Bright light pierced the gloom and the goddess Nu separated from the child. The goddess gasped and a desperate look swept over her features. "My children! Reign, no!"

Children! Reign and Roman. Twice the pain. Revenge delayed is just as sweet. Before Nu could flash, Khuket hurled her weave. Aimed at Nu's chest, the dark ball of energy stopped inches away, snapped opened and wrapped around her. Tendrils, blacker than night, bound her. The goddess collapsed, shrieking in a wail that shattered all the windows in the room and rolled through the house.

Khuket hesitated. Something was wrong. This weak creature could not be the goddess who conquered her kind at the beginning of time. The deity Khuket remembered would never have succumbed so easily. Still, she wouldn't give the Egyptian a chance to recover. She gathered another ball of energy. This one wouldn't bind her. This one would go straight into her heart. "Hello, Great Goddess. Look at me and remember."

CHAPTER THIRTY-SEVEN

A roaring fire blazed in the fireplace, an afghan was wrapped around her shoulders, her feet were in her favorite slippers resting on the ottoman, and she had a cup of tea and a plate of basboosa and baklava made with Egyptian honey. Together, all of these things didn't chase away the loneliness devouring Hathoria Gregory's soul, but they did make this one evening a bit easier to bear. The temptation to reach out to her only child's mind gnawed at her. Tyrone had taken up a quest, one she didn't approve. The day of his blind obedience had ended long ago, yet still too soon.

"He's not a child." She reminded herself and nibbled on the pastry to soothe the ache in her heart. The time to cut the cord had passed, but he was all she had.

She always knew, sooner or later, he would discover the truth—the secret she buried in the shifting sands eons ago. If only *sooner* would wait a bit longer.

"Damn." Her tea was cold. Hathoria peeled off the afghan from her lap, shifted her feet from the ottoman, and stood. She could warm the brew with a thought, but in the waning years of her mortal life, any expenditure of energy taxed her human body and pushed her closer to death. Not for the obvious reasons she didn't want to die. Death would end this life, though not her existence. Once this human form died, the goddess Hathor would return to the Pantheon that would punish her, thus leaving her son unprotected.

Carefully balancing the cup in her trembling hands, Hathoria shuffled off toward the kitchen. Halfway there, Nu's wail stabbed through the protective shields guarding her mind.

It was a psychic scream for help that the goddess dwelling within her couldn't ignore. Hathor peeled away from the mortal shell and caught her human body before it fell.

Gently, she guided her vessel back to the living room and made her comfortable on the sofa in the house which she raised their son. She didn't have time to linger or wonder if she would return. Nu's cries clawed at her. Hathor had no idea why the goddess called, but when the mother of the Pantheon summoned, you came.

Hathor covered the distance between her home and Nu's bedroom at RockGate in a matter of seconds. Nu lay struggling on the carpet, bound by bands of energy with an unknown deity stalking her. A ball of discordant power balanced in the stranger's hands, who stood ready to throw it like a pitcher in the last game of the World Series.

Hathor darted between the two. She stopped the hurled ball by extending her energy around the sphere. Quickly, she studied its erratic pattern to unravel the weave. She'd never seen anything like this energy before. It conformed to no regularity.

The ball burned through Hathor's shield. It knocked her across the room into the wall. She crumpled on the floor and stilled while the energy hovered above, waiting for her to move. The ball spun and tracked back to Nu.

Across the distance, Hathor's and Nu's gazes met. Nu forced her thoughts into Hathor's mind.

No, Hathor answered and ignored the order to leave and stop Reign from whatever disastrous choice he was about to make on the back lawn. Nu tried to compel her, yet she was weak, too weak to command, too weak to save herself. Hathor flashed between the ball and Nu, and deflected it back to its master.

"I did not plan to kill two Egyptians tonight." Balls of energy gathered in the stranger's hand. "Fortune favors me this day."

"Who are you?" Hathor demanded as she collected her vis'Ra.

Red rimmed, pitted eyes glared from an ashen face surrounded by dark pixie hair. The tattered remains of a gown billowed in thick, angry bands stretching yards from the stranger's petite body. "Who am I!" she screeched and the balls increased with her ascending rage. "Ask that bitch!" She hurled the energy, one at Hathor, and the other at Nu.

The Goddess of Love couldn't stop both, not at her present energy level, and this wasn't her fight. Whoever this Goddess was and whatever Pantheon claimed her, she had a serious hard on for Nu.

Hathor could walk away, like Nu walked away and left the Pantheon to wither on the vine. Hathor didn't judge her, at least not as the others judged and condemned because she also left, and found love. Besides, the Pantheon deserved to wither. Those bastards deserved exile in *Duat*.

She couldn't call on them. They'd more than likely take bets than help. By now, they'd all heard Nu's cry. The council would gather, a debate would ensue, and while they argued, she and Nu would die.

Nu chanted, archaic words no longer spoken in the Pantheon. Words Hathor remembered seeing in an ancient scroll that Nu had once snatched from her inexperienced hands. The room shook and dipped like a plummeting elevator. Chunks of plaster fell and the machines attached to the child cried an escalating tune.

"Chant as you will, Egyptian. It will not work. How many millennia have I had to work my spell, this spell that will punish you for your crimes?" Her eyes blazed as she beheld Nu. Then she turned to Hathor.

"I am Khuket, Goddess of Chaos and Darkness. Deity of Ogdoad. I am the last of my kind and the last thing you will ever see."

There was only one road Hathor could take, a path she never thought she would. Steeling her heart, she reached out across the distance and found a source she could use to bolster her energy. So familiar and very similar to her own, except for one key thing. It wasn't Egyptian, not completely, which was a boon. She tapped into her source as the ball struck the shields she had extended around herself and Nu. Fortified, the barrier held…until the whirling mass burrowed through. First, a small fissure, then a wider gap as her weaves melted under the onslaught.

She glanced at Nu. Granite-eyed, Nu watched the second ball do the same to the shield blanketing her. Hathor turned to her source again and drained it of every bit of power. The consequences of this action were unknown. There wasn't anything she could do to change any of it except fight and pray her son would not hate her for her actions this day.

Energy pooled into her, slightly alien, though adaptable. Channeling the force through her body to her palm, Hathor blasted Khuket across the room, smashing her through the farthest wall and into the adjacent bathroom. Pieces of wood, chunks of plaster and paint mixed with a geyser from a shattered sink.

Hathor didn't have a chance to claim victory. Khuket peeled herself from the floor. She levitated back into the bedroom. Wet and filthy, the wreckage followed her, gathered, and became projectiles wrapped in the same vis'Ra as the balls of energy. Hundreds of pieces, big as two by fours, small as splinters, darted toward them. Hathor reinforced her shield with the stolen energy. She slowed the deadly objects.

The bedroom door swung open and Stella stood on the threshold. Her gaze darted between the three Gods and the child on the bed. She rushed toward the child.

Hathor dropped her defenses. A mortal caught between three deities wouldn't survive and Stella's presence would only give Khuket leverage. Power leaped from Hathor's hands. She caught Stella, flung her out of the room, and sealed the door.

Hathor shielded Nu and herself a second before the first projectiles struck. The barrier didn't stop them. Instead of blasting through Hathor's weaves, they pierced the barrier in agonizing increments. Her vis'Ra couldn't defeat this creature, but maybe something else could. Hathor manipulated the spewing water, redirecting the geyser and drenched Khuket. Then she channeled the electricity in the house, pulled it from the nearest sockets, and deflected the streaming arc at her enemy.

The lights in the house flickered wildly. Not far away, a transformer blew and sparks rained on the withered late October grass, throwing the mansion into darkness and cutting off her supply.

Smoking, yet still standing, Khuket wobbled on her feet.

Bent over, hands braced on her knees, chest heaving, Hathor had nothing left. Her shields fell. Hathor deflected the larger pieces of wood and plaster, but the smaller pummeled and stabbed them.

She had to call for help. Together, the Pantheon would destroy Khuket—before they turned their attention to their missing members.

Fingers brushed Hathor's bare feet and Nu's thoughts filled her.

Look to the night.

Hathor glanced out of a destroyed window. A single, dense cloud raced across the moonlit heavens, a spark of lightning crackled within. She raised a hand to the sky, the other to Khuket, and with Nu's help, channeled the lightning through her body and across the room.

Khuket buckled. A bright orange flame ignited within her body. Her mouth opened in a silent scream and the flame consumed her form. She vaporized, leaving twinkling lights hovering in the air. A second passed before Hathor realized what they were. *Hundreds of them.* Somehow, Khuket had unjudged souls encapsulated within her.

Five flickering lights lingered. Denser than the rest, these mini black holes swirled as they hovered.

Hathor gasped. *Sentinels! They were free!* They darted away, each in a different direction before she could capture them. One catastrophe diverted only to have another on the way. Did Khuket know what she'd stolen from *Duat*?

No. If Khuket knew, she wouldn't have wasted time trying to kill two deities. She could've conquered this world and laid waste to Chemmis.

The prophesy came to mind, but Hathor pushed the thought away. The tomb caging the Slayer shifted through time, never in the same place longer than a day, forever lost in the desert. The Rising would never happen.

Hathor kneeled next to Nu. The goddess tried to speak, but her form flickered weakly. Hathor looked to the child and detected a dwindling sliver of life, though the EKG monitor screeched and broad spikes separated by wavy lines appeared on the screen. The goddess and the child were dying. Hathor could heal a broken heart, not an actual body, and not another god, yet she couldn't let Nu die.

"Help them," Nu whispered.

They had to return to Chemmis. It was the only way to save Nu. "I need to help you," Hathor insisted. Feathery fingers brushed her hand and words were no longer necessary. "You're dying. I can't leave you like this."

Nu's grip tightened on Hathor's hand. Hathor tried to repel the urge to obey Nu's wishes, but though she was weak, Nu wasn't dead. Hathor couldn't fight Nu when she merged with her soul.

Outside on the lawn a high-pitched cry ripped through the night. Stella, she was the only woman in the house. Hathor darted to the window.

Damn, she was too late.

CHAPTER THIRTY-EIGHT

The time to explain had ended. Reign gripped Roman's shoulders and flashed them to where Daniel waited, transformed into Alamut. Soon, they would have an audience.

Roman's startled gaze swung to Reign and then landed on the blade humming in his hand.

Reign didn't wait, he couldn't wait, because that one second of indecision would cause him to fail, and lose his brother and Alexis. This was his only chance to save them all.

He buried his blade into his twin's abdomen. Desperately, he wanted to look away from the surprise and betrayal mirrored on Roman's face. Instead, he pulled his brother closer. He wished he could be kinder, gentler, but Roman was just as stubborn as he was. This brutal assault was the only way.

Reign wanted to explain. Alamut standing inches away prevented him from making a sound. But once, they didn't need words to speak to each other. Once, they had entire conversations without saying a word. Reign plunged the blade deeper into his brother's gut and used his power to slice into Roman's mind. Their psychic link connected and unbearable pain blasted through Reign.

His soul's tenuous grip on sanity crumbled chunk by chunk. Roman was dying and taking Reign's mind with him.

He had to hurry. Already the blade had started incinerating Roman from the inside out. Reign ignored Thane and Alamut fighting next to him. He pushed past the fury in his brother's mind and tried to share his thoughts, to make him understand. But Roman fought him, rejected his intrusion. God, he couldn't blame him, and he couldn't stop his brother from dying in front of his eyes.

"I need you to trust me, as you once did, brother." Forehead to forehead, his brother's dying gaze met his as the crimson flames flared, illuminating everything around them. "We are the same. Fight it! Fight me!"

Roman's mouth opened. Flames rushed out and engulfed his brother. When they died—his twin was gone.

Reign dropped to his knees. A sob ripped from his throat. The residual of Roman's pain echoed inside of him, tainting what was left of his soul. That polluted essence slipped a little more as his sanity hung by a slim thread, floating over his own personal hell.

An anguished bellow echoed. Stella, with a blade in her hand, streaked toward him. She swung for his head. He almost let her take it, but ducked and met her challenge blade for blade.

Her strength startled him. Though Reign could see his brother's training in her skill, her parries were wild and unfocused, easy to deflect. When Thane tried to join their battle, Reign drew a protective bubble around them to keep the others out and disarmed her within two moves. She crumpled to her knees and her chin buried in her chest. Wails tore from her throat.

"Kill me." She lifted her head. Stormy gray eyes blazed at him.

Alamut's yell drew his attention. Thane had managed to wound him while Hector hammered against the shield protecting him and Stella. Then Alamut vanished. Reign had to follow or risk losing his chance to save Alexis.

"Forgive me," he pleaded, gazing down into Stella's desolate face.

"Never!"

The word trailed after him as he flashed away.

CHAPTER THIRTY-NINE

Someone must have taken a bat and beaten every square inch of her body, because all of her hurt. Yet all of her aches paled in comparison to the hole in her heart.

Alexis blinked until her blurry vision cleared, though that still didn't help clarify her situation.

Where am I?

Flat on her back and staring straight ahead, the ceiling above her belonged in a mausoleum. All white marble threaded with veins of gold that seemed to resemble the noon sun, with clouds wafting by, and birds soaring between them.

Am I dead?

Alexis inhaled quickly and choked on the strange smelling air. Sulfur—she had just breathed in the poisonous gas. She groaned. The dead didn't breathe and they didn't hurt. She rose and a bout of nausea knocked her flat. At least the bed she lay on cushioned her comfortably. Pieces of memories flashed behind her closed eyelids. The battle with the quimaera, the death of Ruthless, and Reign—how could he? The ache in the center of her chest spread.

Then she remembered the swirling pit of energy and mumbling '*The Lord is my shepherd. I shall not want.*' Next came hazy white noise and nothing.

Reign? Did he follow her in? He had to be near. The tether wouldn't allow them to be separated. Alexis rolled onto her side. Her stomach revolted at the sudden movement and she had to wait before sitting up and swinging her legs over the edge. Her gray matter had turned into cement and her skull threatened to snap right off. She grabbed it to keep it balanced on her neck until the room stopped spinning.

A chill streaked down her spine, raising her hackles. From the corner of her eye, she spotted a shadow sitting in a chair at the foot of the bed, watching. Through the curtain of her hair, Alexis slid her gaze that way for a better look.

A woman studied her every movement. A quick visual sweep and Alexis processed her sky-blue hair, pale skin, and white linen sheath trimmed in blue.

"And who are you?" Alexis eased off the edge of the bed and ignored the warmth seeping from the marble into her bare feet. Glancing around the circular room, she searched for an exit.

"I am the god that is going to kill you, though not presently." She rose from her seated position and approached. Her gown moved like a living being against her skin.

A petite, dainty thing, no more than 5'1", pretty in an obvious sort of way. It was almost comical to think this blue haired, waif–like woman could inflict anything but scorn from anyone taller than her.

"And your name is?" Alexis asked with a tilt to her head.

The woman stopped inches from her. A thin halo, similar to the barrier Reign used to shield them on the golf course, shimmered around her. Faster than Alexis could blink, a hand seized her neck and squeezed. Alexis couldn't move, couldn't defend herself. And she couldn't breathe.

"Killing you would give me no greater pleasure. But having Reign kill you will be better."

Fourth of July sparklers danced in Alexis's vision and the woman seemed to swim.

"I will command my champion to slay you. Then I will judge you. You will remain in the deepest pit of the underworld. " The hand on her throat eased and Alexis sucked in sulfur-tainted air. Rough fingers snagged her hair and tilted her head up. "I am Nephythys, Goddess of the Dead."

This is the goddess that tortured Reign. Alexis wanted a piece of her. Make that a hunk!

"You know of me. I can see it in your eyes. Reign spoke of me?"

"No." She wouldn't give her the satisfaction.

Nephythys's lips thinned. "No matter."

The tinge of despair that replaced the bud of hope in Nephythys's voice frightened Alexis more than her paralyzed body and the hand fisted in her hair.

"You are not pretty enough to satisfy a man's desire. Not a warrior." Her gaze raked over Alexis.

The hand holding Alexis released slowly and trailed across her bare shoulders and arms.

"You are not the young flower I imagined. Many have slid between your thighs. You are unworthy."

Excuse me! I can count the total on one hand. Thank you much, Alexis fumed. Delight sparkled in Nephythys's eyes. The goddess knew her barbs had hit bone.

"Come," Nephythys ordered and a doorway appeared.

Against her will, Alexis stood. Jerky, erratic movements propelled her out of the bedroom and she followed Nephythys. She wasn't afraid. She was pissed. Each step she fought, exhausting her. Now she understood why Pinocchio wanted to be free. After a short tour through a palace—which she would've loved under different circumstances—they stopped in a large room. At one end, a single ornate chair and a raised dais waited. She spotted her gun resting on a matching table against the wall.

Nephythys glided to the table and stopped in front of a large golden bowl. After a few chants and a wave of her hand, she sighed and murmured, "Reign, there you are."

Alexis stopped fighting the strings pulling her along and rushed forward. A frigid glance from Nephythys and Alexis's muscles seized. Her body trembled in protest.

"Do you believe he loves you?" Nephythys purred, gliding around her.

Alexis had no intention of answering the question.

"Come. Peer into the bowl and see who Reign loves."

She didn't want to, but she wouldn't give the goddess the pleasure of seeing her struggle. Besides, her gun was next to the bowl. She stepped close, her heart doing double time, afraid of what she would see. Onyx layered with hieroglyphics coated the inside of the bowl. This priceless antique belonged in a museum. Then again, this place could pass for one.

Who puts muddy water in an antique?

Nephythys' finger stroked the rim of the bowl. The waters swirled and images flickered by like a movie on fast forward until it slowed and settled on Reign's face.

Alexis's heart swelled painfully. His hair was long, flowing past his shoulders, the way she liked it. A shadow of a beard dusted his jaw line. His eyes had that dreamy, sex-dazed appearance she'd seen twice, but wanted to see again. Nephythys lay in his arms. He kissed her, stroked his hands down her naked body.

Alexis nearly looked away, but her gaze caught on the shimmering aura surrounding the goddess, not both of them. Just the goddess.

"He does not love you. Why would he love you, a withering, diseased human when he has had a goddess?" Nephythys smirked and strolled toward the chair on the dais.

"Has he had you?" Alexis whispered through bruised vocal cords.

The question stopped Nephythys in her tracks. Her head whipped around and the tips of her hair flamed. Nostrils flaring, hatred warped her lovely face and she trembled. "You know nothing." Her voice echoed in the cavernous space.

Alexis glanced at her palm. From touching and sifting him, she knew enough. "I know he loved you, once. I know how he hungered for you. A touch, a simple caress, you've never even kissed him. Felt his lips pressed to yours, took his breath into your body. You've never taken any of him inside you...like I have."

The backhand came from nowhere and flung Alexis into the wall above the table. Ribs snapped against the marble. Boneless, she slid down the wall and rolled off the table to the floor. Curled into a fetal position, she didn't move. She couldn't. Pain stabbed her with every breath.

Her ear pressed to the marble, the goddess's soft footstep reverberated in Alexis's head. She tried to turn, but coughed up a mouthful of blood on the beautiful floor.

Nephythys's feet stopped inches from the cooling splatter. "Our love has lasted twenty of your lifetimes. The few moments he spent with you amount to nothing. A speck of time he will quickly forget once he returns to my arms."

"He…hates…you. Disgust…is all he feels…when he sees you," she rasped and coughed droplets of red on the blue hem of Nephythys's gown.

"You lie!" Her hair flamed and writhed like a living being.

"He hasn't loved you in a thousand years. I saw what happened the last time you were together. You, on your knees. Him, flaccid in your mouth." Alexis enjoyed the shock on Nephythys' face. "You know it's true, that's why I'm such a threat."

"You are not my equal." Nephythys spat.

"My love for him makes me more than your equal. Reign is mine," she said with more confidence than she had a right to.

Energy wrapped around Alexis again and she rose from the cool floor. She quelled the bud of excitement pulsing in her chest and waited until her body rose to the perfect level. One chance was all she would have.

Everything inside her stilled. By the confused stare draping Nephythys's face, she felt the strangeness too. Then the air sucked out of the room and Alexis's lungs, pulling at her clothes and whipping her around. Just as her lungs spasmed, a shock wave knocked her flat. The room heaved and fractured the marble beneath her. Too weak to scramble away, she waited for the floor to swallow her and end her torture.

A keening wail lifted the hairs on Alexis's body and caused a shudder of despair to crawl down her spine. The wail didn't cease, but evolved into a lamentation that her voice lifted and joined. She cried out all of her anguish, at her job, Gloria, her father, every hurt, every disappointment and failure, all of it fused into a desperate exclamation that lingered like a forgotten lover, until it finally drifted away.

***

The bastard tried to evade him, flashing repeatedly across New York City. Reign followed the tiny spark of energy left behind from each flash. Each time, he got a bit closer until he caught him back at the factory collecting canopic jars.

"Going somewhere without me?"

No longer able to sustain his form, Alamut devolved into a weakened Daniel. "That was the plan." He shrugged his shoulder and then collapsed on the concrete floor.

This boy tried his patience. Reign snatched Daniel from the ground. Holding him aloft, he easily deflected the knife aimed for his heart. "I am not a novice at this game. Fulfill your promise now." His blade hummed in tune with his rising fury.

Daniel quivered. "All right! We'll go, but I think we should bring along some help." He pointed to the pit with the sleeping quimaera.

Activate the army and have to wonder when they would turn on him? No. As soon as this was over, he would return here and—

what? Slaughter them? He remembered the horror on Alexis's face. "The only aid I need is for you to open the vortex to Chemmis, now." He shook Daniel by his throat.

"Okay," Daniel wheezed.

Reign dropped him and watched him retrieve a wooden box hidden under a canvas tarp in a corner of the factory. A flip of the lid revealed a bowl, oil, and strange herbs.

"What is all this?" Reign studied Daniel's every move while he mixed the items.

"When Anubis summons me, this transfer is automatic. When I request an audience there are rituals I must observe to make the trip. So strip." Daniel yanked his shirt over his head and toed his shoes off. Then unzipped his jeans.

"Stop." Reign ordered. There had to be another way. "Say the words and I will repeat them."

Daniel sighed. "Without the ritual they won't work." He pulled his jeans off.

"For you, no, perhaps they will for me. Say the words." Envy flared in the depths of Daniel's eyes. Reign readied his sword. He couldn't kill him, not yet. "Begin."

Daniel chanted. His words low and hollow. Reign repeated each phrase, concentrating on Chemmis and Alexis's sun-freckled face. His *vis*'Ra coalesced around each phrase, giving the words life. A breeze kicked up, swirled around the enclosed space of the factory. Dirt and debris momentarily blinded him.

Then everything stilled, the air in his lungs, the blood rushing though his veins, his heart beating in his chest, even the dust hung motionless in the air, waiting for this pregnant pause to pass.

The shadows lurking in the corners of the room moved, grew, and stretched towards them.

"What magic is this?" Reign forced himself not to retreat.

"Are you afraid of the dark? You can kill your brother without a thought, but this scares you?" Daniel chuckled.

Reign wrapped his hand around Daniel's throat.

"You're not as cold as I thought." Daniel's irises went vertical. "I wanted to kill Roman."

"You tried. You failed. Too late for regrets." A bit more pressure and Daniel's eyes bulged.

"Relax," Daniel croaked. "And let the dark take you. Don't fight it."

The darkness crept closer, blotting out the moonlight speckled through the damaged roof and shattered windows, casting everything in an inky cloak. Reign struggled to quell the rising tide of fear. It wasn't the darkness he feared, just being entombed, no light, slowly going mad, again. He thanked Nephythys for that also.

The darkness reached his boots and crawled over his feet, up his leg and thigh, steadily coating him in a thick tarry layer. The weight of it nearly buckled him. Up his arms and abdomen, his neck and chin, blanketing his hair until it rushed across his face and covered his nostrils. He opened his mouth to breathe—maybe to scream—and it rushed in to fill that last void.

Reign forgot to blink as he stared at the strange sky above him. A flat, starless gray ceiling hovered oppressively low. Too low. He stretched a hand up and thought he could touch the wet grayness. That simple movement caused something to crunch and rattle beneath him. He rolled over and stared at the suspicious landscape. It took a moment, but when he finally realized what cushioned him, he lurched to his feet.

Bones, bleached white by a non-existent sun, mountains of them surrounded him while he stood in a valley of fragments. He caught movement out of the corner of his eyes. It was

Daniel running toward a cathedral miles away. He flashed, but nothing happened. He tried again to separate his atoms and send them hurtling across the distance which kept him from his prey. Nothing. He glared at Daniel's fleeing back.

Damnation! Reign started after him.

The ground shuddered, swelled, and contracted. He paused, unsure of what lay beneath, but certain Daniel had an idea. That's why he'd left him here. Reign sprinted through the boneyard in the same direction as the traitorous bastard.

The ground surged. Bones and debris flew into the air and he along with it. Cartwheeling haphazardly, he saw a creature.

Reign slammed into the boneyard and stayed. Above him, a monstrosity hovered. Shaped somewhat like a dog, it stood as tall as a three-story house. Empty eye sockets stared down from an ill-shaped head. Bones peeked between bits of flesh and muscle. Rows of teeth, more than any canine should have, grinned. Though no tongue appeared in its hollowed jaw, saliva dripped freely from its jowls. He tried to flash again. Nothing happened.

He didn't moved, didn't dare. Bobbing back and forth, the head weaved. It couldn't see him. This dead thing's eyes had decayed long ago, leaving rotting flesh in vacant sockets. The bit of fresh meat clinging between its teeth didn't mean it couldn't still locate him. Could it kill a god or a demi-god? Did he even have any of his powers here?

His sword appeared in his hand, reassuring him he wasn't alone. The bones lunged. Reign faded and hoped this time the jaws would pass through him. They didn't. Scooped up, he bounced around the hollowed out mouth not understanding how he could still have his sword, but not his powers to evade this thing.

He sliced into the bones surrounding him. His blows had no consequence while each toss of the thing's head moved him from the back of its mouth closer to the three-inch teeth.

Reign grabbed onto the edge of a jawbone. Balancing precariously on the smooth surface, he managed to pull himself up and climb to the back of the throat to where the head met the neck. The first bone that joined the two sections together was dainty compared to the other bones around it. He grabbed the bone that was twice the size of his hand, braced his feet on the flat base of its skull, and pulled. The thing thrashed as if it knew what Reign attempted. Reign held tight, feeling the critical piece of the jigsaw puzzle wiggle, then move and finally, give way and fall with him back into the mouth.

The head separated from the body and the animal collapsed, scattering bones everywhere. Bruised and slightly dazed, he climbed free of the jowls, still holding the linchpin to the creature's demise. He surveyed the wreckage. It wasn't hard to tell beast from battlefield. Though separated, and jumbled, the animal's bones still had life to them. They moved to reform the structure of the thing only to collapse again when the piece he held clasped tightly in his hand couldn't reattach.

I have wasted too much time.

Reign turned to the cathedral. Daniel was nowhere in sight.

CHAPTER FORTY

Dear Ra in all his perfection.

Shaken to her essence, Nephythys stumbled to her feet. The vis'Ra that roiled Chemmis was undeniable. Nu had returned.

A chime sounded. The council gathered and commanded the presence of all of the gods. She glanced at the worthless woman bleeding on her destroyed floor. Nephythys preferred Alexis dead, but she had to keep her part of the bargain until Reign returned.

Alexis's eyes opened. She stared at Nephythys. The woman had more strength than she gave her credit for.

A sharp noise echoed around the chamber and Nephythys's body jerked. Her gaze leveled on Alexis and the object she held in her hand. A gun? How useless.

She glanced down and at the holes in her linen. "You foolish girl. Bullets? Did you really think a bullet could stop a god?" Her laughter peeled across the room. "Worthless human. Reign does not understand the service I am rendering him by removing you from existence."

"He'll never love you," Alexis murmured. Nephythys's hair flamed and her skin mottled. "You, Alexis Lever, stand judged. I cast you to the lowest level of hell where your own desires shall burn you for all eternity. The more you love him, the more you will suffer."

The chime sounded again, more strident than before. Nephythys couldn't linger. She waved her hand and sent her nemesis to the bowels of *Duat*.

From the different corners of the island, twenty gods came together in the solar chamber. Situated in the center of

Chemmis, the golden floor reflected the sunlight burning overhead. Gold obelisks thirty feet tall circled the room at twenty-degree intervals. Symbols of the seasons, harvest and famine, desert and the Nile, beast and man, decorated the eighteen obelisks. And above them, hovered the great symbols of Ra. The one that was always present though no longer seen.

By the time Nephythys appeared, the immense chamber had nearly filled. Still, she paused beneath the symbol of Ra and reveled in the golden shower of light. All were born of the sun. It gave them strength. It gave them life and longevity. It renewed. Even the dark ones gained sustenance from the sun, sought its loving rays.

Nephythys never felt the warmth of Ra. The Goddess of the Dead never basked in the heat of the sun. The dead knew no warmth, no love, and little kindness. She spent most of her life in darkness with her beloved family hounding her heels.

She took her seat and spotted Anubis on the opposite side of the room. Her son seemed oddly subdued and she wondered what had transpired. SET entered in his preferred gaseous state and then solidified into a man. Bare-chested, well defined pectorals and abs surprised her. Muscles bunched his arms and legs. His coal black eyes blazed in a startlingly handsome face. His hostile gaze swept over her, causing an annoying flush to steal over her skin. He smiled. Her stomach rolled.

What game does he play? she wondered as his lips curled into a sneer that doused her body's traitorous response. She returned his sneer with equal fervor.

Whispers circled furiously in the room. She caught a few words from those who couldn't contain their emotions. Younger Gods who didn't participate in the last retrieval. Fear mixed equally with their excitement. Fools.

Aten entered. Dressed in pure white robes and a golden cap on his bald head, he coveted his role as *Rais,* Ra's representative on Earth. He took his elevated seat under the All Seeing Eye and pounded the crystal staff against the marble. Silence blanketed the room.

Patiently, he studied each of them, meeting their gazes with a determination she rarely saw in the titular leader. Once again, he assumed the mantle of leadership none truly wanted him to have, except in times like these.

"Nu has returned!" His booming voice encompassed the room. "Who shall see to her retrieval?"

Several of the younger, bolder gods rose to their feet, eager to prove themselves and be free of the constraints of the Pantheon. Aten ignored the young fools and pointedly turned to the strongest of them: Denwen, the fiery Scorpion God, Mafdet, the Panther Goddess, and Resheph, once a Syrian war god.

All eyes shifted to them. Long ago, upon Nu's first disappearance, the three captured the goddess and together the Pantheon bound her vis'Ras to Chemmis. They spiritually chained her to the island and believed she couldn't leave. How wrong they all were. The three stood. By their hesitant gazes and shifting eyes, Nephythys recognized their unspoken fear.

"By deception, we captured her once," Denwen spoke.

"She chose to release her spirit rather than be bound to the Pantheon and Chemmis," Mafdet added.

"We all heard her wail and felt the force of her despair through the joining link," Resheph said.

"Without her presence Chemmis withers beneath our feet," Aten said.

"To capture her now—" Resheph started angrily.

"—will be the death of you all."

A voice Nephythys had not heard in centuries halted the discussion. Startled gasps swept around the room because Hathor, Goddess of Love entered the chamber. A hiss burned the back of Nephythys's throat as she watched the woman who had joined her to SET, her unbeloved husband.

"You dare to return!" Aten thundered, his face twisted. His staff struck the marble floor again and sparks flew. "For your insolence, disobedience, and betrayal, you, Hathor are condemned to servitude for ten millennia."

Golden thread of light whipped from the staff, leaped across the distance separating Aten and Hathor. The strands caged her body and dragged her to her knees. Nephythys smiled, praying her name would be first on the list of masters for Hathor.

The light restraining Hathor melded together. Armor replaced the strands straining across her chest and abdomen, snaked around her pelvis and down her legs. The bands on her arms transformed into a liquid metal. When the light dulled, every part of her was covered, leaving only her head exposed. Stunned, no one moved to thwart her when she raised her hand and the staff flew to her palm.

Hathor slammed the speared tip into the floor. The building rocked and the foundation fractured. She climbed smoothly to her feet. Slowly her head rose and the goddess standing in the arena, facing all of them, was no longer Hathor. The Goddess of Love had vanished. Nephythys leaned forward and watched Hathor's features morphed into another deity.

Dear Ra. It's Nu!

Nu turned in a slow circle. She met each of their startled gazes. "Now. Let us being this conversation again."

***

Hard and cold. So cold Roman didn't think he would ever be warm again. Yet his gut burned. The fires of hell roasted him from the inside out. He clutched the place where Reign's blade had split his flesh, sure that if he moved an increment his intestines would spill.

Reign. Thinking his name caused more agony in Roman's soul than his body. How could he be so wrong—*again?* No. he wasn't wrong. His first suspicions proved true. Reign had betrayed him, like Daniel, only Reign's betrayal pierced deeper. Memories of a time long past, of bonds which no longer existed, caused him to waver. To believe in something that had died long ago and to offer Reign a place in his home, and by his side.

His twin—beloved, trusted brother—had stabbed him. Cut into his flesh. Ripped through his insides. As Roman clutched the braided handle, the blade had turned neon and melted him from within. His last thought was of Stella. His last sight was of his own face staring back at him as Reign brought him closer. He whispered something, but the words were lost in the agony of death and the roar of rage.

With every heartbeat, Roman's fury had escalated, joining the burning in his gut and the throbbing in his head. Lying on the stone floor, his breath wheezed, cutting off a budding bellow.

His brother had killed him.

Roman opened his eyes. Blackened rock surrounded him, caged him. A torch flickered in the corner of the room, casting an orange glow in the dim chamber.

He wasn't dead.

Curled in the fetal position, he checked the hand pressed to his abdomen. No blood leaked between his fingers. He shifted his palm and braced for the gush of fluid.

Smooth skin.

Stunned, he circled his hand over his flesh and found nothing.

Still, the burn remained, millimeters beneath his unmarred flesh. And instead of fading, it was growing as if a blade were still cutting a bloody path to his spine. He pushed himself up, muscles protesting each movement and stood. He swayed and crashed into the nearest wall. Rough, hot stones cut through his clothing, into his skin. He shook his head to clear the fuzziness and blinked to clear his blurred vision. A sudden weakness drained all the energy from him. He dropped like a stone to the hard ground. His head snapped back to slam into the rock wall behind him.

Sparks ignited in his brain. *Revenge.* That was the word Reign uttered before his insides incinerated. Or was that what he screamed with his dying breath.

REVENGE.

Just thinking the word caused his body to jerk and strength to sputter in his limbs.

"Revenge." Though whispered, the word rebounded on the walls and gained resonance before trailing away. Strength—more than he'd ever known—hummed through him. He surged to his feet. His muscles clenched, straining beneath his skin. He looked down at his fisted hands. Light peeked through his balled fingers. Unafraid, he unfurled his fingers. A faint glow illuminated his palms.

The question his soul always asked, but his mind refused to address, floated to the surface, bloated like a beached whale roasting in the hot sun.

What am I?

Roman pushed the thought away. Self-reflection could wait. Now was the time to scour the earth and wreak vengeance on his enemies. Smoky, iridescent glass barred the exit and hieroglyphics lined the doorway. He approached and the glyphs came alive. They matched the aura radiating from his palms and shifted positions. The glass barrier collapsed back into its natural element, sand. He stepped over the threshold into the corridor. Seven cells lined the wall. Two were empty excluding the one he had exited. The others were occupied, but their barriers prevented him from viewing the residents.

At the end of the corridor waited a cell. Twice as large as the others, the thick glass allowed no light to filter. But there was something there. A presence reached out and brushed across his senses. Male, immensely strong, and it urged him closer. Light bled through the skin of his palms. His hands glowed as if a fire burned within. No longer startled by the display, he ignored his changing anatomy and accepted his evolution.

He focused on the barrier ahead. The thick, opaque structure prevented a glimpse into the interior, yet something studied him, inspected him as he would study an insect under a microscope. The center of the structure weakened and protruded outward. The weaves moved, gave a little. He stopped a yard away and watched as an item appeared. First, a silver handle layered with hieroglyphics, and then a blade composed of light.

Roman caught the sword before it fell. He'd held many blades, and owned an extensive collection of swords. None had ever fit in his hand like an intimate embrace. He considered the barrier again and touched the smooth surface. The presence he felt had retreated, yet the proof of its existence was clutched in his hand.

A hum vibrated through him. An echo of anger that wasn't his reverberated through him. Reign was near. Like a drop of blood trapped in a centrifuge, Roman's cells separated down to the atomic level and sped across the distance separating him and his bastard brother.

CHAPTER FORTY-ONE

Reign raced through the graveyard to the cathedral. The door swung open at his approach, welcoming him inside. He slowed. Anything could be waiting for him. Through the doorway he eased, sword ready. No army. No Alamut or Daniel. Nothing waited but an obsidian altar at the opposite end of an enormous room. A single, sputtering candle bleeding wax over the table and a Scrying bowl, rested on top.

In the silence, the gurgle of flowing water caught his attention as he walked across the threshold. Part way inside, rows of candles lining the walls, flamed. They beat back the gloom and illuminated the wall behind the altar.

He wished they had remained extinguished or that he could look away. Glass walls retained a sea of bodies fermenting in a bloody stew.

Appalled, yet fascinated in a macabre way, he drew closer to the nearest wall. Skeletal heads turned. From every angle sightless eyes leveled on him. Captured by the strange display, Reign couldn't look away. Bits of tattered clothing clung to their decomposing bodies. Emblems and insignia decorated a few. That's when he noticed these weren't just any corpses. A wail rose behind him. Reign spun and faced his constant nightmare.

No longer ghostly, the Vanquished gathered behind him, weapons ready and pointing at him. Together they charged.

In an instant, he relived each battle, grieved each senseless and justified death, mourned the loss of comrades he vowed to protect, and failed. The memories tore through him, nearly bringing him to his knees. He couldn't let them take him down.

His eyes opened. Back pressed against the wall, Reign had no idea what his next move would be. Or theirs.

Alexis, they screamed. Her beautiful face appeared in his mind. The freckles sprinkled across her cheeks. The twinkle in her coppery eyes as she gazed at him. Her lush, kissable lips. He concentrated on her and counted on the anguish in his heart to bring him to her side. He dug into his core and the power waiting. His body unraveled and his atoms scattered.

Intense heat blasted him to his knees. A barrier appeared over his skin, saving him from roasting. *Please God, tell me she didn't place her here. Not here.*

His eyelids refused to blink as he took in the smoldering landscape he'd once inhabited. The damned—condemned here by Nephythys—were chained to one of the vertical volcanic tubules and hung over vents spewing lava. His flesh crawled from the memories of the eons he spent chained, cooked until charred and resurrected. No respite before the cycle repeated. He thought he deserved the everlasting anguish. Thought, his failure as a warrior, had brought him to this fate.

He endured, expecting nothing else for the rest of eternity. Until Nephythys appeared as a saint and his savior. He took her hand, accepted the slavery she offered and allowed her to lead him out of this hell—where his will was tested and his flesh was stripped—into purgatory, where the Goddess of the Dead dined on his heart and called it love.

A garbled cry echoed in the vast chamber. A backwash of pain knifed him. He collapsed onto the sulfuric ash littering the floor. *Alexis!* They were still tethered, psychically instead of physically. Her pain became his. It reverberated, magnified in his skull until he threw back his head, and bellowed. The shield coating him buckled, thinned precipitously. At the last moment, he quelled his agony, shuffled it to a section of his brain, and slammed the door shut.

Reign lurched to his feet as the echo faded. He wiped the sweat from his eyes and ignored the wave of exhaustion threatening to drag him under. He had to find her. NOW.

He stretched his senses again, to no avail. Other than the shield protecting him, this place voided his powers. He couldn't pinpoint her location, but his gut guided him to the left through the fields of lava and the damned.

"Alexis!" Desperation chipped away at his control. His speed increased at each turn until he ran, past the pitiful residents. The wails for mercy, the pleas for death, one of the damned touched him. He stopped and looked at the scorched being that reached out to him. No recognition jarred him. Reign turned away. He hadn't come for them.

A weak murmur stopped him. His head tilted. Fifty feet up, dangling over the opening of a vent, Alexis hung from a chain. Her dress had melted into her, leaving blistered, red and black skin, and nearly unrecognizable. Except for her eyes. They remained the same coppery gems he fell in love with.

The ground rumbled. Steam rushed from the vent, followed by a geyser of lava. Her cry was lost in the roar of the eruption; still he heard it, felt it in his core. When the geyser receded, all of her was aflame.

And so was he. Crimson flames leaped from his core as his *vis 'Ra* shattered the weaves caging it and rippled from his skin. He reached for her, tried to flash, and sweep her into his arms.

Nothing.

His *vis 'Ra* bubbled through his veins, verifying Mrs. Kelly's words. He had the power to save her. Yet he could not. The Goddess of the Dead ruled here.

The flames died and her head slumped against her bound arms. Vacant eyes stared, but did they see him? Know he was here for her?

Alexis. His soul reached for her.

Tears dropped from her eyes, hissed, and steamed when they met her charred skin.

She didn't know he was there. Didn't know he had failed her again. He gritted his teeth and sucked a harsh sulfur-filled breath. On his life, she would not remain here.

Only one could rescue her from this hell. The one who put her here.

His atoms scattered to plead with or to kill his blue-haired demon.

***

Nu had forgotten how light the armor was on her petite frame. Molded to her body, the Armor of Ra did more than protect. Impenetrable in sunlight, it also gave the wearer additional strength and agility.

She studied the startled glances of those gathered. Not often can one stun a group of gods. Appearing in Chemmis cloaked in Hathor's body was a brilliant strategy, but one that wouldn't last. Two gods stuffed into one form created impossible tension. Even though Hathor had submerged her consciousness, every few seconds her subconscious sparked with queries.

Ember was much more a convenient host. The mousy child submitted to her will without complaint. Again, Hathor's mind probed her with questions. Nu battled to ignore the prattle and focus on the enormous tasks ahead.

Defeat the Pantheon. Save all her children from ripping each other apart. Whether birthed from her body or fashioned by Ra, they were all hers, descendants of Ra. None of their deaths would be tolerated. As she stared at her offspring and their equally stubborn progeny, the tasks she had set before her appeared insurmountable. Nu had to find a way.

"You have kept my chair warm long enough, Aten. Step down." She focused her attention on him, their leader. If he fell in line, the others would follow.

"Being a fugitive has agreed with you and Hathor," Aten answered from his perch above her.

Nu ground her teeth. It gave him pleasure to look down at her, from the chair she vacated eons ago. "Being free of Chemmis has agreed with both of us."

From her peripheral vision, Denwen, Madfet and Resheph encroached. With a single thought, she could kill the trio who'd once captured her.

She'd cursed Ra when he abandoned the pantheon. Now, she envied his wise decision. *Where once they worshiped, now they seek to conquer.* He would've had no qualms decimating every member of the Pantheon and starting anew. As a goddess of creation, her *vis'*Ra could create and destroy, yet she couldn't bring herself to that deadly point. No matter the circumstances, they were all her children, though some she would prefer not to claim.

Nu lifted the staff again. Sunlight struck the cosmic dust and the particles of a dying star encased in the center. She slammed it into the marble. Rainbow sparks flew before she extended the tip and drew a wide circle around her. This added layer of protection guaranteed none would gainsay her intentions.

An unexpected light brightened the room behind her.

"Nephythys! Where are you?"

Nu spun. Reign stalked into the room. His sword glowed in his hand and sang an ominous tune. And he glowed! A vibrant crimson! His vis'Ra was no longer buried behind the protective barricade she wove at his birth. From his incandescent eyes to his shimmering skin, and the fury leaping off him in waves, Reign looked like a god. All that she had done to hide him was undone.

The Pantheon would shred him. Though her power flowed through his veins, he was a demi-god and no match for one god, never mind all of them. She hadn't risked all to have his insides coat the walls of the chamber.

"Reign, no!" Nu cried.

He spared her a glance, but there was no flare of recognition in his eyes. No warmth. No love for the one who had risked so much for him to exist.

"Whose *Get* is this!" Aten shouted above the raised voices of pantheon.

Reign's gaze shifted around the room, searching until he settled on the one he sought. "Where is Nephythys?" he snarled.

Embarrassment more than shock froze Nephythys's features into a comical mask. Her gaze darted to her husband. Nu followed and gasped. Darkness pulsed beneath his translucent skin. He knew! Dear Ra, SET knew of Nephythys's infidelity, but worse—now the Pantheon knew.

Before Nu could move, SET exploded. Gone was the human shell, leaving a swirling dark mass hurtling toward Reign. Reign leveled his blade and braced for impact.

Nu pierced the protective circle with the staff. Denwen, Madfet, and Resheph reached her, but she flashed in front of

Reign. At the last second, she formed a new circle around them. SET repelled off the shield and slammed into the opposite wall.

Gods dropped from their perched seats to the Atrium floor and surrounded them. Each gathered their vis'Ra to attack. Hathor shrieked inside her head, tearing at her control. Next to her, Reign beat against the shields.

"Release me!" Reign bellowed much too near her ear for shouting.

"Foolish child. I'm trying to save you," Nu said.

"I want no help from your kind." He towered over her.

My kind? "Just what do you imagine you are?"

"I am Reign, son of Helios. I am Thracian and I am here to claim what is mine."

Hearing her lover's name after so many years drove a knife into her heart. "I know very well who your sire is. This is not the way to claim your birthright." Nu shook her head.

"Birthright? I seek no rights from this place," he snarled, his eyes feral.

His anger and stubbornness smacked her, reminding her of his father, and—to her shame—herself.

"I am Nu, your—"

"I care not who you are! I am here to free Alexis, the woman I love, from Nephythys."

"Alexis is here?" Nu stretched her weakening senses across the island. She found the girl in the lowest level of *Duat* and brought her to them.

The girl was alive. If you could call being nearly roasted, living. The fire pits on the lowest levels were for the worst of humanity. Souls kept at the highest level of torture forever. Her charred hair smoked. Her pale skin was orangey in places and bright red and black in others. The stench of cooked flesh had Nu covering her nose and mouth. Alexis didn't deserve this and neither did her son. She had failed them both.

Nu looked at the horde outside her protective circle. No, not only her natural born sons. *I've failed all my children.*

CHAPTER FORTY-TWO

Reign gathered Alexis to him. Her muscles turned rigid and she convulsed in his arms. A guttural moan tore from her throat and her eyelids fluttered. He focused and pinpointed his vis'Ra into her. His aura bathed her, soaked into her charred body, but when it faded, nothing had changed.

"Have you forgotten about the Vanquished? Only I can free you from your demons. Your life belongs to me," Nephythys said from her seat in the gallery.

No, he hadn't forgotten. He'd rather bed down with his demons than cozy up to Nephythys once more.

"Let me try." Nu knelt next to him. She stretched out her hand. If he wasn't so desperate, he would've slapped it away. He wanted nothing from these gods, except Alexis. For her life, he would beg.

"Heal her, please. My life for hers."

Judging by the sympathy in Nu's eyes and her quick nod, he almost wanted to trust her. And there was something familiar about her brown eyes and sun-kissed skin. Her familiarity teased him, pushed at the boundaries of his mind.

A memory surfaced. Reign tried to stop it, but he couldn't halt the earthquake rumbling through his core. "I know you."

She smiled. Tears gathered in her eyes. Her hand hovered over Alexis's forehead and her face scrunched, concentrating. Nothing happened. Her gaze darted to his. "She's been judged. I can't heal her. Reign, I'm so sorry."

The same hand that tried to heal Alexis cupped his face. Calm poured into him, but rage was all that fed him. He jerked away. Alexis convulsed in his arms again and clung to him until her shudder faded, and her hand slid limp to the marble. Fear gripped him hard and he touched a finger to the pulse under her chin. A faint thread flickered beneath her broiled skin.

"Death would be a kindness, but she won't die. She'll live like this forever. And there's nothing I can do." Nu's voice cracked.

"Reign?" Alexis murmured.

Her weak voice surprised him. "I'm here."

Scorched eyelids peeled open and her milky gaze roamed until it landed on him. "You came. For me?"

Tears pricked his eyes. "Always." The haze cleared, revealing the coppery gaze he loved.

A hand touched his face. Her breath came in short bursts. "I understand...now, why you tried to leave me...I didn't want you to go. I should've known things aren't...always what they seem. You thought you were right killing that quimaera while all I saw was a boy. Maybe you were...maybe I was...doesn't matter anymore," she whispered. "I want you to go."

Her voice wavered, yet he heard every word. "And leave you here? I refuse to live without you. Where you go, I go."

"I love you...want you to know..."

He wanted to say the words, yearned to shout the desires of his heart. He thought of Nephythys and swallowed the bile rising in his throat. He wouldn't give her more ammunition against him to hurt Alexis. Gently, he pressed his cheek into her burned hand. He felt her inside him, first a tentative flutter, then a deeper sifting. No longer did he hide what was secreted in his soul. He wanted, needed her to know. Reign opened his heart and welcomed her inside.

Tears welled in her eyes. A broken smile cracked her face.

"I didn't mean to make you cry," he whispered. "I will not leave you here." As he watched Alexis, pink skin replaced scorched and her melted dress peeled away from her flesh and returned to normal. "What has happened?" He looked at Nephythys.

"She's in a healing cycle. It is a part of the judgment. Never-ending suffering for loving you. The more she loves you. The brighter the anguish. It will end when the love in *your* heart for her dies."

"You cannot do this!" he choked.

"You are my slave and she has been judged." Nephythys's eyes sparkled. Her chest heaved.

Murmurs rumbled through the room as the gods whispered amongst themselves.

"Aten, she has judged a human, non-Egyptian, non-worshiper." Nu glared arrogantly at Aten. "Prove you are a leader and not a wet nurse."

Attention swung to Aten. It seemed forever before he turned and faced Nephythys. "Will you offer no defense against the accusations Nu brings forth?"

Nephythys seemed to wither under the glare of so many stares. Aten glanced at Alexis. He stepped closer to the protective barrier and scrutinized her as one would road kill. Nephythys squirmed. She shifted in her seat while her trembling hands fisted her gown.

"You interrogate the Goddess of the Dead at the behest of a criminal?" SET spoke and the power of his voice made the hairs on Reign's arms stand at attention. Waves of darkness radiated from the deity. The Vanquished responded with a call for destruction. He wanted to release them, but not yet.

"You cannot call Nu a criminal and not label your wife the same." A goddess spoke from her seat in the gallery. Her glare nailed Nephythys. "She will answer the question."

Reign studied the play of emotions crossing Nephythys's face as her gaze swept the room, searching for aid. Scorn was all they offered. She glanced at SET. The God of All Evil simmered with rage. Her spine stiffened and finally, she turned to Aten.

"No." One single word was all she gave. But that word whipped around the room as gossip spread from mouth to ear.

"Nephythys! You cannot refuse!" the goddess demanded.

"I will not answer to you, Bastet, Avenger of Ra," Nephythys hissed, her hair writhing with anger.

"Heal her." Aten spoke and the chamber vibrated.

"No. She has been judged." Eyes narrowed, lips firm, Nephythys stared from her perch and refused to budge.

"Then I will take her place." Reign shouted. "I agree to stay with you for as long as you desire. As your lover, your pet." He spat. "You will have all of my undivided attention. My love will be yours alone." He glanced at SET, hoping his words had the desired effect. The swirling tide under the god's translucent skin had ceased. He appeared a marble statue, molding by a sculptor's hand, instead of a deity.

"I won't let you do this." Alexis clutched his arm. Her fingers scored his flesh.

He felt her inside him, pushing at his will. With so much at stake, he couldn't allow her to sway his decision. And this was the only way he could save her.

"Agreed." Nephythys jumped to her feet, her grin eager.

A gasp circulated and set off another round of chatter.

"Have you lost your senses?" Bastet clucked and shook her head.

"I am the Goddess of the Dead." Nephythys descended to the chamber floor. "A Primal. Who here can punish me? Nu is weak and in a borrowed body. Osiris is imprisoned. Without the staff, Aten speaks, but none listen. Who here would depose me and claim my throne in *Duat*?" Her gaze circled the room. "Who here wants to rule at SET's side in the bowels of hell?" No one answered.

"I have given up my freedom for hers. Heal her, Nephythys, and let her return to her world." Reign had enough of listening to her voice. Gently, he lay Alexis on the marble floor. Then he steeled his heart and stepped away.

Nephythys gave Alexis a scornful glance. "She may return, but I will not heal her. She will be a testament to my mercy and a reminder of my wrath to all who see her."

"That was not our bargain!" Reign blasted through the shield. He flashed between the crowds of gods aimed to take a chunk out of Nephythys's hide.

Claws pierced his side, flipped him into the air. Pain seared through flesh and bone, weakening his body. He landed on his side, rolled across the floor, and gained his footing in one fluid motion. His blade appeared in his hand. Heat surged from within, erupted from his pores. The crimson glow swept over his body, shielding him, healing him. He faced his opponent.

Sleek fur, eight legs, lots of claws and rows of teeth in a head. A big fucking head. Four large eyes, two on each side, all focused on him. SET, in his Typhon form moved closer. Reign wasn't surprised. All of the gods had animal forms.

SET charged. His many legs resounded like a stampede. Reign's sword screamed as he rushed forward, blade raised, aiming for the space between SET's eyes.

SET faded.

Reign spun, searching. *Where is he!* He spotted Nu, immobilized by three gods, her staff gone. A force knocked him off his feet. He hit the ground. His head cracked against the marble, stunning him.

Four of SET's legs pinned Reign's limbs to the marble. Two landed on his chest. Claws burrowed through his shield, causing the barrier to sizzle and buckle. Then they buried deep into his muscle, while the remaining two legs shredded everything they touched.

Reign flashed. SET blocked his power. He faded. SET blocked him again. He looked up into the drooling jowls of the Typhon. No tongue. Just teeth. Rows of them gleamed.

Damnation. He was in this same predicament at the cathedral. Though this time, fate had upped the ante.

A spatial distortion followed by a blinding light warped the space near him. A whirling vortex opened. SET shrank from the aura and a tremor rippled through his body.

Awareness froze Reign in place. Only one person affected him this way. From the corner of his eye, he glimpsed a man.

Roman. It worked.

A white sword glowed in his hand. He leaped for SET's back, blade clutched and raised in both of his hands.

SET reared, exposing his vulnerable underbelly. Reign thrust his sword into SET's unprotected hide. The beast shuddered. Roman landed on SET's back. His weapon sliced straight through, exiting SET's furry skin a hairs' length from Reign's neck.

Light emanated from both blades. His, blood red. Roman's, pure white. SET disintegrated into a cloud of inky smoke and dashed to the other side of the room. Roman dropped to his feet next to Reign. The flat of Roman's sword reflected the blinding rays of the sun, casting a kaleidoscope of color around the chamber.

Reign stared into Roman's stark face. What brotherly affection existed between them had vanished. Bitter hatred was all that remained. If it wasn't for Alexis, he would lay there and let Roman have his due. But he couldn't. If he died, she'd be alone to face life in *Duat* at the mercy of the gods.

He rose. Face to face, he met his brother's glare. Roman looked at Reign. Memories of their childhood, their inseparable bond tightened Reign's heart. War with his brother was not how he planned this journey to end. He came to this world to save Roman, not to kill him. There was a time when they didn't need words. They spoke in their own language, shared thoughts through silent communication. Especially on the battlefield. Now, Reign didn't need to link their minds to understand his brother's intent. Roman wanted his blood.

Teeth bared, hate bled from Roman's eyes. "I trusted you and you betrayed me," Roman stated.

"I had no choice. It was the only way—"

"After this is over, we finish it." Roman growled.

With lead in his heart, Reign gave a single nod. "Agreed."

"Where did you get The Blade of Osiris?" SET ended their reunion.

SET's voice cut through Reign's thoughts and his standoff with Roman. The god's Typhon form had been replaced by a dense, churning cloud.

Reign's gaze darted between SET and Roman as the two glared at each other. How did these two know each other? Movement made him glance up into the gallery of gods. All of the gods stood, their palms exposed, and glowing in a multitude of colors. All of their eyes were trained on the blade in Roman's hand.

Reign glanced at his brother and winked—their designated signal for an attack plan they'd created eons ago. Roman gave a single nod and they separated, each walking in the opposite direction. The cloud fanned out to track both of them.

"The sword. Where did you find it?" SET's voice emanated from the center of the dark mass.

"What's it to you?" Roman demanded.

"Give it to me and I will let you live." A hand formed and extended from the clouds.

Roman rotated his wrist. The blade spun, seemed to capture the sun and reflect the beams back in a dizzying array. He flipped the sword to his other hand. His gaze flicked to Reign. "And what about him?"

"He will breathe his last tonight," SET said. "I claim the rite of Infidelitatis al Mawte." The cloud pulsed and lightning streaked in the center.

"I agree. Tonight will be his last, but not by your hands. I claim the rite of retribution. He fucked me over first. After I kill you—" Roman pointed his sword at his brother. "I kill him."

Lightning crackled again in the center of the cloud. "So be it." SET's voice filled the chamber.

Reign braced. Together they would defeat SET and afterwards he would face Roman. He wanted to look at Alexis, but didn't dare take his eyes from the enemies facing him.

In a blink, the cloud swelled, slammed into him, and swallowed. The living, breathing, thing, melted his shield and clung to him like tar smothering a dying animal. He spotted Roman. The light radiating from his sword repelled the darkness, making him a beacon in a sea of blackness while Reign couldn't move. Worse, he couldn't breathe. His lungs struggled to draw air. Fear gnawed at his reasoning, threatening to overwhelm. He fought the urge. There was too much at stake. SET could not win. He glimpsed Alexis climbing unsteadily to her feet.

And Nephythys...

She closed the distance between her and Alexis.

CHAPTER FORTY-THREE

Reign strained to break free from the encompassing cloud while SET's voice filled his head, laughing. Mixed with the chants of the Vanquished, his sanity splintered. All of him collapsed, the physical and the mental, which comprised of what he was. Pitched into the abyss, the complete darkness shredded him and hauled him to the bowels of his soul. At each passing level, calm stole over him. Languid and soothing, death approached with empty promises and a treasure chest of lies.

Alexis doesn't love you. LIE. He heard the love in her whisper and her coppery eyes.

Alexis doesn't need you. LIE. She couldn't defeat Nephythys alone.

Proclaim your submission and SET will allow you to live. LIE. SET wanted him dead and was seconds away from achieving his goal.

His conscience crashed in a heap in the last place he wanted to be. Home. The familiar mountain range and the lush valley below gave him the location. Weary, he climbed to his feet. The Vanquished littered the ground. In the distance, the rubble of his childhood home loomed.

He walked through the field of bodies to the single, crumbling wall still standing. A mural came into view, the same mural that once graced the dining hall of his father's home in homage of the woman who birthed his sons, Roman and Reign.

She has not changed much. Sun-kissed skin, sad, lonely eyes. *Damnation!* "He told us you had died," he whispered to the image. *Why?*

Everything Mrs. Kelly had said was true. Worse, everything he suspected, yet refused to question was true. So many lies and half-truths had brought him and his brother to this point. Why?

The wall disintegrated to ash, leaving the Vanquished. Their bodies were discarded like unwanted timber. They climbed to their feet and stood at attention. Each nailed him with a fierce gaze. Their right hands fisted and landed over their hearts. Readiness hummed, overlaid with tempered rage. His demons, for eons they'd tortured him. Now, their silent plea overwhelmed him. This couldn't be what they wanted.

Feet leaden, Reign walked amongst the warriors. So long a part of him, yet he had never accepted his hand in their demise. Cursed with a conscience, *he,* not the Vanquished, tortured himself.

This life wasn't what he wanted. Born of an unknown goddess and warrior father, fate decreed his birthright of blood and death.

His head spun. Everything dimmed and he stumbled. Arms caught and cradled his body, refusing to let him fall. Set back on his feet, he looked to the men he had damned. Now, his life was in their hands.

Join me and end this divided existence, he commanded.

En masse, they kneeled and accepted his dominion. Weaves extended in vibrant crimson threads, binding each of the Vanquished to his soul. No longer separate, they forged into one being, making him as strong as the blade singing in his fist.

***

Stretched out on the floor, barely clinging to consciousness, Alexis hurt in places she hadn't known existed. Broiling in lava had ravaged her body and carved a canyon in her soul. Memories of Reign kept her sane. His barely there smile and beautiful eyes. The way he looked the first time she'd seen him sprawled on her sofa. She hadn't appreciated the moment then. If she could just hold on to that slice of time, maybe she'd survive this hell.

Grunting and the echoes of flesh hitting flesh gave her a reason to force her eyes open. A battle unfolded somewhere within the dense fog bank a few yards away, but all Alexis could see was delight on Nephythys's face. The excitement etched on her features sickened Alexis. She couldn't let her win. But how to defeat the goddess when Alexis had nothing to bargain with.

Except her life.

She didn't belong in this realm. She'd never prayed to these gods. If she died, *Duat* was not her hell. Possibly, a different hell awaited her. At least she wouldn't be here, used as a tool to bind Reign to Nephythys. She wanted him to have a life…and find love. He deserved that much after spending an eternity with a blue-haired witch.

Alexis pushed herself into a seated position. Patches of burned skin on her arms cracked and flaked away, leaving angry blotches. The healing prepared her for another round of torture. Not. Today.

She panned the room, taking in the avid spectators while searching for a final glimpse of Reign. A hint of crimson is all she caught as she scanned the dense, churning cloud. *And Roman? Both must be inside.*

Favoring her left side, she struggled to her feet. Nephythys's gaze landed on her. Her lips curled into a sneer.

"Ready to have my foot up your ass, Nephythys?" Goading worked in high school, why not here? "You and me, bitch. Right here. Right now." Nephythys flinched as if the words had landed a body blow.

"No," came from the woman pinned to the floor. Her golden armor had vanished, leaving her dressed in a simple brown sheath. Alexis wanted to help her, but had no help to give. She ignored the woman and focused on dying.

"You challenge me!" Energy pooled in Nephythys's palms. Her hair blazed along with her eyes and her gown billowed from an unseen force.

Being a martyr wasn't on Alexis's bucket list. If only she could get one solid punch in and knock the heifer back a few feet. Then she would die with a smile. A burst of adrenaline made her heart speed, her blood rush, and the hairs on her limbs stand at attention. Balanced on the balls of her feet, Alexis took a steadying breath. Her hands curled into tight fists.

Wait for it. Wait. For. It.

Nephythys hurled a ball of energy. Alexis feinted left, but the energy tracked her movement. She dove right and hit the ground hard, rolled and staggered to her feet.

"Alexis, look out!" Someone shouted.

She leaned in time to avoid a direct hit, but the glancing blow tore through her side. Agony burrowed through her and wiped coherent thought from her brain. She collapsed next to the woman, their faces inches apart. Heat leeched out of her, turning every part of her body cold. Guessing at the injury was better than actually seeing her insides ventilated. And lying here dying didn't feel like victory. But she was done. She had nothing left.

The woman's gaze darted to Alexis's cleavage. Her kohl-lined eyes widened.

Alexis dreaded the damage she would find, but she had to see. A slight tilt of her head brought her face to face with her grandmother's bracelet. Peeking from the glove nestled between her breasts, its ruby eyes twinkled. The woman chanted in a strange language. Low and rhythmic, the words washed over Alexis.

It moved! In front of her startled eyes, the small jeweled head lifted. Bobbing and weaving, it mesmerized Alexis.

Nephythys's rustling skirts snapped her out of the trance. "You will have plenty of time to lie down and die. Now, you will stand and face your punishment."

"Alexis, we don't have much time. My *vis* 'Ra is fading quickly. I can't help you. The bracelet. It is all you need to defeat them." The words rushed from the woman.

Mrs. Kelly's speech on the golf course returned to her.

The woman glanced over Alexis's shoulder. "She nears. Trust the Serpent. It won't lead you astray."

A force gripped Alexis and dragged her from the floor. Hovering, every nerve screamed in excruciating pain as she rotated and faced her executioner.

Nephythys stood a few feet away. The flames in her hair danced with unabridged mayhem in tune with the energy crackling in the palms of her hands.

Too close to miss, Alexis thought and prepared for the end. Warmth coiled in her cleavage and snaked up her chest. Her heart hiccuped, then steadied into a heavy beat. Her muscles relaxed, bones straightened, flesh and skin knit together. The torment stopped and strength returned in a sweet rush.

The power in Nephythys's hands sputtered and faded, but the astonishment on her face remained. A gasp circled the room followed by cries of dismay. She wanted to glance down and see what caused the panicked look on the goddess's face, but couldn't take her eyes off her nemesis.

The sensation continued around her neck. A force took control of her arm and extended her hand. The delicate golden head snaked over her shoulder. As it twined around her arm, the body elongated and thickened. Gone was the dainty piece of jewelry she coveted. Now the size of a cobra, it reared back and turned toward the woman. Fangs dropped from its peeled back lips. The three men holding her stepped away.

"You gave this human an *Anu*-Ra!" Aten held the staff in front of him like a weapon.

"Step away, Aten." The woman climbed to her feet.

"How many times must you be punished before you obey, Nu?" Aten growled.

"Does the moon obey the tide? Does the sun follow the flower? You command obedience from the one who created you?" Her voice vibrated and though low, the words echoed in the chamber. "You overstep your station."

"My station is leader of this Pantheon. Granting humans power is forbidden."

"Then punish me." Nu grinned and her gaze swept the room. "I await all of your judgments."

"My *vis'*Ra is gone!" A god cried.

"As is mine." Whispers echoed. Alexis looked up at the gallery filled with deities. Where once eternal youth and beauty dwelled, haggard, wizened faces leered. Without access to their *vis'*Ra, they withered. Now—they were mortal—and destructible.

The Serpent flattened against her skin, becoming an intricate tattoo rather than a piece of jewelry, as if it knew her intention.

Nephythys stared, her eyes wide in her wrinkled, sallow face. Her hair had flamed out, leaving listless blue coils. Alexis almost pitied the frightened *elderly* goddess. However, '*but*' always follows '*almost*'. She *almost* pitied Nephythys . . . *but* putting the bitch in her place was too tempting to resist.

Alexis's hands curled into tight fists. She stepped into the punch, pivoting at the right moment and delivered a right hook to the goddess's jaw. The resounding crunch satisfied a multitude of wrongs, though not all.

Nephythys stumbled. Wobbled. But, she didn't go down. Her appearance was another lie. Blood trickled from the corner of her mouth. She wiped it clean with the back of her hand and launched into Alexis with a barrage of wild punches.

You fight like a girl, Alexis thought, jabbing between blocking Nephythys's ineffectual punches. One lucky blow connected with Alexis's temple. She weaved and came back with a right cross, left hook combo. Nephythys's head bobbled. Alexis danced back, grateful for the secret sparing lessons from Thomas.

A kick to Alexis's stomach did more than knock the wind out of her. She landed on her back and skidded across the floor. Nephythys plopped her butt on Alexis's stomach. She grabbed two handfuls of hair and beat Alexis's head into the marble.

Alexis bucked and rolled, but Nephythys clung to her. Her fist connected with a glancing blow to Alexis's cheek and jaw. Alexis blocked the next punch with her forearm. Nephythys grabbed Alexis's arm and clawed at the image of the Serpent. The tattoo didn't budge.

Alexis wrapped her hand in Nephythys's hair and dragged the goddess to the side. Nephythys's claws dug into Alexis's scalp and grabbed a fistful of hair. As Alexis pulled, so did Nephythys. Hair snapped and yanked free from the scalps of both women. Having survived a few catfights, Alexis gritted her teeth through the pain.

Nephythys shrieked. The high pitched, girly cry ended when Alexis plugged her mouth with a fist, loosening several teeth.

Alexis hauled Nephythys up by her hair. "Stay. Away. From. Reign!" She accentuated each word with her fist meeting flesh.

"No," Nephythys gurgled and spit a mouthful of blood onto the marble.

Alexis shoved her away. "You pathetic...Ugh! I can't even call you a woman! Why would you want a man that clearly doesn't want you?"

"You know nothing. He loved me once and he will again. And he gave me his word."

"It's true, Alexis. He did give his word. And once given it cannot be broken," the woman said.

"Of his own free will he agreed to stay with me. He gave his word and I will not allow him to break it." Nephythys chuckled.

"You are gonna pay for everything you've done." Alexis grabbed Nephythys by the throat and shook her.

"You stupid ape. I am a god!" Nephythys shrieked.

Alexis cocked her arm, ready to pummel Nephythys again. A soft hand on her shoulder stopped her. The tattoo flexed and her muscle suddenly weakened. Nephythys slipped from her numb fingers. "What!" She whipped around.

The woman who helped her sidled between her and Nephythys. "You're not a killer and she is needed here."

The Serpent twisted around her arm, hummed at the nearness of the woman. Wary, Alexis backed away. "Who are you?" She demanded.

"She birthed them. Like a beast in a field, they crawled out of her," Nephythys spat. Bloody and disheveled, the goddess had fallen on hard times.

With new appreciation, Alexis studied the woman and found no resemblance between her and her sons. Their mother's tan skin and cinnamon-hued eyes were the complete opposite of their coloring.

The woman's spine stiffened and she glowered at Nephythys. "I proudly bore two beautiful children who I left so they would be safe from this cesspool."

Alexis muttered a curse. "You two can fight later. Answer my question, who are—" A ribbon of smoke wormed its way around her waist and dragged her backward into the dark recesses of the churning cloud.

CHAPTER FORTY-FOUR

Reign opened his eyes. Flat on his back, SET's inky smoke blanketed him. But now, he could see through the acrid smoke to the entity within. He breathed the evil in and didn't choke on the foulness. It entered his nose and mouth, filled his lungs on one long draw that lasted forever.

"W-what are you doing?"

SET's voice echoed in Reign's head.

"Killing you." Accepting this much malevolence had to tip his soul back into the abyss. Yet as he continued to pull SET into him, his soul attenuated the weight. The burden settled around him.

"You can't kill evil, boy."

"Let's see if I can prove you wrong." Reign continued to draw him in.

SET retreated and tried to retrieve what Reign had taken in. But Reign held on. He wouldn't return what he'd swallowed. He leaped to his feet and entered the heart of the dark.

A storm raged at the center of the mass. Wind tore at his skin. His sword deflected bolts of lightning aimed at his heart. No matter how many forms SET took, today the god would die.

A scream froze him. It dwindled to a muffled cry that had no direction. Dread pumped through his veins. He stilled. Listening, he caught a soft groan and spun in that direction. The smoke parted.

Alexis.

Her body bobbed like a piece of driftwood in a raging sea. His vision tunneled and pinpointed her split lip and the bruise coloring her cheeks. His hand tightened on the handle of the blade until his fist ached. Whoever touched her would feel its edge.

Behind her, the lightning gathered into a form. Reign hurled his blade. The sword tumbled, handle over tip and embedded in the center of the mass. The burst of light and following concussion wave burned away the smoke holding her captive. Reign dashed beneath Alexis and caught her before she fell.

His weapon returned to his hand, humming. He spotted Roman a few feet away, his sword still glowing as he raised it. Across the room, SET—once more in the form of a man—slumped against a wall. Chest heaving, limbs trembling, the god had lost his aura of invincibility. Yet his eyes blazed. *You have taken what was mine. Soon, I will take what is yours.*

SET's thoughts echoed between Reign's ears. The malevolent muck, the part of SET Reign consumed, throbbed within him. His arms tightened around Alexis.

"I know how to kill you." Certainty settled in Reign's bones adding weight to his words. "Touch her and die."

Your confidence is misplaced—

"Is it?" Reign inhaled a sharp breath. SET's essence stirred inside his lungs. A bit of it escaped from his mouth and nose, curling in the air.

Indecision and fear swiped the arrogance from the god's features, and Reign didn't hide his smile.

SET exploded again. This time his smoky form streamed past Reign. Nephythys screeched as SET smothered her. When the smoke cleared, they were gone.

Nu rushed over and kneeled opposite him. She touched the strange tattoo on Alexis's arm. The one-dimensional Serpent came alive, separated from her skin and slithered from Alexis to her new host.

The animal grew from a few inches long, to five feet of coiled menace. Nu nuzzled both jeweled heads. "Hello, Tirrika. I've missed you so." The Serpent glowed and shared the aura with Nu.

Nu stood and faced the gallery of gods still gathered. The words she spoke were strangely melodic, but the room trembled with each syllable. Gods scattered, climbing over each other to escape.

"We have to leave. Once, I could blanket the entire island and nullify their *vis'*Ra. Now, as soon as they leave the grounds, their Godhoods will return, as will their quest for vengeance."

A light enveloped and transported them to a bedroom. Dark blue marble dotted with jewels created a starry night pattern. Large soft cushions were next to him but he was reluctant to let Alexis go. Nu crouched next to them and placed her hand on Alexis's shoulder. The ruby and emerald eyes of the Serpent sparkled and light passed through Nu to Alexis.

The point of a blade lifted Reign's chin and pressed against his throat. Roman stood over him. His face was devoid of emotion, but his eyes were eerily bright.

The light bleeding from the edge of the sword sizzled Reign's skin. He wouldn't fight Roman. Not again. Reign couldn't take from his brother what he sought to gain for himself, life with the woman he loved. Gently, he lowered Alexis to a cushion. If he was to die, it wouldn't be on his knees. He started to rise, but Roman pressed the blade into his neck.

Roman's gaze shifted from Reign to Alexis. "You love her?"

"With everything I have." Before he existed. With Alexis, he lived.

"As I love my wife who you would've made a widow. You sacrificed me! And like a lamb to the slaughter I went, because I trusted you!" The room shook.

The blade seemed to ignite Reign's blood. He didn't budge. Retribution demanded he accept this final judgment. Though, he did turn his head a notch so his last vision would be of Alexis.

"Roman! I command you to cease!" Nu said.

"Who are you to order me?" he snarled.

"She's...your m-mother." Alexis croaked weakly.

Both men pivoted.

Time stretched. In the heat of the battle, Reign didn't have the luxury of staring at the woman. Now he tried to absorb everything about her and burn it into his memory. The mural hadn't lied and his father's memory was accurate. Her skin was the color of the sun the moment before it sets. Her hair brushed her shoulders in auburn waves. And her eyes, they were chocolate, rich and mysterious, yet welcoming. His father always said he took after him with their fair skin and blue eyes.

"You are not our Mother." Roman glared at Nu, and the tip of the sword still dug into Reign's neck.

"Open your eyes, brother, and remember the mural in our father's home." Reign tried to share his thoughts with Roman, recreate the bond they once had, but the merging of their minds couldn't breach Roman's hatred.

Seconds ticked by while Roman studied the goddess in their midst. His struggle was portrayed on his shifting features. He shook his head. "I don't believe it."

Her shoulders slumped, then quickly stiffened. "Your belief matters not. I will not allow you to harm each other." Nu raised her hand and moved Roman yards away. He raged against the restraints, and nearly broke free. With a wave of Nu's hand, he disappeared.

"Where have you sent him?" Reign demanded.

"I returned him to RockGate. I pray time will cool his anger, though he has every right to hate you."

Though she was correct, Reign squared his shoulders. "I did what I had to."

"I understand your motives. I can't say I wouldn't have done the same for your father. But Dear Ra, I have given up too much to see you at each other's throats." Her eyes watered and her form flickered.

Reign swallowed the lump in his throat. He could guess the answer, still he had to ask. "What did you give up?"

Nu's eyes darkened and despair glazed over her face before she turned away, wiping her eyes. Suddenly, she stumbled and sank to the floor.

Reign caught her before she crashed. Her form flickered, vanished for a second, and then solidified.

"What has happened?" Reign held her slight form close, afraid to let her go.

"My host, that willful child. I must return." She patted his arm and briefly rested her head against his chest. "Thank you...son." She pushed away and rose to her feet.

He studied her golden skin. "Forgive me...Goddess—" The word mother stuck in his throat. "I do not resemble you in any way."

Nu sighed. "That was intentional. For added protection, I buried your true nature. You and your twin favor your father." She turned away. "This palace was once my home. Now, it is yours, and your brother's when his temper cools. The palace is on a different plane of existence. None of the other Gods can find it." She faced him again, her beautiful face suddenly old and withered.

"I will not stay here." He wanted nothing from the Egyptians, even if he was part of them.

She studied him. An ethereal light shone in her cinnamon eyes. Reign steeled himself against her intrusion into his soul, but none came. Instead of an intrusive invasion, sadness took hold and the light dimmed before she looked away. "As you will, yet know this. By obtaining Osiris's sword, SET is no longer chained to Chemmis. Your brother has freed the God of Evil from this realm to walk the earth. Though you stopped him, as long as evil exists, you can't kill him. He draws his *vis*'Ra from a different source so Tirrika cannot stop him. Making his wife pay for her public insult will be his first priority. His second will be you. This place is a sanctuary to do with as you please."

"You may call it a sanctuary, I call it a prison. No gift is given without a price, usually, steep and painful," Reign replied bitterly.

Her lips thinned and Reign was certain she bit back a sharp retort. "Come, Tirrika," she called to the giant snake curled in the corner of the room.

Nu walked over to Alexis's bedside. "She rests and heals. What will you do now?"

He couldn't do what his heart longed for. To keep her with him forever. He didn't know what the future held and after today's events, he wasn't sure he could keep her safe. Every God in the pantheon wanted him dead. At the top of the list,

SET. Then there was Roman. His brother would seek retribution, and Reign would not stop him from spilling his blood.

Damnation! He'd entered her life and destroyed it. He never wanted to hurt her, cause her pain, but that's exactly what he'd done. And after everything he'd put her through, she would never agree to stay.

"I will return her to her home and use all I have to protect her from afar." Just saying the words opened a cavern in his chest.

"But—she's given up everything to be you. *Everything.* I know how that is for a woman. How hard it is…" Nu murmured as she touched Alexis's hand.

The wistful edge to Nu's voice made questions rise. So many times his father's voice held the same notes as he stared at the tiled image on the wall.

"Returning her will protect her from all of this. *Starting with me.* She did not ask for this to befall her and I will not force her to stay with me." It was the only decision he could make.

"She won't accept it. She will hate you. Like your father hated me."

Reign steeled himself against the surge of emotions. He didn't see hate in his father's gaze when he caught him staring at the mural, but this was not about his parents. "She won't have a chance to refuse. And her hate will help her forget me."

"It won't be enough," Nu whispered. "You could keep her here, to ensure her safety."

"Keep her here, as I was kept? Never. I will not force her to accept my will." *And she would not tolerate it if I tried.* Too independent, too headstrong, which was exactly what he loved about the detective.

"Sometimes, that is all we can do to protect those we love." Nu sat bedside Alexis. "Wake up, dear." Garden snake-sized again, the Serpent slithered into Nu's lap.

"What are you doing?" Reign moved closer.

Nu began chanting. Alexis roused enough to open her groggy eyes. "Tirrika is my gift to you. She's a marvelous friend. For many years, she was my only friend. She will take care of you, defend you when others cannot, and she will never leave you. Trust her. Keep her close." She placed the Serpent around Alexis's neck and stepped away.

Alexis's gaze followed Nu. "Sleep, child." Nu murmured and Alexis's eyes closed. Nu turned to her son. "You're a fool," were her last words. She vanished like fog in a stiff breeze.

The bed creaked as Reign sat beside Alexis. He took her hand and brought her fingers to his lips. "Yes, I am a fool."

CHAPTER FORTY-FIVE

Alexis sprang upright. Wrenched from oblivion, her gaze lurched around the bedroom. She took in the Baroque armoire and dressing table, the velvet curtains and brocade chairs. This wasn't her grandmother's bedroom with its worn Colonial set.

Am I still on Chemmis? Could this be a new torture designed by Nephythys? But most importantly, w*here was Reign?* Her gaze swept the room, searching for her weapon, any weapon.

She shoved the heavy blanket to the side. Someone had dressed her in jeans and a sweatshirt, Reign, she hoped. She touched her side, the spot where Nephythys had wounded her. Solid, but a bit tender. Being sore beat being dead. A glint of gold stopped her as she crossed in front of the dresser mirror.

The Serpent lay coiled loosely around her neck. Its twin heads—facing each other—rested in the slight dip between her collarbones. Slowly, her trembling hand rose to yank the jewelry from her throat. Ruby and emerald eyes twinkled, seemed to study her. Calm steadied her nerves.

Alexis stroked the delicate heads and filigreed scales. A ripple traveled through the serpentine body and tickled her skin. The head separated and the Serpent slid harmlessly into her palm. The deceptive piece of jewelry coiled, waiting. Reign's mother had called it Tirrika. She'd said '*Trust the Serpent,*' '*Keep it close*' and something else. If only she could remember.

"I never had a pet before." Gloria wouldn't allow one in the house. "At least I won't have to feed you live animals. I guess you can stay."

She placed the jewelry around her neck and swore the thing purred.

Alexis opened the bedroom door. An ethereal barrier barred her way. The gossamer strands pulsed. Tentatively, she stretched out her hand. The weaves parted before she touched them. She stepped through the doorway and into a familiar hallway. Mrs. Kelly's humming emanated from the kitchen downstairs.

Alexis walked downstairs, expecting to find Reign in the living room. He wasn't there. She passed through the dining room, entered the kitchen, and caught Mrs. Kelly in mid-scoop of dough onto a cookie sheet.

"You're awake! How do you feel?" She wiped her hands on her apron before hustling over.

"Where's Reign?" She ignored Mrs. Kelly's questions.

"Are you hungry? Thirsty?" Mrs. Kelly ushered Alexis to the dinette tucked in a corner of the room. "I'll get you something."

A chill cooled her blood as she watched her neighbor flit nervously about.

Something's happened!

The last thing she remembered was beating the crap out of Nephythys. Everything was spotty after that. Reign…he could be—*NO.*

Mrs. Kelly placed a glass of milk and a plate of cookies in front of her. Alexis grabbed Mrs. Kelly's bare arm and jumped to her feet.

"Tell me. Where is Reign?" Her voice quivered. The sadness in Mrs. Kelly's eyes nearly choked her.

She sat and forced Alexis to sit opposite her. "He brought you here a few days ago."

Days? "Was he hurt?"

"No, he is fine."

"So, what did he say? Why did he leave? Where is he?" Mrs. Kelly's hesitation drove her crazy.

"He said to tell you thank you…for your help and that you are safe. None of the Egyptians, including Nephythys, will ever hurt you again."

Everything inside her stopped. "That's it," she whispered.

Mrs. Kelly nodded.

Why would he leave? Dump her here without a word. Without a goodbye. Goodbye?

The word carved a hole in her heart. "I have to get out of here." Alexis needed air. She dashed through the kitchen to the front door and yanked it open.

"Alexis Lever! The house is warded. But if you step off the porch, the world will see you."

She wiped the tears from her eyes and saw the barrier. God, she was twice trapped. Bent over, hands on knees, she sucked in the crisp evening air. Her mind tumbled, along with her heart. Mrs. Kelly rubbed her back, but nothing could soothe this ache.

No. This couldn't be the end. Not after she'd told him she loved him. He wouldn't just walk away. Tears streamed from her eyes, blurring her vision. She'd given her heart, given up everything she had, burned all bridges tying her to New York City, and her family, only to have him dump her. He got what he wanted. She was no longer needed.

She let Mrs. Kelly lead her back into the house and up the stairs. They passed through the barrier to the bedroom. Alexis sat on the edge of the bed, hysteria beating on her senses. Mrs. Kelly fussed around her. The woman's incessant chatter didn't help.

"I can't stay here." "But there's nowhere for you to go, dear." Mrs. Kelly sat beside her and handed her a box of tissues.

"What?"

"Or there's everywhere that you *could* go."

Now was not the time for riddles.

"You're a wanted woman, Alexis. Your picture is on every TV, all over the internet. There isn't a place on the continent that doesn't know who you are. There's nowhere you can hide."

Deep down, she knew this would be the outcome, but still, Dear God, what had she done?

"On the other hand, you never have to hide again."

"What?" Mrs. Kelly's words made no sense. They jumbled together in her mind.

Mrs. Kelly touched the Serpent necklace. "This is a gift from the gods, Alexis. And they let you keep it. You, a mortal. They favor you."

Alexis yanked the necklace off and tossed it into Mrs. Kelly's lap. "I don't want anything from them."

"Alexis, it's not what you think."

"Please just go."

The door closing behind Mrs. Kelly was a blessing.

Alexis tried not to think. It's not as if she hadn't been here before. This time was no different. One good cry and she would be over it. Then she'd focus on what to do next. She'd allow herself ten minutes, not a second longer.

Ten minutes turned into hours of racking sobs until her tear ducts had nothing left to give. Her eyes were swollen, her throat burned, and her lungs ached. All of her hurt. When sleep finally took her, she didn't fight it.

A cool breeze fanning her face roused her. Yet when she opened her gritty eyes and focused on her surroundings, no one was there. She wasn't fooled.

"Stay away from me. Y-you coward." She shoved her aching body upright. And turned on the bedside lamp. The empty room threatened fresh tears.

He did come? He was here? She didn't buy it. The silence lied. He came to spy on her. To see how much damage he'd caused. After Paul, she swore she'd never fall in love again. But she had fallen. Hard. She loved the bastard more than humanly possible.

She raised her hand to brush her hair out of her face and saw Tirrika around her wrist. "I told her I didn't want it!" She yanked it off again and tossed it onto the dresser.

God, she was so tired. She glanced at the clock and realized she'd slept for hours. A lot of good it did. A rustling sound jerked her around. Tirrika slithered across the bed. Alexis scooted away until the headboard stopped her escape. Tirrika leaped. A scream of terror streaked up her throat. The snake wrapped around her arm again. A purr vibrated through her. Was this her stalker? Maybe Reign wasn't here. An ache swelled in her heart, which she couldn't push away. She'd give anything to forget him. No. She needed to remember so she'd never repeat the mistake again.

She stared at the serpent and recalled how it grew, changed, evened the playing field, and gave her a chance to survive. *She will take care of you, defend you when others can't, and she will never leave you.* The words floated across her brain.

Reign had said nearly the same thing. She remembered the love in his eyes. And the truth in his touch, and when she sifted through him, she found the truth.

He loved her! She knew he did. So why did he leave?

"Oh God." She smacked her forehead with the heel of her hand. She was as much of an idiot as he was. She had to find him. He owed her an explanation. And she'd be damned if she didn't get one. She jumped up and snatched a jacket.

Nu said to trust the serpent. Okay, I will trust it to take me to Reign. She concentrated, centered her thought on Reign. The sensation started in her abdomen, first a tingle that morphed into a thousand pinpricks that spread down each limb. She dematerialized. Her atoms scattered and sped across town.

She materialized in a dark place. It took a moment of focusing on the faint sunlight peeking through the Swiss-cheesed roof to realize she had flashed to the factory. Nothing here had changed. Gloom still clung to each corner. Dust still coated every surface. Rain drizzled through the roof and a stiff wind howled through the cracks in the boarded windows. This is where the journey started. Where she first met Reign and everything changed. She peered into each pit. Empty. Their inhabitants were gone, leaving goo lining the walls and a puddle at the bottom. Reign had already done it. He had come and gone.

She settled back on her haunches. Disappointment ate at her. After everything, he still hadn't thought enough of her wishes to spare them.

"I did not kill them."

His voice came out of the shadows. She closed her eyes and listened to the deep timbre before turning her head toward him.

"The quimaera were gone when I arrived. I suspect Alamut found a way to awaken them."

She couldn't see his face, but enough light draped across his body. He was dressed differently. Instead of jeans, black leathers stretched across his muscular thighs, a dark muscle shirt hugged his chest, outlining his pecs and abs, and a long leather coat completed his new look.

"Why should I believe you?" Her heart raced. God, she wanted to believe him.

Slowly, Reign approached. "I've given you no reason to believe me, but I speak the truth."

A shaft of light from the tattered roof illuminated his face. His beard had grown back and his hair brushed his shoulders. His blue eyes were bottomless pools of pain, threatening to drown her. She had to resist.

"You left. You dumped me at Mrs. Kelly's and left." She blurted. Her fist curled with the need to beat some sense into him.

"I warded the house to alert me to any threat breaching the barrier, and you. If you left."

"So you knew I wasn't at Mrs. Kelly's anymore. Why? I'm not your responsibility."

"I will always protect you, Alexis."

"Why?" She stepped closer. "You owe me nothing."

"I owe you in more ways than I can count." He cupped her face and leaned in.

"Try," she ordered when all she wanted to do was throw herself into his arms and bring his lips to hers.

He touched her hair, tugged gently on a loose curl. Tension vibrated through him. "You gave me a reason to live, a reason to fight. You gave me your love. I only want to keep you safe. Away from me is the only guarantee, but I can't think without you, can't breathe when you're not near." A soft glow pulsed within his eyes.

Alexis drew closer. "You can't keep me safe if we're not together."

He reached for her, but then his hand dropped to his side. "I will not have you in danger. I cannot lose you. The pantheon is fractured. Roman wants me dead—"

She cupped his face between her hands. "Do you love me?"

His body jerked at her touch and his answer reflected in his heated gaze. But worry creased his brow. He pulled away and reluctantly her hands slid from his face and settled on his pecs.

"Sometimes love is not enough. Alexis, you do not know how close I came to hurting you."

A knot formed in her heart. "What are you saying?"

He closed his eyes and his chest expanded with a slow breath. But then his cold gaze landed on her. A chill raced down her spine.

"The Vanquished are a part of me now, but on the golf course, after we argued and you walked away, something snapped inside me. My mind turned chaotic. Hurting you was all I could think of." A shudder ran through his body and anguish replaced his frigid stare. "So close...the Vanquished stopped me. I would thank the gods if I knew which one to pray to." His hands dropped from her hips and he stepped away.

Alexis followed his retreat. She fisted his shirt, grabbed the back of his neck, and hauled him close. Wary blue eyes studied her face. "Reign, the Vanquished were always a part of you. They didn't save me. It was you."

A grimace tightened his features. "I wish that were true. I saw them. They saved me from killing you. Since then, my demons and I have merged, but they are still with me. I fear what I will do without them to stay my hand when my mind turns chaotic once more."

"Sweetheart, every time I've touched you there has been only one person I sensed and that's you." She brought her hands up to his lean cheeks. His shadow of a beard brushed her palms. Mrs. Kelly kept telling her how powerful she was. Now was the time to see just how much.

Alexis opened her senses. In an instant, her sight, hearing, smell, and touch tripled in intensity. System nearing overload, she focused on Reign and reached within herself for the power gifted by an unknown ancestor. Reign dropped his mental shield, laid himself bare, and welcomed her intrusion.

She hated invading his privacy, but she had to prove to him what she already knew. Like an onion, she sifted through each layer, until no territory lay undiscovered. She saw his

childhood with Roman. His father's brutal death. The many
battles fought and won. Nephythys...her betrayal scarred him
for centuries. Ashes had replaced the love he once had. And
what he did to his brother. Weakened, she slumped in his arms.

"Alexis, are you injured?" Gently, he tapped her face.

"I'm fine, and so are you. Sweetheart, there are no
vanquished. I don't think there ever were." On her feet again,
she processed the effects of deep sifting for the first time.

Reign pressed his fingers against his temple and gave his
head a vicious shake.

"Whenever I've touched you all I have ever sensed, is you.
Nothing else. I suspect Mrs. Kelly didn't sense them either
'cause she certainly wouldn't have held her tongue," Alexis
said.

He scrubbed a hand across his face and grew distant.

"Do you believe me?"

Seconds stretched in silence between them. "When I think
back to my first encounter with my demons, your words seem
credible. My weakness manifested the Vanquished."

"Reign Nicolis, there is nothing weak about you. You are
strong and your heart is good. Whatever happens, we're in this
together. Understand? Because I don't want to live without
you."

Hope lurked within the depths of his blue eyes. But then he
shook his head. "You do not know what you are saying. Roman
and the Pantheon hate us. Nephythys will kill you and SET is
free to leave Chemmis and wreak havoc where he wills.
Danger surrounds you because of me. That I cannot accept."
The desperation in his voice tore her heart. He took her hand.
"I will take you back to Mrs. Kelly and draw these forces
away—

"I love you."

He jerked as if slapped, as if the three words were body
blows. "The Egyptians have declared war on me." His nostrils
flared and raw aggression rolled off him in waves. His eyes
glowed neon.

In this moment, any lingering doubt about him being a
demi-god, vanished. "You want this war?"

"They want it and I will not retreat," he growled.

"I expect no less." Alexis cupped his face and felt a shudder race through him. His hand gripped her hip.

"There is a place I can take you. A sanctuary created by Nu. You will be safe there." His voice was strained, tight with need.

"Not without you. You can't watch your back and your front and watch me from a distance. SET will stop at nothing to make you pay." Just barely, she brushed her lips across his and trailed her tongue along his seam. "You need me."

"Will you stand with me?" His hoarse voice told her more than his words.

She brought his head to hers, touching their foreheads together. "Always. Besides, you couldn't get rid of me if you tried."

"I love you with all that I have." His voice broke on the last note.

"I know." Alexis's lips touched Reign's. At first a slight kiss, teasing a sigh from him. Then she lingered, kissing the man who had changed her world and stolen her heart. His arm banded around her waist and pulled her into the shelter of his big body as she wrapped herself around him. She slanted her lips across his and bound their souls in a moment that lasted forever.

EPILOGUE

Particles of flickering darkness, too small to see with the naked eye, floated in the evening air of the destroyed room. This was how Khuket began, as nothing more than glimmering randomness as the earth was formed.

She collected herself, gathered the particles together and slowly coalesced into a grayish, misshapen cloud and swept out of the smashed window. The wind battered her, tossing her about. She welcomed the chaotic dance and siphoned some of its kinetic energy to keep her alive long enough for her nourishment to return to Rockgate.

She didn't have long to wait as she rested on the roof. Her prey exited the house and strolled into the backyard with his brothers. He was a fine specimen of male virility. Muscles bulged beneath his tattooed skin and added to his tasty aura. Tonight, she would feed. Tomorrow, Khuket would begin her revenge.

GLOSSARY

Anubis- Egyptian God of the Underworld. Son of SET and Nephythys

*Anu-*Ra- Sacred relics of power.

Avery Nicolis- Adopted member of the Nicolis family. Older brother of EJ Nicolis.

Cartouche- Frame containing a name.

Duat- The Underworld.

Eidos- Race of Elementals conquered by the Egyptian.

EJ Nicolis- Adopted member of the Nicolis family. Younger brother of Avery Nicolis

Ember Walker- Human host of the Goddess Nu.

Flail and Crook- Egyptian royal symbols of power.

Hathor- Goddess of Love. Mother of Tyrone (Tau) Gregory.

Hathoria Gregory- Human host of the Goddess Hathor and mother to Tyrone Gregory.

Khuket- Eidos Goddess of Chaos.

Nephythys- Goddess of the Dead. She sits in judgment of dead souls. One of the five original Gods created Nu and Ra.

Nu- Goddess of Heaven and Sky. Matriarch of the Pantheon. Mother of Roman and Reign Nicolis.

Nulls- Descendants of the Eidos and slaves of the Egyptian gods. To touch them is to own them.

Osiris- God of the Underworld. Former lover of Nephythys. Husband of Isis. Imprisoned in the bowels of Duat.

Quin (Joaquin)- Adopted member of the Nicolis Family.

Quimaera- Hybrid beasts transformed from humans. Part man, crocodile, and cobra.

Roman Nicolis- Twin to Reign. Owner of Nicolis Security INT.

Reign Nicolis- Twin to Roman.

Sentinels- Keepers of the Egyptian Realm.

Serpent Bracelet Tirrika- Personal Anu'Ra of Nu.

SET- Egyptian God of all Evil. Son of Nu. Husband of Nephythys. Father of Anubis.

Sifting- the power to read a person's mind.

Summoning- Calling a human to the Egyptian Realm.

Thane Nicolis- adopted member of the Nicolis family.

The Rising- When all the souls of the dead rise.

vis'Ra- power, energy. Your personal essence.

TMONIQUE'S BIOGRAPHY

Tmonique Stephens wrote her first novel about a reporter and a hockey player after the U.S. hockey team won gold in the 1980 Olympics. She loves writing flawed characters who reflect the emotional baggage we all carry. She writes complicated stories for complicated people. Paranormal romances and fantasy novels are her favorite genre.

Eternity and *Everlasting* are the first two novels in her *Descendants of Ra* series. *Evermore*, the third novel will be released in July 2014. Currently, she is working a contemporary revenge series and *Encore*, the fourth novel in the Descendants of Ra series. She will read anything about fairies, demons, or angels. She also enjoys Stephen King, Dean Koontz, and Preston and Child.

She has a Bachelor's Degree in Creative Writing from City College of New York where she won an English Department Award for her play *Tea with Salt* in 1987.

Born in St. Thomas USVI, Tmonique Stephens grew up in The Bronx, New York one mile from Yankee Stadium. She loves SyFy, the History channels, and also Asian cuisine. But her heart and stomach longs for anything from the Caribbean.

Website: http://tmoniquestephensauthor.com/
Facebook:
http://www.facebook.com/TmoniqueStephens
Fan page: https://www.facebook.com/pages/Author-Tmonique-Stephens/334686337991
Twitter: https://twitter.com/Tmoniquebooks
Pinterest: http://pinterest.com/tmoniquestephen/
Email:Tmoniquebooks@gmail.com